About the Authors

Andrea L ... orary author wh ... tories since she ... st girl transplant ... trying to develop ... ng for her boyf ... ontact Andrea at her website ...

USA TODAY Bestselling Author **Jules Bennett** has penned more than fifty novels during her short career. She's married to her high school sweetheart, has two active girls, and is a former salon owner. Jules can be found on Twitter, Facebook (Fan Page), and her website julesbennett.com. She holds contests via these three outlets with each release and loves to hear from readers!

Addison Fox is a lifelong romance reader, addicted to happy-ever-afters. She loves writing about romance as much as reading it. Addison lives in New York with an apartment full of books, a laptop that's rarely out of sight and a wily beagle who keeps her running. You can find her at addisonfox.com, facebook.com/addisonfoxauthor or on Twitter (@addisonfox).

Indecent Proposals

Indecent Proposals:
The Fake Engagement

ANDREA LAURENCE

JULES BENNETT

ADDISON FOX

MILLS & BOON

First Published in Great Britain 2022
By Mills & Boon, an imprint of HarperCollins*Publishers,* Ltd
1 London Bridge Street, London, SE1 9GF

www.harpercollins.co.uk

HarperCollins*Publishers*
1st Floor, Watermarque Building,
Ringsend Road, Dublin 4, Ireland

INDECENT PROPOSALS: THE FAKE ENGAGEMENT
© 2022 Harlequin Enterprises ULC.

One Week with the Best Man © 2015 Andrea Laurence
From Friend to Fake Fiancé © 2016 Jules Bennett
Colton's Deadly Engagement © 2018 Harlequin Enterprises ULC.

Special thanks and acknowledgement are given to Addison Fox for her contribution to *The Coltons of Red Ridge* series.

ISBN: 978-0-263-30490-9

MIX
Paper from
responsible sources

FSC
www.fsc.org

FSC™ C007454

This book is produced from independently certified FSC™ paper to ensure responsible forest management.

For more information visit: www.harpercollins.co.uk/green

Printed and Bound in Spain using 100% Renewable electricity at CPI Black Print, Barcelona

ONE WEEK WITH
THE BEST MAN

ANDREA LAURENCE

To my baby sister Hannah—

Being a girl is tough. Surviving your teenage years with your self-esteem intact is a major feat. You've got a long way to go, but no matter what, I want you to remember: you are smart enough, you are talented enough and you are pretty enough. Don't let anyone tell you otherwise. You can do anything you put your mind to, and if and when you choose to fall in love, that man will be damn lucky to have you in his life. Don't settle for someone that treats you like anything less than the best thing that has ever happened to him.

One

"Pardon me," Natalie said, leaning in toward the man sitting across from her. "Could you run that by us again?"

Gretchen was glad Natalie had said it, because she was pretty darn confused herself. The four owners and operators of From This Moment wedding chapel were seated at the conference room table across from a man wearing an expensive suit and an arrogant attitude she didn't care for. He wasn't from the South; that was for sure. He was also talking nonsense.

Ross Bentley looked just as annoyed with the women's confusion as they were with him. "You advertise From This Moment as a one-stop wedding venue, do you not?"

"Yes," Natalie said, "but usually that means we'll handle the food, the DJ and the flowers. We've never been asked to provide one of the wedding guests a date. This is a wedding chapel, not an escort service."

"Let me explain," Ross said with a greasy smile that Gretchen didn't trust. "This is a very delicate arrangement, so this discussion will need to fall within the confidentiality agreement for the Murray Evans wedding."

Murray Evans was a country music superstar. On his last tour, he'd fallen for his opening act. They were having a multiday wedding event at their facility next weekend, the kind the press salivated over. Those weddings usually required a confidentiality clause so that any leaks about the event are not from the venue. Frankly, Gretchen was getting tired of these big, over-the-top weddings. The money was nice—money was always nice, since she didn't have much—but carefully addressing thousands of invitations in perfect calligraphy wasn't that fun. Nor was dealing with the high-and-mighty wedding guests who came to these kinds of shindigs.

"Of course," Natalie replied.

"I represent Julian Cooper, the actor. He's a long-time friend of Mr. Evans and will be attending the wedding as the best man. I'm not sure how closely you follow celebrity news, but Julian has just had a big public breakup with his costar of *Bombs of Fury,* Bridgette Martin. Bridgette has already been seen out and about with another high-profile actor. As his manager, I feel like it would look bad if Julian attended the wedding alone, but he doesn't need the complication of a real date. We just need a woman to stand in and pretend to be with him throughout the wedding events. I assure you there's nothing inappropriate involved."

Gretchen knew of Julian Cooper—it would be impossible not to—although she'd never seen any of his films. He was the king of dude films—lots of explosions, guns and scripts with holes big enough to drive a truck through them. That wasn't her thing, but a lot of people loved his movies. It seemed a little ridiculous that he would need a fake date. His sweaty, hard abs were plastered all over every billboard and movie preview. While Gretchen might not appreciate his acting skills, she had a hard time discounting that body. If a man who looked like that couldn't get a last-minute date, she was doomed.

"What kind of woman are you wanting?" Bree, their photographer, asked cautiously. "I'm not sure I know many women who would look natural on the arm of a movie star."

"That's understandable," Ross said. "What I'd really prefer is an average woman. We don't want her to look like an escort. I also think it would go over well with Julian's female fan base for him to be seen with an everyday woman. It makes them feel like they have a shot."

Gretchen snorted, and Ross shot a cutting look at her across the table. "We'd be willing to handsomely compensate her for the trouble," he continued. "We're willing to pay ten thousand dollars for the woman's time. Also, I can provide additional funds for salon visits and a clothing allowance."

"Ten thousand dollars?" Gretchen nearly choked. "Are you kidding?"

"No," Ross said. "I'm very serious. Can you provide what we're asking for or not?"

Natalie took a deep breath and nodded. "Yes. We'll make arrangements and have someone in place to meet with Julian when he arrives in Nashville."

"Very good. He flies into Nashville tonight and he's staying at the Hilton." Ross reached into his breast pocket and pulled out a leather wallet. He extracted a handful of cash and pushed it across the table to Natalie. "This should cover the incidentals I discussed. The full payment will be provided after the wedding is over."

Without elaborating, he stood up and walked out of the conference room, leaving the four women in stunned silence.

Finally, Bree reached out and counted the money. "He left two grand. I think that will buy some really nice highlights and a couple fancy outfits, don't you, Amelia?"

Amelia, the caterer and resident fashionista, nodded. "It should. But it really depends on what we have to start with. Who can we possibly get to do this?"

"Not me," Bree insisted. "I'm engaged, and I've got to be able to take all the pictures. You're married and pregnant," she noted.

Amelia ran her hand over her rounded belly. She had just reached twenty-two weeks and found out that she and her husband, Tyler, were having a girl. "Even if I wasn't, I've got to cook for five hundred guests. I'm already in over my head on this one, even with Stella's help."

They both turned to look at Natalie, who was frantically making notes in her tablet. "Don't look at me," she said after noticing them watching her. "I'm the wedding planner. I'll be in headset mode keeping this show on track."

"There's got to be someone we could ask. A friend?" Gretchen pressed. "You grew up in Nashville, Natalie.

Don't you know anyone that wouldn't mind being a movie star's arm candy for a few days?"

"What about you?" Natalie fired back.

"What?" Gretchen nearly shrieked in response to the ridiculous question. They'd obviously lost their minds if they thought that was a viable solution. "Me? With Julian Cooper?"

Natalie shrugged off her surprise. "And why not? He said they wanted a normal, everyday woman."

"Just because he doesn't want a supermodel doesn't mean he wants...*me*. I'm hardly normal. I'm short, I'm fat and never mind the fact that I'm horribly awkward with men. I clam up whenever Bree's musician fiancé comes by. Do you really think I can act normal while the hottest star in Hollywood is whispering in my ear?"

"You're not fat," Amelia chastised. "You're a normal woman. Plenty of guys like their women a little juicy."

Juicy? Gretchen rolled her eyes and flopped back into her chair. She was twenty pounds overweight on a petite frame and had been that way since she was in diapers. Her two sisters were willowy and fragile like their ballerina mother, but Gretchen got their father's solid Russian genes, much to her dismay. Her pants size was in the double digits, and she was in a constant state of baking muffin tops. *Juicy* wasn't the word she would use.

"You guys can't really be serious about this. Even if I wasn't the last woman on earth that he'd date, you forget I work here, too. I'll be busy."

"Not necessarily," Bree countered. "Most of what you do is done in advance."

Gretchen frowned. Bree was right, although she didn't want to admit it. The invitations had gone out months ago. The programs and place cards were done. She would need to decorate the night before, but that didn't preclude her from participating in most of the wedding day activities. "I handle a lot of last-minute things, too, you know. It's not like I'm sitting around every Saturday doing my nails."

"That's not what I'm implying," Bree said.

"Even so, it's ridiculous," Gretchen grumbled. "Julian Cooper? Please."

"You could use the money, Gretchen."

She looked at Amelia and sighed. Yes, Gretchen was broke. They'd all agreed when they started this business that the majority of their profits would go into paying off the mortgage on the facility, so they weren't drawing amazing wages. For Amelia and Bree it didn't matter so much anymore. Bree was engaged to a millionaire record producer, and Amelia was married to a rare jewels dealer. Gretchen was getting by, but there wasn't much left over for life's extras. "Who couldn't?"

"You could go to Italy," Natalie offered.

That made Gretchen groan aloud. They'd found her Achilles' heel without much trouble. She'd had a fantasy of traveling to Italy for years. Since high school. She wanted to spend weeks taking in every detail, every painting of the Renaissance masters. It was a trip well out of her financial reach despite years of trying to save. But Natalie was right. With that cash in her hand she could immediately book a flight and go.

Italy. Florence. Venice. Rome.

She shook off the thoughts of gelato on the Spanish Steps and tried to face reality. "We're overworked. Things are slower around the holidays, but I don't see a three-week Italian vacation in my future. He could give me a million bucks and I wouldn't be able to take off time for a trip."

"We close for a week between Christmas and New Year's. That would cover some of it," Natalie said. "Or you could go later in the spring. If you work ahead with the printing, we can get someone to cover the decorating. What matters is that you'd have the money in hand to go. What can it hurt?"

"Yeah, Gretchen," Bree chimed in. "It's a lot of money, and for what? Clinging to the hard body of Julian Cooper with a loving look in your eyes? Dancing with him at the reception and maybe kissing him for the cameras?"

Gretchen tightened her jaw, choking down another argument, because she knew Bree was right. All she had to do was suck it up for a few days and she could go to Italy. She'd never have another opportunity like this.

"Besides," Bree added, "how bad can faking it with a sexy movie star really be?"

If Ross hadn't been personally responsible for Julian's career success, Julian would throttle him right this second.

"A date? A fake date? Really, Ross?"

"I think it will be good for your image."

Julian sipped his bottled water and leaned against the arm of the chair in his Nashville hotel suite. "Do I look that pathetic and heartbroken over my breakup with Bridgette?"

"Of course not," Ross soothed. "I just want to make sure that her management team doesn't outsmart us. She's already been seen out with Paul Watson. If you don't move on fast enough, you'll get painted as lovesick for her."

"I don't care," Julian exclaimed. "Despite what everyone thinks, I broke up with Bridgette six months ago. We only went out publicly because you insisted on it."

"I didn't insist," Ross protested. "The studio insisted. Your romance was a huge selling point for the film. They couldn't have you two break up before it even came out."

"Yeah, yeah," Julian said dismissively. "If I ever even look twice at one of my costars again, you haul me off and remind me of this moment. But now it's done. I'm over Bridgette and I'm *way* over dating someone just for the cameras."

Ross held up his hands. "It won't be like that. I swear. Besides, it's already done. She'll be here to meet you in about five minutes."

"Ross!" Julian shouted, rising to his full height to intimidate his short, round manager. "You can't just do stuff like this without my permission."

"Yes, I can. It's what you pay me to do. You'll thank me later."

Julian pinched the bridge of his nose between his finger and thumb. "Who is it? Some country music singer? Did you import an actress from Hollywood?"

"No, none of that. They tell me she's one of the employees at the wedding chapel. Just your everyday girl."

"Wait. I thought after what happened with that waitress you didn't want me dating 'regular' women. You said they were a bigger security risk than another star with her own career to protect. You said I needed to stick to women that didn't need my money or my fame." Julian had been dealing strictly with high-and-mighty starlets the past few years at Ross's insistence, but now, a regular girl was okay because he said so?

"I know, and normally that's the case. That waitress just wanted to dig up dirt on you to make a buck with the tabloids. There are a million women just like her in Hollywood. But in this scenario I think it's a smart choice. Women in Nashville are different, and it's an unexpected move. Your female fans will like it, of course, and so will the studios. I've been trying to get you a role as a true romantic lead. This could do it."

Julian didn't really want to be a romantic lead. At least not by Ross's definition. His manager's idea of a romantic film was one where the sexy blonde clings to his half-naked body while he shoots the bad guys. He'd already played that role again and again. When he'd pushed Ross on the topic a second time, he got Julian the "romantic" lead in a movie about male strippers. Not exactly hard-hitting, award-winning stuff. Hell, he'd be thrilled to just do a light romantic comedy. Something without explosions. Or machine guns. Or G-strings.

"I should fire you for this," Julian complained as he dropped down into his chair. It was a hollow threat, and they both knew it. Ross had made Julian's career. He might not be creatively fulfilled by big-budget action films, but the money was ridiculous and Julian needed every penny.

"It will be fine. I promise. It's not a real relationship, so I can break my own rules this once. In a few days, you can go back to Hollywood and date whomever you want."

Somehow, Julian doubted that. Since moving to Hollywood, he hadn't had the best track record with the ladies. The waitress had sold the story of their romance to the newspapers with some other juicy tidbits she'd gotten out of him. The dancer was just looking for a guy to pay for her boob job. So many others were after either his money or his leverage to get into show business.

Ross encouraged him to date other actresses to reduce that issue, but either way, there was usually some kind of confidentiality contract involved. Even with that in place, he'd learned quickly to keep private things private. He didn't talk about his family, his past…anything that he couldn't bear to see in the papers. An after-the-fact lawsuit wouldn't undo the damage once it was out there.

Since his breakup with Bridgette, he hadn't really shown any interest in dating again. It was too damn much work and frankly, just not that fun. How was he supposed to find love when he couldn't even find someone he could trust?

Ross got up from his seat and put his drink on the coffee table. "Well, that should do it."

"Where are you going?"

"I'm leaving," Ross said.

"Leaving? I thought you said my date was on her way over."

"She is. That's why I'm leaving. Three's a crowd, after all. You two need to get to know each other."

Julian's jaw dropped as he watched his manager slip out of the hotel suite. He should've throttled him. He could get a new manager.

With nothing to do but wait, he slumped into his chair and killed time checking his smartphone for missed calls or updates from his family. His mother and brother lived in Louisville, and that was the easiest and most secure way to keep up with them, especially with his brother James's condition. James's attendant usually kept him up to date on how his brother was doing and shared any funny tidbits to make him feel more connected. Today, there were no messages to worry him.

About four minutes later, there was a knock at the door to his suite. His new girlfriend was punctual if nothing else.

Julian got up and went to the door. He looked through the peephole but didn't see anyone there. Confused, he opened his hotel room door wide and realized it was because his guest was very petite. She was maybe five foot two if she had good posture, and she didn't. In addition to being petite, she was curvy, hiding most of her body under an oversize cardigan. She had the look of the average woman on the street, nothing like he was used to seeing around Malibu.

What really caught his attention, however, were her eyes. She had a dark gaze that watched him survey her with a hint of suspicion. It made him wonder what that was about. Shouldn't *he* be suspicious of *her*? Julian had been a part of the Hollywood scene for several years and had seen his fair share of staged relationships. The women were usually attractive and greedy, hoping they might actually charm their fake boyfriend into falling for them so they could take advantage of California's community property laws.

He waited for her to say something, but she just stood there, sort of awkwardly hovering outside his door. "Hi," Julian finally offered to end the silence. "I'm Julian, although you probably already know that. Are you the one the wedding company sent over?"

"Yes." She nodded, her dark brown curls bouncing around her round face. He expected her to say something after that, but she continued to just hover. It made him think that at any moment, she might turn and bolt down the hallway. He was used to his fans being nervous around him, but not skittish. He was certain Ross would blame him if he ran off the woman his manager had so carefully arranged for him.

Julian didn't want a fake girlfriend. He would gladly send this poor woman back home with an apology, but Ross wouldn't have set this up without a good reason. He paid the man to make smart, strategic decisions about his career, so he had to be nice and make this work. Or he'd hear about it.

"And your name is…?" he prompted.

She seemed to snap out of her nervous daze. "Gretchen," she said, holding out her hand. "Gretchen McAlister."

Julian shook her hand, noticing how ice-cold her skin was and how her fingers trembled in his grip. This woman seemed terrified of him. Women usually had a much…warmer reaction to Julian. He had to pry them from his neck and wipe away their lipstick from his cheeks at movie premieres. He needed to warm her up or they were never going to convince anyone—much less a skeptical press—that they were dating.

He took a step back to let her into the hotel room. "Come on in, Gretchen." He shut the door behind them and gestured for her to take a seat in the living room of his suite. "Can I get you something to drink?"

"Something alcoholic would make all this easier," she muttered under her breath.

Julian's lips twisted in amusement as he went over to the minibar. That wasn't a bad idea to help break the ice. At least for her. He didn't drink, but certainly the hotel would've stocked the room with something useful. He wished he *could* drink, but that was on his personal trainer's list of no-no's: no alcohol, no sugar, no carbs, no dairy, no preservatives, no artificial colors, flavors or anything else remotely interesting or tasty.

Unfortunately, he didn't know where to start with a drink for Gretchen. "There's a collection of tiny bottles in here. Feel free to pick whatever you'd like."

Gretchen watched him curiously as she walked over to the bar and pulled out what looked like tequila. He expected her to mix it with something, but instead, watched in surprise as she twisted off the lid and threw back the tiny bottle in a few hard draws. She really must be nervous if she was doing tequila shots just to be in the same room with him.

"You know, you look like you could use one of these yourself. I'm not getting the feeling that you're very happy about this," she said as she looked at him out of the corner of her eye. She tossed the empty bottle into the trash and turned back to sit on the couch. "I know I probably don't meet your standards for a woman you'd date. Mr. Bentley specifically requested an everyday woman, but I assume I'm not what he had in mind. I'm obviously not a Bridgette, so if that's going to be a problem, just say the word and I'll go on my way."

He was doing a crappy job at making her feel welcome. "No, no. I'm sorry," Julian said, sitting down in the chair to face her. "My manager informed me about this whole arrangement literally minutes before you showed up. My reaction has nothing to do with you and the standards you seem to think you fall short of."

"So you're not on board with Mr. Bentley's plan?"

"Not really," he replied. There was no sense in sugar-coating it. "I'll do what I need to do, but this isn't my choice, no. It's pretty common in Hollywood to contract relationships, but that's not my style. I'd rather go to an event alone than with some woman I don't even know. That's probably why Ross sprang this on me—I couldn't get out of it quickly enough. But now, here we are, and I find I'm just not as well prepared as I would like to be."

"Neither am I," she said. "Does one ever really get used to being pimped out by your friends for something like this?"

"Pimped out?" Julian chuckled. The alcohol seemed to loosen her tongue. "That's one way to put it. Welcome to the Hollywood game, Gretchen McAlister. We've all sold ourselves for success. How much did it take for you to toss your good sense out the window and end up on my couch?"

A flicker of irritation crossed her face, blushing her cheeks an attractive pink. It might have just been the tequila kicking in. He'd bet her hands weren't cold any longer. He fought the urge to find a reason to touch her again.

"Apparently, ten grand for my time and another two grand to make me more presentable."

Julian looked over his date of the next few days and frowned. It shouldn't take two thousand to make her presentable, and he hoped Ross hadn't been rude enough to say such a thing. Ross was usually brutally honest, with a set of unrealistic Hollywood ideals. Whereas Gretchen wasn't the kind of woman Julian was normally seen with in LA, she wasn't unattractive. Her skin was creamy and flawless, her lips full and pink. Her eyelashes were so long and thick, he thought they might be fake, but she didn't strike him as that type.

He supposed anyone could use a haircut and a manicure. She could take the rest of the money and buy clothes. Tonight she was dressed as though she'd come straight from her work at the wedding chapel, wearing a plain green shirt and khakis with a brown cardigan, a pair of loafers and argyle socks. Appropriate for winter in the South, he supposed, but not overly dressy. She looked nice. She actually reminded him a lot of his mother when she was younger and life hadn't completely sucked away everything she had.

But instead of complimenting Gretchen the way he knew he should, he went the other direction. He felt himself being drawn in by her shy awkwardness, but Julian had no intention of getting chummy with this woman. She may not be a part of the Hollywood machine, but she'd use him just like everyone else. She was only here because she was being paid a ridiculous amount of money to do it.

"You should've held out for more. Ross would've paid twenty."

Gretchen just shrugged as though the money didn't mean much to her. He knew that couldn't be true. Who would sign up for something like this if it wasn't because they needed the money? He was a millionaire, and he still wouldn't turn down a well-paying role. There was always something he could do with it. Even socking it away in the bank put it to good use.

He doubted that was the case for her, though. She certainly didn't seem to have agreed to this because she was a fan. She was lacking that distinctly starry-eyed gaze he was used to seeing in women. The gaze that flickered over him was appreciative, but reserved. He sensed there was a lot going on in her mind that she wouldn't share with him. He knew he shouldn't care;

she was just a fleeting part of his life this week, but he couldn't help but wonder what was going on under that curly mop of hair.

"Well, now that we've established that I've been had cheaply, do we need to work out any details?"

Yes, Julian thought. It was better to stick to the logistics of the plan. "I came out a few days early to hang out with Murray before the wedding, so you've got some time to buy clothes and do whatever grooming women do. The first event for the wedding is Wednesday night. They're holding a welcome barbecue out at Murray's house. That will be our first official outing. Maybe we should get together here on Wednesday afternoon and spend some time on our story for anyone that asks."

Gretchen nodded. "Okay. I'll get the event schedule from Natalie, the wedding planner. Any special requests?"

Julian's brows went up at her question. "Like what?"

She shrugged. "I've never done this before, but I thought you might have favorite colors for me to wear, or find acrylic nails to be a turnoff, that sort of thing."

He'd never had a woman ask him something like that before. Despite how often people told him they were there for him, they rarely inquired or even cared what he might really want. He had to think about an answer for a moment. "I only have one request, really."

"What's that?"

"Please wear comfortable shoes," Julian said. "I don't know how many events I've sat through where the woman did nothing but complain about her expensive, fancy, painful shoes the whole night."

Gretchen glanced down at her practical and comfortable-looking brown leather loafers. "I don't think that will be a problem. Well, I'll get going." She got up from the couch and held out a card to him.

He accepted it, turning it over to find it was her business card. The design of it was very intricate but delicate, with a shiny ivory damask pattern over a flat white card. The text was in a blush pink, as was an edging of abstract roses, screaming wedding, but not cliché wedding.

"You can reach me at the chapel number during the day or my cell phone the rest of the time. If nothing comes up, I'll see you Wednesday afternoon before the barbecue."

Julian took her hand in his. It was warmer now, and this time, he noticed how soft her skin was against him. He swallowed hard as his palm tingled where their skin touched. His gaze met hers, and he watched her dark eyes widen in surprise for a moment before she pulled her hand away.

"Thanks for doing this, Gretchen," he said, to cover his surprising physical response to her touch. "I'll see you in a few days."

She nodded and bit at her lip as she made her way to the door. After she slipped out, he bolted the lock and turned back to face his room. It suddenly felt more empty and cold than it had when she was here with him.

Perhaps this setup wouldn't be as bad as he thought.

Two

Gretchen felt as if she'd just lived through that make-over montage from the movie *Miss Congeniality*, al-though it was more painful than funny. Amelia had scheduled her appointments at the day spa they con-tracted with for bridal sessions, and they were happy to fit in Gretchen for a full day of beauty.

She was expecting a hair trim and some nail polish. Maybe a facial. Gretchen wasn't a movie star, but she didn't think she needed that much work.

Instead, she'd had nearly every hair on her body ripped out. The hair that was left was cut, highlighted and blown into a bouncy but straight bob. Her skin was buffed and polished, her clogged pores "extracted," and then she was wrapped like a mummy to remove toxins, reduce cellulite and squeeze out some water weight. They finished her off with a coat of spray tan to chase away the pastiness. She got a pedicure and solar nails in a classic pink-and-white French manicure that she couldn't chip. They even bleached her teeth.

Thankfully Gretchen didn't have much of an ego, or it would've been decimated. It had taken about seven hours so far, but she thought she might—*might*—be done. She was wrapped in a fluffy robe in the serenity room. Every time someone came through, they took her into another room and exposed her to another treatment, but she couldn't come up with anything else they could possibly do to her.

This time, when the door opened, it was Amelia. If Gretchen's lady parts weren't still tender, she'd leap up and beat her friend with an aromatherapy pillow for putting her through all this. Instead, she sipped her cucumber-infused mineral water and glared at her.

"Don't you look refreshed!" Amelia said.

"Refreshed?" Gretchen just shook her head. "That's exactly the look I was going for after seven hours of beauty rituals. Julian Cooper's new woman looks so well rested!"

"Quit it, you look great."

Gretchen doubted that. There were improvements, but "great" took it a little far. "I should, after all this," she joked. "If this is what the women in Hollywood go through all the time, I'm glad I live way out here in Nashville."

"It wasn't that bad," Amelia said in a chiding tone. "I've had every single treatment that you had today. But now is the fun part!"

"Lunch?" Gretchen perked up.

Amelia placed a thoughtful hand on her round belly.

"No, shopping. They were supposed to feed you lunch as part of the package."

"Yeah, they did. Sort of." The green salad with citrus vinaigrette and berries for dessert hadn't really made a dent in her appetite.

"If you promise not to give me grief while we're shopping, I'll take you out for a nice dinner."

"I want pretzel bites, too," Gretchen countered. "Take it out of my makeover money."

Amelia smiled. "Fair enough. Get dressed and we'll go buy you some clothes and makeup."

"I have makeup," Gretchen complained as she got up, realizing as she spoke that she'd already broken her agreement not to give Amelia grief. It just seemed wasteful.

"I'm sure you do, but we're going to have the lady at the counter come up with a new look for you, then we'll buy the colors she puts together."

In the ladies' locker room, Gretchen changed back into her street clothes, all the while muttering to herself about Italy. It would be worth it, she insisted. *Just think of the Sistine Chapel*, she told herself.

She continued the mantra as the woman at the department store did her makeup. The mantra got louder as Amelia threw clothes at her over the door of the changing room. Gretchen wasn't really into fashion. She bought clothes that were comfortable, not too expensive and relatively flattering to her shape, such as it was.

But as she turned and looked at herself in the mirror for the first time today, something changed. She was still the Gretchen she recognized, but she looked like the best possible version of herself. Those hours in the salon had left her polished and refined, the makeup highlighting and flattering her features. And although she wouldn't admit it readily to Amelia, the clothes looked really nice on her, too.

It was an amazing transformation from how she'd woken up this morning. This department store obviously used fun-house mirrors to make her look thinner.

"I want to see," Amelia complained. "If you don't come out, I'm coming in."

Reluctantly, Gretchen came out of the dressing room in one of the more casual looks. She was wearing a pair of extremely tight skinny jeans, a white cotton top and a black leather jacket. It looked good, but the number of digits on the price tags was scaring her. "I only have two thousand dollars, Amelia. I don't know how much we blew at the spa, but I'm certain I can't afford a three-hundred-dollar leather jacket."

Amelia frowned. "I have a charge account here. They send me a million coupons. We'll have enough money, I promise. You need that jacket."

"I'm going to a wedding. Isn't it more important for me to get a nice dress?"

"Yes, but all the formals are marked down from homecoming, so we'll get one for a good price. You're also going to the welcome party and the rehearsal dinner. You need something casual, something more formal and a few things in between just in case you get roped into the bridal tea or something. And you're going to own this stuff long after this week is over, so it's important to choose good bones for your wardrobe. I like that outfit on you. You're getting it."

"It's too tight," Gretchen complained, and tugged the top away from her stomach. "I'm too heavy to wear clingy stuff like this."

Amelia sighed and rolled her eyes. "I'm sorry, but wearing bulky clothes just makes you look bigger than you are. I wore a 34F bra *before* I got pregnant, okay? I've tried hiding these suckers under baggy sweaters for years, but I wasn't fooling anyone. If you've got it, flaunt it. Well-fitting clothes will actually make you look smaller and showcase your curves."

Gretchen just turned and went back into the dressing room. There was no arguing with her. Instead, she stripped out of the outfit and tried on another. Before they were done, she'd gone through about a dozen other outfits. In the end, they agreed on a paisley wrap dress, a gray sweaterdress with tights, a bright purple cocktail dress, and a strapless formal that looked as if it had been painted with watercolors on the full silky skirt. Gretchen had to admit the gown was pretty, and appropriate for an artist, but she wasn't sure if she could pull any of this off. In the end, she needed to look as though she belonged on the arm of Julian Cooper.

She didn't think there were clothes for any price that would make the two of them make sense. Julian was…the most beautiful man she'd ever seen in person. The movies didn't even do him justice. His eyes were a brilliant shade of robin's-egg blue, fringed in thick brown lashes. His messy chestnut-colored hair had copper highlights that caught the lights and shimmered. His jaw was square and stubble-covered, his skin tan, and when she got close, she could smell the warm scent of his cologne. It was intoxicating.

And that wasn't even touching the subject of his body. His shoulders were a mile wide, narrowing into a thin waist and narrow hips. He'd been wearing an untucked button-down shirt and jeans when they met, but still, little was left to her imagination, they fit so well. The moment he'd opened the door, her ability to perform rational speech was stolen away. She'd felt a surge of desire lick hot at her blushing cheeks. Her knees had softened, making her glad she was wearing sensible flats and not the heels Amelia had nagged her to wear.

When it came down to it, Julian was…a movie star. An honest to God, hard-bodied, big-screen superstar. He was like an alien from another planet. A planet of ridiculously handsome people. And even though she looked pretty good in these expensive clothes with expertly applied makeup, Gretchen was still a chubby wallflower with no business anywhere near a man like him.

Men had always been confusing creatures to Gretchen. Despite years of watching her sisters and friends date, she'd never been very good with the opposite sex. Her lack of confidence was a self-fulfilling prophecy, keeping most guys at arm's length. When a man did approach her, she was horrible at flirting and had no clue if he was hitting on her or just making conversation.

At her age, most women had a couple relationships under their belts, marriages, children… Gretchen hadn't even been naked in front of a man before. On the rare occasion a guy did show interest in her, things always fell apart before it got that far. Her condition seemed to perpetuate itself, making her more unsure and nervous as the years went by.

Being close to any man set her on edge, and a good-looking one made her downright scattered. Julian just had to smile at her and she was a mess. She couldn't find a normal guy to be with her; how would anyone believe a shy, awkward nobody could catch Julian's eye? It was a lost cause, but she couldn't convince anyone of that.

An hour later, they carried their bags out to Amelia's car and settled on having dinner at a restaurant that was a few miles from the mall, near the golf course.

"I'm glad we could have a girls' day out," Amelia said as they went inside. "Tyler had to fly to Antwerp again, and I get lonely in that big house by myself."

Amelia's husband, Tyler, was a jewel and gemstone dealer who regularly traveled the world. They'd hired a woman named Stella to help with catering at From This Moment, so Amelia occasionally got to travel with Tyler, but the further she got in her pregnancy, the less interested she was in long flights. That left her alone in their giant Belle Meade mansion.

"In a few more months, that little girl will get here and you'll never be alone again."

"True. And I need your help to come up with some good names. Tyler is terrible at it." Amelia approached the hostess stand. "Two for dinner, please."

"Good evening, ladies."

Gretchen turned at the sound of a man's voice and found Murray Evans and Julian standing by the entrance behind them. Before she could say anything, Julian approached her and she found herself wrapped in his arms. He smiled at her with a warmth she would never have expected after their awkward first meeting, and he hugged her tight against the hard muscles of his chest.

She stood stiffly in his arms, burying her surprised expression in his neck and waiting for him to back off, but he didn't seem to be in a rush. When he did finally pull away, he didn't let her go. Instead, he dipped his head down and pressed his lips to hers. It was a quick kiss, but it sent a rush down her spine that awakened her every nerve. She almost couldn't grasp what was going on. Julian Cooper was kissing her. Kissing her! In public. She couldn't even enjoy it because she was so freaked out.

He pulled away and leaned down to whisper in her ear. "You need to work on that," he said. Then he wrapped his arm around her shoulders and turned to Amelia with a bright, charming smile.

"What good fortune that we'd run into you tonight. It must be fate. Do you mind if Murray and I join you for dinner?"

"Not at all, please," the redhead said with a smile that matched his own. "Gretchen said the boys would be out and about today, but we didn't expect to run into you down here in Franklin." She had a twinkle of amusement in her eyes that made her seem like the savvy type who knew how to play the game. But judging by the curve of her belly and the rock on her hand, he knew why the redhead had been taken out of the running for his fake girlfriend.

"Excellent." Julian turned to ask the hostess to change the table from two to four, ignoring the woman's stunned expression. He was used to that reaction when he attempted to live a real life outside Hollywood. What bothered him more was the wrinkling of the woman's nose as her gaze shifted to Gretchen in confusion. It made him pull her tighter to his side and plant a kiss in the silky dark strands of hair at the crown of her head.

"What are you two doing out in Franklin?" Gretchen spoke at last, squirming slightly from his arms.

"Well," Murray began, "we wanted to play some golf. Since I live in Brentwood, coming down here to Forrest Hills is easier and we're less likely to run into any photogs."

The hostess gestured for them to follow her to a corner booth in the back of the restaurant. Gretchen slid into one side, and he sat beside her before she could protest. She might not be ready for their ruse to begin, but they were together in public. He hadn't seen any photographers, but one could be around the next corner. The nosy hostess could tip someone off at the local paper. If anyone saw them together, they needed to be playing their parts.

"What are you ladies up to today?" Julian asked after the server took their drink orders.

"It's makeover day," Gretchen said. "Julian, this is Amelia Dixon. She's the caterer at From This Moment. She's also very fashionable and helped me with my full day of beauty and shopping."

Julian shook Amelia's hand, but he found it hard to turn away from Gretchen once he started really looking at her. She looked almost like a different woman from the one who had shown up at his hotel room the day before. He hadn't even recognized her when they first walked in the restaurant. It wasn't until Murray pointed out that they were the women from the chapel that he realized it was Gretchen. The changes were subtle, a refinement of what was already there, but the overall effect was stunning. She was glowing. Radiant. The straightening of her hair made an amazing difference, highlighting the soft curve of her face.

"Well, she did an excellent job. You look amazing. I can't wait to see what you guys bought for the wedding."

Gretchen watched him with wary eyes, as though she didn't quite believe what he'd said. She'd looked at him that way the first night, too. She was an incredibly suspicious woman. He smiled in an attempt to counteract her suspicion, and that just made her flush. Red mottled her chest and traveled up her throat to her cheeks. It seemed as though she blushed right down to her toes. It was charming after spending time with women too bold to blush and too aware of their own beauty to be swayed by his compliments.

He'd argued with Ross that he didn't think this was going to work after their short, strained meeting, but maybe he was wrong. They just needed to deal with her nerves so her physical reactions to him were more appropriate. She went stiff as a board in his arms, but he had some acting exercises that would help. It was probably fortuitous that they ran into each other tonight. Better they work these issues out now than at an official wedding event.

As the evening went on, it became clear that Julian knew the least about everyone there. Murray had met both women at the various planning sessions leading up to the wedding extravaganza. Julian was starting with a completely clean slate where Gretchen was concerned. Ross hadn't even told him his date's name before they met, and their first conversation hadn't been particularly revealing. They wouldn't just be posing for some pictures this week. They'd have to interact as a couple, and that meant they needed to learn more about each other if they were going to be believable.

"So you said Amelia is the caterer. What do you do, Gretchen?"

Gretchen got an odd look on her face as though she

wasn't quite sure how to describe what she did for a living. It wasn't a very hard question, was it?

"Gretchen is our visual stylist," Amelia said, jumping in to fill the silence.

"I have no idea what that is," Julian admitted.

"Well, that's why I hesitated," Gretchen said. "I do a lot of different things. I design all the paper products, like the invitations and programs. I do all the calligraphy."

"So you designed Murray's invitations?"

A wide smile crossed Gretchen's face for the first time. "I did. I was really excited about that design. I love it when I can incorporate something personal about the couple, and musical notes seemed like the perfect touch."

"They were just what we were looking for," Murray said.

"They were nice. I wouldn't have remembered them otherwise."

"Thank you. I also do a lot of the decorating and work with the various vendors to get the flowers and other touches set up for the wedding and the reception. I'm a jack-of-all-trades, really. On the day of the wedding, I might be doing emergency stitching on a bridesmaid's dress, tracking down a wayward groomsman, helping Amelia in the kitchen…"

"Or pinch-hitting as the best man's date?" Julian said with a chuckle.

"Apparently." She sighed. "I was the only one that could do it."

"You mean, you ladies weren't clamoring over who got to spend time with me? I don't know if I should be insulted or not."

Gretchen shrugged and looked at him with a crooked smile that made him think maybe he should be insulted. "It's got to be better than stitching up a torn bridesmaid's dress, right? It's not so bad to be around me. At least I don't think it is. I'm fun, aren't I, Murray?"

"Absolutely. You're going to have a great time with Julian. Just don't get him talking about his movies. He'll be insufferable."

"What's wrong with my movies?" Julian asked with mock injury in his voice. He didn't really need to ask. He knew better than anyone that all the films he'd done in the past few years were crap.

He'd started out at an acclaimed theater program at the University of Kentucky. He'd gotten a full scholarship out of high school, praised for his senior performance as the lead in *The Music Man*. He'd intended to go on to graduate and do more stage work. Maybe not musicals—he wasn't the best singer—but he enjoyed the acting craft. Then his life fell apart and he had to drop out of school. Desperation drove him to commercial acting, and with a stroke of luck, he ended up where he was now. It wasn't the creative, fulfilling career he'd dreamed of when he was younger, but his paycheck had more zeroes than he'd ever imagined he'd see in his lifetime.

Everyone laughed and they spent a while critiquing the plot of *Bombs of Fury* as their food arrived. The conversation continued on various subjects throughout the evening, flowing easily with the group. Gretchen had been quiet at first, but after talking about her work and mocking his, she started to warm up. Julian actually had a good time, which was rare, considering he was having to eat salmon and steamed broccoli while the rest of them were enjoying tastier foods. It should be against the law to be in the South and not be able to eat anything fried.

When it was over, they headed out to their cars as a group. He walked Gretchen to the passenger door of Amelia's SUV and leaned in close to her. "I had fun tonight."

"Yeah," she said, nervously eyeing him as he got close to her. "It was a pleasant surprise to run into you."

"I guess I'll see you tomorrow afternoon." Tomorrow was the welcome party and their first official time out as a couple.

"Okay. Good night."

"Good night." On reflex, Julian leaned in to give her a kiss good-night. He was stopped short by Gretchen's hand pressed against his chest.

"You know, no one is watching us. You don't have to pretend to want to kiss me."

Julian smiled. "If there's one thing I've learned in my years in LA, it's that someone is always watching. But even then, I would still kiss you."

"Why?" Her dark eyes searched his face in confusion, her brows drawn together.

She honestly didn't think she was kissable. That was a shame. She was very kissable, with pouty lips glistening from just a touch of sparkly lip gloss. If he were interested in that sort of thing. Tonight, however, he was more focused on their cover and getting it right.

"I'm going to kiss you again because you need the practice. Every time I touch you, you stiffen up. You've got to relax. If it means I have to constantly paw at you and kiss you until you loosen up, so be it." He'd had worse assignments.

Gretchen bit her bottom lip. "I'm sorry. I'm just not used to being touched."

He wrapped his hand around hers and pulled it away from his chest, where she'd still been holding him back. "It's not that hard. Just take a deep breath, tilt your head up to me and close your eyes."

She did as she was instructed, leaning into him like a teenage girl being kissed for the first time. He shook away those thoughts and pressed his lips against hers. He'd intended it to be a quick kiss, knowing it would take a while for them to work up to a convincing one. But he found that once they touched, he didn't want to pull away.

Gretchen smelled like berries. Her lips were soft, despite the hesitation in them. A tingle ran down his spine, the kind that made him want to wrap his arms around her and pull her soft body flush against his hard one. He settled for placing a hand on her upper arm.

She tensed immediately, and in an instant, the connection was severed. He pulled away and looked down at her, standing there with her eyes still closed.

"You did better this time," he noted.

Her dark lashes fluttered as her eyes opened. A pink flush rushed across her cheeks as she looked up at him with glassy eyes. "Practice makes perfect, I guess."

He laughed softly. It certainly did. "I'll see you tomorrow afternoon. Be sure to bring extra lipstick."

"Why?" she asked, her brow furrowed.

Julian smiled wide and took a step back toward where Murray was waiting for him. "Because I plan to remove all of it several times."

Three

Gretchen made her way back up to Julian's hotel suite the next day. This afternoon, she wasn't as nervous as her first visit, but she still had butterflies in her stomach. She was pretty certain that last night's kiss had something to do with it. She'd been kissed by only four men before last night, and none of them had been movie stars.

She couldn't even sleep last night. His threat to remove her lipstick several times over lingered in her mind. He was going to kiss her again. She felt a girlish thrill run through her every time the thought crossed her mind, quickly followed by the dull ache of dread in her stomach.

There was nothing she could do about it, though. She had to live through this. It was only four days. She could make it through four days of almost anything. She knocked at his hotel room door and waited, anxiously tugging at her paisley wrap dress.

"Hey, Gretchen," Julian said as he peeked around the door with a head of damp hair. "You'll have to excuse me—I was running late. Come on in. I've just got to finish getting dressed."

He stepped back and opened the door wider. As Gretchen entered the suite, she realized he'd been hiding his half-naked body behind the door. Just his hair wasn't wet; all of him was. He had a bath towel slung low around his waist, but otherwise, he was very naked.

She didn't even know what to say. As he closed the door behind her, all she could do was stare at the hard, tanned muscles she'd seen in the movies and on advertisements. His body didn't even look real, although she could reach out and touch it. It was as if he was Photoshopped.

"Gretchen?"

She snapped her head up to see Julian watching her with amusement curling his lips into a smile. She could feel the blood rush hot into her cheeks when she realized she'd been caught. "Yes?" she said.

"Go ahead and grab a seat. I'll be right back."

"Yeah, okay."

Turning as quickly as she could, she focused on the couch, gluing her eyes to the furniture so they couldn't stray back to Julian's naked, wet body.

He disappeared, thankfully, into the bedroom. The moment the door closed, she felt the air rush out of her lungs. Sweet Jesus, she thought as her face dropped into her hands. She was about as smooth as chunky peanut butter. There was no doubt that Gretchen was miserably in over her head. There had to be a better person to do this than her.

"Sorry about that," he said as he came out a few minutes later. He was wearing a pair of charcoal dress pants and a navy dress shirt that made his eyes seem as if they were an even brighter blue. "I didn't want to leave you out in the hallway while I got dressed. I hope that was okay."

"It's fine," she said dismissively. Hopefully convincingly. "It's not like you don't run around like that in half your movies anyway. Nothing I haven't seen."

He chuckled as he settled down on the couch beside her. "Yeah, most of my modesty went out the window a few years ago. Once you film a sex scene with thirty-five people watching, then millions watch it on the big screen, there's not much left to worry about."

"Do you do a lot of sex scenes?" Gretchen asked. She couldn't imagine how invasive that would be. She couldn't even work up the courage to take her clothes off in front of one man, much less a roomful.

"There's usually one in every film. I typically save the female lead from the bad guy and she thanks me with her body. It's always seemed a little cliché and stupid to me. You'd think someone would be too traumatized for something like that, but apparently I'm so handsome, they can't help themselves."

"I'm sure most women in real life couldn't help themselves either. You're in…excellent shape."

He grinned wide, exposing the bright smile that charmed women everywhere. "Thank you. I work very hard to look like this, so it's nice to be appreciated."

"I can't imagine what it would take."

"I can tell you. I do high-intensity interval training four days a week and run about ten miles a day the other three. I have given up all my vices, and my trainer has me eating nothing but lean protein, vegetables and some fruits."

Gretchen's eyes grew larger the more he talked. That sounded miserable. No pizza, no bread, no cookies. He looked good, but what a price. "I, obviously, am not willing to put that much work in."

"Most people aren't, but I make my living with these abs. It's not exactly what I'd planned when I moved to California, but it's worked out. Even then, there are days where I'd kill for a chocolate chip cookie. Just one."

That just seemed sad. She was no poster child for moderation, but there had to be some middle ground. "I guess the wedding cake is out, then. That's a shame. Amelia does amazing work."

Julian narrowed his gaze at her. "Maybe I'll make an exception for a bite or two of her amazing cake. I'll let you feed me some of yours so I'm not too tempted."

She couldn't even imagine feeding Julian cake while they sat together at the reception. That seemed so intimate, so beyond where they were together. She knew nothing about him, aside from the fact that he was out of her league.

"I need to tell you something," she said. The words shot out of her mouth before she could stop them.

His dark brows went up curiously. "What's that?"

"It may be painfully obvious to you, but I'm not very good with this kind of thing. I haven't been in many relationships, so this whole situation is alien to me. I don't know if coaching will be enough for me to pull this off." She stopped talking and waited in the silence for him to put an end to this torture and terminate the relationship agreement. If they hurried, maybe they could find a more suitable replacement before the welcome dinner. Anyone would be better than Gretchen.

"I think that's charming," he said with a disarming smile. "Most of the women I know mastered flirting in kindergarten. But no worries. I'll teach you what you need to know."

"How can you teach me how to have a relationship in only a few hours if I haven't mastered it in almost twenty-nine years?"

He leaned in and fixed his bright blue gaze on her. "I happen to be an actor," he confided in a low voice. "A classically trained one at that. I can teach you some tricks to get through it."

Tricks? How could a few acting drills undo fifteen years of awkwardness around men? "Like what?"

"Like reframing the scene in your mind. For one thing, you've got to stop thinking about who I am. That's not going to help you relax. I want you to look at the next few days like a play. You and I are the leads. I'm no more famous than you are. We're equals."

"That's a nice idea, but—"

Julian held up his hand to silence her. "No buts. We're actors. You are a beautiful actress playing the role of my girlfriend. You're meant to be here with me and you're perfectly comfortable with me touching you. That's how it's supposed to be."

Gretchen sighed. It would take more than a little role-playing for her to convince herself of that. "I'm not a beautiful actress. I can't be."

"And why not?" He frowned at her, obviously irritated by her stubbornness to play his game.

"To be a beautiful actress, one must first be beautiful. Only then are acting skills relevant."

Julian narrowed his gaze at her. She squirmed under the scrutiny. They both knew she wasn't Hollywood starlet material; there wasn't any need to look so closely and pick apart the details of her failures.

He reached out and took her hand in his. "Did you know that Bridgette has a mustache she has to get waxed off? She's also not really a blonde, and most of her hair is made up of extensions. Her breasts are fake. Her nose is fake. Everything about her is fake."

"And she looks good." The money was well invested in her career if what he said was true. If Gretchen had a couple grand just lying around, she might make a few improvements herself.

"Julia Monroe is legally blind when she isn't wearing her contact lenses. If her makeup artist doesn't contour her face just right, she looks like a guy after a losing boxing match."

Julia Monroe was one of the biggest and most sought-out actresses in Hollywood. Gretchen had a hard time believing she could look anything but stunning.

"Rochelle Voight has the longest nose hairs I've ever seen on a woman, and her breath is always rancid. I think it's because all she ever eats or drinks are those green juices. I hate when I have to kiss her or film close scenes."

Was he serious? "Why are you telling me all this?"

"Because you need to know that it's all an illusion. Every single one of the Hollywood beautiful people you've compared yourself to is a carefully crafted character designed just for the cameras. We're far from perfect, and more than a few of us couldn't even be described as beautiful without our makeup and hair teams."

"You're telling me everyone in Hollywood is secretly ugly, so I shouldn't feel bad."

He smirked and leaned in to drive home his point. "I'm saying you're an attractive woman—a realistically attractive woman. You shouldn't put yourself through the wringer comparing yourself to an unrealistic ideal. It's all fake."

Gretchen's brows went up in surprise. Even with her makeover, she felt as if Julian were only tolerating her because he couldn't get out of the arrangement. Could he actually believe what he said, or was he just trying to boost her ego enough to get them through this week together?

"Everything about me is fake, too," he said.

It was easy to believe the women he'd spoken about were painted to perfection, but everything on Julian looked pretty darn real to her. "Come on," she chided, pulling her hand from his. She knew he was putting her on now.

"No, I'm serious. These baby blue eyes are colored contacts. The highlights in my hair are fake. My teeth are porcelain veneers because my parents couldn't afford braces when I was younger. My tan is sprayed on weekly. Even my accent is fake."

"You don't have an accent," she argued.

"Exactly. I'm from Kentucky," he said with an unmistakable twang he'd suppressed earlier. "I have an accent, but you're never going to hear it from me because I hide it like everything else."

Gretchen sat back against the cushions of the couch

and tried to absorb everything he was telling her. It was a lot to take in all at once.

"We may all have fake hair and wear makeup and put ourselves through all sorts of abuses to chase the elusive beauty and youth, but we're all actors. This is just our costume. So think of your new makeover as your costume. You've been given all the tools you need. Are you ready to play the role of Julian Cooper's girlfriend?"

She took a deep breath and straightened up in her seat. "I think so."

He cocked his head to the side and lifted a brow at her in challenge.

"I *am*," she corrected with faux confidence in her voice. "Let's do this. Where do we start?"

Julian smiled and turned to face her on the couch. "Okay. When I was in acting school, one of my professors was adamant about throwing the hardest scenes at us first. He didn't let us warm up or start with a less challenging part. We had to open with the dramatic soliloquy. His theory was that once you did that, everything else would come easier. So we're going to start with the hardest part of your role."

Gretchen tensed beside him. The hardest part? It all seemed pretty challenging. She'd be much happier working her way up to the comfort level she needed to pull this off. "How are you—"

He lunged forward and pressed his lips to hers, stealing the question from her lips. Unlike their quick, passionless pecks at the restaurant the night before, this kiss packed a punch. Julian leaned into her, coaxing her mouth open and probing her with his tongue.

She wanted to pull away, but he wouldn't let her. One of his hands was at her waist and the other on her shoulder, keeping her from retreating. Closing her eyes, she remembered she was an actress playing a part. She stopped fighting it and tried to relax. Maybe she could let herself enjoy it for once.

When her tongue tentatively grazed along his, he moaned low against her mouth. The sound sent a shock wave of need through her body making her extremities tingle. She wrapped her arms around his neck and pulled him closer to her. When she'd relaxed against him, his grip on her lessened and his hands became softer and exploratory. They slid across the silky fabric of her dress, finally coming to rest as they wrapped around her waist.

Just when Gretchen had relaxed into his arms and was enjoying their experimental kiss, she felt him tug hard against her. Mercy, but he was strong. Those muscles weren't just for show. The next thing she knew, she was in Julian's lap, straddling him. Her dress rode up high on her thighs and she could feel the warm press of his arousal against her leg.

She almost didn't believe it at first. Gretchen hadn't felt many erections in her time. She hadn't anticipated feeling one here, for sure. Could Julian really be turned on by their kiss, or was he just a very convincing actor? The concerning question startled her enough to make her break away from the kiss. The second her eyes opened, she regretted it. In the moment, things had felt right. Exhilarating and scary, but right. Once she pulled away, all she could do was look awkwardly at the man in whose lap she was sitting. It was a decidedly unladylike and bold place to be, and she wasn't comfortable with either of those adjectives. She could feel the heat in her chest and throat and knew she was blushing crimson in her predicament.

Julian didn't seem to mind. Their awkward parting and her extra pounds in his lap were irrelevant if the pleased grin on his face told her anything. She couldn't tell if he was happy she was doing so well, if he was that good an actor, or if he really was having a good time with it.

"Excellent work," he said. "You're an A pupil."

"Does that mean I should get off your lap so we can move on to the next lesson?"

He shook his head and wrapped his arms tighter around her waist. "Not a chance. Just because you're a quick study doesn't mean you don't need the lessons. We're going to work on this a little more."

"How much more?"

"We're going to sit on this couch and make out until it feels like the most natural thing in the world for us both. If you're going to fool the cameras, we can't stop short of anything less than authenticity."

Gretchen swallowed a chortle of laughter. She wasn't sure that making out with a man like him would ever feel natural, but she wasn't about to complain any time soon about extra lessons.

Julian's rental car was only a few miles from Murray's house, where they were hosting the welcome barbecue. Julian had spent a good part of the past hour going over their manufactured backstory with Gretchen.

"Okay, tell me again how we met. People are going to ask."

She sighed and turned to look out the passenger side window. "You came out here to visit Murray a few weeks ago and happened to join him on a trip to the venue, where you met me. We hit it off, you asked me out for a drink. We've been texting and talking since you went back to LA, and you came back to Nashville early for us to spend time together."

She nailed it. He knew she would. Beneath that shy buffer, Gretchen was one of the smartest, funniest women he'd ever met. It just took a while to get through the nerves. She could handle this; she just couldn't let her anxiety get in the way. "Have we slept together yet?"

Gretchen looked at him with wide eyes. "No, I doubt it. I think we may have traded some saucy texts, but I'm making you wait a little while longer."

"You're a little minx. Good to know."

Julian slowly pulled the car into the driveway and stopped at the large wrought-iron fence, where a small crowd of camera-toting men and fans were loitering. "Smile, you're on *Candid Camera*."

"What do I do?" she asked.

"Just pretend they aren't there. That's the easiest thing to do. Maybe play it up for them a little bit." He reached out and took her hand, holding it in an effortless way as they waited for security to open the gates. Once they pulled through there, they followed the circular driveway to the house, where a valet was waiting. He left the keys in the ignition and turned to look at her. "Any last questions before we do this?"

"Who knows the truth about us?"

That was a good question. "Murray, obviously. And I'm sure he told his fiancée, Kelly. That should be it since Ross won't be at the festivities. Everyone else here thinks you're my new girl."

She nodded and took a deep breath. "Let's get our party on, shall we?"

The valet opened her door and she stepped out, waiting for Julian to walk around and meet her. Together, they walked up the stairs to the front door. When the massive oak doors swung open, they were bombarded with a cacophony of sounds and delicious smells. Murray had spared no expense with even the smallest of events. There were easily a hundred people throughout the large open areas of the ground floor and more outside on the heated deck. A bluegrass band was playing in the gazebo in the backyard, and parked out there was a barbecue truck, smoking ribs and brisket for everyone.

There was a large bar set up in the dining room, just past the buffet of goodies that he knew was only to hold people over until the main course was ready. Shame he couldn't eat any of it.

"Would you like a drink?" he asked, leaning down to murmur in her ear.

"Please."

They went over to the bar, where he got her a margarita on the rocks and got himself sparkling water with a twist of lime. They had a huge keg of beer from a local Nashville microbrewery, which he'd love, but he knew he shouldn't. There would be enough temptations this week without starting off on the wrong foot. As it was, he hadn't worked out since he got here.

"So you don't drink?" Gretchen asked. "Is that a health thing or a moralistic thing?"

"Health. Too many empty calories. One too many beers and all my dietary rules will go out the window. You don't want to find me passed out in a half-eaten pizza, I assure you."

"Scandalous!" she mocked.

"I know, right?" He looked around and spied Murray and Kelly out on the patio. "Have you met Kelly?"

"The bride? Yes. She's been to the facility several times going over details."

"Okay, good. Let's go say hi to the happy couple, then we can find a comfortable place to hang out and hide from most everyone."

"You don't have friends here?"

Julian shook his head. "Not really. Murray and I were roommates in college. When I dropped out and moved to LA, we kept in touch, but I don't really know any of his Nashville friends. I'm mostly here for moral support."

They stepped out onto the deck and greeted the engaged couple.

"So, this is the new lady Murray has told me so much about," Kelly said with a wide smile and a twinkle in her green eyes. "It's good to see you outside of work, Gretchen. I have gotten so many compliments on the invitations. I can't wait to see what you've got in store for the wedding. I think the programs are going to be fabulous."

"Thank you," Gretchen said with a smile.

Julian watched the two women as they chatted about wedding details. From that night at the restaurant, Julian had noticed that Gretchen's reluctance faded away when she talked about her work. She was like a totally different person. She nearly radiated with a confidence that vanished the moment the attention shifted from her art back to her. He understood that. He'd much rather talk about his films, such as they were, than talk about his family or his upbringing. Those were tales better left untold.

"Do you mind if I steal her away?" Kelly asked. "I want to introduce her to my bridesmaids."

"Sure." Julian bent down and planted a kiss in the hollow just below her ear. She shivered but didn't pull away or tense up. Bravo. "Hurry back."

Gretchen gave him a wave and disappeared into the house with Kelly.

"How's that going?" Murray asked.

"Better than expected. I've got her loosened up, so that's helped."

"You're doing a good job, whatever it is. When you came out on the patio together, there wasn't a question in my mind that you two were a couple."

"Really?" Julian smiled. He was pleased they'd come so far, so quickly. Perhaps he wouldn't have to deal with Ross's sour disposition later in the week if this worked out. "I am an award-winning actor, you know."

"The golden popcorn statuette from MTV for Best Fight Scene doesn't really stack up to a Screen Actors Guild Award."

"Don't I know it," Julian grumbled. One day, he wanted a real award for a movie with substance. Once he'd told Ross he wanted to do a movie with depth and the next thing he knew, he was in a movie about terrorists who take over a submarine. Just another flick where he lost his shirt eventually.

"It didn't look like acting to me," Murray said. "You two really look like you've got some chemistry between you. Real chemistry. I'm surprised. She didn't strike me as your type, but stranger things have happened. I, for one, never thought I'd end up with my opening act."

Julian listened to his friend and thoughtfully sipped his drink. He was right. There was something building between them. He didn't know what it was—novelty perhaps. Gretchen was nothing like any of the women he'd ever dated before, and it wasn't just physical differences.

For one thing, she wasn't a vain peacock of a woman. Julian spent his fair share of time in the hair and makeup trailer during films and for official appearances, but it was always a fraction of the time his female costars put in. He got the feeling that Gretchen's day at the spa was a rarity for her. She took care of herself, but her whole self-worth was not wrapped up in her appearance. She was a skilled artist, a savvy businesswoman, and that was more important to her than clothing designers and a close, personal relationship with her colorist.

She also didn't seem that impressed by him. Gretchen was nervous, to be sure, but he got the feeling she was that way around most men. She was aware of his celebrity status, but he couldn't tell if it just didn't impress her, or she didn't care for his body of work. He'd been greeted by plenty of screaming, crying women on the verge of passing out when he touched them. If Gretchen passed out at his touch, it was probably because she'd tensed up and locked her knees.

It had been a long time since he'd been around a woman who didn't care about his money or what he could do for her. She didn't secretly want to act. He wasn't aware of her carrying around a screenplay in her purse for him to read and pass on to a producer. Gretchen was real. She was the first authentic woman he'd spent time with in a really long while. He'd been in California so long, he'd forgotten what it was like to be with a woman instead of a character.

He turned and glanced through the wall of French doors into the house. He spied Gretchen and Kelly standing by the buffet chatting with another woman. Gretchen was smiling awkwardly, carrying on the conversation as best she could. He knew the exact moment the discussion shifted to her work, because she lit up like the sun. She might not think she was a beautiful woman, but he'd never seen anyone more radiant in that moment.

Gretchen was slowly drawing him in. He never intended to let himself get that close to his fake date, but he couldn't help it. He fought the urge to text his brother and tell him about her. James always loved it when his aide would relay stories about Julian's escapades, and he thought his brother would take to Gretchen. She was a talented artist with a quick wit and coy smile. She seemed to enjoy the pleasures in life, drinking her margarita and nibbling on goodies without remorse. She knew who she was, and she lived the life she wanted to.

It was an attractive quality that made him both extremely jealous of her and desperate to have her all at once.

Four

Gretchen crept quietly into the office Thursday morning. She didn't have any wedding-related activities with Julian today, so she wanted to get some things set up for the weekend. Despite the assurances from her coworkers that she didn't have much to do the day of the event, there was plenty that needed to be organized beforehand. And the more she could get done without her coworkers knowing she was there, the better. She wasn't ready for the inquisition.

"Look at you," a woman's voice called down the hallway just before Gretchen reached her office. "Creeping around in the hopes we wouldn't see you. Your hair might be different, but we can still recognize you, you know."

Turning around, Gretchen saw Bree standing outside her office. There was a knowing smirk on her face, and her arms were crossed over her chest.

"Morning, Bree," Gretchen tried to say brightly.

"Don't 'morning' me. You go ahead and get settled, but you'd better know we want to hear all about it."

With a sigh, Gretchen nodded and continued into her office. She hoped it would be quick. They did have a huge, expensive wedding this weekend. Amelia, especially, didn't have time to waste with all those people to feed.

Setting down her things, Gretchen didn't even bother getting on her computer. Instead, she went to the door that led to her storage area. She scanned the various box labels on the shelves, finally identifying the box with the Murray wedding paper goods.

She put it on her desk and lifted the lid. Inside were the wedding programs she'd had printed weeks ago. Beside them were the name cards, table markers and menus. Gretchen had thoroughly gone over everything when they arrived, so she knew they were good to go. She carried the programs into the chapel and left them on the small table just inside. The name cards were left on the round table outside the reception hall. Once the table linens were put out and the centerpieces placed, the cards would be laid out alphabetically for attendees to find their table assignment.

Gretchen continued on through the glass double doors into the reception hall. The large, open room was just a shell of what it would be. The bones were there—sparkling chandeliers and long draped panels of white fabric were hanging overhead, the stage and the dance floor cleared and ready to be occupied by tipsy revelers. The cleaning crew had already been through the day before to vacuum and arrange the tables and chairs.

It would take hours of work to decorate the room. She

hoped to get a head start on some of it today, although a lot of things were last-minute, such as the dishes and the floral arrangements. The wedding was black and white, following along the musical note theme, so the dry cleaning company would deliver their cleaned, pressed white and black table linens sometime this morning. Some custom hand-beaded sheer overlays were ordered to be put over them, making the white tables look like sheet music. The napkins needed to be folded. Several hundred white pillar candles had to be put out.

Gretchen nervously eyed the bare ballroom. The list of things she had to do was staggering. How had she allowed herself to get roped into this romance charade? Just because things were handled the day of the wedding didn't mean she wasn't running around like a chicken with its head cut off the days leading up to it.

"Gretchen, the dry cleaning delivery is here." Natalie stuck her head into the ballroom. She was wearing her headset, as usual, as she was constantly on the phone. She was the command center of the entire operation, coordinating vendors, talking to clients, booking future events and managing the bookkeeping.

"Awesome, thank you."

She helped unload all their clean linens into the ballroom and decided she wanted to start laying them out. She didn't have time to waste.

"I'm ready to hear about yesterday." Amelia walked into the ballroom with Bree on her heels. "My cakes are cooling and I've got some downtime."

Downtime? Gretchen tried not to snort. "Well, I don't have downtime, so if you want to hear about yesterday, you can listen while you help me drape all the tables."

"Fair enough." Bree shrugged. She reached for a tablecloth and flung it over the nearest table.

"We're alternating black and white," Gretchen explained, and they all started at it. They got through about a third of the tables before Bree gently reminded her that they weren't helping out of the goodness of their hearts.

"So, spill it. Did you kiss him?"

Gretchen felt her cheeks turn crimson again. "Yes. I kissed him a lot. He insisted we kiss until I could relax while I was doing it."

"That is just crazy," Bree said. "You're getting paid to make out with Julian Cooper. How did this even happen?"

Shaking her head, Gretchen covered another table in black linen. "I recall you all twisting my arm until I agreed to it."

"Are you getting more comfortable?" Amelia asked, ignoring Gretchen's pointed accusation.

"Yes. I think we're finally to the point where people might actually believe we know each other."

"Biblically?"

"Ugh," Gretchen groaned. "I haven't known anyone biblically, so I can't really say."

"Say what?" Bree stared her down, the linen in her hands pooling on the table. "Did you just say what I thought you said?"

Amelia narrowed her gaze at Gretchen, too. She should've kept her mouth shut about the whole thing. She'd gotten good at it after all these years, even keeping the truth from her best friends. Now the cat was out of the bag.

Gretchen straightened the cloth on the table and admitted the truth, reluctantly. "Yep."

"You're a virgin?" Bree nearly shouted. "How could we not know that you're a virgin?"

"Hush!" Gretchen hissed. "Don't shout it across the ballroom like that."

"I'm sorry," she said, her blue eyes as big as saucers. "It just never occurred to me that my twenty-nine-year-old friend was keeping a secret that big. Did you know?" Bree turned to Amelia.

"I did not."

"You didn't tell any of us?"

"She told me," Natalie said, coming into the room. "It's been a long time, but I haven't gotten any updates that would lead me to believe things had changed."

That was true. Natalie was the only one she'd told, and that had been on a long-ago college night where they'd stayed up late studying, ended up getting into a cheap bottle of wine and spilled their secrets to each other. Natalie was the right person to tell. She wasn't a hopeless romantic like Amelia or pushy like Bree. She took the knowledge at face value and didn't press Gretchen about it.

Bree dropped the tablecloth and sat down in the chair. "Stop, everyone, stop. You all sit down right now and tell me what the heck is going on. How could you keep that from us? And why would you tell Natalie, of all people?"

"Hey!" Natalie complained.

Gretchen frowned at Bree and dropped into a nearby chair. "Bree, how could you not tell us that Ian was your ex before you went up into the mountains to take his engagement photos?"

Bree's nose wrinkled, and she bit at her bottom lip. "It wasn't relevant at the time."

"And neither is my sexual inexperience."

"It might not be relevant to running the business, but as your friend, it seems like something we should've known."

"Known what? That I'm so incredibly awkward with men that I've driven them away since I was fourteen? That my self-esteem is so low that I can't believe a guy could really be interested in me and I look suspiciously at their motives?"

"You're a beautiful, talented woman, Gretchen," Natalie said. "You may not have felt that way when you were a teenager or just in college, but you're on the verge of being in your thirties. Don't you feel differently about yourself after your successes in life?"

"I did. I thought I was doing better and I was even considering putting up an online dating profile, but I have to tell you there's nothing quite like a movie star to bring out your insecurities."

"May I ask how you've gotten this far in life without losing your virginity?" Amelia looked at her with concern in her eyes. It was the same look guys tended to give her when she told them the truth. Like she was damaged somehow.

Gretchen shrugged. "I didn't date in high school. College was hit-or-miss, but nothing ever got serious enough. As I got older, it got harder. It felt more like a burden, which made it even harder to admit to it. With the few guys I've dated in the last couple of years, they push for sex until they find out I haven't done it before, then they back off. They don't want the responsibility for being my first, or they think I'm going to get clingy because of it… I don't know. It just seems like the longer I wait, the harder it is."

"We can fix this," Bree said brightly. "With your new makeover and your new attitude, we can get you a hot guy, pronto."

"I don't want a—" Gretchen tried to argue, but was drowned out.

"We don't just want to get her laid, Bree," Amelia argued. "We want her to find real happiness in a healthy relationship that includes sexual intimacy."

"I'm not sure I'm—"

"She's waited this long, it should be special."

"Just stop!" Gretchen shouted. The others were working hard at fixing all her problems, but that wasn't what she wanted. "See, this is what I wanted to avoid. I don't need to be fixed up or pimped out. It just is what it is."

"Are you happy with the status quo?" Amelia pressed.

"Some days yes, some days no. But the point of this whole thing is that it makes it harder for me to pretend with Julian. I am awkward enough without being around someone that is completely unattainable in real life."

"I don't know," Bree said thoughtfully. "I think you could have him. You're looking mighty fine today."

"You've lost your mind," Gretchen muttered. If there was one thing she hated, it was being the center of attention. It made her extremely uncomfortable. She was desperate to shift this conversation in another direction. "Now you all know my deep dark secrets, so either help me put out tablecloths or return to your battle stations. There's nothing more to see here."

Bree finished laying out one more tablecloth, then she joined the other two as they slipped out to their offices and kitchen to return to work. Gretchen was relieved to be in the ballroom by herself again.

That was uncomfortable, but it was over, thankfully. She'd never have to confess it to her friends and coworkers again. But she was sure she hadn't heard the end of it. Once this nonsense with Julian wasn't taking up her time, she had no doubt one of them would try to fix her up. They'd tried before, just attempting to help her find a guy, but now it would be a mission.

Laying out the last tablecloth, she looked across the room, which was like a checkerboard stretching out in front of her. In two days, she would be in this room as a guest instead of an employee. It was an odd thought, especially considering she'd be on Julian Cooper's arm.

She couldn't believe Bree actually thought that Julian could be the one to relieve her of the burden of her virginity. That was ridiculous, even with her secret knowledge that he was aroused by kissing her. There was a far leap between those two things. She was paid to be his date in public, not in private. If he actually slept with her, it would be because he wanted her.

There was no way in hell he wanted her. Or did he?

Julian pulled his nondescript black rental SUV into the parking lot at From This Moment. He really didn't need to come here today. Today was a day of relaxation, small errands and final preparation for the big event. At least for the men. The women had gathered for a spa day in the morning, and this afternoon, they were having a bridal tea downtown. That left their male counterparts a day to themselves.

The day had started for them at the golf course. The weather at that hour was a little brisk for Julian's California blood, but the skies were clear and they had a good time playing. They'd all had lunch at some famous hole-in-the-wall barbecue joint, where Julian had a grilled chicken breast and one glorious hush puppy, and then they returned to the hotel and went their separate ways.

With that done, Julian was able to clean up and get ready to do a few chores for the day. There were no messages on his phone from his family, nothing to concern him, so he could focus on wedding preparation. He needed to pick up the tuxedos and get the wedding rings from the jeweler. As the best man, Murray didn't ask much of him. Running a couple errands and throwing a decent bachelor party Friday night were all that was required. It wasn't hard.

And yet he found himself thinking he should pick up Gretchen and bring her along with him.

She wasn't expecting him to show up. He knew she had work to do and his sudden arrival would likely throw her off her game. He told himself he needed to keep her on her toes, because the press certainly would, and she had to be ready for anything.

But in truth, he just wanted to see her again.

It was hard to explain—a feeling he hadn't experienced in a long time. Lately, he'd dated his costars, women he saw on the set every day. He'd gotten used to that sort of immersive dating pattern. So last night, when he'd realized he wouldn't see Gretchen until Friday evening at the rehearsal dinner, he'd felt a little… lonely. He found he missed her awkward smiles and sarcastic comments under her breath. He wanted to wrap his arms around her waist and kiss her until she blushed down into her cleavage.

He didn't realize he was driving to the wedding chapel until he saw the sign ahead of him. By then, he figured it couldn't hurt to pop in and see if she had the time to join him.

Turning off the engine, he climbed out of the SUV and went in the front entrance. The lobby was huge and shaped almost like a cross, with four arched doorways leading to different areas of the chapel. In the center was a round table draped in white with a sheer fabric over it. It looked as if tiny musical notes were stitched all over with shiny black thread, beads and crystals. A tall silver tree branch came up out of the center. Hanging from it were strands of crystal, musical notes and little white cards with people's names on them.

Fancy.

To his left was the wedding chapel, and straight ahead was the reception hall, so he opted to go right, where the offices were. He found a closed door with Gretchen McAlister's name on it and knocked softly.

"No, I don't want to date your cousin!" he heard her shout from the other side of the door.

With a smile, he opened the door, peeking his head in to see her sitting at her desk, tying black and white ribbons around glass cylinders with candles in them. "But you've never even met my cousin. You might like him."

Gretchen's gaze shot up at the sound of his voice, her eyes widening. "Julian! Sorry about that. I thought you were Bree. What are you doing here? Is there a problem? I thought we weren't getting together until tomorrow."

"No problem," he said, slipping into her office and shutting the door behind him. "I just thought you might like to hang out with me today."

Her gaze narrowed at him. "Hang out? Do you mean practice some more? Go over our cover story again?"

Julian shook his head. "No, you've got that covered, I think. I've got to run a couple errands today and I thought you might like to join me, that's all."

Her eyebrows drew together as she considered his offer. She seemed genuinely confused by it. That, or suspicious again. He still didn't understand that. "I'm not dressed up for an official day out with you."

Her hand ran self-consciously over her hair, which was pulled back into a butterfly clip. Her makeup was done, but not heavy-handed. She was wearing a pair of skinny jeans and a simple V-neck sweater with boots. The dark brown of the sweater matched her eyes and made her skin look even creamier against the rich tones. She looked great to him. He actually had a hard time tearing his gaze away from the tantalizing glimpse of cleavage that her sweater teased at, without being too blatant. "You look great," he countered.

"I've also got a lot to do," she said, uncertainty in her voice.

"Well, it just so happens that I don't have a lot to do. How about a little trade-off? You come with me to do a few wedding-related chores, and then I'll come back here with you and help you do whatever it is you do."

A delicate dark eyebrow raised at him. "You're going to help me?"

"Sure," he said with a winning smile. "I have no clue what needs to be done, but I'm an actor. I can fake it."

Gretchen snorted and shook her head. "Well, I'm not sure how much help you'll be, but any help would be great."

Julian chuckled. "Well, thank goodness you have

low standards. Let's go. I have to pick up the tuxedos and the rings."

He helped Gretchen into her coat, and they left the chapel a moment later. As they got into his rental, he admitted, "I also have no idea where I'm going. Do you know where Couture Connection is? That's where I have to get the tuxedos. I can look it up on my phone if we need to."

Gretchen nodded and pointed to the right. "I know where it is. It's just a couple miles from here. Go out to the right."

That part of the day went smoothly enough. They found the store and waited a few minutes to pick up their suits. It wasn't until they were getting ready to leave that Julian noticed the guy across the street with a camera.

He sighed. They'd finally found him. It had actually taken longer than he expected. "Someone tipped off the paparazzi," he said to Gretchen, although he gave a meaningful glance at the girl behind the counter. She'd been in the back room far, far too long in his opinion. She bit her lip and handed over the suits without comment.

"What do we do?" Gretchen asked. "I told you I'm not camera-ready today."

He shrugged. "We do what we need to do. If life stopped just because someone was taking my picture, I'd never get anything done." Julian draped the suits over his arm and reached out to grasp Gretchen's hand. "Off we go," he said.

By the time they reached the jewelry store, there were three cars tailing them, and they were bolder than before. Julian hadn't even opened the car door for

Gretchen before there were four guys swarming the car with cameras, snapping pictures and asking questions.

"Who's the lady, Julian?"

"Her name is Gretchen McAlister," he said, opening the door and helping her out of the car. Normally he would just ignore them, but what was the point of having a fake girlfriend if he wasn't going to publicize that fact?

"Is this your new lady love?" another one prompted, making Gretchen blush.

Julian took her hand and looked into her eyes. It was easy to get lost there, the feelings she evoked in him lately hardly an act. "She's very special to me," he answered with a sincere smile.

"What do you think Bridgette will think of your new relationship?"

"I really don't care what she thinks," Julian said and leaned into Gretchen's ear. "Let's get inside."

The cameras stayed outside while they met with the jeweler. The woman at the counter left them for a moment to go back and find the owner. Julian watched Gretchen peruse the case, her eyes lighting up as she spied something interesting. It was always dangerous to go into a jewelry store with the women he dated. It almost always cost him more than he expected.

"What do you see?" he asked, curious as to what would spark such a reaction in Gretchen. She didn't seem to wear much jewelry.

"That necklace," she said, pointing out a teardrop-shaped opal, speckled with blue and pink fire. "That's my birthstone. I've never seen a natural opal with such bright fire in it before."

It was pretty, and not at all what he expected her to

choose in the case of flashy diamonds and other glittering and expensive gemstones. He doubted Bridgette even knew what an opal was. Julian hovered, waiting for the expectant look he was used to seeing, but Gretchen just shrugged and continued down the case. She continued to surprise him. Perhaps she deserved a surprise in return.

"Mr. Cooper," the owner of the store greeted them as he came out from the back room. "Come with me. I have everything ready for you."

They were taken to a private room in the back where they could inspect the rings and sign for them. There was a lot of gold and a lot of diamonds involved, so he wanted to make sure everything was perfect for Murray and Kelly.

"Is there anything else I can do for you today, Mr. Cooper?" the jeweler asked.

"Actually, yes. That opal teardrop necklace in the case. I'd like that for my companion, please."

The man nodded. "An excellent choice." He called out to the woman at the counter to bring it back to them.

Julian ignored the stunned look on Gretchen's face as the jeweler presented the necklace on a velvet tray. "It looks perfect, thank you."

"Would you like it boxed up?"

"No, we'll be wearing it out." Julian reached for the necklace and unfastened the clasp. Before Gretchen could breathe a word of argument, he rose from his chair to stand behind her. He gently brushed a loose strand of dark hair from her neck, then draped the necklace at her throat. When fastened, the gem fell right beneath her collarbone and was highlighted nicely by the low plunge of her sweater.

"Lovely," the jeweler said. "I'll put the box in the bag with the rings for you."

Julian handed over his black American Express card as the jeweler left the room.

"What is this for?" she finally said when they were alone. "This necklace was super expensive."

He could only shrug and dismiss it the same way she'd dismissed the idea of getting the necklace. "It made you smile," he said. "That was worth every penny."

Gretchen gripped the pendant in her hand, shaking her head. "I'm already being paid a ridiculous amount for this. You don't have to buy me anything."

Julian tried not to flinch at that unfortunate reminder. He'd nearly forgotten that she was being paid to be with him. She was so unlike all the other people in his life with their hands out that it was an unwelcome shock to remember she was getting her piece of him just like the rest. And yet he somehow knew that she was different.

In the end it didn't matter. He wanted to buy the necklace and he bought it. "It's a gift. Enjoy it."

The jeweler returned with his card and receipt. "Anything else I can do for you today?"

As they stood, Julian considered the reporters outside waiting for them. He'd spied a little café up the block, but he didn't want them following the two of them there. He wanted some quiet time with Gretchen before the wedding chaos began.

"Just one more thing. Do you have a rear exit we could use?"

Five

"Is that all you're going to eat?" Gretchen asked. "Seriously, I can't have those camera guys show up and document me here with a full plate while you pick at a spinach salad with no dressing."

"I told you," he said with a smile, "I'm saving up for that cake of Amelia's."

Gretchen looked down at her sandwich and shrugged before taking another bite. "You could at least have the decency to order more food for appearances and just not eat it."

"No one is looking at us, Gretchen. We're hidden in the back corner of a tiny café. Relax and enjoy your food."

Gretchen took a few more bites before she worked up the nerve to ask Julian a question. "Do you ever get tired of it?"

"Tired of what?"

"Tired of being treated like a piece of meat?"

Julian smothered a snort of laughter. "Actually, yes, I do. But I won't look like this forever. I'm young, in my physical prime, so I thought I should make the most of it while I can. I suppose I can tackle some meatier scripts when I'm older and people aren't that interested in my biceps anymore."

"It's not your biceps," Gretchen corrected. "It's the abs."

One of Julian's dark eyebrows went up. "Well, thank you for noticing."

Gretchen blushed. "I didn't. I was really just saying that I…" Her voice drifted off as she ran out of argument.

"It's okay, Gretchen. You're allowed to admire the abs. It would be hypocritical of me to use my body to make money, then criticize someone for noticing it. Maybe someday I'll be known for something else."

"Have you considered doing different kinds of films now? I mean, how many big action flicks can you make in a year? You'd think you'd have time to do something new every now and then."

Julian sighed. "I'd love to. I've actually got a script in my hotel room for something I'm really excited about. It's totally different for me. A real, meaty role. The kind that might earn critical acclaim for my acting."

Gretchen noticed Julian perk up in his seat as he talked about the plot of the script. He was eyeing the role of an alcoholic who loses everything and returns home to face the family he'd left behind. It sounded like an amazing role, the kind that could change the whole trajectory of his career. "Why don't you do it?"

"My manager doesn't think it's a good idea. And

he's right. The more I think about it, the more I know it isn't the right time."

"Why? What could it hurt to try it?"

Julian got a distant look in his eyes as he turned to glance out toward the front of the café. "It could hurt everything. I'm blessed to have what I do now. I have enough money coming in to care for my family, live an amazing life and never worry about how I'm going to pay for something. But this industry is fickle, and you can lose it all in an instant."

"How could you possibly do such a terrible job that you could sink your entire career?"

"It's been a while since I've stretched my serious acting muscles, Gretchen. I may not have even been any good at it to begin with. I landed my first movie role for my body, and little has changed. What if I…" His voice trailed off. "What if I tried to do a serious movie and I'm no good? What if I get panned left, right and center, ripped apart by critics for thinking I could do anything more than shoot a gun or fly a helicopter?"

"At least you will have tried. Pardon me for saying so, but these action movies don't really seem to fulfill you. As a creative person, I understand how that can be. If you're compromising and not doing what you love, eventually you'll lose your joy for the work."

"You enjoy your work, don't you? I can tell by the way your whole demeanor changes when you talk about it."

Gretchen hadn't noticed that before, and she was surprised Julian had paid that much attention. "I'm not sure about how it changes me, but I do love my job. I'm not necessarily a traditional artist that paints or sculpts, but I get to do so many different and creative things. I never get bored. And I get to work with my best friends, so that makes every day fun."

"I have to admit I'm jealous."

Gretchen looked up at him, her eyes wide in surprise. "You're jealous of me? Really?"

He nodded. "Absolutely. You're living the life you want. You're doing the job you enjoy. You seem to be living so authentically, doing what makes you happy."

"Well, I'm also not a millionaire. There's probably a trade-off in there somewhere."

"Money isn't all it's cracked up to be. It's necessary, and I'm thankful to have enough to do what I need to do, but the thought of losing it can become what holds you back. I mean, look at me. I'm in a delightful-smelling café, near drooling over some berry tart in the case that I won't let myself have. I don't eat what I want, I don't do what I want, I don't act in the films I'd like to…all because of the money."

Gretchen shook her head. "Only someone with money could ever consider it a burden."

Julian watched her curiously for a moment. "May I ask why you agreed to participate in this charade with me?"

She had to laugh at his query. She was surprised it had taken him this long to ask. "That's a good question. For the first few days, I was asking myself the same thing. Part of it was being in the right place at the wrong time, but in the end, I'm ashamed to admit it came down to the money. It was a few days out of my life and when it was over, I'd have the opportunity to take the trip I've always dreamed of taking. Without it, who knows when, if ever, I'd get another chance."

"I love to travel," Julian said, scooting aside his half-eaten salad and leaning closer to her. "Where are you wanting to go?"

"Italy," she said with a wistful sigh. "It's been my dream since high school when we studied the Renaissance. I want to go and just suck up all the beauty there. The paintings, the architecture, the food and the people. I want to experience it all, and this money will make that possible."

Julian nodded as he listened to her speak. "Italy is beautiful. You'll love it."

"Have you been?"

"Once. We filmed for a few weeks in Tuscany and I got to visit Florence. It's an amazing place. I've always wanted to go back, but I haven't had the time."

Gretchen understood that. "I know how you feel. Even with the money, taking the time away from From This Moment is hard to do. It's been my life since we started the place."

"Well," he said, "I think you need to make the time. If you've got the money, do it. There's never going to be a perfect time, and before you know it, life will dwindle away your savings and you'll miss your chance."

"I don't think I—"

"I dare you to go next spring," Julian said with a conspiratorial smile. "Maybe late April or early May. It will be perfect. Good weather and not too crowded yet."

Gretchen nearly choked. "You *dare* me?"

"I do," he said, his blue eyes focused intently on her in a way that made her spine soften and her chest tighten. "You don't seem like the kind of woman that would back down from a dare."

She eyed him with a twist of her lips. She hadn't played many games of truth or dare in her time, but she was certain that two could play at this game. "Very well, I accept. But I have a dare for you as well."

"Oh, you do now?" He sat back in his seat and crossed his arms over his chest as though he couldn't be intimidated by her challenge. "I can't wait to hear what it is. Back in college, I always opted for the dare over the truth. I haven't turned one down, ever."

That might be true, but he hadn't gone up against Gretchen before. "Okay, Mr. Confident. I dare you to go back to the counter, buy that berry tart you want so badly and eat every bite of it. Live on the wild side for just today, Julian. Who knows, one day it's berry tarts, the next day it's a film premiering at Sundance."

Julian watched her face for a moment. She knew that he was fighting with himself, but a dare was a dare, right?

She decided maybe she should throw him a bone. She of all people knew what it was like to try to diet and have family and friends unintentionally sabotage her plans. "I'll share it with you, if you want."

At that, his expression brightened. "Done." He got up and left her alone at the table for a few minutes to secure their pastry prize.

Alone, she sat back in her chair and took the first deep breath for nearly half an hour. Julian was so intense, she sometimes found it hard to breathe when he was around. But she liked it. She liked being with him. She'd never expected that to be the case. They were so different, or so she thought.

Beneath it all, she realized they had more in common than she expected. The more time they spent together, the more easily she was able to see the man behind the actor.

As nice as that was, they were dangerous, pointless thoughts. They'd just discussed what she was going to do with the money he was paying her to be around him. Once the wedding was over, so was their time together. It might feel as if they had a connection, but he was an actor. Gretchen couldn't let herself forget that. In a few days, he would return to LA and forget she ever existed.

It was just her luck that the first guy she'd really felt comfortable with in years turned out to be a Hollywood actor who would disappear and want nothing more to do with her.

At this rate, she was never going to get laid.

Julian nearly groaned as he took the last bite of the berry tart. It was the best thing he'd tasted in…a year, maybe? Most days of his life, he didn't control what he ate. His trainers and personal chefs took care of that for him and kept the temptations far away. Bridgette was even more strict with her eating, so it was easier to get through the day knowing he wouldn't be exposed to the things he really wanted. Out of sight, out of mind.

Gretchen wasn't hung up on all that. She indulged when she wanted to indulge, and the satisfied smile on her face was evidence of that. So what if it cost her a few extra pounds? Her soft, womanly figure with a sincere smile was far better than rail-thin Bridgette and her pinched, anxious look. She never smiled with contentment. She was always looking for something more in life.

This berry tart may have been that very thing.

"So naughty," Gretchen said, putting her fork down on the empty plate. "I bet you gain three whole pounds eating that."

Julian sat up sharply. "That's not possible. Is it?"

She laughed at him and shook her head. "No. You're fine. Half a berry tart isn't the end of the world. You did get a serving of fiber-rich fruit out of it, after all."

That's when Julian noticed a small dab of strawberry glaze at the corner of her lips. He reached for his napkin to dab it away, but hesitated. He had a better idea.

"Hold still," he said, leaning across the table toward her. With one hand gently caressing her neck, he pressed his lips to the corner of her mouth, removing the last of their dessert before moving over and kissing her.

Just like every time he touched her, Julian immediately responded to Gretchen. With her soft lips pressed against his and the scent of her skin filling his lungs, he couldn't pull away. Every muscle in his body tightened with a building need for her. Each time they kissed, his desire for her grew. He knew that this was a business arrangement, but he couldn't help his reaction to her. He wanted her more than he'd wanted any other woman before.

But unlike the other times when they were practicing making it look good for the cameras, this time Gretchen pulled away from him.

He wasn't expecting it, and her sudden withdrawal left him hovering, vulnerable, over the table. "What's the matter?"

She watched him with wary dark eyes. "What was that about?"

His brows went up. "What was the kiss about?"

"Yes." She glanced around the café, her gaze dropping into her lap. "I thought you said we were done practicing that. There's no one watching us right now."

Gretchen couldn't fathom that he would kiss her just

because he could. Because he *wanted* to. "That kiss," he said, "wasn't for the cameras. That one was for me."

Her eyes met his with a narrowed gaze and a frown wrinkling her nose. "I don't understand."

Julian reached across the table and took her hand. "What is there to understand, Gretchen? I like you. I wanted to kiss you, so I did. That's pretty simple boy-meets-girl kind of stuff."

She nodded, although he wasn't entirely sure she felt better about the whole thing. "I told you before I'm not that good with the boy-meets-girl thing."

She had told him, but he didn't realize until that moment how serious she was about it. How was it possible that she couldn't understand why he'd want to kiss her? Was her self-esteem so low that she didn't think she was worthy of his attention? If so, he'd see to correcting that assumption right away.

"You said you like me. What did you mean by that?"

"I mean that I like you. And yes, that I'm attracted to you. I know this arrangement is mostly about business, and I don't want to make you feel uncomfortable, but I'm into you, Gretchen. Truly."

She responded with silence, reaching out to take a sip of her iced tea. It was almost as though she didn't know how to respond, as if he'd said "I love you" too soon in a relationship. Had he read the signals wrong? He didn't want her to think that he presumed their contract extended to extracurricular activities in the bedroom. He was about to say something to soften the statement when she looked up at him with an intensity in her chocolate-brown eyes.

"I'm attracted to you, as well," she said boldly.

Julian shelved the instinctual smile. He didn't want

her to think he was laughing at her. It was anything but. He had suspected that she was turned on by him, but he couldn't know for sure. Knowing made him feel lighter somehow. "I'm glad we got that out there."

She nodded, and her gaze returned to her lap. Any fantasies he had about taking her back to his hotel room and making love to her that instant fizzled away. One step at a time, he reminded himself. Besides, they had work they were avoiding. Even if she wanted him as desperately as he wanted her, there was a wedding coming up, and the ballroom needed to be decorated sooner rather than later.

"I guess we'd better get back to the chapel," he said. "I promised I'd help you set up all those decorations, remember?"

"You don't really have to," she said dismissively. "You bought my food, and more importantly, this necklace. I'll happily stay up all night decorating on my own to make up for the lost time."

He shook his head. "You're not getting rid of me so easily. I may not have an artistic eye, but I'm helping you and that's final."

Gretchen nodded and placed her napkin on the table. "It's been over an hour. Do you think the photographers have given up or are they still sitting outside the jewelry store?"

Julian shrugged and got up from the table. "It doesn't matter. I'm happy we had the hour alone that we had." He took her hand and led her out of the café. The cameramen had given up, and their vehicle was waiting patiently for them down the block.

The return to the chapel was uneventful, yet awkwardly silent. Not since their first night together had there been this weird energy between them. It continued until they were back in the ballroom and the work began. They lost themselves in tying a black organza bow around the back of each chair. Julian was quickly removed from that task—apparently he didn't tie bows, just knots—and he was given the job of folding all the linen napkins. Thank goodness there wasn't some fancy fabric origami going on, just a simple fold that created a rectangle with a pocket.

When the bows were finished, Gretchen laid a glass charger with silver beaded accents at each place setting. Julian followed behind her, draping the napkin across the charger and slipping the menu into the pocket. He helped her carry in about forty of the decorated hurricane vases, placing them on the stage along with some large silver vases and candelabras.

"What next?" he asked. "Do these need to go on the tables?"

Gretchen sat down on the edge of the stage and shook her head. "Not tonight." She glanced at her cell phone. "It's getting late. I'll do that tomorrow."

Julian sat beside her and eyed the room. They had gotten a lot done, but if he knew Gretchen, there was a lot more in store for the decor. "Are you sure? I can stay as late as you need me to."

"Aren't you here for Murray? Shouldn't you guys be hanging out and playing poker or something? Guy bonding?"

He shrugged. "Not really. We golfed and ate barbecue today before I came over. Tomorrow, there's just the rehearsal, the dinner and the bachelor party."

Gretchen gave him a knowing smile. "Whatcha got planned? Strippers and beer?"

"No," he said with an offended tone to his voice. "It's going to be classy! I've rented out an old piano bar downtown. I've also got a Cuban guy coming in to roll authentic cigars and a local microbrewery doing flights of all their best beers. A few ladies from the burlesque show will be performing." He tried to say it all with a straight face, but it didn't last long. She had him pegged the first time. "Okay, yeah," he laughed. "Strippers and beer. But they're expensive strippers and beer."

"I'm sure that makes it a much classier affair," she said with a smile.

"I thought so."

"We'd better get you home, then. You'll need your rest for a long night of debauchery." Gretchen stood up and dusted her hands off on her jeans.

Julian followed her out of the ballroom, waiting as she switched off lights and locked doors behind her. When they stepped outside into the parking lot, he noticed the temperature had really dropped since they went inside. In just a few short hours, it had gone from a California November day to a November day anywhere else. He snuggled into his leather jacket, but all it really did was keep the wind from cutting through him.

Gretchen seemed more prepared. She stepped outside in a dark burgundy peacoat and a scarf. He walked her over to her tiny sedan, hesitant to say good-night and hesitant to say what he needed to say to make the night last. He moved close to tell her goodbye, her back pressed to the car as she looked up at him with the overhead lights twinkling in her eyes.

"Do you have a real coat?" she asked when she noticed him start to shiver.

"Not with me. I have one I wear when I go skiing

in Aspen, but I didn't think I'd need it here." Looking at the space between them, he realized he could see his breath. It was darn cold. He should've looked more closely at the forecast before he packed.

"Well, maybe tomorrow you should take a trip to the store and pick up a nice wool coat. We can't let the best man catch cold the day before the wedding."

"That's a good idea. Perhaps you can just help me stay warm in the meantime."

With a smile, Gretchen wrapped her arms around his neck and pulled him close. Her lips mere centimeters from his, she asked, "How's this?"

Julian pressed the full length of his body against her and wrapped his arms around her waist. "Definitely getting warmer. Still a little cold, though."

Holding his face in her hands, she guided his lips to hers. A surge of heat shot through his veins as they touched. When her tongue grazed along his own, he was nearly warm enough to take off his jacket. That simple, innocent touch was enough to set his blood to boiling with need for her.

He traveled the line of her jaw, leaving a trail of kisses until he reached the sensitive curve of her neck. Gretchen gasped and clung to him as he nibbled at her flesh. The sound was like music to his ears, sending a chill through his whole body. Desperate to touch more of her, he moved one hand from her waist, sliding it up her side until it cupped her breast.

He was rewarded with another gasp, but it was quickly followed by insistent palms pressing against his chest. He moved back, dropping his hands to his sides. "What's the matter?" he asked between panting breaths.

"I…" she started, then shook her head. "It's just a little too fast for me, Julian."

Fast? "It's Thursday, Gretchen. By Monday, I'll be back in California. I don't want to make you uncomfortable, but we don't have forever."

Gretchen sighed and shifted her gaze to look over his shoulder. "I know."

"What's really bothering you?" It didn't seem as though her body and her words were lining up. "Tell me."

Swallowing hard, she nodded. "I told you I hadn't dated much, but it's more than that, Julian. It's not that I don't want you. I do. Very badly. And I would gladly take this as far as you're willing to go. But I think if you knew the truth, you'd…"

"I'd what?" He couldn't think of anything she could say to smother his desire for her.

"I'm a virgin," she said, almost spitting out the words as if to get them out before she could change her mind.

Julian's eyes widened and he stumbled back, as though her words had physically hit him. Was she serious? "A virgin?" he asked.

"Yes. Like I said, it isn't a problem for me. Frankly, you'd be doing me a huge favor by ridding me of this burden I've carried around for all these years. But I find that people don't react well to the news."

He could understand that. He wasn't reacting that well himself. It wasn't as though she'd just announced she was a hermaphrodite or something, but still, it had caught him off guard. In an instant, the idea of a fun, casual romance while he was in Nashville had just gotten instantly more complicated.

"Damn," Gretchen whispered.

Her curse snapped him out of his own head. He looked at her with a frown. "What?"

"It's happened again," she said. "I've scared you off. You can't get away from me fast enough. I can see it in your eyes."

"No, no," he said, shaking his head adamantly. "It's just not what I was expecting. But I should've…" His voice trailed away. All the signs had pointed there; he just hadn't thought it was possible.

"Well, it's getting late and you're probably freezing," he said, the words sounding lame even to his own ears. "We've got a long night tomorrow, so I'll let you get home. I'll see you here at the rehearsal at six?"

"Yeah." Gretchen didn't even try to hide the disappointment on her face and in her voice. His quick backpedaling had hurt her feelings, but he didn't know what else to do. "Good night, Julian."

Without so much as a goodbye peck on the cheek, she opened her car door and got inside. He'd barely closed the door when the engine roared to life and she backed out of the parking space.

As her taillights disappeared into the distance, Julian realized he was a schmuck. Apparently he was much better with women when he had a script to follow.

Six

Gretchen should've kept her damn mouth shut. That was it—she wasn't telling a guy the truth again. The next time she got someone interested in sleeping with her, she'd let him find out the hard way. It might be rough going, but by the time he realized it, it would be done and she wouldn't have to go through this embarrassment again and again.

At the moment, it would be easy to believe that nothing had happened last night. She and Julian were seated together at a table with a few other members of the wedding party. The rehearsal dinner was wrapping up, and waiters were coming around with trays of desserts. His arm was draped over her shoulder, a devoted smile on his face whenever he looked at her. Ever the actor, this was easy for him. It wasn't so easy for her, especially with Bree hovering around the edge of the room taking pictures and smiling knowingly at her.

Just when she thought she'd overcome all the potential problems with this fake dating scenario, she'd screwed it up. She should've just kept it fake. By admitting in the coffee shop that she was attracted to him, it had opened up the charade to more. He liked her, she liked him…what was stopping this public relationship from becoming a private one?

A hymen, that's what.

The look on Julian's face when she said the words had been heartbreaking. One minute, he'd looked at her with blue eyes hooded with desire. She had no doubt in that moment that he sincerely wanted her. Not even her fragile ego could believe otherwise. Then, in a flash, it was replaced by panic. She knew the moment the words left her mouth that it was a mistake.

Julian wanted fun, flirty sex. A hot wedding hookup. Deflowering some thirty-year-old virgin probably didn't line up with his plans. She'd accused him of trying to escape, but at that point, she wanted out of there more desperately than he did. She needed plenty of time to get home, lie in bed and kick herself.

Fortunately, today had been about wedding preparations. She spent most of the afternoon getting things in place in the chapel before the rehearsal. That kept her busy enough that she could keep her embarrassing incident far out of her mind. When she did see Julian again, there wasn't much time to talk. First was the rehearsal, and he was on the platform with Murray and Kelly. After that, they all got ushered onto a limo bus and taken to the restaurant for the rehearsal dinner. They hadn't had two seconds alone, much less time to talk.

Part of her was okay with that. She didn't feel the need to analyze last night with him. She just needed to get through the next two days and put all of this behind her. But it was hard when he was always touching her. Holding her hand, hugging her to his side, whispering in her ear. It just made her want what she was destined not to have that much more intensely.

One of the waiters placed a piping hot ramekin of peach cobbler in front of her with vanilla bean ice cream melting over it. It looked amazing, and the thought of a tasty treat was enough to rouse her from her dark thoughts. She needed to play the happy girlfriend regardless of what was going on between them.

"That looks good," Julian said, leaning in to examine her dessert. "Decadent, actually."

"Didn't you get dessert?" she asked, already knowing the answer but trying to make polite conversation.

He shook his head and took a sip of his water. He'd spent the evening nibbling on blackened tilapia and roasted vegetables. "Just because you dared me to eat that berry tart doesn't mean I've thrown my clean eating lifestyle out the window."

"Would you like just one bite? I mean, I know you don't want to be first, but I thought you might want the second bite." She couldn't help getting that dig in under the veiled discussion of dessert so the others at the table couldn't follow the twists and turns of their relationship.

A look of surprise lit up Julian's face, his lips twisting into an amused smile. "For the record, I don't mind having the first taste. I just feel guilty getting the first bite when I know I can't stay around to eat the whole thing."

"The cobbler won't be offended, I assure you. It just wants to be eaten while it's still hot and juicy. Before long, it's going to be a cold, crusty, bitter mess."

"I sincerely doubt that. I know turning that treat down last night was a mistake, but as it was, I spent two hours in the hotel gym last night."

Her gaze met his. "Feeling guilty?"

He nodded. "I had a little pent-up energy after I left you. Ten miles on the treadmill helped, but I still felt like crap when I was done."

"You can run all you want, but if you're on a treadmill, you aren't getting any farther from your problems."

"Wise words," he agreed. "Exercise does help me think. If nothing else, I got some...clarity."

Gretchen narrowed her gaze at him, her heart suddenly leaping to life in her chest. "What does that mean?"

"It means we need to talk."

She rolled her eyes and turned back to her dessert. Talk? She'd done plenty of that already. If all he wanted to do was talk, she was going to save this poor cobbler from her own fate. She picked up her spoon and scooped up a bite, stopping as Julian leaned in.

"Soon," he whispered into her ear. The spoon trembled in her hand as she held it in midair. "I don't know when, but soon. Don't you worry about that dessert going uneaten."

Gretchen drew in a ragged breath. Suddenly, she wasn't that hungry for cobbler anymore. The idea that she might be naked in front of him in the near future was an appetite killer.

"So, Julian," one of the bridesmaids called across the table. "Are you guys ready for the bachelor party tonight?"

Julian sat up and flashed his charming smile at the

others seated with them. "Absolutely. I've got a great night planned for the boys."

One of the other women looked at her date with a warning glance. "Try to limit yourself to one lap dance, please."

The man laughed. "Why? I'm not the one getting married tomorrow. You afraid I'll be tempted by the goods?"

The brunette shook her head. "No, I'm worried you'll stick your whole paycheck in her panties and come back to me broke."

"Well, if I do, maybe Julian can help me out. I heard you made fifteen million for your last movie. Is that true?"

Gretchen felt Julian stiffen beside her. For the first time while they were together, he was the nervous one. He'd mentioned a few times about how people seemed to come to him with their hands out. This guy didn't even know Julian, not really. It was veiled as a joke, but it wasn't funny. She didn't like seeing Julian react that way.

"And exactly how much money did *you* make last year?" she piped up before Julian could respond.

The man's eyes grew wide at her sharp tone and he immediately held up his hands in surrender. "Sorry," he said. "It was a joke. I mean, if I made that much money, I'd be shouting it from the rooftops."

"And everyone, including the IRS and some guy you don't even know at a rehearsal dinner, would be knocking on your front door looking for their piece."

The large, burly groomsman seemed to disappear into himself. "I'm going to go get a drink from the bar," he said, getting up and crossing the room. The other people turned to each other and started talking among themselves to avoid the awkward turn in the conversation.

"Rawr." Julian leaned in and growled into her ear. "I didn't know you were such a tiger."

Gretchen chuckled. "Neither did I. But I couldn't sit there and say nothing. Just because you're a public figure doesn't mean it's any of his business how much you make."

Julian smiled. "It isn't as exciting as it sounds anyway. I mean, I have plenty, don't get me wrong, but the bigger the life, the bigger the expenses. The mortgage on my house in Beverly Hills is nearly thirty thousand a month."

Gretchen nearly choked on her sip of wine. "That's insane."

"That's California real estate for you. Add in the ridiculous property taxes and insurance, security, staff… it adds up. Uncle Sam gets his whopping cut, then Ross, then my accountant."

"Do I need to give this necklace back?"

"No, of course not. I wouldn't live in a five-million-dollar house if I couldn't afford to. Life is just on a different scale when you live this way, is all."

Gretchen shook her head and reached into her purse to find her phone. It was getting late. As much as she was enjoying the dinner and curious to finish her interrupted conversation with Julian, she needed to get back and finish up the ballroom for tomorrow. "I'd better go."

Julian pouted, the frown pulling at the corners of his full mouth. Gretchen wanted to kiss it away, but resisted. Instead, she leaned in and pressed a kiss to his cheek. "You have fun with the boys tonight. Don't let Murray get too hungover. Natalie hates it when the wedding party is teetering on their feet all day."

"Yes, ma'am. I'll walk you out."

"No, no," she insisted, pushing him back into his seat. "I can make it just fine. Your loyalty is to Murray tonight."

Gretchen stood up, and he scooped her hand into his own. He brought it up to his lips, placing a searing kiss on the back of her hand. The heated tingle radiated up her whole arm, making her flush pink against the deep shades of purple fabric that made up her dress.

"I'll see you *soon*," he said, emphasizing the last word. That was the same word he'd used earlier when they spoke about their physical relationship.

She pulled her hand away and tried to cover her reaction with a smile. "Okay," she said. "Good night."

Gretchen gave a parting wave to Murray and Kelly before slipping out. It wasn't until she stepped out that she realized they'd all come in the limo van, including Bree. With a shake of her head, she called a cab and waited patiently outside for it to arrive.

It was just as well. She needed the cold air to cool the fire Julian had so easily built inside her.

Julian was over the bachelor party scene. He'd done his duty and set up a great send-off for Murray, complete with alcohol, scantily clad women and billiards, but it wasn't really where he wanted to spend his time. Not since his discussion with Gretchen at the rehearsal dinner.

He'd relived that moment by her car over and over in his head since it happened. He had expected a lot of different reasons for why she shied away from him, but none of them included the fact that she'd never been with a man before. In this day and age, that sort of thing was almost unheard of.

Admittedly, he hadn't reacted well to the news, and he felt horrible about it. He'd told her about his two-hour treadmill penance, but that wasn't the half of it. He'd barely slept that night thinking about how badly he handled her confession. It hadn't been because he felt as if there were something wrong with her, or that she was strange, but because he'd felt this sudden pressure he wasn't expecting.

Being a woman's first lover was a big responsibility. When he was sixteen and horny, he hadn't thought about it that way, and he knew of at least one girl who'd had a less-than-stellar first time because of how he'd handled it. Now he was a grown man. An experienced lover. It was bad enough that he had a reputation because of his films that he was some hard-bodied Casanova. Adding the delicate handling of a woman's first time on top of that made his chest tighten.

Gretchen had made it sound as though she would be happy to be rid of the burden of her virginity. It would be doing her a favor, somehow. And he wanted her. There was no doubt of that. But was making love to Gretchen selfish? Was taking her virginity and then returning to LA a horrible thing to do, even if she'd asked him to? Just the thought of it made him feel sleazy.

Speaking of sleazy, a woman in a corset and a thong was making her way over to him. She had multiple bills tucked into her G-string and a coat of glitter across her tan skin, reminding him of his own ill-fated turn as a stripper in a movie. The kind of movies he hated.

The kind of films Gretchen encouraged him to branch out from.

The burlesque dancer wrapped her feather boa around Julian's neck to pull him closer. Putting a few obligatory dollars beneath the strap at her hip, he waved her back toward the groom. Murray was the one who deserved the attention tonight, not him.

Julian looked down at his phone to check his messages. He didn't want anything to be wrong at home, but it would give him an excuse to leave. Murray had been his roommate in college, so he knew all about Julian's family and how things tended to crop up. Thankfully, all was well, but unfortunately it was only a little after ten. Was that too soon to leave? He sighed and put his phone away. Probably. The cigar roller hadn't even finished making all the cigars yet.

Then he caught Murray's gaze across the room. His friend smiled and shook his head. "Go," he mouthed silently, then turned back to the busty blonde vying for his attention.

That was all it took. He stood and walked toward the edge of the room, trying to slowly slip out without making a big deal of it. Once he made it out the door, he climbed into his SUV, thankful that they hadn't taken the limo bus directly from the rehearsal dinner so he had a vehicle to make his escape. Inside his car, he texted Gretchen.

Where are you?

As the engine warmed up, he got a response. In the ballroom hanging seventy thousand crystal pendants. Care to join me?

He did. Putting the phone aside, he pulled out of the parking lot and headed back to From This Moment. Once again, Gretchen's little green sedan was the only car in the lot when he arrived. Apparently everyone else had already given up for the night.

He headed straight for the ballroom, as she'd said she'd be there, but he didn't see her. Her handiwork was evident, though. The room had been absolutely transformed since he'd been there the day before. The tables now had an assortment of glasses and flatware at each place setting. The tall silver candelabras he'd moved the night before stood in the center of some tables. Others had slim silver vases or small silver bowls. There were candles scattered all over and tall white trees in the corners, dripping with crystals. It looked as though the only thing missing was the fresh flowers.

"Just wait until the pin lights are on and all the candles are lit," Gretchen said, coming in behind him with a box in her arms. "It will be magical."

"I bet. You're very talented."

Gretchen snorted and moved past him to set the box on the edge of the stage where the band would set up in the morning. She was still wearing the flirty purple dress she'd worn to the rehearsal dinner, only now she was barefoot, having cast aside her heels for the sake of comfort. "You're very kind, but it's a table setting, not a Picasso."

Julian followed her path, slowly coming up behind her as she unpacked tiny attendee gifts to place on the tables. When she stood, he snaked his arms around her waist and pulled her back tight against him. The soft curve of her backside pressed into his desire, suppressing all the reasons why he couldn't be with Gretchen.

What if he could give her something without taking anything away? It might take every ounce of restraint he had, but he wanted this so badly. "I've thought a lot about our discussion at dinner."

Gretchen gasped softly, although he wasn't certain if it was his words or his obvious need for her. "And?" she asked in almost a hushed whisper.

"And it made me wonder." Julian nestled into her neck, planting warm kisses under her earlobe between phrases. "You said you're a virgin, but have you ever had an orgasm before?"

Gretchen chuckled. "Yes, I have. I might be a virgin, but I'm also a grown woman perfectly capable of managing my needs when necessary."

Now Julian had to laugh. She always surprised him, especially with her bold honesty, even in the face of potentially embarrassing questions. "Has someone else ever given you one?" he pressed.

"No."

"I'd like to."

She shivered as he pressed another kiss along the soft skin of her neck. "Um…right now?"

Not the ideal location, but why the hell not? "Yes, right now." His palm slid across her torso, venturing to her low belly, then to the side of her hip and down. He moved until he reached her smooth bare thigh, shifting the hem of her dress a few inches higher to stroke it. Then he stopped. "Unless you'd rather wait," he said.

After a slight hesitation, Gretchen arched her back, pressing the curve of her rear firmly against his erection. "I think twenty-nine years is long enough to wait, don't you?"

"I do."

Julian turned her in his arms so she was facing him. Despite her bold declaration, he could still sense anxiety in her. She bit at her bottom lip, her dark eyes both challenging him and nervously flickering toward the door and back. He could imagine that the mix of emotions was confusing, but he wouldn't let her psych herself out about this. It was happening.

Dipping his head down, he kissed her. She started to relax with the familiar activity, wrapping her arms around his neck. She let her tongue slide boldly along his own, eliciting a low groan deep in his throat. Keeping this all about her pleasure would be hard when she touched him like this, but he could do it. He was determined.

Julian encircled her waist, pulling her toward him and guiding her backward toward the stage. Once her calves met with the wooden platform, he eased her back until she was sitting on the edge. He tore his lips away from hers, lowering himself to his knees in front of her. Gretchen's eyes grew wide as she watched him put his palms on each bare knee.

With his eyes trained on hers, he pressed gently, parting her legs little by little until he could move between them. He slid his hands up her thighs, pushing the purple fabric of her dress up and out of his way, stopping just short of exposing her. He could feel her muscles tense beneath his touch, so he changed his tactic. Julian wanted her fully relaxed for this.

He kissed her again, distracting her with his lips and tongue as he slipped the straps of her dress off her shoulders. It didn't take much for the fabric to slide down, exposing the bra beneath it. He cupped one breast, slowly stroking and teasing at the nipple through the sheer black fabric. Gretchen groaned against his mouth, her reaction encouraging him to break away from the kiss and draw her nipple into his mouth.

Gretchen's head went back, a cry of pleasure escaping her lips. It echoed in the large ballroom like music to his ears. He continued to tease her through the moist fabric, the distraction it provided allowing him to move his hand beneath her skirt. He found that the panties were made of the same sheer material. When his fingers brushed across her most sensitive spot, Gretchen gasped, her hips rising up off the stage.

Julian eased Gretchen back until she was lying on the stage. She protested at first, but he didn't want her nervously watching everything he did. "Just lie back, close your eyes and enjoy it," he said soothingly until the tension eased from her body.

He started by removing her panties. He slid them down her legs, tossing them out of his way. Then he crouched down and started a trail of kisses that ran from the inside of her ankles, up her calves, to her inner thighs. He let his hot breath tease at her center. She squirmed beneath him, the anticipation of it likely building inside her.

Without warning, he let his tongue flick across her flesh. Gretchen cried out, her fingers grasping fruitlessly at the stage beside her. Julian gave her a moment to recover before he did it again. He pressed her thighs farther apart, exposing more of her to him. His fingers and tongue started moving over her in earnest now, the relentless pursuit of her release foremost in his mind.

Gretchen's gasps and groans were an encouraging melody. As they escalated in pitch and intensity, he knew she was getting close. Her thighs were tense beside him, as though they were made of steel. He re-doubled his efforts until a desperate "yes, yes!" filled the room.

Gently, he slipped one finger inside her, knowing it would put her over the edge. He felt her muscles clamp down on him and half a second later, she came undone. She gasped and cried, writhing on the hard stage even as he continued to work over her with his tongue.

It wasn't until she collapsed back against the stage, her thighs trembling, that he pulled away. Her ragged breath was the only sound in the massive ballroom as he smoothed out her skirt and sat back on his heels.

Several minutes later, Gretchen pushed herself up to look at him. Her pale cheeks were flushed red, her eyes glassy, but she was smiling. It made his chest ache to see it. The women in his life always seemed to de-mand so much from him. Gretchen appreciated even the tiniest of gestures.

"Well," she said at last. "I'm never going to look at this ballroom the same way, ever again."

Seven

"Take me to the hotel, Julian."

Julian's gaze met hers, a heat in them she couldn't ignore. And yet he hesitated, swallowing hard before he spoke. "Are you sure?"

"I am." She'd never been so certain of anything in her whole life. She wasn't foolish enough to think this relationship would last past the weekend, or that she would be anything more than a faint memory in Julian's mind, but she couldn't pass this chance up. Even if she *had* been with a man before, making love to a movie star was every woman's sexual fantasy.

And yet the doubts plagued her. Of course she wanted him. But his wanting her was another matter. "Unless you don't want to," she added in a quiet voice.

Julian rolled his eyes and took her hand, tugging her up off the stage. "I want to. You have no idea how much I want to. I just don't know that I should. I can't promise you anything."

Gretchen gazed up at him and shook her head. "All I want you to promise me is a night of hot sex and enough orgasms to last me until the next guy comes along."

Julian smiled, making her relax into his arms. He wasn't turning her down, thank goodness.

"That," he said with a wicked glint in his blue eyes, "I can do."

They left the chapel so quickly, Gretchen barely had time to grab her heels and switch off the lights. The drive to his hotel seemed to take an eternity. In the dark of the car, Gretchen bit at her lower lip and tried to stay in the moment. While her body was still pulsating from the orgasm he'd given her it was easy to propose they go further, but the reality was creeping in with every mile they came nearer to his hotel. She was about to have sex. The idea of it both thrilled and terrified her.

As they walked the length of the hotel corridor together, hand in hand, she could feel her heart pounding in her chest. On the other side of the door was what she'd been fantasizing about since she was sixteen years old.

"Would you like a glass of wine?" he asked as they stepped into his suite.

"No," she shook her head. "I'd rather just…get to it."

Julian frowned at her and crossed his arms over his chest. "Gretchen, this isn't a sprint, it's a marathon."

"I know," she replied, knowing it had come out wrong and right at the same time. She wanted it done so she could put the anxiety aside and enjoy herself.

Julian dropped his arms at his side and approached her, stopping just short of them touching. He placed his large, warm palms on her bare upper arms, rubbing them in a soothing rhythm. "Relax. Enjoy yourself. Unless you change your mind or the hotel catches fire, I guarantee it's going to happen."

Gretchen let out the ragged breath she didn't realize she'd been holding in. As the air rushed from her lungs, so did the tension that had built up in every muscle. "You're right, I'm sorry. I'm just so—"

Julian's lips met hers in an instant, stealing the words from her mouth. His touch made all her worries disappear. She melted into his arms, pressing into the hard body she couldn't get out of her head. Even when she heard the sound of her zipper gliding down her back, she didn't tense up. The glide of his tongue and the hungry press of his fingertips into her flesh made her whole body soften like butter.

He tugged the straps of her dress and bra down her shoulders, planting a line of kisses along her throat and across the newly exposed skin. Julian's hungry gaze flickered over her breasts before he dipped his head to taste the flesh that threatened to spill over the top of her bra.

With her dress open in the back, she could feel the fabric slipping down, pooling at her waist, but she fought the urge to stop it. By all indications, Julian liked what he saw. Tonight it was all coming off, no matter how anxious she might be about it.

Reaching behind her, Julian unfastened the clasp of her bra, sliding it down her arms and draping it across the nearby chair. Her nakedness was immediately covered by his hands and his mouth. Gretchen's eyes fluttered closed as he drew one hard pink nipple into his mouth. A bolt of pleasure shot right through her, mak-

ing her core tighten and ache and her legs start to tremble beneath her.

She was so lost in the moment that when Julian
crouched down and lifted her up into the air, she was
caught completely off guard. With a cry of surprise, she
wrapped her arms around his neck and her legs around
his waist. "You're going to throw your back out or something," she complained as she clung to him. She wasn't
some skinny-minnie supermodel, as though he could
forget with her half naked in his arms.

He narrowed his gaze at her, a challenge in his eyes.
"Gretchen, even on a bad day I can bench press twice
what you weigh. Stop worrying and let me carry you
into the bedroom to ravish you properly, all right?"

Squeezing her eyes shut, she buried her face in his
neck. She couldn't let her stupid insecurities ruin this
moment. With one arm wrapped around her waist, Julian's other slid along her outer thigh, gripping one
round cheek beneath her cocktail dress. She felt his
palm explore her skin in a curious fashion before he
spoke.

"Naughty," he whispered as they started toward the
bedroom.

"What?" She didn't know what he was talking about.

"You never put your panties back on."

Gretchen straightened up in his arms, her eyes wide
as she gasped. "Oh, my God. I left them on the floor
of the ballroom."

Julian chuckled and shook his head, continuing into
the bedroom. "Someone's going to get a surprise first
thing in the morning."

Thoughts of Bree or Natalie running across those
sheer black panties in the ballroom suddenly consumed

her. How embarrassing. Then Julian lowered her onto the bed and her bare back met with the soft, plush fabric of the comforter.

She watched as he unbuttoned his dress shirt and slipped it off, exposing the famously familiar muscles beneath it. God, he was beautiful. There was a Michelangelo-like quality to the definition of his body, as though each muscle had been carved out of flesh-colored marble with a fine chisel.

Her eyes remained glued to his hands as he unbuckled his belt, unzipped his trousers and let the last of his clothing fall to the floor. He kicked off his shoes and stepped out of it all, taking a step toward the bed in all his naked glory.

"Well?" he asked after giving her a moment to take in every inch of the glorious sight. "Will I do?"

Gretchen laughed in a nervous titter. The man was beautiful, rock hard and very aroused. Any doubts she had about his attraction to her were instantly quelled. They were replaced by the anxiety of realizing he was a large specimen of man. She covered her nerves with a wide smile and a nod. "I suppose so."

One dark brow shot up at her blasé assessment of his manhood. Without responding, he approached the bed and reached for her waist. He gathered her dress and gave it a firm tug to slip it over her hips. When he dropped it to the floor, his gaze returned to her fully naked body.

Gretchen took a deep breath and fought the urge to cover herself. Instead she raised her hand and crooked her index finger to beckon him to her.

He didn't hesitate. Julian covered her body with his own, every inch of his blazing-hot skin touching hers.

The firm heat of him pressed at her thigh, urging her to open herself to him, so she did. He slipped between her legs and rested there. She could feel the tip of him teasing at her, but he didn't press forward. Not yet.

Instead, he hovered over her, lavishing more attention on her breasts. He kneaded and tasted her flesh, nipping at the tight peaks and flicking over them with his tongue until her back arched off the bed. Then, with one nipple drawn into his mouth, his hand slid down her stomach to delve between them. As he had at the chapel, his fingertips sought out her most sensitive flesh. He stroked over her in soft circles, building up another climax.

He slipped one finger inside her, stroking in and out of her tight body while his thumb still teased at her apex. The sensations coursing through her were so intense. She was desperate to keep her eyes open, yet no matter how hard she fought, they kept closing so she could savor the feeling.

He added a second finger, stretching her body wider and intensifying the ache in her belly. She easily accommodated him, anxious and ready for everything he had to offer.

That was when he pulled away. Gretchen's eyes flew open in time to see him reach for something beside the bed. A condom, she realized, as he quickly applied it and returned to the bed. As he moved across the mattress, his hands slipped behind her knees and bent them, drawing her legs up and spreading her wider for him.

Julian hovered over her then, watching her with a curious expression on his face. Then he lowered his face to hers and kissed her. Gretchen wrapped her arms around his neck and gave herself over to the kiss.

He rocked forward in short, slow strokes, rubbing the tip of his erection against her, picking up where his hands had left off a moment ago. She felt the orgasm building up inside her again. He sped up, rubbing over her sensitive flesh again and again as her cries escalated.

She was about to come a second time. She could feel the tension in her, about to break. "Julian," she gasped, clinging to his neck. "Yes, yes!" she cried out as she went over the edge.

That's when he entered her in one quick thrust. Pleasure. Pain. It was so fast, she almost didn't realize what had happened until it was done. She gasped with a mix of surprise and release as the last tremors of her orgasm traveled through her body.

Julian held himself remarkably still, even as he was buried deep inside her. His eyes were closed, a look of near pain on his face.

"Are you okay?" she asked.

His brows drew together as he looked down at her. "Aren't I supposed to be the one asking that question?"

"I suppose, but you're the one that looks like you're being hurt."

He shook his head. "Oh, it doesn't hurt. Not at all. I'm just trying to restrain myself a little."

Testing the waters, he eased out slowly and thrust forward again. Gretchen's body lit up with tiny pinpricks of sensation, most of them wonderful. "Don't. It's done. Now make love to me, Julian. Please."

With a curt nod, he shifted his weight and moved in her again with agonizing restraint. Now it was his turn to groan aloud. The feeling was amazing, but Gretchen couldn't help watching Julian's responses. She loved that she was able to give him pleasure, something she hadn't entirely considered before this moment.

Any residual soreness faded away as his movements came faster. Feeling more bold, she drew her knees up, cradling him between her thighs. The movement allowed him to move deeper, and she gasped as she adjusted to the feeling.

Julian swore against her cheek, a low rumble of approval that vibrated to her core. "You feel so amazing, but if you keep moving like that, I'm going to lose it."

"Lose it," she encouraged. She wanted him to lose control because of her. "Like you said earlier, we've got all night."

"Yes, we do."

Closing his eyes, Julian moved harder into her, the quick thrusts pushing him over the edge in mere minutes. His muscles tensed beneath the skin, his breath labored. She watched as he surged into her one last time, his jaw dropping open with a silent groan and shudder that ran through his whole body.

And then it was done. It was official. Gretchen was no longer a pathetic twenty-nine-year-old virgin. Julian rolled off onto his side and collapsed back against the bed with ragged breaths.

Gretchen could only lie there and smile as she gazed up at the ceiling. They'd just finished, and she couldn't wait to do it again.

A familiar sound roused Julian from his satiated sleep. One eye pried open to look at the screen on his cell phone as it charged on the nearby nightstand. It was the last number he wanted to see, especially at such an early hour, but it was the one he'd been anticipating all week. He'd had a feeling something wasn't quite right with his brother, and he was usually spot-on with that.

Shooting up in bed, he grabbed the phone and answered.

"Hello?" he said in a sleepy, gravelly voice.

"Mr. Curtis?" the woman said, using Julian's real last name.

"Yes?"

"Mr. Curtis, I'm sorry to call at such a late hour, but this is Theresa from the Hawthorne Community."

He knew that. He knew the minute he picked up the phone. Now get to the point. "Is James okay?"

A hesitation, slight but noticeable, preceded her answer. "He's stable," she said. "He's developed pneumonia and we're going to be transferring him to the hospital for observation."

Julian fought the confusing mix of sleep and panic. "Do I need to come? Is he going to be all right?"

"We don't think you need to come yet," Theresa said. "Right now he's stabilized. We're going to see how he reacts to treatment. He already has so much difficulty breathing, this just makes things that much harder for him."

"Yes, I know. Someone will call me as soon as there's a change?"

"Yes, Mr. Curtis. That's what James's file says, which is why we called you at such a late hour. You're to be notified any time there's a major medical change for him."

Julian nodded at the phone. That was the way he wanted it. If anything went wrong, he wanted to know. He couldn't be there with him, but he could make sure

James had all the best doctors and treatment that a movie star's salary could provide. "Thank you."

The call ended. Julian dropped the phone into his lap and took a deep breath to expel the fear that held his lungs captive. It was only fair—if James couldn't breathe, Julian shouldn't be able to breathe, either. That was never the way it was in reality. Julian was perfect. Healthy and able-bodied. James was not. The constant stream of late-night calls over the years had proven that much.

"Julian?" Gretchen's soft, concerned voice called to him from the pillows. "Is everything all right?"

A sudden feeling of dread, more powerful than the one that rushed over him as his phone rang, overcame Julian. Gretchen was in bed beside him. She'd heard everything. This situation had the potential to go horribly wrong.

"Uh, yeah," he said dismissively, hoping she would let it go. Very few people in his life knew about James's situation. Hell, almost no one knew about James at all. Julian kept it that way on purpose. He certainly didn't need the press exploiting this story. James had never asked for anyone's pity, and making him a headline could potentially have millions of people looking at his brother as though there was something wrong with him. He didn't want that. Despite everything, James had always just wanted to live a normal life. Being at the Hawthorne Community had given him that. He had his own apartment, his own helper and a staff of professionals to care for him when he needed it. Julian didn't want to ruin that for his brother.

Gretchen sat up beside him in bed and leaned her

bare shoulder against him. "For an actor, you're not a very good liar."

Julian chuckled softly. "Three a.m. is not the peak hour for my craft, I suppose." He turned to her, planted a soft kiss on her lips and ignored the concern in her eyes. "It's nothing. You can go back to sleep."

He expected her to lie down, but instead he felt her arm wrap around his shoulders. "Julian, I told you my secret and you were able to…uh…help me out. Tell me what's going on and maybe I can help you in return."

He shook his head. "Gretchen, if this was as simple as making love to you, I'd tell you in a second. But this can't be fixed by you or anyone else." Julian returned his phone to the charger and lay down in the hopes she would do the same.

She did, pressing her naked body against his and resting her head on his chest. Normally, thoughts of desire would've rushed through his mind and he would've made love to her again, but there were too many worries in his mind now.

"Tell me," Gretchen said. "It's dark. We're both half asleep. You don't have to look at me while you say it. Just get it off your chest. You'll feel better."

Julian had never told anyone about this situation aside from Ross and the people who were a part of his life before he became a star, like Murray. Ross needed to know why he was so driven. But tonight, under the cover of darkness, he wanted to tell Gretchen the truth. She wasn't like those other women, mining for a story they could sell. If there was one person he could tell, it would be her. He didn't want to keep it from her.

"My brother is in the hospital," he said simply.

"I'm sorry to hear that. Is it serious?"

"Unfortunately, everything is serious when it comes to my brother." That was true. A run-of-the-mill cold could be near fatal, much less the pneumonia he currently had.

"Tell me," she pressed again.

He wanted to, but he had to be careful. "If I do, you have to swear that you'll never tell a single soul what I've said. It's absolutely critical that no one know about this."

"Okay," she said. "You have my word."

Somehow, Julian knew that Gretchen wouldn't spill his secrets, but he had to put it out there and let her know how serious it all was. "I have an identical twin brother named James."

"I didn't realize you had a brother, much less an identical twin."

"No one knows. I try to keep my life before I went to Hollywood very quiet for my family's sake. They didn't ask for this spotlight to be shone on them. And since my brother has so many issues, I'm all the more protective of him."

"What's wrong with him?"

Julian sighed. There were so many things. James had never had a chance to live the truly normal life he wanted, no matter how hard they tried or how many specialists they brought in to see him. "My brother has a severe case of spastic cerebral palsy. The doctors said that he sustained some kind of brain injury in utero or during his birth that impaired his ability to function."

Gretchen didn't respond. He wasn't sure if she was surprised by his tale or wanted to let him just get it all off his chest.

"He was diagnosed when we were about two. My mom was in denial, thinking he was just slower to crawl and get around than I was, as though the two minutes older I was than James made that big of a difference. She finally took him to the doctor when she couldn't ignore the disparity any longer. The diagnosis was devastating, but the hardest part was not knowing how it would fully impact him until he got older. The severity of cerebral palsy can vary widely based on the injury. Some people can live normal, long lives with only a few limitations. My mother hoped for that, but by the time we were getting ready to start kindergarten and his problems became more pronounced, it was easy to see that it was getting harder for her to stay positive. She cried a lot when she thought I wasn't looking. James was wheelchair-bound and needed constant supervision. He had an aide at school that stayed with him and helped him through his day.

"The medical bills were crippling. Even though my father had a good job at a nearby production facility with solid benefits, it didn't cover everything. James went through so many surgeries and treatments. Hours of therapy and trips to the emergency room. Cerebral palsy doesn't get worse, you see. But the complications can. He'd had trouble swallowing and breathing since he was a baby. James nearly choked to death a couple times, and every time cold and flu season came around, we lived like a quarantine facility to keep him from catching anything. Eventually, when he was about ten, they had to put in a tracheostomy tube.

"As we got older, it got harder. James wasn't a little boy anymore—he was a growing teenager. Simple things like getting him out of his chair and into bed, or giving him a bath, got so difficult. We got a home health nurse to help out when we were in high school, but by the time I went off to college, Mom just couldn't handle it anymore. He had a really severe bout of pneumonia and he ended up in the hospital. The doctors told us that he needed better care than we could provide, and they recommended we put him in a state facility that was better equipped to handle James's treatment."

Finally, Gretchen spoke. "That must've been a very hard decision for your parents. Hard on all of you."

"You have no idea. I've lived my whole life with this guilt."

"Guilt? Why would you feel guilty? You didn't do anything wrong."

Julian stroked his hand over Gretchen's soft curls. "I was healthy. I was everything James wasn't. We were identical, we started absolutely the same in every way, and yet something went wrong—something I could've caused before we were even born. It's very easy to feel guilty."

"Did the doctors ever say that? Did they ever directly blame you for it?"

He shrugged. "If they did, my mother would never tell me. It wouldn't matter, though. I was still active and went out with friends and did all the things he couldn't do. When I went off to college and he went into a state hospital, the disparities were painful. And then my father died my junior year of college. In addition to our grief, we had to cope with the fact that now the family had no income and no insurance. My father's life insurance policy was barely enough to pay off the mortgage so my mother wasn't homeless. Something had to be done, so I dropped out of school and moved to LA."

"Really?"

"Stupid, right? I was convinced that I would go out

there and get acting work and be able to support my family. I could've just as easily landed a long-term role as a waiter who couldn't afford his own rent. But I met Ross. He saw potential in me. He might be a jerk sometimes, but he got me into some commercials, then small roles in movies. The next thing I knew, my parts were getting larger, and then I was offered a lead role. I wasn't an overnight success, but it only took a few years before I started making seven figures on a film. I wasn't thrilled with the parts, but they allowed me to move James to a private residential facility that special-izes in patients with cerebral palsy. I was able to buy private health insurance for all of us and send my mom money to live on. I'd achieved my goal."

"That's why," Gretchen said with an enlightened tone.

"Why what?"

"Why you don't want to take those other roles. You said you worried about screwing up and damaging your career. It has nothing to do with your ego and every-thing to do with supporting your family."

Julian sighed. "Yes. They depend on me. I can't, won't, do anything to risk my career. Or to risk anyone finding out about James and turning him into a tabloid headline." As he said the words, he realized just by tell-ing Gretchen this story, he'd compromised his brother. She might not mean to tell, but things could happen. If Ross knew, he'd insist on a confidentiality agreement. Not exactly his usual pillow talk, but he supposed ev-erything was different with Gretchen.

"I know I made you promise not to tell anyone, but to tie up loose ends and ensure my brother's protection, I'll probably need to have Ross draft up a confidentiality agreement in the morning. I know he'll insist on it. I'll also see to it that he adds another five thousand to your payment to compensate for your cooperation. It's not your fault I dumped this on you."

He felt Gretchen stiffen beneath his fingertips, and then she raised her head to look at him. "Are you serious?"

Julian frowned. "This is the way my life works. Contracts and compensation, even in my personal life."

She just watched him for a moment, but her body remained stiff as a board. Finally, she said, "I'll sign your stupid agreement, Julian." The tone of her voice was sharp. He could tell he'd offended her. "But I'm not taking any more of your money."

Eight

Any second now, someone was going to wake Gretchen up. She sat in front of her vanity applying her makeup the way the woman at the department store had told her to. Draped across the bed behind her was the gown she was wearing to the wedding as Julian's date. That was surreal enough on its own. Knowing she'd slept with him the night before was completely in the dream realm.

She'd waited years for that moment, never once anticipating that she would end up in the arms of one of the sexiest men alive. Gretchen still couldn't quite understand why he wanted her. It annoyed him when she mentioned it, so she'd stopped. But even if she'd had a healthy sense of self-esteem going into this scenario, it would be unbelievable.

The only thing about the past few days that convinced Gretchen that all of this was real was their awkward discussion after his call about James. She had been high on the excitement of having sex for the first time and thrilled that Julian was willing to share something that personal with her. Then he started talking about confidentiality contracts and worse—paying her to keep quiet about it.

The longer they were together, the easier it was for her to forget that none of this was real and that she was being compensated for her time. She hadn't liked the idea of this from the beginning, but as they went on, she liked it even less. With sex added to the mix, she was starting to feel very *Pretty Woman* about the whole thing. The additional money for her silence just rubbed salt in the wound and reminded her that she was that much closer to being a whore.

"Ugh," she said as she applied the last of her mascara and threw it down onto the table in disgust. She needed to get out of here and distract herself with the chaos of the wedding so she didn't stew in those thoughts any longer.

Looking into the mirror, she admired her handiwork. It wasn't bad at all. She'd already straightened her hair and wrapped it into a French twist with a crystal barrette securing it. Having her hair up made her neck look longer and her face look thinner, which was great. She anticipated a lot of cameras being around today since it was the big event they'd been building up to. She had to be believable as Julian's girlfriend, and a double chin wouldn't help her case at all.

With her undergarments in place, Gretchen slipped into the gown she'd chosen with Amelia. It was strapless with a sweetheart neckline and a high waist that fell right under her bust. The top was a shiny black ruched satin, but below the waist, it was flowing white satin, painted in purple, blue and black almost like a wearable piece of watercolor art. It was beautiful and fit her perfectly.

The last piece she added was the necklace Julian had given her. The fiery opal rested nicely on the bare expanse of her chest, falling right below her collarbone.

Admiring herself in the full-length mirror on her closet door, she was stunned by what she saw. This wasn't the mousy, awkward Gretchen from a week ago. She looked confident, radiant and even beautiful. Gretchen was ready to walk out the door and be Julian's girl, which was a good thing, because it was time to go. She needed to get back to the facility.

It felt weird enough already that she wasn't there helping the others, but she'd done her part, including buzzing by this morning to meet the florist and snatch up those wayward panties. Now she was returning as a guest. Since Julian was the best man, he wasn't able to pick her up. He was in the groom's room, likely doing a shot of whiskey with Murray and helping him with his tie. They had to be ready early so Bree could take pictures of the wedding party before the ceremony.

Just in case, Gretchen threw a few last things into an overnight bag she'd packed. If she did end up staying with Julian again, she wanted to be ready and not slink back home in the morning in a gown. She had all her toiletries, a change of clothes and a slinky little red lace chemise that had been rotting in her closet since she'd impulse-purchased it several years back. She was looking forward to someone actually seeing her in it, aside from her.

After loading everything into her car, she returned

to the chapel. Gathered on the curb outside the facility was a crowd of photographers. The location had leaked, as expected, but they weren't allowed on the grounds. With very little activity outside with the winter weather, all they'd get were shots of people coming in and out. They paid little attention to her in her cheap sedan. She was able to slip in the back door as usual.

"Wow."

Gretchen paused outside her office where she was about to stow her overnight bag. Turning, she saw Natalie watching her from the hallway. She was all geared up with her headset, her tablet and fierce determination to tackle the day, but the expression of awe on her face was new.

"Do I look okay?"

Natalie nodded, coming close to admire the dress. "You look amazing. Every bit the girlfriend of a movie star, no doubt."

Gretchen beamed. She thought she looked nice, but was nice good enough? It seemed so, at least in Natalie's opinion.

"I especially like the well-bedded glow. Is that a bronzer or an all-night lovemaking session?"

Gretchen's eyes widened and she brought her hand to her lips to shush her. "Bronzer," she said pointedly. "We'll discuss the brand and how well it was applied later."

Natalie gave her a wicked grin and swung her dark ponytail over her shoulder. "You bet we will. The ballroom looks great, so relax and have fun today."

"I'll try." Gretchen put her things into her office, then went around the facility checking on a few last-minute things. All was well in the ballroom. The pin lights were perfect, and the floral arrangements added the ideal touch. Amelia's wedding cake was an eight-tier masterpiece nestled in a bed of white pastillage roses. All that was left was for the servers to light the candles and the guests to mill in.

She crossed the lobby and found Julian, Murray and the other groomsmen in the chapel taking photos with Bree and another guy who was probably from the magazine that had the exclusive to the event. Gretchen couldn't help the wide smile on her face when her eyes met Julian's, especially when his own smile returned her excitement. He looked so handsome in his tuxedo, as if he were auditioning to be the next James Bond. And he was hers, at least for now. Their relationship might be short, but it was special, and she'd always think of it that way.

Natalie followed her into the chapel, this time on official planner duties. "Okay, gentlemen, we need to get all of you except the ushers back into the gentlemen's suite. The guests are about to arrive. Ushers, please meet me back here so we can go over your instructions one last time."

The men filed out, Julian pressing a kiss to her cheek as he went by, so as not to mess up her lipstick. "I'll meet you in the lobby after these two get hitched."

"I'll be waiting," she said, trying out a seductive smile. She wasn't entirely sure that it worked, but Julian sighed and reluctantly followed Murray out of the chapel. That was proof enough for her.

"All right," Natalie shouted. "Ushers at the doors. Musicians, please cue up the string medley to take us through to the groom's entrance. Gretchen…do something with yourself. Let one of the ushers seat you. They need practice." Without another word, she disappeared from the room.

As she was told, Gretchen returned to the entrance and approached one of the ushers with a polite smile.

"Are you a guest of the bride or the groom?"

"The groom."

He nodded, handed her one of the programs she'd made and took her arm to lead her down the aisle and to a seat on the right side of the chapel. She wasn't alone for long. Guests started arriving in huge waves. This was a big wedding, putting the facility's capacity limits to the test. Every spot in the parking lot, every seat in the chapel, would be taken, and taken by Nashville royalty.

The room filled quickly. Gretchen tried not to act out of place as different country music stars were seated around her. Before long, the chapel looked like the audience at the Country Music Awards. She was pretty certain Garth Brooks and Trisha Yearwood were sitting right behind her. It was odd, but that hadn't fazed her when she was working—a guest was a guest—but as a guest herself, it felt extremely bizarre to be sitting among them. She had to keep reminding herself that her date was a movie star and she needed to be cool.

The string quartet's music medley faded, and she recognized them changing to the song they played when the parents were escorted in, then the officiant and the groomsmen entered. Julian sought her out in the crowd and gave her a sly wink as he went by. It was enough to make her heart flutter in her chest.

They assembled on the raised platform, and the music announced the arrival of the bridesmaids, then Kelly with her father. Gretchen stood with the crowd as the bride walked down the aisle in a lace-and-crystal extravaganza, custom-made for a country music diva.

As the wedding began, Gretchen felt her mind stray. Her gaze drifted to Julian, standing by with the ring and to catch Murray if he fainted. He looked so calm, so natural, compared to Murray, who'd started to sweat and could barely make it through his vows his voice was shaking so badly. Of course, Julian wasn't the one getting married.

She imagined he'd still be calm at his own wedding. Even if he felt nervous, he'd fall back on his actor training and play the part of a confident groom. He'd speak the words to her without faltering, with nothing but love and adoration on his face and in his voice…

Oh, no. She stopped herself. Gretchen might be in the midst of a lusty haze, but she wasn't letting herself go *there*. She wasn't a naive girl who thought the man who took her virginity would love her forever and marry her and they'd live happily ever after. She knew the truth and she'd accepted it, despite the ridiculous tangent her brain had taken. Like it or not, she was a paid companion. He wouldn't be looking adoringly at her and speaking vows of any kind, ever.

With a sigh, Gretchen let her gaze drop into her lap as she pretended to study the program. Maybe it was a good thing that their time together was coming to an end. Keeping her heart out of the arrangement with Julian was getting harder and harder.

He needed to get on that plane back to Beverly Hills before she lost the fight.

Julian couldn't wait for the ceremony and all the pictures to be over so he could hold Gretchen in his arms again. She'd hovered on the fringes during the photo shoot, watching with adoration in her eyes, as she was instructed.

Their progressing physical relationship had certainly made their public appearances easier. Neither of them really had to act anymore. They just did what felt natural and it translated beautifully. He'd already had several people ask him about Gretchen, and he couldn't help boasting about how smart and talented and beautiful she was.

It was all true.

At last, Julian's duties were over, save for his toast at the reception. The wedding party finally made their way over to the ballroom and took their places to welcome the happy couple and witness their first dance. That done, they were allowed to take their seats, eat their dinner and finally relax. The round of toasts was completed during the salad course, effectively allowing Julian to be off duty the rest of the night. Weddings were exhausting, almost a bigger production than some of the movies he'd starred in.

"You look amazing," he leaned in and said to Gretchen as the wedding cake was served. Julian wasn't interested in dessert. He had a hard time tearing his eyes away from the exposed line of her neck and shoulders. He ached to run his fingertip along her bare skin and leave a line of kisses in its wake.

Gretchen smiled at his assessment, her cheeks blushing adorably. "Thank you. You're looking pretty dapper yourself."

"Meh." He dismissed it. He wasn't interested in talking about himself tonight. He wanted the focus to be on her. "I can't wait to get you out on the dance floor and show you off to everyone."

Gretchen stiffened slightly, looking at him with concern in her dark eyes. "Dancing? We've never discussed the subject of dancing before. I've got a lovely pair of two left feet."

"You can't be that bad," he dismissed.

"No, you don't understand. My mother was a professionally trained ballerina. She tried to teach me to dance for years, then finally declared I was about as elegant and graceful as a rhino in heels."

Julian flinched. That was a horrible thing to say to someone, much less your own daughter. No wonder she'd gone this long thinking she wasn't worthy of a man's attentions. "We're not doing that kind of dancing," he insisted. "I'm going to hold you close and we'll just lose ourselves in the music. Nothing fancy, just dance floor foreplay."

"Foreplay?" Her arched brow raised curiously.

"You betcha." Julian knew a lot of guys didn't like to dance, but those guys were damn fools. If they only knew how a good slow dance could prime the pumps, they'd all sign up for ballroom dancing lessons.

As if on cue, the bandleader invited the whole wedding party out onto the dance floor. "Here's our chance," he said.

"Aren't you supposed to dance with the maid of honor?"

He turned to see her step out onto the floor with another man. "I guess not. Would you care to help a lonely gentleman out?"

Gretchen nervously took his hand and let him lead her out onto the dance floor. The song was slow and romantic, allowing him to take full advantage of the moment. He slipped his arms around her waist, pulling her close. It took a minute for her to relax, but eventually, she put her arms around his neck and took a deep breath to release the tension.

"See? This isn't so bad."

"You're right. And if it wasn't for the frantic flashing of cameras taking pictures, I might be able to relax."

Julian shrugged. He'd learned long ago to tune all that out. It was hard for an actor to stay in the moment if he couldn't ignore the camera in his face, the lights shining on him and the boom mike hanging overhead. There were really only two photographers tonight; the rest were just guests taking photos like at any other wedding. They were harmless.

"This moment is what the whole week was about. Let them take their pictures. Let them plaster it across their celebrity gossip magazine pages and make you a household name if that's the price for bringing you into my life."

Gretchen gasped softly at his bold words. He'd surprised himself with the intensity of them, but it had felt right at the moment. As time went on, he realized that he just couldn't let this go when he returned home. He didn't know how they could manage it or if it would work at all, but he wanted to try. He would be a fool to let such a sweet, caring woman drift out of his life.

The moment was perfect, like one carefully crafted by one of his directors. The lighting was dim with the occasional beam dancing across them. The music was soft and seductive, their bodies moving in time with it. Every inch of her soft curves was pressed against him. When she laid her head on his shoulder, it was as if the world had ceased to exist. The wedding guests, the cameras...all of it felt as if it was suddenly a million miles away and they were dancing all alone.

Her touch made his skin prickle with sensations,

but none could come close to the lightness inside him. With Gretchen in his arms, he felt as though he could do anything. He could take on that gritty script, he could pursue a more serious acting career without compromising his brother's care, he could have everything he wanted...including her.

It had been only a few days, but he had Gretchen to thank for opening his eyes to the possibilities. He intended to talk to Ross about it tomorrow morning. That script was everything he wanted, and a part of him needed to try out for it. He might not get it, or he might wish he hadn't when the critics got a hold of him, but he needed to try.

The song came to an end, and Julian could feel the spell drift away with the last notes. This night could only be more perfect with Gretchen in his bed again. He wanted to get out of here before something interfered.

"Are you ready to go, Cinderella?" he asked as he led her off the dance floor.

"I don't know," she said with a wrinkled nose. "The minute we step out the door, it's over, isn't it? Our little fantasy relationship turns back into a pumpkin at midnight. If leaving means it's over, then no. I want to stay and dance until the band unplugs and goes home."

Julian pulled her tight against him and kissed her. A tingle traveled straight to his toes, making his feet feel as though they were asleep. "I'm not sure what time period Ross negotiated, but I really don't care. If we walk out of this ballroom, I intend to take you back to my hotel and make love to you all night. And I'm going to keep doing that until I have to get on a plane and go back to LA. I don't know about you, but to me, what's going on between us has nothing to do with any business arrangement."

"It's not for me, either."

Julian smiled. "Then slip out of this ballroom with me right now."

Gretchen looked around the dim ballroom at the crowd on the dance floor and the others milling around their tables. "Isn't it too early to leave? Isn't there anything else you need to do as the best man?"

Julian shook his head. "I'm done. We'll see them tomorrow morning at the farewell brunch."

She was biting her lip, but he could tell he'd won the battle by the naughty glint in her eye. "Okay, let me go get my bag out of my office and we can go."

Julian took Gretchen's hand and they made their way out of the ballroom. He was moving quickly, weaving through the other guests. He couldn't wait to peel that dress off her tonight. In the lobby, he waited while she dashed down the hallway to grab her things.

Then he heard it: the special ringtone designated for his brother's care facility. Reaching into his tuxedo pocket, he grabbed his phone and said a silent prayer.

"Hello?" he said, wishing the voice on the line would tell him it was a wrong number or something.

"Mr. Curtis?" the woman said, dashing his hopes.

"Yes?"

"Mr. Curtis, I'm sorry to have to call again, but this is Theresa from the Hawthorne Community. James's condition has gotten substantially worse since we spoke last."

"He's in the hospital, isn't he?"

"Yes, but he isn't responding quickly enough to treatment. The doctors think they might have to put him on a ventilator to keep his oxygen levels high enough while the pneumonia clears up."

Julian should know more about his brother's condition and what all this would mean for him, but he didn't. His brother's tracheostomy was supposed to solve his breathing problems, but apparently it wasn't enough this time. "What does that mean? Is he going to be okay?"

"We don't know. We called to give you the status and let you know that your mother is with him and hopes you can come as well. Do you think that will be possible?"

"Yes, I'm in Nashville right now. I can be there in a few hours. Which hospital is he staying in?"

"He's at the university hospital. I'll be sure to let your mother know you're on your way."

"Thank you. Goodbye."

Julian hung up the phone and slipped it back into his pocket. He looked over his shoulder as Gretchen came from her office with her purse and a small duffel bag.

"Gretchen…" He stopped. He hated to derail everything, but he had no choice. "I'm going to have to cancel on tonight. I just got a call about James and I'm leaving for Kentucky as soon as I walk out of here."

Her dark eyes widened with concern lining them. "Is he going to be okay?"

Julian felt a tightness constrict his chest, making it almost impossible for him to get out the words. "I… don't know. I just know that I have to go. I'm so sorry. This isn't how I wanted tonight to end."

"Then let's not let it end. Let's go."

"Go?" he asked in confusion. "You mean you want to go to Kentucky with me?"

She nodded quickly, without hesitation. "Absolutely." Walking up to Julian, she placed a reassuring kiss on his lips and then took his hand to tug him toward the door. "Let's get on the road."

Nine

Julian hated hospitals. A lot of his childhood had been spent in one while his brother was tested and treated. Julian was the lucky one—no one ever came after him with needles and scalpels—but the scent when they exited the elevator was unmistakable. Bleach and blood and God-knows-what-else.

Having a firm grip on Gretchen's hand made it easier. He'd never considered bringing her here until she suggested it, and then he'd realized he didn't want it any other way. For all his muscles, having her here made him feel stronger. He wanted to introduce her to his family; he wanted to share this secretive part of his life with someone.

As they approached the waiting room outside the ICU, he heard his mother's voice calling to him. Turning, he saw her pick up the coffee she was making and head their way.

His mother had been—and in his eyes still was—a beautiful woman. Time and stress had aged her faster than they should've, but you could still see the sparkle of the vibrant young woman beneath it all. Her wavy dark hair was more gray than brown anymore, but she still had the same bright smile, and her blue-gray eyes lit up when she saw him. Julian had her eyes, his own color much more sedate without his colored contacts.

"I'm so glad you could make it." She smiled as she approached, wrapping him in a big hug, then turning to look at his unexpected companion. "And who is this?"

"I'm Gretchen," she said, reaching out to take the woman's hand. "It's nice to meet you, Mrs. Cooper."

His mother smiled and shook her head. "It's Curtis, dear. Cooper is Julian's stage name. You can just call me Denise."

"Mom, Gretchen and I are seeing each other." It may have only been for a week, but it was true. This was more than just a setup relationship to him.

His mother looked them both up and down. "We've interrupted something important, haven't we? You two look like you came here straight from an awards show or something."

"Just a wedding that was winding down anyway," Julian insisted. "You remember Murray, my roommate in college?"

She nodded. "Oh, yes, I bought one of his albums for James to listen to. That explains why you were in Nashville. Convenient timing, although there's never really a good time for this." His mother smoothed over her hair, which was pulled back into a bun.

"How is he doing?"

She shrugged, drawing her oversize cardigan tighter

around her. "It changes by the hour. Doctors keep waiting, hoping his blood oxygen levels will start coming back up without further intervention, but they could decide to go ahead and put him on the ventilator. They worry that if they take that step, he might be on it permanently. I just hate it. He was doing so well."

His mother shook her head sadly. "That trip to Europe for the Botox treatments made a huge difference. He was able to stretch his legs out, and the casts corrected some of the alignment problems he had in his legs. We were hopeful that with enough therapy we might get him walking, but this will set him back again. He's always had the breathing troubles."

Over the years, the spastic nature of his brother's cerebral palsy had worsened as his underutilized muscles started to atrophy. He'd undergone multiple surgeries and years of therapy to lengthen his muscles in the hopes he could walk or manage other dexterity tasks on his own, but they always drew back up. The controversial Botox treatments weren't legal in the States, but they'd taken the risk and traveled to a doctor who could try it. It had cost a fortune, but James had done so well afterward, it had been worth every penny.

"Can we see him?"

His mother bit at her bottom lip, reminding him of Gretchen. "Visiting hours are over, but maybe we can talk to someone." His mother disappeared, returning a few minutes later with an encouraging smile on her face. "They're going to let the two of you go back now, but just for five or ten minutes. You'll have to come back again in the morning. He's in the bed at the far end of the unit on the right. I'll wait here for you and drink some more coffee. It's going to be a long night for me."

"Okay, we'll be out in a minute." Julian hugged his mother, then led Gretchen with him through the double doors of the ICU. They walked around the nurse's station and to the end of the hall. Taking a deep breath, he pushed back the curtain and found his identical twin lying in a hospital bed. It was such a familiar sight, he almost didn't react to it the way he should've. His brother's eyes fluttered open, then a lopsided smile spread across his face.

"Julian," he mouthed with a raspy whisper, breaking into a fit of coughing.

"Try not to talk too much, James. Use your signs." He let go of Gretchen's hand to walk to his brother's bedside. He scooped up James's clenched fist and patted it. Both the boys had learned sign language when they were young to help James communicate without speaking. It was helpful when the tracheostomy made it that much more difficult for him to speak. "Mom says you're having trouble breathing. Have you been sneaking pot again?"

His brother smiled at his joke and shook his head. "Can't get any. Mean nurses," he signed. James took a few rattling, wheezing lungfuls of air through the tracheostomy tube in his throat, making Julian more worried the longer he stood there.

Most people with a tracheostomy could speak by covering the tube with their finger or chin. Because James had such limited control of his hands and arms, that hadn't been an option for him. Instead, they'd adjusted the valve in his windpipe so he could get just enough air to whisper between breaths. Even then, his speech was limited by muscle control in his throat and face. He tended to sign most of the time to get his point across, but occasionally, he'd speak a few words. It had never taken much for Julian to understand him. They were identical twins; Julian knew his brother inside and out. He just couldn't help him.

"James, this is my friend Gretchen. She wanted to meet you."

James's head was almost always cocked unnaturally to the side with a pillow supporting his neck, but his gaze traveled past his brother to Gretchen. His left arm was drawn to his chest, but he waved his fingers at her. "Pretty," he signed.

"Yes, she is. She's very pretty."

"I'd hit that," James whispered with a smile.

Julian and Gretchen both broke into unexpected laughter. Despite everything, James always had a sense of humor. Whatever trauma that had impacted his ability to control his body had left his cognitive powers intact. He was smart and funny, and it made Julian sad that the world would miss out on what James could've done if he'd been born healthy like his brother.

"Uh, thank you, James," she said, blushing at his amusing compliment. "How are you feeling?"

James shrugged. His brother probably didn't know what it was like to feel good. He had okay days and bad days, but even his best days could be hard on him. Those were the days when he felt well enough to think about how he was trapped in a body that couldn't do what he wanted it to do.

A loud, wheezing breath rattled through James's trach tube, but it was quickly drowned out by a shrill beeping noise that sounded from the machine by James's bed. Julian looked up, noting that the blood oxygen percentage on the screen was blinking red.

The nurse came in a second later, checking the screens.

"You two will have to leave. We've got to get the ventilator hooked up."

Two other nurses and a resident came in behind her, and Julian was pushed out into the hallway with Gretchen. As he watched them work on his brother, Julian realized that his fantasies of doing serious films were just that—fantasies. Hard-hitting, low-budget indie films might reap all the awards and get the buzz at Sundance, but they wouldn't pay these bills. They wouldn't cover charter flights to Europe for experimental treatments. Giving James the absolute best quality of life was his number one priority. His vanity and his artistic needs would always take second place to that.

"We'd better go," Gretchen said, tugging at his arm.

Reluctantly, he followed her out of the ICU, dreading the news he'd have to share with his mother in the waiting room. The woman hadn't gotten a stitch of good news in almost thirty years. He hated to pile more on top of it.

But he knew that with the news would be his promise that he'd take care of it. Just as he always had. And always would.

They stumbled into a Louisville hotel room near the hospital at almost three in the morning. Gretchen was exhausted down to her bones, and yet too much had happened for her to sleep anytime soon. She could tell Julian was feeling the same way after how he'd paced in the hotel lobby while they got a room. Even if they went straight to bed, they'd both likely lie there with their brains spinning.

Gretchen flipped on the lights of their suite, revealing a tasteful and modern room. It had a separate sitting area from the bedroom, like Julian's room in Nashville. He carried her bag into the bedroom and laid it out on the bed. They'd left in such a rush, he didn't have a bag of his own. All he'd had was a small leather travel case he'd taken with him to the wedding chapel with things he might need throughout the day.

Now he stood at the foot of the bed, silently tugging off his bow tie and slipping out of his tuxedo jacket. She could tell he was distracted and worried about James. Gretchen knew that if one of her sisters were in the hospital, she'd be beside herself.

Instead of watching him undress, she took her bag into the bathroom to change. She'd spent far too many hours in this strapless bra, and she was ready to be done with it all. Unzipping her bag, she looked inside and groaned. Unfortunately, when she'd packed, she'd packed for a sexy night at his hotel. A detour to Louisville to see his sick brother hadn't been on the radar. The only pajamas she had were of the sexy red lace variety. With the dark cloud looming over Julian, she doubted he would be interested.

But with limited options, she slipped into the chemise and pulled the fluffy hotel bathrobe over it. When she returned to the bedroom, Julian's suit was lying across the chair and he was gone. She found him in the living room, standing in front of the minibar clad in just a pair of boxer briefs as he held a tumbler of golden liquid in his hand. Scotch, she'd guess.

"You're drinking?" she asked. That was the first thing she'd seen him drink aside from water since they met.

"Yeah," he said, looking thoughtfully at the glass. "My trainer can punish me later. That's the beauty of being able-bodied. I just… I just needed something to numb all the feelings inside me. A bottle of water and a protein bar wasn't going to do it."

Gretchen nodded. She hated to see him like this, but there wasn't much she could do. Instead, she sat down on the couch and beckoned him to sit beside her. He slammed back the rest of his drink and left it on the counter before he came over and collapsed onto the pillows.

Without saying anything, Gretchen snuggled up beside him. He wrapped his arm around her shoulder and hugged her tight against him.

"I want to talk about something other than my brother," he said after a long silence. "Tell me…" Julian hesitated. "Tell me about how someone so beautiful and full of life could be so awkward and inexperienced with men."

Really? That was the last topic she wanted to discuss, but if it would take his mind off James, she would confess it all. With her face buried against his chest, she started the not-so-interesting tale of her life. "My mother was a ballerina. She toured with a company for several years before she broke her ankle and retired. She met my father, a physical therapist, while she was doing rehab on her leg. She was tall and willowy, educated in the classics, and he was shorter and stockier, with more knowledge about football than anything else, but for some reason, they hit it off.

"They married and had three girls. I was the middle child. My sisters were always so much like my mother, so graceful and so skilled when it came to charming men. I took after my father. I was always chubby, always clumsy. I actually got kicked out of kinder ballet classes because I kept knocking over the other children. To say I was a disappointment to my mother was an understatement."

"Did she actually say that to you? That you were a disappointment?"

"No. But she always pushed me to be more like my sisters. She didn't seem to understand me at all. Even if I hadn't been stockier or uncoordinated, I was very shy. I was much more comfortable with my art and my books than with boys. I really didn't have much in common with anyone in my family. And when I got old enough to date, I don't know, I guess I sabotaged myself. I didn't feel pretty, I didn't feel confident and so guys never noticed me. I was so quiet, I could virtually fade into the background, unseen and unheard. It just continued on like that and after a while, I decided that maybe I was meant to be one of those suffering artists, destined to be alone."

"That's ridiculous." Julian eased back and lifted her chin with his finger until she had no choice but to look him in the eye. "There's no way a woman like you would end up alone. You're beautiful, talented, smart, passionate… You've got way too much to offer a man. He just has to be smart enough to see you when others don't. I'll admit that I probably wouldn't have been that guy. I'm always on the move, always too distracted to see things that aren't right in front of my face. And if Ross hadn't set up this date, I would've missed out on a wonderful few days because of my blindness."

Gretchen felt the blush of embarrassment rise to her cheeks. She wanted to pull away, to avoid his gaze, but he wouldn't let her.

"I mean it. You don't know how much it meant to

have you here with me tonight. I'm always the one that comes in to save the day. It was nice, for once, to have someone to hold my hand, to support me when I needed it. It's so hard watching James's health deteriorate, but having you there made all the difference."

"I'm glad I could be there. No one should have to go through that alone."

His blue eyes focused on hers, and she noticed for the first time that he'd taken out his contact lenses. The stunning Caribbean blue eyes she was used to looking at were now the soft blue-gray of the northern seas. The color suited him more, and she liked seeing him without part of his Hollywood facade. "Your eyes are a beautiful color," she said.

"They don't pop on camera," he said, deflating her compliment.

"That's the camera's loss."

He watched her for a moment before he spoke. "Gretchen, I don't want this to end."

The surprise shift in the conversation threw her off and she sat up, pulling away from him and taking a few seconds to respond appropriately. "Neither do I, but what choice do we have? You're going back to LA, and my business and my life are in Nashville."

He nodded in agreement, but he had a firm set in his jaw that told her he wasn't giving up that easily. "It would be complicated, yes, but I want to try. I can't just walk away from you like this. Say you want to be with me—no contracts, no faking it for the cameras."

Gretchen almost couldn't believe her ears. He was serious. He wanted to be with her, truly be with her, and not just because his manager was behind it or they were enjoying the benefits of their arrangement. A woman like her being with a man like Julian was some kind of fantasy come to life. How could she say no to that, especially when just a look from him could make her chest so tight she could barely breathe? She certainly wasn't looking forward to letting Julian go. She'd tried to keep her heart out of this short-term scenario, but with every minute that ticked by, she was losing the fight. Was it really possible that she wouldn't have to give him up when his plane took off on Monday?

"I want to be with you, Julian," she said, and she meant it. "I don't know how we'd manage, but I don't want to let this go, either."

"Then don't." Julian leaned into her and pressed his lips against hers. He kept advancing, easing her back until she was lying on the cushions of the couch. His hands fumbled with the tie of her belt, opening the robe and pulling back to admire what was beneath it.

"Holy hell," he said, running his fingers over the red satin-and-lace chemise. "You've had this on the whole time?"

"Just since we got here."

"And we've been talking? If I'd known what you had under that robe, we could've found some more pleasurable distractions than talking."

His lips met hers. Unlike the night before, there was less tenderness in his touch. There was a tension there, and she knew it was stress. He needed a distraction, and she was happy to be that for him tonight. She wanted him to lose himself in her and forget about all his troubles.

His hand glided up her outer thigh, pushing the robe out of the way and brushing against the lace edges of her negligee. "Did you know," he asked, as his hand ran across her stomach, caressing her through the fabric, "that red is my favorite color?"

Gretchen smiled, parting her legs for him to draw closer. "Is it really?"

"It is now." He punctuated the words by burying his face in her neck. He tugged at the plunging neckline of her nightie until her breasts were exposed and he could tease at them with his rough palms.

She still hadn't quite adjusted to the idea that she was a sexually active woman now. She still felt as though she was fumbling around, but being with Julian made it so easy. All she had to do was close her eyes and do whatever felt right. So far, that hadn't steered her wrong, and Julian certainly seemed to like it.

Drawing her leg up, she hooked it around his hip, pulling his firm desire closer to the slip of satin that separated them. Julian groaned when they made contact, rubbing himself across her most sensitive spot. The tiny panties that came with the chemise were hardly clothing, more an eye patch in matching fabric, but she supposed they weren't intended for everyday wear.

Julian gripped the panties in his fist and tugged at them. They tore away without hesitation, and he tossed them onto the hotel room floor. Gretchen gasped in surprise, then started to giggle. There was a reason they were so flimsy. The giggles were abruptly stopped when the panties were replaced by Julian's hand.

Her back arched up off the couch, her hips both drawn to and shying from the powerful feelings his touch roused inside her. It was amazing just how quickly he could bring her to the edge. He'd learned her body's responses after only a few encounters.

Gretchen clenched her eyes shut, hovering on the

verge of release, when she felt cold air rush across her skin. Her eyes opened and she found that Julian had pulled back and was watching her as he lay against the far arm of the couch.

He slipped out of his briefs and beckoned her to join him. "Come here," Julian said.

Gretchen shook out of the robe, nervously took his hand and covered his body with her own. "What are we doing?"

"I'm not doing anything," he said with a sly smile. "I'm going to lie here and watch you while you take the lead."

Her jaw dropped in surprise. They'd moved on to an advanced class without warning. The idea of sitting astride Julian during sex while he watched her was incredibly unnerving. And arousing. She knew instantly that she wanted to do this. She could do this. She wouldn't let nerves get the best of her.

Julian reached for his toiletry case sitting on the coffee table and pulled out a condom. "Care to do the honors?"

She took it from him, determination setting in her jaw. Opening the package, she put it in place and slowly rolled it down the hard length of him. Julian let out a hiss as her hands worked up and down. His jaw was tight, his body tense. It was then that Gretchen realized she liked being in charge. This might be nerve-racking, but it was also going to be fun.

She rose up onto her knees, and Julian helped guide her movements as she lowered herself onto him. She moved slowly, painfully slow, as her body stretched to accommodate him. Then, at last, she found herself fully seated. Her core was already throbbing and prickling with the sensation of his previous touches. She couldn't imagine she would last long like this.

Biting her lip, she braced her hands on Julian's bare chest. She leaned forward and rocked back once, testing the waters. It was a delicious feeling, and judging by Julian's fingertips pressing fiercely into the flesh of her hips, she was doing something right.

Gretchen did it again, this time faster. Gaining confidence, she fell into a pleasurable rhythm with Julian muttering encouraging words to her.

His hands stroked the silk-and-lace fabric of her chemise as she moved, rising up to cover her breasts as they spilled over the top. She placed her hands over his and thrust her hips harder and faster against him.

"Julian," she whispered as she felt the release building up inside her.

"Yes, baby," he encouraged. "Just let go. Take me with you."

So she did. With renewed enthusiasm, she moved over him, opening the floodgates so that every ounce of pleasure, every emotion she held back, rushed free. In the moment, it wasn't his touch or her movements that sent her over the edge, it was the warm heat in the center of her chest.

She'd never felt this sensation before, but she knew what it was. Now that she and Julian had a future, she'd finally allowed herself to feel what she'd been fighting. Love. It was love that pushed her over the edge, crying out his name as the tremors of pleasure washed through her. As he followed suit, thrusting into her one last time, she looked down at him, placing her hand over his heart until they were both still and silent.

It was then that she collapsed against him. Gretchen

buried her face in his neck, breathing in the scent she'd become so used to so quickly.

This. The sex was nice, but *this* was what she'd truly waited twenty-nine years for.

Ten

Monday morning was a reality that neither of them really wanted to face. James's condition stabilized with the ventilator, and the doctors were extremely positive about his prognosis. He was moved out of the ICU, and his mother ushered Julian and Gretchen out the door and back to Nashville Sunday evening.

That night together had been a somber one, both of them knowing what Monday brought. Gretchen had to be in the office for her weekly staff meeting, so she slipped out of bed, leaving him a kiss as she ran out the door. She promised she would return after the meeting to say a proper goodbye before he had to leave for the airport.

They'd agreed they would give their relationship a real try, long distance be damned, but they both knew it would be hard. And different from how they'd spent the past few days. Julian worried about how they would pull it off. He had some time before his next film started shooting, but if he spent those weeks in Nashville, Ross would undoubtedly start complaining. He would want Julian in LA, doing readings, lining up his next part and being "seen." Unfortunately, he would probably want him being seen out on the town with a woman. That wasn't an option.

The only thing that got him up and dressed that morning was the knowledge that Ross was coming by to meet with him before he flew on to New York to arrange for a few press appearances. He'd much rather stay in bed and wait for Gretchen to return so he could make love to her one last time before he left.

He was drinking a protein shake he'd had stashed in his refrigerator when he heard his manager's knock on the door. Right on time, as usual. Julian opened the door, letting the short, squat man in the expensive suit into the room.

Ross wandered over to the sofa and sat down. "So, how'd the fake date go? The pictures I've seen looked pretty convincing, so good work. I know that couldn't have been easy to keep up."

Julian wasn't sure what his manager meant by that, but they should've been convincing. Every moment together was authentic and amazingly easy. "Actually, it was the easiest role I've played in years. After the first two days, I wasn't acting at all. In fact, Gretchen and I have really hit it off. I've asked her if I can continue to see her after this week."

The smug smile faded from Ross's face the longer Julian spoke. "Are you serious?"

Julian frowned at his manager. "I'm absolutely serious. She's a great woman. I've never dated anyone like her."

Ross sighed and ran his hand over his bald head. "I know that I set this up and I said that you dating a normal, everyday woman would be good for your image. But I never intended this to be a long-term arrangement."

"What does it matter if it's long-term or short-term? You wanted me to be with someone. I'm with someone. You should be happy."

"Not with her," Ross complained. "She's…"

Julian stared Ross down, daring him to insult Gretchen so he'd have a good reason to punch him. "She's *what*, Ross?"

Ross looked at him, preparing the words carefully. "She's not the kind of woman you'd want on your arm when you walk the red carpet at the Golden Globes. That's all I'm saying."

Julian snorted in contempt. "And when, in my illustrious career, have you ever booked me into a role that would get me invited to the Golden Globes?"

Ross shook his head. "You're missing the point. I'm sure she's a perfectly nice girl—the type you'd want to take home to meet your mother. But she's not the kind of girl that will take your career to the next level. Think Brad and Angelina. Tom and Nicole."

"Tom and Nicole are divorced."

"So it didn't work out," he said with a dismissive wave of his hand. "My point is that their high-profile marriage boosted their acting careers."

"There are plenty of famous actors and actresses with spouses that aren't in the business."

Ross leaned forward and rested his chin on his

pointed index fingers. "Julian, I'm your manager. You pay me to know what's best for your career. And I'm telling you—she is not the kind of woman Julian Cooper is supposed to be with."

If that was true, Julian wasn't certain if he wanted to be Julian Cooper anymore. His alter ego was becoming the kind of person he didn't even like. "You might be right, Ross, but I'm telling you that Gretchen is *exactly* the kind of woman that Julian *Curtis* wants to be with. This isn't a role, Ross, it's my life. I pay you to manage my career, but my private life is private. I'll date whomever I want to, and I'd appreciate it if you'd keep your mouth shut on the matter."

Ross's cell phone chimed and he looked down at the screen. Julian was happy for the interruption. The energy in the room had gotten far too tense. Ross was a good manager, but he needed to know he had boundaries.

Ross frowned at the phone and then let it down by his side. "You can date whomever you like, Julian, you're right. But you may want to reconsider choosing Gretchen."

"Why?"

"Did you tell her about James?"

Julian stiffened. "I had to. She was there when I got the call about him going into the hospital. But I told her she'd need to sign a confidentiality agreement."

"Did she?"

"Not yet. I was going to have you draw it up today."

Ross sighed and handed his phone over to him. "It's too damn late. The tragic story of Julian Cooper's secret twin has just hit the papers."

No. That wasn't possible. Julian scanned over the

article, looking for some kind of evidence that would prove that Ross was wrong. The sinking ache in his stomach didn't fade as he read the article. It was a huge, in-depth story about James, including his illness and recent hospital drama. Whoever had leaked the story had very up-to-date information about his brother.

"Who else knows about James?"

Julian shook his head. No one knew. "Just you and Murray. And Gretchen."

"Well, *I* certainly didn't leak the story."

He knew that was true, and with Murray on his honeymoon and worrying about anything but Julian and his brother, that left an unacceptable alternative. He just couldn't believe that Gretchen would sell him out and leak that story. She'd hardly seemed interested in the money he already owed her. But how much would the press be willing to pay for a story like this? Perhaps more than she could turn down?

"No," he insisted with a shake of his head. "I've been with her nonstop until this morning when she went to work. There's no way she could've contacted a reporter and sold that story without me knowing it."

Ross rolled his eyes. "Don't be so ignorant, Julian. You weren't with her every single second. You showered, you used the restroom, you slept. For all you know, she slipped out of bed in the night and emailed a reporter while you were satiated and unconscious."

Julian dropped into the chair beside him, the doubts finally creeping into his mind. He'd trusted her. Could Gretchen really have sold him out just like all the others?

A sad expression lined his manager's face as he reached out and patted Julian's shoulder. "I'm sorry, I really am. I know you think I'm a cold, heartless businessman, with all my confidentiality contracts and arranged relationships, but I've been in this business a long time. I've seen a lot of my clients get sold out by the people they trust the most. I try to protect my clients, but there's only so much I can do."

There was only one person who knew about everything that had happened with James over the past few days. The idea of that betrayal made his protein shake threaten to rise in the back of his throat. He didn't want to believe it. Every fiber in his being screamed that it couldn't be true. But Ross was right. There was no other answer.

"We've got to figure out how you want to handle this. Ignoring the article will make it seem like you're ashamed of your brother, which we don't want. It's probably best that we set up a tell-all interview of some kind, where you talk about him and explain why you tried to keep him out of the harsh spotlight."

"That sounds fine," Julian said in a flat tone. He really wasn't listening. At the moment, damage control was the last thing on his mind.

"While I'm handling that, you need to talk to Gretchen." He laid a fat envelope on the table. "Here's the money we owe her. Pay her and make her go away. Or I will."

Julian nodded. He knew Ross was right, but he didn't relish that conversation. "She's supposed to be coming over here today."

"When?"

Julian looked at the clock hanging on the hotel room wall. "Soon. She was coming back over before I left for the airport."

Ross nodded and stood up. "I'm going to head out, then. While I'm in New York, I'll see who I can talk to about that interview. When you get back to LA, call me and let me know how it went with Gretchen."

His manager slipped out of the room, but Julian hardly gave him any notice. The pain in his chest had subsided, leaving only the numbness of disassociation and the faint heat of anger licking at his ears. He knew what he had to do, and it was a role he didn't want to play. But play it he would to remove the malicious cancer from his life.

Gretchen had a hard time walking down the hallway to Julian's hotel room. A half hour ago, she'd damn near skipped down the same path, arriving earlier than she'd intended. She'd been so excited to see Julian one more time before he left that Natalie had let her cut out of the staff meeting early.

As she'd raised her hand to knock, she'd heard the sound of two men arguing loudly. She hadn't intended to listen in, but there was no way she was going to interrupt their argument. She'd decided to wait for a lull, then knock, but instead, she'd overheard more than she'd bargained for.

Ross's words haunted her, even now. *She is not the kind of woman Julian Cooper is supposed to be with,* he'd said. That hadn't surprised her. But when Julian said that he might be right, she'd felt her heart break. He'd done nothing over the past few days but tell her how beautiful she was, how worthy she was. To hear he really felt otherwise was a crushing blow to her fragile ego. She'd rushed to her car, sobbing against the steering wheel until she saw Ross leave.

She took a few minutes to recover from her tears and then headed back upstairs. She hadn't wanted to go back after that, but she knew it would be suspicious if she didn't show up. Taking a deep breath, she knocked on the door, more anxious than she'd been the very first day.

Julian was slow to answer, and when he did, she wished he hadn't. The light in his eyes was gone, his smile a distant memory. His jaw was tight in anger, his gaze burrowing into her as though he were searching her soul for some kind of guilt.

"Come in," he said, stepping back to let her inside.

This wasn't the reception she was hoping for, but she wasn't surprised. She sat down on the couch, clutching her purse in her lap. Without even speaking, she knew their relationship was about to unravel.

Julian picked up his phone from the coffee table and hit a few buttons. He wordlessly handed it to her, his blue eyes daring her to take it.

Gretchen hesitated, finally accepting the phone from him. When she looked down on the screen, she felt the air get sucked from her lungs. It was an article about James. She knew how hard Julian worked to maintain his brother's privacy, but now the secret was out. No wonder Julian was angry.

"How awful," Gretchen said, her hand coming up to cover her mouth. "How could anyone have found out about James? You were so careful. Could it have been one of the nurses at the hospital?"

"Good try," he said with a deadly cold tone. "I'm the actor in the room, not you."

Gretchen's gaze tore away from the phone to meet

his accusatory one. "What is that supposed to mean? Do you think I'm the one that leaked the story?"

Julian crossed his arms over his chest, looking larger and more intimidating than he ever had before. He looked as if he were about to mow down a field of terrorists with an automatic weapon, as in one of his films. "I don't have a lot of people to choose from, Gretchen. You're the only one who knows everything. You're the only one that's ever met my brother. No one else would have all these details."

Gretchen stood up. She was shorter than he was, but she couldn't just sit there and let him hover over her intimidatingly. "Just because I had the information doesn't mean I would've shared it. I told you that I wouldn't tell anyone about James and I meant it. I said I'd even sign your stupid agreement."

He nodded. "It never occurred to me that you'd manage to sell your story before I had time to draft the paperwork. A brilliant way to get around it, I have to say."

"Get around it?" she said, surprising herself with her own shrill tone. "I didn't get around anything, Julian, because I didn't sell this story. Did Ross feed you all these lies? I don't understand how you could think I'm capable of something like that."

"I didn't think you were capable of it, either." Despite his hard expression, Gretchen detected some hesitation in his eyes. He didn't seem to believe his own accusations, and yet he wouldn't back down.

"You're just using this as an excuse," she said, trying to bait the truth from him.

His brows went up in surprise. "An excuse for what?"

"To get rid of me," she accused. Ross's cruel words echoed in her head, fueling her own anger. "Despite all those promises you made in Louisville, you know I'm not the kind of woman that will boost your career."

Julian seemed baffled by her allegation. "What makes you say that?"

"I heard you talking to Ross," Gretchen said. "I got off work early and heard you arguing. I know I'm not the right kind of woman for Julian Cooper. I'm fat and I'm awkward. I don't have an elegant or graceful bone in my body. I know that. I don't need Ross or you or the press to point that out to me."

Julian shook his head angrily. "I don't know what you heard, but I can assure you that isn't what that discussion was about."

"It wasn't? Come on, Julian, be honest. As much as you claim you want to be this serious actor, you're hooked on that blockbuster lifestyle. You claim you can't quit because of your brother, but how much could his expenses possibly be? Are they as much as your Beverly Hills mansion? Your sports cars? Personal trainers and private chefs? Expensive baubles for your expensive women? I bet not. You're going to use this story to drop me because I don't fit into that lifestyle. I'm not going to help you become a bigger star."

"You know, this doesn't have anything to do with my lifestyle or my career. You obviously didn't hear the whole conversation with Ross or you wouldn't accuse me of such a thing. I would've happily walked the Gretchen I knew down any red carpet. I thought you were beautiful. Special. I meant every word I said to you, Gretchen. But that entire discussion I had with Ross is moot now, because I can't stand by and let you hurt my family."

Angry tears threatened to spill from Gretchen's eyes.

She didn't want to cry. Not in front of Julian, but the harder she fought it, the harder it became to hold the tears back. "I would never do that to you. Or to James. Or your mother. And if you think that I would, then you don't know me as well as you think you do."

"I guess not, but it's only been a few days, right? It's not like we were in love."

Gretchen flinched at how ridiculous he made the idea of love sound. She was grateful she had kept her budding feelings to herself. The last thing she needed was for him to throw that in her face.

"What did they offer you, Gretchen?" he taunted. His face was so twisted with anger and betrayal he didn't look anything like the Julian she knew. "Money? Was the ten grand I'm paying you not enough?"

"No, it isn't about the money. I don't care how much they would've offered me, I wouldn't have sold that story to the press. I don't even want the money from this week."

Julian rolled his eyes and picked up an envelope from the table. He thrust it into her hands and stepped away before she could reject the parcel. "Why don't you want the money? Don't need it after your big story payout?"

Gretchen was so upset, she didn't even look down at what he handed her. "There is no payout. There is no money. I don't know how to convince you of that. And I don't want your money because it feels wrong to take it when it felt like we were…more than just some fake Hollywood relationship."

His blue gaze tore away from hers, focusing on the beige carpet of the hotel room. "It was just acting, Gretchen. By making you think it was real, you were far more relaxed for the cameras. We never would've pulled this fake relationship off if you didn't think I really liked you."

That struck Gretchen dumb. Could he really mean that? Had he just played her because she was so stiff and awkward? She knew she wasn't good with men, but could she really be fooled that easily? He was an actor, after all, but she couldn't believe he'd misled her like that. He couldn't make eye contact when he said it. She was certain that there was more between them, but for some reason, he wouldn't let himself admit to the truth.

Her chin dropped to her chest, her gaze finally falling on the package in her hand. "What is this?" she asked.

"Ten thousand dollars, as agreed. You fulfilled your end of the bargain, and quite pleasurably at that." There was a gloating expression on his face that she didn't like. She'd been desperate to rid herself of her virginity, but she couldn't stand to have him gloat over taking it so easily.

"Obviously," he added bitterly, "the five-thousand-dollar bonus for keeping quiet about my brother was forfeited when you spilled your guts to that reporter."

Gretchen closed her eyes. She could feel her heart crumbling in her chest. There was no other explanation for the sharp sensation that stole her breath from her lungs. She had no words, but it didn't matter because she knew her words wouldn't make any difference. He'd decided she was guilty, and nothing would convince him otherwise.

And even if it did...what would it change? If he'd been pretending to like her just to get through the week, there was nothing between them to salvage. All she could do was hold it together long enough to get out of this hotel room with some of her dignity intact.

"Obviously," she said, steeling her nerves and matching his bitter tone.

When she opened her eyes, Julian was emerging from the bedroom with his rolling suitcase. Once again, he avoided her gaze, making a wide berth around her as he made his way to the door. "Enjoy Italy," he said. "I hope you can put that blood money to good use." Julian grabbed the handle of the door and flung it open, walking out of the hotel suite without so much as a backward glance.

Gretchen wanted to chase after him, to convince him that she was telling the truth, but her legs just wouldn't cooperate. She might not think much of herself, but she had too much pride to beg. Instead, her knees trembled and gave out, her body collapsing into the cushions of the couch. Her face dropped into her lap, this morning's second round of tears flowing freely and wetting the envelope in her hands.

She was a fool. A fool to believe that a man like Julian would ever want something to do with a woman like her. A fool to think that she could find happiness with a person so unobtainable. He was a fantasy.

And now, it had all come to an end.

Eleven

Gretchen had buried herself in work this week. It was easy with her job—there was always a wedding to decorate for, a consult with a couple, some design work to finish and send to the printers. Thank goodness. She needed the distraction.

Her two days off had been awful. She'd pretty much sat in her apartment crying and eating cookies. That wasn't going to help matters at all. But by the time she returned to the office, she had that out of her system. She was ready to focus on work and forget all about Julian Cooper.

Unfortunately, it wasn't that easy. Not with three nosy friends and coworkers who immediately noticed that the romantic bubble had burst. She'd left their staff meeting on Monday almost beaming and came back Thursday morning in mourning. She'd fought off the questions but gave them enough information to satisfy them: it was over. She didn't want to talk much more about it when it was so new. So far, they'd backed off, but only because they were busy preparing for the next wedding, too.

When the time came, she wasn't entirely sure what she would tell them. Getting up from her desk and going into her supply closet, she pulled down the bin labeled for this weekend's autumn-themed wedding. As she sorted through the paper products, she tried to work out the tale in her mind.

"He accused me of leaking a story to the press and we broke up," she said aloud. "And really, we were never actually together. He was just playing me." That sounded silly, especially out loud, despite every word being true.

Of course, the supposed truth was nothing compared to her secret worry. Would he really have used all that as an excuse to break up with her because when it came down to it, he needed to date a pretty actress, not a frumpy artist? He'd insisted that wasn't true. He'd done nothing but tell her how pretty she was while they were together, but was he just buttering her up for the part? She couldn't dismiss what she'd heard between him and Ross.

The worst part of it was that she had to admit that Ross was probably right. She wasn't what people expected. Vain, painted-up Bridgette made a lot more sense in their business, even if Julian didn't like it. As hard as he worked to keep his brother and family out of the spotlight, protecting Gretchen would be harder. While early press might be positive, eventually, she'd find herself on a cover with a headline that declared Julian demands she lose weight or it's over.

It would never work between them; she knew that now. It was a pipe dream, a fantasy that lasted only while he was playing the role of the adoring, doting boyfriend.

Her fingers went to her throat and sought out the opal necklace. She'd worn it nearly every moment since he bought it for her. She loved it. But it was time to take it off. She unlatched the clasp and let it pool in her hand. Looking down at the beautiful, ruined necklace, she opened her desk drawer and dropped it in with her pens and paper clips.

That done, Gretchen picked up the box of paper products and carried them out of her office. She quickly divided them up among the chapel, the entryway table and the ballroom.

The ballroom was still bare bones. This weekend's wedding was smaller and far less grand compared to Murray and Kelly's event, but there was still plenty to be done.

"Gretchen?"

Gretchen set down the programs and turned to find Natalie in the doorway behind her. "Hey."

"The linen delivery is here. Do you need help?"

She shrugged. "Sure, if you've got time."

Natalie nodded and they both went to the back to get the cleaned, pressed linens from the delivery truck. They rolled the cart back into the ballroom and Gretchen started laying them out on the tables. She could tell Natalie was lingering purposely, but she wasn't about to start the conversation she was dreading.

Her coworker joined her in laying out linens, this wedding using a chocolate brown with an ivory-and-gold lace overlay. After a minute, Natalie said in a quiet voice, "Are you okay?"

Gretchen sighed and finished spreading out the tablecloth. "No, but I'm getting there."

Natalie nodded. The wedding planner at From This Moment was the quiet, observant type. She did a lot of listening, both in her job and in her daily life, something most people didn't really do. By listening, she noticed a lot, most importantly what people weren't saying.

"How long do you think I have before Bree and Amelia will try to fix me up with someone else?" Gretchen had hoped that losing her virginity would take that pressure off her friends and their quest to get her a man, but she doubted that would be the case. With that sexual burden gone, they could just hunt down a normal guy for her, not some superhero worthy of her first time.

"I think you're safe through the holidays. It's too busy a time to try fixing someone up, although I wouldn't put it past Amelia to throw a Christmas party at her house and casually try introducing you to a couple single guys while you're there."

Gretchen could handle some awkward conversations at a party. That gave her a few weeks at least. She always liked Christmas, so having that distraction would keep her busy. She'd just have to be super careful about how many sugar cookies she consumed. She didn't need these twenty extra pounds turning into twenty-five.

"You could always take a page out of my book and go into holiday hibernation. Don't surface until the New Year's Eve hangovers fade away."

Gretchen had too much family for that, as nice as it might sound. Natalie was different; she had divorced parents and a general disdain for the holidays, so it was easier to fade away for a week or so. "Not everyone hates Christmas, Natalie. I can deal with the match-making as long as all the holiday festivities distract me."

"Maybe you should take some of that money and go on a little trip. You don't have enough time for Italy, but what about New York City or Vegas?"

Gretchen chuckled. "After what happened to Amelia in Vegas? No, thanks."

"I doubt you'll elope while you're there. But maybe you'll meet a hot distraction and spend some time catching up on all those vices you've missed out on."

Gretchen eased down into one of the chairs and shook her head. "I don't think I can spend any of that money. It feels…tainted somehow."

"What about Italy?"

"I'll get there someday. Just not any time soon. If I go now, all I'll see is old ruins and shells of what was. But if I wait long enough, maybe I can go with a man that loves me and I'll be able to see the beauty in it again. That would make the trip better, don't you think?"

Natalie smoothed out the fabric in front of her. "It sounds nice," she said with a noncommittal tone. Natalie was nearly as enthusiastic about love as she was about Christmas.

"If this last week taught me anything, it's that I'm worth more than I think. I just need the confidence to put myself out there and maybe I can have a healthy relationship with a normal guy."

"Absolutely," Natalie agreed. She came over and knelt beside Gretchen, giving her a comforting side hug. "You'll find someone if you want to. You can do anything you want to."

Gretchen had said the words, but she didn't entirely

believe them yet. Not even Natalie's assurances convinced her, but she would try. She wouldn't let her heart be trampled on by someone like Julian. She'd just reached too high, like Icarus, and crashed to the ground. If she'd opted to date someone safer, it might not have hurt as much to fall.

"Thanks, Natalie."

"I've got an appointment in a few minutes, but I'll try to check back and help you later."

Gretchen waved as Natalie slipped out of the ballroom. She watched her go and let her gaze drop into her lap. She would go to Italy someday, she knew that. But she wouldn't do it with the money Julian gave to her. He thought she was a sellout, and if she spent it, maybe she was.

Getting up, she went into her office and sat down at her desk. She opened the bottom drawer and pulled out her purse. Inside, she could see the thick wad of cash she'd stashed there in an envelope. She felt ridiculous walking around with ten grand in her bag, but it was all she could do until she made her decision.

Bree insisted that she go to Italy and drown her sorrows in a hot Italian lover. Amelia suggested that she mail it back to him if it bothered her to keep it and take her trip. While the idea of sipping prosecco in Capri as a sexy man who spoke very little English rubbed suntan lotion on her body seemed nice, she knew she couldn't do it. But sending it back would likely result in Julian rejecting the delivery, and she'd never get rid of the money.

That left a third option—to do something positive with the money, so no matter what, some good would come from the whole thing. If Gretchen did something worthwhile with the money, maybe it would purify it somehow. Make the past week have purpose. Julian might think she was a sneaky liar willing to sell him out, but nothing could be further from the truth. There was one way to make sure he knew it, too.

Logging on to her computer, she looked up the website for the Cerebral Palsy Foundation. With just a few clicks she found what she was looking for—a solution and a little peace of mind. All she had to do was deposit the money in her account and put the wheels in motion.

She might not get to go to Italy, but she would get the final word.

This script sucked. Julian could barely stand to continue reading the crap that Ross had couriered over this afternoon. It made *Bombs of Fury* look like Shakespeare.

A week ago, he would've accepted the offer without question, but that was before Gretchen had gotten under his skin. She'd planted those seeds of hope that he could have a serious acting career, then turned around and poured gasoline on the buds as they broke through the earth. Ross and his publicist were already scrambling to shift attention away from James and find a way to suppress the story without making it look as if Julian was embarrassed of his brother. He was anything but. He just didn't want press camped outside the Hawthorne Community or reporters pressing Julian for a sob story. He'd already gotten a call from Oprah to share his secret pain.

Despite Ross's assurances that it was the right path to take, Julian didn't want to share his secret pain. He wanted to keep his brother out of the spotlight, and he'd failed when he'd spilled his guts to Gretchen. He'd trusted her. Those big brown eyes had pleaded with him to confide in her. Then she'd turned around and stabbed him in the back just like all the others. He still couldn't quite believe it.

He tossed the offensive script onto the kitchen table and shook his head. He'd do it. He knew he would. But he'd loathe himself even more than he already did. Getting up from the table, he planned to march into the kitchen and make himself a stiff drink when he heard the sound of footsteps on the tile of the entryway.

No one was in the house but Julian. Before he could react, the intruder sauntered around the corner in a crop top and a pair of yoga pants. Bridgette.

"What the hell? How did you get in here?" Julian clenched his teeth at her bold move.

"I still have a key," she said, swinging her blond ponytail over her shoulder and smiling at him with a sweetness he didn't trust. She held up a bundle of letters in her hand and set them on the counter. "I brought in your mail. I came by because I heard you were back from the wedding and I wanted to see you."

She took a step toward him, but Julian stepped backward. He didn't like this. Bridgette was far too calculating to just pop in to be sociable. "Why?"

Bridgette pouted, her collagen-plumped bottom lip thrusting out. "Because I miss you, Julian. These last few weeks have been really hard on me."

"We broke up six months ago. Last I saw, you had your tongue down Paul's throat. You didn't seem like you were suffering to me."

She frowned, but the movement didn't translate to a furrowed brow because of all the Botox she injected.

"I was using Paul as a rebound. I was just trying to get over you, and it didn't work. When I saw those pictures of you and that fat girl, my heart nearly broke. I—"

"Stop," he interrupted, holding up his hand. Julian might be upset with Gretchen, but he wasn't going to let anyone else tear her down. He'd lied when he said she hadn't meant anything to him. It hadn't been acting, but it was the best thing to say. It convinced her, and him, that there was nothing to fight for. But despite all that, she still meant something to him. More than Bridgette ever had. "Gretchen is a beautiful, smart, sensitive woman that I cared about quite a bit. Be respectful of her or leave." He preferred she just leave, but he doubted he'd get rid of her that easily.

"Cared for her?" Bridgette whined. "You barely knew her. She must've worked hard to get her hooks into you that quickly. I could tell she was up to no good. I knew I had to find a way to get you back."

"You don't know what you're talking about. Gretchen didn't have hooks, much less ones in me. And even if she did, I don't need you to save me. If the choice were between the two of you, Gretchen would win." Even with the media leak and the lies, she was more genuine than Bridgette. In fact, that kind of thing was what he would've expected from his ex, which was why he'd never so much as breathed James's name in her presence.

"How could you still think that way about her after what she did? Selling the story about your brother to the press is just unforgivable."

Julian was about to argue with her when he stopped short. The article never mentioned the source for the story. Even if Bridgette had read the magazine from cover to cover, why would she presume that Gretchen had been the one to spill the news? How could she even know that Gretchen had knowledge of James to begin with? There was only one good reason for that.

"You did it." The sudden realization made his heart drop into his stomach with a nauseating thud.

Bridgette eyed him, a practiced look of vague innocence on her face. "I did what?" she asked with all the sweetness she could muster.

He didn't know how she'd dug up the truth, but he knew down to the depths of his soul that Bridgette had been the one to betray him. "You're the one that leaked the story about my brother."

"Me? How could I do that when I didn't know you had a brother? You never mentioned him or anything else about your family to me. I read about it in the gossip pages just like everyone else."

"No. You did this." Julian wasn't about to fall for her protests; they were far too polished. She was an actress, after all. "There's no way you could know that I'd blamed Gretchen for leaking the story unless you'd deliberately set it up to look that way. You got so jealous you did it deliberately to break up Gretchen and me. Admit it, or I'll track down the journalist and find out for myself. And if it was you, and you lied to me, every secret you've ever told me will be front-page news."

Bridgette's mouth dropped open, her eyes darting around the room in a panic. Nothing here was going to help her now, unless she was willing to bludgeon him with the ceramic jar on the countertop.

"I had to," she admitted at last. "It was the only way to get you away from Thunder Thighs. I had a detective following you in Nashville. I'd hired him just to keep tabs on you and get a feel for whether or not we had a chance to reconcile. Then he tailed you to Louisville and uncovered the truth about your brother. I wouldn't have said a word about it, but then I realized that you took her with you. You'd never said a word about James to me in over a year together and yet you took *her* to meet him. I was devastated, Julian. I didn't know what to do. I thought if the story leaked, you'd blame her and come home so distraught I could comfort you and we'd get back together."

Bridgette was crazier than even he gave her credit for. "You plan is flawed, Bridgette. I did blame her and I did come home distraught, but I don't want you to comfort me. I want you to go away."

"Please, Julian. We could be a Hollywood power couple. Admit it, we just make sense together. A heck of a lot more sense than you and the pudgy artist."

"Get out!" he roared, his anger turning on like the flick of a switch. He wasn't going to have her in his presence insulting the woman he loved for one more minute.

"Julian, I—"

Julian lunged forward and snatched his house keys out of her hand. He wouldn't make that mistake twice. "Get out before I call the cops *and* the press so they can photograph you getting arrested for trespassing."

Her eyes widened. He could tell she was trying to figure if he was bluffing or not. After a moment, she decided not to press her luck. Flinging her hair defiantly over her shoulder, she spun on her heel and marched down the hallway, proudly displaying the word JUICY in big letters across her rear end. Julian watched as she opened the front door and looked back at him. "You'll regret losing me one day, Julian."

Instead of responding, he waved his fingers in a happy dismissal. She stormed out, slamming the door shut behind her. Julian followed her path down the hallway, flipping the dead bolt and arming the perimeter alarm system in case she tried to sneak back in and boil a rabbit or something.

With a heavy sigh of relief, he traveled back to the kitchen. He tossed the keys down by the stack of mail and started sorting through the letters that Bridgette had no doubt snooped through before bringing them inside. The last letter in the stack had the logo of the Cerebral Palsy Foundation on the front.

Setting the rest aside, he opened the envelope. It was a letter informing him that an anonymous donation had been made to the foundation in his and James's names. That brought a smile to his face. Perhaps having James's story hit the news wasn't bad after all. Now that it was done, perhaps being vocal about it would bring some much-needed attention to the cause. The foundation had even featured a story about them on the site with the link to donate to the cause in their name. If someone had seen the story and made a donation because of it, perhaps it was worth the angst that came along with it.

Turning to the next page, he saw that the amount donated was ten thousand dollars. That was no paltry donation. His eyes remained glued to the number, a nagging feeling prickling at the back of his neck.

Ten thousand dollars. That was exactly how much he'd left in cash for Gretchen when he'd stormed out. She'd said she didn't want his money, but he'd forced it on her. Was this her way of giving the money back and proving she was the bigger person at the same time?

Julian suddenly felt weak in the knees. He wasn't

used to experiencing that feeling outside of the gym. He slumped down onto a stool at the kitchen counter and looked over the letter again. The timing was far too perfect for it to be from anyone else.

He was a jerk. He knew that now. The only reason she'd gotten involved in this whole mess was because she'd wanted to take that money and go to Italy. All the drama and the heartache were for nothing. She'd handed the money away along with her dream.

Julian dropped the letter onto the counter and squeezed his eyes shut. Gretchen was the only person in his life who didn't want or need anything from him but his love and his trust. Without realizing the depths of his feelings for her, he'd given her both, then snatched them away, accusing her of terrible things and throwing cash at her as he left as though she were a common whore.

Picking up his phone, he dialed his travel agent. He didn't stop to think or worry about what Ross would say. He didn't care. All Julian knew was that he needed to get back to Nashville as soon as possible.

Once his arrangements were made, he started to formulate the rest of his plan. There were several hours before his flight, and he needed to make some important stops on the way to LAX.

He just prayed it wasn't too late to make this right.

Twelve

The red-eye from Los Angeles landed Julian back in Nashville around sunrise on Saturday morning. He grabbed his rental car and tore off in the direction of the chapel.

He was expecting the place to be mostly empty given that it was just past 7:00 a.m., but the lot was filled with vans and trucks with vendor logos on the side. Wedding preparation apparently started early. Among them was Gretchen's green sedan.

Parking his rental out of the path of the big trucks, he followed a man with a giant vase of deep red, orange and yellow flowers through the back door and over to the ballroom.

The room was bustling with people. There were men on lifts adjusting the lighting in the rafters, at least half a dozen people handling flowers, an orchestra setting up on stage, and a few people setting out glassware and other table decor. In the middle of all the chaos was Gretchen. Despite everything going on around them, his eyes went to her in an instant.

Her hair was curly today. He'd gotten used to her straightening it while the cameras were around, but now that their farce of a relationship was over, she'd let it just be curly again. Julian liked it curly. The other style was chic and fashionable, but the wild curls were more suited to the free artist he saw in Gretchen.

She had on a pair of dark denim skinny jeans with ballet flats and a sweater in a rusty color that seemed to go with the fall decor of the day's event. Her back was to him when he came in. She was busily directing some activity in the corner where Murray and Kelly had placed their wedding cake.

With determination pumping through his veins and pushing him forward, he meandered through the maze of tables and chairs to the far corner of the room. No one paid any attention to him. He was only ten or so feet away when Gretchen finally turned around. As her eyes met his, she froze in place, clutching her tablet to her chest as though it was the only thing holding her on the Earth.

Julian smiled, hoping that would help soften the shock, but it didn't. She did recover, but it only resulted in a frown lining her brow and tightening her jaw. He wouldn't let that deter him, though. She was angry. She had a right to be angry after he turned on her like that. He'd expected this response when he got on the plane. But he would convince her that he was sorry and things would be okay. He was certain of it.

"What are you doing here, Julian?" Her voice was

flat and disinterested, matching the expression on her face. The only thing that gave her away was the slight twinkle in her dark eyes. Was it interest? Irritation? Attraction? Perhaps it was just an overhead pin light giving him hope where there was none to be had.

"I came back to talk to you," he said, taking a step toward her and hoping for the best.

Gretchen didn't retreat, but her posture didn't welcome him closer, either. "I think we've done plenty of talking, don't you agree?"

"Not about this." He took another step forward. "Gretchen, I'm so sorry about Monday. The whole situation with Ross, the news article… I know now that none of that had to do with you, and I'm sorry for blaming you for it. You were right when you said you would never do anything like that to me. And I knew it. But I've had so many people betray my trust in the past. Someone had to be to blame, and I didn't know who else could possibly be involved."

She nodded, setting down her tablet so she could cross her arms over her chest. "Jumping to unfounded conclusions tends to cause problems. I'm glad you found the real culprit. I hope you made them suffer the way you made me suffer the last few days. It seems only fair."

Julian watched a flicker of pain dance across her face, and he hated that he was the one to cause it. He had to fix this. "It was Bridgette," he admitted. "She had a detective following me around Nashville and up to Louisville. He dug up the whole story, and then she leaked it because she was jealous of you and wanted to break us up."

Gretchen snorted at his words. "Bridgette Martin…

is jealous…of *me*? How is that even possible? She's one of the most beautiful women I've ever seen."

"Like I told you before, Gretchen, it's all an illusion. I work in a business where everyone tries to tear you down. Even someone like Bridgette isn't immune to scathing critique, and their ego can be fragile because of it. You were a threat to her. She's a woman used to getting what she wants, and she was going to get me back by any means necessary."

"Those silicone implants must have leached chemicals into her brain."

Julian smiled. "Perhaps. But I wanted you to know that it didn't work. Even before I knew the truth about what she'd done, I didn't want her. I still wanted you."

Her dark gaze narrowed at him. "No, you don't," she said with certainty in her voice.

"I do," he insisted. "I did then and I still do. Even when I was angry at you, I only pushed you away because I knew I had to or risk another story in the papers. I didn't want to let you go, though. These days without you have felt so empty, like I've just been going through the motions. I miss having you in my life."

He expected Gretchen to echo his words, to say that she missed him, too, but she stayed silent.

"And then, just when I didn't think I could feel like a bigger jerk, I got the letter from the Cerebral Palsy Foundation. When I saw it, I knew the donation had come from you."

"How do you know it was from me? It was anonymous."

Julian shook his head. "It was, but it had you written all over it. I made you take the money when you didn't want it, so you returned it in a way that even I couldn't argue with. It was brilliant, really, but it just confirmed in my mind that I had been right about you all along."

Her brow went up slightly. "Right about what?"

"Right when I thought that you were one of the sweetest, most giving creatures I'd ever met. That you didn't want anything from me but my love, unlike so many others in my life. You could've taken that money and blown it and forgotten all about me. But you didn't. You couldn't return it, so you used it in the best possible way. A way that could help my brother."

"I hope it does," she said. "Something good should come of the last week's chaos."

Julian's chest clenched at her words. Did she really think what they had was nothing more than a muddled mess? "It might have been chaotic, but I loved every minute of it." Julian hesitated and took a deep breath before he said the words he'd been waiting to say. "And I love you, Gretchen."

Her eyes widened at his declaration, but the response stopped there. No smile, no blush, no rushing into his arms. She certainly didn't respond in kind, as he'd hoped. She just stood there, watching him in her suspicious way.

"I mean it," he continued in a desperate need to fill the silence. "You've changed me in such a profound way that even if you throw me out of here and never speak to me again, there's no way I can go back to living life the way I had before. I've told Ross that I want to take the role in that independent film we discussed. They're going to be filming in Knoxville, Tennessee, in the summer. I've got some re-shoots between now and Christmas, and then another shoot-'em-up movie to film this spring, but after that I'll be out this way for months."

Gretchen swallowed hard, her throat working before she spoke. "You'll like Knoxville," she replied casually.

"What I'll like is being closer to you."

"For a few months. And then what?" she pressed.

"And then I move to Nashville."

That got her attention. This time it was Gretchen who took a step forward, stopping herself before she got too close. "What are you going to do here?"

Julian shrugged. He didn't have all that worked out yet, but he knew that he wanted his home base to be here with Gretchen, even if he had to travel to the occasional movie set or publicity event. "Whatever I want to do. Theater. Television. Smaller-budget films. I could even teach. You were right when you said I was using my brother as an excuse. I have plenty of money to care for him. Even if I just invested the income from *Bombs of Fury* and never acted again, I could probably keep him comfortable for the rest of his life. The truth is that I was scared to try something new. Afraid to fail."

Gretchen's expression softened as she looked at him. "You're not going to fail, Julian."

"Thank you. You believe in me even when I have a hard time believing in myself. You give me the strength I didn't know I was missing. Having you there by my side when we visited James...you have no idea how much that meant to me. I need you in my life, Gretchen. I love you."

He reached into his pocket and grasped the ring he'd hidden there. As he pulled it out, he closed his eyes and sank to one knee, praying that his words had been sincere enough to quell her doubts so she could accept his proposal.

He opened the lid on its hinge, exposing the ring he'd

selected specially for her. The large oval diamond was set in delicate rose gold with a halo of micro-diamonds encircling it and wrapping around the band. The moment he saw it, he knew the ring was perfect for her. "Gretchen, will you—?"

"No!" she interrupted, stealing the proposal from his lips.

Julian looked startled at her sudden declaration, but Gretchen was even more surprised. The word had leaped from her mouth before she could stop it.

His mouth hung agape for a moment, and then he recovered. "The jeweler recommended this cut for a woman who was artistic and daring. I thought that suited you perfectly. Do you not like it? We can get a different one. You can pick whatever you want."

Of course she liked it. She loved it. It was beautiful and sparkly and perfect and she wanted to say yes. But how could she? "It isn't about the ring, Julian."

"Wow. Okay." He snapped the ring box shut and stood up. He glanced around the room nervously, as though he hoped none of the suppliers had witnessed his rebuff. Thankfully everyone was too busy to notice them in the corner.

"Julian." She reached out to touch his arm. "We need to talk about this."

His jaw flexed as he clenched his teeth. "It sounds like you've said all you needed to say. You don't want to marry me. That's fine."

"I never said that."

His blue eyes searched her face in confusion. "I proposed and you said no. Quite forcefully, actually."

Gretchen sighed. She'd botched this. "I wasn't saying no to the proposal. I wanted you to stop for a minute so I could say something first."

The lines in his forehead faded, but he didn't seem convinced that she wasn't about to drop him like a rock. "What do you want to say?"

"I care about you, Julian. I'm in love with you. But I'm not sure if that's enough to sustain a marriage. How can I know that you love me? Truly? How does either of us know that you don't just like the way I make you feel? Yes, I support you. I care about you and make you feel ten feet tall when everyone else is trying to tear you down or get something from you. Are you proposing to that feeling you get when you're with me, or are you actually proposing to me?"

"I'm proposing to you. Of course I am." He seemed insulted by her question, but it couldn't be helped. She needed to know before she fully invested not only her heart, but her life in this relationship.

"That all sounds wonderful. This whole speech of yours has been riveting. Award-caliber material. I think you'll do great in that independent film. But standing here, right now, how can I know that you mean what you say and that it's not some over-rehearsed script? You said that I wasn't the kind of woman Julian Cooper should be with. I heard you agree with Ross when you thought I wasn't listening. For you to turn around and propose not long after…it doesn't leave me feeling very confident about us. Are you going to drop me when the next hot young thing hits the scene and Ross pushes her at you?"

Julian closed his eyes a moment and nodded. "I did say that to Ross. You're not the kind of woman international action star Julian Cooper should be with. But if you'd stayed one moment longer, you would've heard me say that you're the perfect woman for Julian Curtis. And that Julian Curtis wasn't interested in his manager's opinion of his personal life."

Gretchen gasped. She didn't even know what to say to that. Could he really mean it?

"Gretchen," Julian said, moving close to her and placing his reassuring palms on her upper arms. "This isn't a rehearsed script. This isn't Julian Cooper standing in front of you right now reciting lines. This is Julian Curtis, a guy from Kentucky," he said with his accent suddenly coming through, "telling you how he truly feels and asking you to marry him. Do you believe me?"

Her head was spinning. With Julian so close, the warm scent of him was filling her lungs and his touch was heating her skin through her sweater. She could resist him from a distance, but when he stood there, saying all the right words the way he was now, she had no defenses. All she could do was nod.

Julian smiled and slipped back onto one knee. "Now, I'm going to try this again and I want you to let me finish before you answer, okay?"

Gretchen nodded again as Julian pulled out the ring box and opened it a second time. He took her hand in his and looked up at her with his soulful blue eyes.

"I love you, Gretchen, with all my heart. I know there are going to be people out there that think you're so lucky—a regular woman from Tennessee landing a big movie star—but they're wrong. If you accept my proposal and agree to marry me, I can assure you that I'm the lucky one. Every morning I wake up with you beside me is a day I count my lucky stars that you're in my life and have chosen me as the man you love.

Gretchen McAlister, would you do me the great honor of being Mrs. Julian Curtis?"

Gretchen waited half a heartbeat to answer. Not because she didn't want to say yes, but because she wanted to make sure she didn't interrupt him this time. When she was certain he was finished, she said "Yes!" with a broad smile spreading across her face.

Julian slipped the ring onto her finger, the tears in her eyes blurring her view of the sparkly jewelry. It didn't matter. She had a lifetime to look at it. Once he stood up, Gretchen launched herself into his arms. She wrapped her arms around his neck and pulled him close. There, with her nose buried in the hollow of his throat, she finally got to return to a place she thought she might never visit again.

Julian hugged her fiercely and then tipped her head up so that he could press his lips to hers. The kiss was gentler, sweeter, more wonderful than she could've expected.

What an emotional roller coaster the past week had been. She'd gone from the top of the world to the pits of despair and back in only a few days' time. Gretchen was no expert on this love business, but she hoped that it would level out. Her heart couldn't take the drama. But she could take fifty or sixty more years in his strong arms.

"We need to go to Italy," Julian proclaimed, drawing Gretchen from her spinning thoughts.

"Right now?"

Julian smiled and shook his head. "No, not right now. Unless you want to hop on a plane and elope… It might be the only way we can manage to get married without the press finding out."

Elope? She wasn't so sure about that. Amelia had not recommended her quickie Vegas wedding to others. "I'd rather not elope," she said, "but if you want to get married in Italy, that sounds amazing."

"That's what we'll do, then. You gave away your chance to go to Italy when you donated all that money, so it only seems right that we go there to get married, or at the very least, for the honeymoon."

Gretchen could just envision it in her mind. "A tiny rustic chapel in Tuscany. Or maybe a winery on a hill overlooking the poppies and sunflowers."

Julian tightened his grip on her waist. "Anything you want. You're marrying a movie star, after all. There's no cutting corners for an event like this. I can even call George to see if we can have it at his place on Lake Como if you want."

George? She blinked and shook her head. She would be perfectly comfortable as Mrs. Julian Curtis, but it would take a while for her to get used to the idea of their public lives as Mr. and Mrs. Julian Cooper, friends of movie stars, musicians and other famous people.

"That's probably a little more over-the-top than I was thinking," she admitted. Marrying Julian was enough of a fantasy come true. Having the wedding in Italy was more than she could ever ask for. She wanted to keep it simple, though. She didn't want to burn through a fortune on the first day of their marriage. They had a long life together ahead of them, and she wanted to celebrate every day, not just the first. "I just want something small with all our family, some amazing food and wine and scenery that can't be beat by any decoration you could buy."

"I think I can handle that. I'll add that I want to see

you in a beautiful gown that showcases all those luscious curves. I want flickering candles all over to make your skin glow like flawless ivory. And after we eat all that amazing food, I want to dance with you under the stars. This spring, I'll have a month off between filming. How does May sound to you? We can get married and then spend a few weeks exploring every nook and cranny Italy has to offer."

"Perfect," she said, and she meant it. She couldn't imagine a wedding or a husband any more wonderful.

A sound caught her attention. Looking around Julian's broad shoulders, Gretchen noticed three women hovering in the doorway of the ballroom, not working like the others. A blonde, a redhead and a brunette. Even from this distance she could hear the high twitter of their fevered discussion of Julian's return. He'd probably slipped in the back door, but it didn't matter. You couldn't get anything past those three. She also knew that they wouldn't go away until she told them what they wanted to know.

Raising her left hand in the air, she flashed the sparkling diamond at them and wiggled her fingers. It was a large enough setting that even from across the ballroom, the gesture was easily decipherable. A whoop and a few squeals sounded from the entrance.

Gretchen turned away to look up at her fiancé and smiled. "Block a week off the calendar next spring, ladies," she shouted while she focused only on him. "We're all going to Italy for a wedding!"

Epilogue

"Christmas is coming."

Gretchen's brow went up at Natalie's morose declaration. "You sound like a character in *Game of Thrones*. Of course Christmas is coming. It's almost December, honey, and it's one of the more predictable holidays."

Her friend set down her tablet and frowned. Gretchen knew that Natalie didn't like Christmas. She'd never pressed her friend about why she despised the beloved holiday, but she knew it was true and had been since back when they were in college. Every year, the chapel would shut down for the week or so between Christmas Eve and New Year's Day. Natalie claimed it was a built-in vacation for everyone, but Gretchen wondered if there wasn't more to it.

Natalie was a workaholic to begin with, but when December rolled around, she redoubled her efforts. She claimed that she wanted to get a head start on the accounting and taxes for the end of the year, but Gretchen was certain that she was trying to avoid anything to do with Christmas.

While Bree might stroll into the office wearing reindeer antlers that lit up and Amelia might try to organize a holiday party, Natalie did not participate. She insisted they not exchange gifts, arguing they were just passing money around and it was pointless.

Natalie wasn't a Grinch, per se. She wasn't out to stop everyone from having a good holiday. She just didn't want others to subject her to their merriment. That usually meant she hid in her house and didn't leave for a solid week, or she went on a trip somewhere.

Even then, she couldn't avoid everything. Always the professional, Natalie usually had to coordinate a couple winter- or holiday-themed weddings this time of year. There was no avoiding it. Especially when one of this year's weddings was the wedding of Natalie's childhood best friend, Lily.

Natalie leaned back in her office chair and ripped the headset off, tossing it onto her desk. "It's bothering me more than usual this year."

"Are you taking a trip or staying home?" Gretchen asked.

"I'm staying home. I was considering a trip to Buenos Aires, but I don't have time. We squeezed Lily's last-minute wedding in on the Saturday before Christmas, so I'll be involved in that and not able to do the normal end-of-year paperwork until it's over."

"You're not planning to work over the shutdown, are you?" Gretchen planted her hands on her hips. "You don't have to celebrate, but by damn, you've got to take the time off, Natalie. You work seven days a week some-times."

Natalie dismissed her concerns. "I don't work the late hours you and Amelia do. I'm never here until mid-night."

"It doesn't matter. You're still putting in too much time. You need to get away from all of this. Maybe go to a tropical island and have some kind of a fling with a sexy stranger."

At that, Natalie snorted. "I'm sorry, but a man is not the answer to my problems. That actually makes it worse."

"I'm not saying fall in love and marry the guy. I'm just saying to keep him locked in your hotel suite until the last New Year's firecracker explodes. What can a night or two of hot sex hurt?"

Natalie looked up at Gretchen with her brow fur-rowed painfully tight. "It can hurt plenty when the guy you throw yourself at is your best friend's brother and he turns you down flat."

* * * * *

FROM FRIEND TO
FAKE FIANCÉ

JULES BENNETT

There's no greater happily-ever-after than sharing the journey with your best friend. Love you, Michael.

One

"All I need you to do is play the part of my boyfriend for the next week."

"Let me get this straight. You had me fly to Bora Bora so we can make your ex believe you've moved on. We'll be pretending to shack up in this romantic hut. And in the midst of all of that, you'll be doing the flowers for your sister's wedding?"

Okay, when Mac O'Shea phrased the question like that, the situation did sound rather ridiculous. But she had her reasons, damn it. Good reasons. Reasons that justified making her very best friend pose as her boyfriend.

Standing in the cozy hut that was her home for the next week, Jenna LeBlanc adjusted the strap on her favorite coral sundress and stared at Mac. "Listen, you love to travel and I'm giving you a free trip. Stop complaining."

Shoving his suitcase out of the way with the toe of his shoe, Mac stalked toward her. Emerald eyes held her in her place, as if daring her to move until he got to the bottom of this. Mercy, that man was potent. Her best friend was sexier than any other man she'd ever encountered and now she needed him to pretend to be madly in love with her because she trusted nobody else. Sure. This should be no problem.

"I can afford my own damn trip." He propped his hands on his hips as he stopped right before her. "I want to know why you didn't tell me the full reason you needed me down here when you called."

Humiliation? Fear? Too many emotions swirled around, leaving her more desperate than she'd like to be. The need to keep her sister's wedding perfect and her mother's past demons from creeping up had Jenna putting everything on the line. Heart, sanity…everything.

"Listen, Martin is still attending because he's the best man," she explained. "We broke up two weeks ago and he wants me back. He won't take no for an answer. There's no way to avoid him here, so that's where you come in."

Mac's dark brows drew in as the muscle ticked in his square jaw. "You told me you broke things off with him, but you never said why."

"Well, you were gallivanting around the world—"

"In Barcelona."

"And you didn't return my call when I tried to reach you."

"Because I was in a meeting when you called and your message said to come here." Mac sighed. "Now, tell me what the hell is going on and why we're dating, because if we are, my family needs to know. My sister will be thrilled."

Jenna narrowed her eyes. "Now is not the time to be snarky."

Mac crossed his arms over his massive, broad, extremely chiseled chest. She couldn't help but stare as the material strained across his shoulders. They may be only friends, but that never stopped her from eyeing the goods. Mac made thirty-two look damn sexy.

"Martin was screwing his assistant."

It hurt to say those words. Not because she'd been madly in love with him; they'd only been dating a few months. But to know he didn't feel she was worthy enough for him to break up with first? Did men not consider women's feelings anymore?

"He was a jerk anyway," Mac commented. "Want me to rough him up?"

She laughed, though she knew he wasn't kidding entirely. Rumors of the O'Sheas' infamous ways of conducting "business" were strong enough that his words rang true. Mac's father, Patrick, had passed away less than a year ago and the man wasn't known for his gentle hand or kind mannerisms. Mac's brother Braden had taken over as head of the family, and he and his fiancée, Zara, were much more personable, but Braden was still a formidable presence. He wasn't a man to mess with, either, but had more tact, self-control—and quite possibly more power—than Patrick did.

"Seeing Martin in pain would be lovely, but no thanks." Jenna patted his cheek and went on. "But since he has to be here, I refuse to have him believe I am available. As far as he's concerned, I've moved on and I'm head over heels for you. He's nothing but a bad memory."

"And this is where my undying love comes in."

Jenna swallowed hard. "If you want to put it that way, then, yes. But I really just need a favor without the sarcastic comments."

Jenna didn't want to think of Mac and love in the same sentence. That would be a cruel trick to play on herself.

Yes, they'd been best friends since he tried to pick her up years ago at the party of a mutual friend. She'd blown him off, thinking there was no way a guy like that would ever find her attractive. Added to that, she'd been in Boston long enough to know the O'Shea name and hadn't wanted to associate herself with people who were synonymous with "mafia" and "mob."

Apparently he'd found her bold rejection appealing because he'd pursued her anyway. She'd told him she was a long-term type of girl, and he'd said he admired that but he wasn't in the market for a relationship. Now she laughed at the fact that they were indeed long-term, but as friends only.

Jenna had to admit, he was like no other friend she'd ever had. She'd seen a side to him that didn't seem ruthless or conniving at all. He made her laugh, made her relax. She didn't know when the switch occurred, but one day she knew who her best friend was and that he would do anything for her. And his friendship wasn't a bad connection to have. Mac wasn't just a jet-setting playboy, his family owned auction houses around the globe, brought in billions each year and were a force to be reckoned with in the international business world.

Yet, after all these years of knowing him, she still wasn't sure which side of the law the family truly operated on. Jenna had brought that topic up only one time in the past decade—a mistake she wouldn't make again. She'd asked about his family business, why all the traveling and secrecy. Mac had turned almost cold and made it perfectly clear that topic was off limits and not to be approached ever again. Which is why she wasn't asking about the Barcelona trip or the meeting he'd been in.

Mac stared at her for a moment, then hitched his hip onto the bamboo-and-wicker barstool at the island in the kitchen of her bungalow. "If your sister isn't getting married for another week, why are we here now?"

Because her perfect sister wanted the perfect wedding to go along with her perfect life. Jenna loved her sister more than anything, but Amy seriously had it all. Jenna had...no. She wasn't going to start down that path because she was happy for her sister and that's why she was here. Jenna didn't want to be the bitter bridesmaid simply because she had a cheating ex. Amy had actually found true love and this was going to be the best week of her life. She deserved perfect.

Jenna hadn't told her family why she and Martin parted ways. A fake boyfriend would really go a long way to keep everyone all smiles until this wedding was over.

"Amy wants her wedding party and guests to enjoy the island. Kind of a mini-vacation for them and a giant party building up to the main event."

When Mac didn't say anything, Jenna sighed and tugged the top of her dress up another inch. Damn boobs. These little sundresses always looked so good on those plastic, size two models but were hard to pull off in reality.

"You don't have to. I know it's silly and desperate and ridiculous to ask—"

"What would you expect of me?" he asked, a naughty smile spreading across his face. "And don't skimp on the details."

Letting out an unladylike growl, Jenna rolled her eyes and marched through the luxurious hut and straight out the door leading to a small, straw-covered deck overlooking the crystal-blue water. Heavy footsteps sounded behind her and seconds later a familiar, firm hand settled over her shoulder.

"I'm not in the mood to be made fun of."

With a gentle squeeze, Mac turned her around. "Fine. Tell me what you need me to do."

She stared up into the emerald eyes she'd found herself getting lost in more than once. "You'll have to stay in this hut with me."

"Done."

She swallowed. "There's only one bedroom."

His mouth quirked up. "Then try to keep your hands to yourself."

"Can you focus?"

Jenna couldn't help but laugh. He flirted with any woman between eighteen and death. He had no filter and she never took him seriously. The man loved life, loved women and loved his family. He was loyal to a fault. If she thought for even a second he could do long term, she could fall so easily for him. But she kept her heart guarded and firmly planted on the friendship side.

"I'm focused," he insisted, holding his hands out. "One bedroom. I understand what we won't be doing in there, so tell me what we'll be doing outside our little house."

"You'll need to come to the evening events with me. There are only a few." Jenna ran the list down in her head. "I'm doing all the flowers for the ceremony, so if you could make some trips with me to assist with the arrangements, that would look all boyfriend-ish. Oh, there's the rehearsal dinner and ceremony, too, of course. But during the day, we may need to be seen on the beach together holding hands. I don't know…doing lovey-dovey things."

"Lovey-dovey? Whatever you mean by that, I can handle it." He glanced out at the water for a second, then back to her. "There's only one problem."

Her heart sank. She didn't have time for problems. Her mom was arriving in the morning and who knew when her ex would show his cheater face. Stupid guy had to be the best man, which meant she'd be walking down the aisle with him…she'd rather walk barefoot on broken glass.

"I've known you for ten years and you're not the affectionate type."

Jenna swallowed and nodded in agreement. There was a reason she wasn't all touchy-feely. She couldn't afford to be.

"I can be," she assured him.

"Really?" He took a step forward, instantly filling the gap between them.

His hand came up to her face as he trailed his fingertips down her cheek, to her jawline and down her neck. She couldn't suppress the tremble that racked her body.

"You think you can handle me touching you in public?" he whispered. "Kissing you? Acting like I'm your lover and pretending to know every single detail about your body?"

Jenna's breath caught in her throat. The idea of Mac knowing every inch of her body both thrilled and terrified her. She had no doubt this man knew how to bring pleasure, but at the same time, she'd be mortified if he saw her naked and looked disappointed. Her body wasn't perfect, far from it. The curves, the dips and rolls, everything about her physique was the exact opposite of the women she'd seen him with.

"I bet you that I can fool anyone who sees us," she told him, trying to catch her breath. "So long as Martin thinks we're an item, that's all I care about."

"I've never turned down a bet." He continued to stroke her skin. Her collarbone, her jaw, the sensitive spot behind her ear. "What does the winner get?"

Jenna swallowed, forcing herself to focus. "If we pull

this off, I win and you'll owe me another favor, which I can redeem at any time."

His brow quirked up. "And if I win?"

"You won't. I plan on being very convincing."

Mac's warm breath tickled her cheek as she shifted under his touch. He slid one palm up the side of her face, his fingers threading through her hair. "Then we better practice before he arrives."

Before she could ask what he meant, his mouth claimed hers.

What. The. Hell?

Mac's question to his own sanity quickly evaporated the second Jenna opened to him. He swallowed her gasp and kept his hand firm on her jaw, as if daring her to pull away.

Finally, after all these years of wondering how his best friend would taste, now he knew and the fantasy didn't even come close to touching reality. And he'd had a multitude of fantasies regarding this stunning woman.

Jenna stiffened against him, then melted. There was no other word for what happened with her body— those curves would be the death of him.

For years he'd kept his distance out of respect to their friendship and because there was no way in hell he'd let her in deeper…not when his family had secrets he could never share. His father had been a killer, though Patrick O'Shea could justify each and every death. Mac had actually made the decision himself twice before, when Braden wouldn't do it and Patrick was forcing their hand. Mac didn't look back, though. No regrets. Regrets meant living in the past. His family was looking toward the future, looking to go legit. The idea seemed so simple, but the execution—no pun intended—was proving to be a bit harder to pull off.

Mac's family was cunning; they got what they wanted. They stole, lied and would betray anyone to get where they needed to be. On the flip side, the O'Sheas were fiercely loyal to their allies. They wouldn't hesitate to help anyone legitimately in need. But pity those foolish enough to cross them.

There were so many family secrets, Mac knew full well he'd never put a woman he loved in a position of having to lie to the cops or keep the darkness of their deeds hidden.

For the most part, the O'Sheas put up a great front. Yet beneath the surface they were always watching, waiting, ready to strike at any threat to their family.

Braden had found love, but Mac wasn't so sure such a thing existed for him. He didn't do relationships. Jenna was a relationship type of girl, so friends was all they could ever be. Because he wasn't letting her out of his life. She got him. She knew his family was…unique, and she didn't pry.

But playing boyfriend to her for a week? Now that he could totally get behind. The green light to touch her, to kiss her, was the stuff of fantasies and he planned on making every second count. Because if he was going to play this role, he intended to take it all the way. He hoped like hell she knew what she was getting into.

After their little charade was over, she'd be out of his system and they could go back to being friends. He'd pushed for more years ago, but she'd shut him down, stating she was only looking for something long term. Now she'd made the first move and all he had to do was follow her orders…and touching Jenna after all this time would be one benefit he'd never forget.

And when the ex showed up, Mac planned on having a little one-on-one chat with the bastard. Nobody hurt Jenna and lived to tell about it. And no one made her feel less about herself. She was a beautiful, vibrant woman deserving of a man who would appreciate her.

And for a week, Mac would be that man...in theory.

Mac tipped his head, rubbing his lips against Jenna's before capturing her mouth once again. Her fingertips curled into his shirt as he slid his hands down that sultry, killer body. If he was going to pretend to be her boyfriend, he wanted all the perks that came with it.

"Oh. I'm sorry!"

Jenna jerked in his arms. Mac didn't let her go as he glanced toward the doorway where Jenna's mother and sister stood. They were clearly embarrassed, seeing as how neither of them were making eye contact. Mac didn't care that they were seen during a very private moment, he actually found it rather amusing.

Besides, getting caught in the act was something he'd grown used to over the years, considering his family's activities. Thankfully, with the right law enforcement and powerful people in his family's back pocket, he'd never been arrested or faced charges.

When Jenna started to shift away, Mac tightened his grip. Might as well practice now, if they were going to pull this charade off for the ex. If they could make her mother and sister believe, then the ex would be no problem whatsoever. And after this week they could simply tell Mary and Amy that he and Jenna had decided they were better off as friends. An easy fix and they'd both still get everything they wanted: Jenna would get her ex to stay away and Mac would get her in his bed.

"We didn't mean to..."

"I had no idea you two..."

Mary and Amy spoke at the same time and Mac laughed. "You're fine. I just arrived myself and I was giving Jenna a proper hello."

Mary's eyes widened as she stared at her daughter. "You just broke up with Martin two weeks ago."

Jenna remained frozen at his side and he knew she was struggling with how to explain this scenario to her family. Coming to her defense was easy.

"Martin is an ass," Mac stated. "Jenna and I have danced around our attraction for years and we thought spending some time here away from work and reality would help us figure out if we should take things to the next level."

"What are you two doing here?" Jenna croaked out.

Mary nodded. "I thought we could get some girl time in before the guests started arriving. I didn't know you'd already had company, but I'm glad Mac is with you. Martin was a nice guy, but Mac is…well, you know I love him."

Mary smiled and Mac knew he had them fooled. These three women were strong, united and had a bond that rivaled that of his own family. He hated lying to Jenna's family. But it was necessary and nothing he and Jenna couldn't get out of later.

Amy let out a little squeal as she stepped forward and wrapped her arms around Jenna, spinning her in a circle. "I knew you two would end up together. I'm so happy for you guys. I'm sorry Martin is the best man and you have to walk with him, but I promise you and Mac will have an amazing time."

Jenna glared at Mac over her sister's shoulder and he knew he'd crossed the line. He was going to have some explaining to do once they were alone.

He sent her a wink and a grin, which only earned him a narrowed gaze. Oh, yeah. This boyfriend scenario was going to be fun.

Two

"What the hell was all of that?"

Okay, he'd expected her to be pissed. He'd kissed her, lied to her family and then she'd had time to stew about everything once her mother and sister had whisked her away for a family dinner. The ladies' dinner conversation was a no-brainer. He had no doubt Jenna had been bombarded with questions that she likely didn't have answers to all because of that kiss.

He wasn't sorry.

Mac quirked a brow, knowing his silent action would get under her skin. It was just too easy to push her buttons... and she was sexy as hell all fired up like this.

Throwing her arms in the air, Jenna growled and slammed the door to their hut. "Do you have any idea what I just had to endure, all because you couldn't keep your lips and hands to yourself?"

So what? She had to discuss the kiss with her sister

and mother. He'd had to sit here in the silence and replay it over and over in his head. He could still taste her if he licked his lips, could still feel her when he clenched his fists.

"Are you going to say anything?"

"Did you bring me anything to eat?" he asked. "I'm starving."

She crossed the room in two strides and shoved at his chest. "My mother wants to know how serious we are and my sister is already making plans for a double date with her fiancé and us. Are you ready for this?"

Mac wouldn't be pushed, literally or figuratively, by anyone—even his best friend. He gripped her wrists, tugging on her until she fell against him. Perfect.

"You got this ball rolling, I only gave it an extra nudge. If you want your ex to believe we're lovers, then practicing on your family is the perfect place to start."

Jenna stared into his eyes. "I don't like lying to them."

"We're not lying. I fully intend to take you for my lover."

Her body stilled against his, her eyes widened. "Wh-what?"

"You heard me." He was confident the shock in her eyes only masked her desire. She'd kissed him with too much passion, had practically melted against him. No way could he ignore her response. "I plan on fully experiencing being your lover, and when the week is over we'll go back to being friends. That way nobody will be lying to your family."

She jerked away from him, raking her shaky hands through her hair. She twisted it up into a knot and closed her eyes. Mac crossed his arms while he waited for her to process the kink he'd just put into her plans.

With a sigh, she dropped her arms and her hair fell all

around her shoulders in messy waves. "We aren't sleeping together. I need a friend, Mac. I take sex seriously. I know you can detach yourself from the emotions that come with intimacy, but I can't."

Knowing he was on shaky ground here, Mac closed the gap between them until he was so near she had to tip her head to look up at him. Her face was totally devoid of makeup, yet the tan she'd gotten was all the glow she needed to be even more radiant. Women he dated tended to use spackling to enhance their beauty, but Jenna needed nothing extra. He preferred a woman who wasn't all made up in an attempt to gain attention.

"I know you want long term, Jenna. But this week is all about special circumstances. You invited me here." He purposely used a softer tone. "Let's see where this goes. I promise, when this is over we'll go back to being friends. Nobody will get hurt, Jenna."

"Says the man who has women strewn throughout the world."

He suppressed a smile. "Despite what you think of my travels, most of the time it's business and I'm too damn tired to entertain."

She shook her head and took another step back, hitting the wall by the front door. "Sex implies…"

He quirked a brow. "Lust, desire, passion? I'm willing to admit you're hot and any man would be lucky to have you in his bed."

She put her hands on his chest. When she didn't push him away, he reached out, curling his fingers around her bare shoulders.

"Don't," she warned. "We're not sleeping together. We're not doing anything but pretending to be lovers. After this week, my family will think we just decided to stay friends. That's all. I can't do more and if you're honest with yourself, you can't, either."

Oh, he could do plenty more. Starting with peeling that dress from her curvy body. But he wouldn't push her. She was already feeling stressed and recovering from the betrayal of her asshat ex. The last thing she needed was for her best friend to force her into anything. But that didn't mean he would stop his attempts to get her into his bed. For years he'd wondered how it would feel to have his best friend in every way possible and now he had this week to seduce her. Bora Bora provided the perfect backdrop for temptation, with its sultry nights and lazy days on the beach. Seducing Jenna would be so easy, so perfect. Before these seven days were up, he'd know exactly how amazing they were together.

But Mac didn't want her to feel forced, to feel pressured. He wanted her willing and aching for him. He wanted her to admit that the attraction was mutual. There wasn't a doubt in his mind she wanted him. She may be lying to herself, but her actions spoke volumes.

Stroking his thumbs along her delicate skin, Mac bent slightly to hold her gaze. "I'm not putting any pressure on you. You've got enough going on now."

Beneath his palms, her shoulders relaxed. "I still have all those flowers to do and Amy has changed her mind about the arrangements twice already. My ex will be showing up any day and I'm exhausted from my mother's questions. If you add more stress on me, I'm going to smother you in your sleep."

Laughing, Mac pulled her in and wrapped his arms around her. She literally fell against his chest as if the fight had gone out of her. This would be the perfect opportunity to seduce her…if he wanted to be a complete, uncaring jerk. He'd already planted the seed. She knew exactly what he wanted. Now he had to let his actions speak louder than his words. Not a problem at all. In his line of work, actions always got the job done.

"Why don't you go out on the deck and relax?" he suggested, rubbing his hand up and down her back. "I'll bring you some tea. I'm sure you packed an assortment."

Jenna wasn't a drinker, not of alcohol, anyway. Her mother had once battled alcoholism, but had been clean for the past several years. So, while booze was off the table for Jenna, Mac knew the girl never went out of town without her tea collection. It was one thing she took quite seriously. No doubt she'd brought the antique tin that he'd gotten her for Christmas several years back. She'd seen the piece before an auction and had coveted the item, so Mac had anonymously placed the bids and gotten it for her as a surprise.

Nearly all bidding was anonymous.... But in this instance, he'd simply done something for his best friend, not for a billionaire client or the good of the family business.

Jenna pulled away and offered him a tired smile. "You're too good to me."

"I'll let you return the favor one day when I need you to pretend to be my fiancée," he joked. "Do you want a particular flavor?"

He watched the sway of her hips as she walked away. "Surprise me."

Mac laughed. She'd better watch what she asked for. Because by the end of this week, she'd be surprised all right. Seduction would never taste sweeter.

This might be the only chance to be this close to her, at her invitation. He planned to take full advantage of this week posing as her boyfriend. This was the exact opportunity he needed to get closer, by her invitation. He planned on playing his role flawlessly every minute of the next seven days.

* * *

Jenna crossed her ankles and stared out at the sparkling water just beyond her deck. With bright blue skies, the sun just on the horizon and her best friend brewing her tea, Jenna should be the most relaxed woman in the world.

Unfortunately, she couldn't relax when her lips were still tingling, her body was still aching and her mind was still reeling from her best friend's bombshell admission that he wanted to sleep with her.

She hadn't seen that coming. Yes, he'd tried to pick her up with some overly cheesy line many years ago, but Mac was a professional flirt. And they'd agreed not to take things in that direction back then. She'd told him she only wanted long term and she knew he couldn't offer permanence. No way would she make herself vulnerable when she knew nothing serious could come of her attraction to Mac.

But the way he'd kissed her, held her and stared into her eyes when he delivered that shocking blow…this man wasn't joking anymore. He was full-on trying to get her into his bed, and if she wasn't careful that's exactly where she'd find herself. Talk about an awkward morning after, and she just couldn't risk their friendship.

Stretching her arms out, she clasped her fingers behind her head. She really needn't get too worked up, though. Mac loved women and women, understandably, loved Mac. He had charm, power, a killer body and a smile that could melt the clothes right off your body.

But she had to remind herself the proposition had nothing to do with her personally. Mac was a world-renowned playboy. He'd earned his reputation by his actions over the years and Jenna wasn't naive. She'd seen firsthand what a damaging relationship could do. Granted, her parent's situation was much different, but her mother had still been crushed, destroyed and ultimately had turned to the bottle when Jenna's father walked out. Jenna didn't think she'd ever be dependent on alcohol, but she was vulnerable to the same emotional damage her mother had suffered. Jenna knew if she allowed herself to be intimate with Mac two things would happen: she would love every single erotic moment, and he'd leave her wanting more as he walked away. She refused to be dependent on her feelings, to let her emotions lead her common sense around on a leash. Jenna had to keep a level head about this and remember everything going on here was all for show.

So, while her lips may still be tingling from their earlier encounter, she had to ignore the urge to take what he so eagerly offered.

Mac's heavy footsteps hit the wood deck. "Here you go."

After handing her a glass of iced tea, peach she guessed from the scent, he walked to the edge of the deck and took a seat. With the huts and decks built right on the water, his feet rested in the crystal-clear ocean. His black T-shirt pulled across his broad shoulders. His dark, unruly hair curled just slightly on the ends. Jenna didn't care that she was checking out her best friend. She'd done it for years, and the older he got, the sexier Mac O'Shea became. This combination ocean/hottie view was definitely one she would be enjoying all week.

"So, tell me what's on the agenda for tomorrow." He threw a glance over his shoulder, offering her an evil, lopsided grin. "Kissing on the beach, you unable to keep your hands off me, frolicking in the ocean?"

Jenna took a hearty drink of her iced tea and rolled her eyes. "I think we'll stick with hand holding, a few hugs and some lingering glances. Can you handle that?"

With a shrug, he turned back to the ocean. "I can handle anything. I'm in Bora Bora with my best friend and I have everything under control with the upcoming auction. I could use a few days to rest up, even if I'm pretending to be in love."

A sliver of guilt started to course through her. "I know I'm putting you in a weird position, so if you want to back out, do it now before we get too far."

Mac turned, rested his back against one of the posts and drew one knee up as he met her gaze. "Jenna, I came here for you. If you need me to hold your hand, literally, to get through this next week, that's what I'm going to do. Stop worrying about my feelings or whatever else is going through that head of yours."

She sat up in her lounge chair and swiveled her legs to the side. Clutching her glass, she watched the drops of condensation slide down it, disappearing beneath the pads of her fingers. Worry gnawed at her and she knew she could be totally honest with Mac about her deepest concern.

"I don't want things to get awkward between us."

"Then stop analyzing it to death," he commanded. "We'll be fine. The ex will think you've moved on, your sister's wedding will be over and done, and you'll be back in Miami by next week."

In theory everything sounded so perfect and easy. Reality always had other plans, though.

Jenna took another drink before looking over to Mac, who was still staring at her. "Do you want something to eat? The resort actually stocked our kitchen. I don't even want to know what Amy paid for all of this."

Mac shook his head. "Nah. I was joking earlier. I'm too tired to eat, anyway. That whirlwind trip to Barcelona wiped me out."

"I'm sure the lovely Lolita you left behind with a smile would take that as a compliment."

Mac pulled his other foot from the water and hopped to his feet. "Lolita was nowhere to be found," he retorted as he took a seat beside her on the lounge chair. "The trip was all business. I didn't see one naked woman the entire time."

Gasping, Jenna mocked him. "No wonder you're so cranky. And here I'm putting a damper on your social life because you have to pretend to be taken."

"We don't have to pretend," he replied with raised brows. "Say the word and we'll make use of this lounge chair."

Jenna sprang to her feet and headed toward the open doorway. "Chill out, stud. I have enough to handle without feeding your overactive hormones."

Mac followed her into the hut. Jenna rinsed her empty glass and just as she went to set it on the counter, it slipped from her hands and shattered all over the ceramic tile.

Cursing beneath her breath, she glanced down, trying to figure out how to get out of the mess without cutting her bare feet.

"Don't move."

Mac stepped carefully around the shards and seconds later lifted her into his arms.

"Put me down. I'm heavy."

Halting his steps, Mac met her gaze, his face mere inches above hers. "You're not heavy, Jenna. You're perfect. I won't want to hear that from your mouth again."

Closing her eyes, praying for the humiliation to pass, Jenna sighed. "Just put me down. I'll put some shoes on and get this mess cleaned up."

"I can get it."

"You're going to cut yourself," she argued, though the point was moot now.

"Better me than you."

He placed her on the sofa and stood back, his hands on his hips, his narrowed eyes daring her to argue. Jenna held her hands up in defeat. She wasn't fighting with him. She chose her battles wisely. Besides, she had to admit she rather liked this whole knight-to-her-rescue thing.

Moments later, once the glass was all discarded and he'd swept the floor thoroughly, Mac returned and sat on the table in front of the sofa. Straddling her legs, he reached down and placed one of her feet on his leg. When he started to examine her, she pulled her foot away.

"I'm fine. I wasn't cut."

"You're sure?"

Jenna snorted. "I think I'd know, Mac. Calm down. Were you cut?"

He merely shrugged. The man was infuriating at times.

"You know, you could've called someone to come clean that up."

Shaking his head, he replied, "By the time someone came, I would've been done. It's not a big deal."

Mac O'Shea might have been a billionaire, he might have been a mysterious, powerful man, but he wasn't lazy. He worked hard and always remembered that just because someone had money didn't make them better than anyone else. His father had instilled that value in all of the kids, and Jenna admired Mac and his siblings for being so conscious of other people's feelings…unless those people crossed the line. Then the O'Sheas left no room for negotiation, if the rumors were correct. Still, overall they were good people. She knew about the charities they silently donated to. She'd overheard Mac talking on the phone once to Laney, his sister, but Jenna hadn't said a word. She was proud the family didn't boast about the fact they shared their wealth. That's what giving was all about.

The sun had sunk lower, sending a soft glow into the hut through the wide opening leading to the deck. Fatigue was starting to take over and she was running out of steam. She needed to rest up if she was going to pull off this charade for the next seven days. Who knew when Martin would arrive, and she wanted to be ready.

"I'll sleep here on the sofa," she told Mac. "Actually, I'm so tired, I think I could pass out on that hammock out on the deck."

Mac simply shook his head. "You're sleeping in the bed and so am I. We're adults, Jenna. We've been friends for years."

Yeah, well, she'd never lain next to her best friend and attempted to sleep after he kissed her as if he needed her more than air. How could she sleep if his hard body brushed against hers in the middle of the night? What if she rolled over and her parts touched his parts? Because then a new level of awkward would settle in and that was the last thing she wanted.

"Whatever you're worried about, stop." His demand was loud and clear. "Go to bed. I'll be in later."

Yeah, that's precisely what she worried about.

Three

"We may have found something."

Mac sat up straighter and glanced toward the closed bedroom door where Jenna had disappeared over an hour ago.

"The scrolls?" he asked his associate Ryker in a hushed tone. But Ryker was so much more than an associate. He was a brother, a friend, an enforcer. He might not share the same blood, but he was practically family.

And he'd found information on the infamous scrolls. The nine pieces of family heritage they'd been chasing for decades. Their ancestor was an Irish monk who'd been chosen to transcribe Shakespeare's early works. The scrolls were invaluable…and still missing. They'd been in the O'Shea family up until they'd lost everything in the Great Depression, then they'd vanished.

Under the direction of their father, they'd followed countless leads. Once Patrick had passed and Braden had taken control, he'd gone to the point of origin at an old estate in Boston that used to be owned by the O'Sheas. The scrolls were last known to be there, yet his family was still on a damn wild goose chase. Granted, had he not gone to the starting point, Braden never would've met Zara, the love of his life. Zara now owned the home which used to be in their family. Even she had searched her home, but nothing had turned up.

Mac, his brother Braden and their sister Laney were ready to fulfill their late father's request and find these missing heirlooms, but so far they'd had no luck. Ryker, the go-to guy who was more like a brother than an employee, had proved himself to be relentless in finding the scrolls, in fulfilling a dying man's wish—no matter where in the world he had to follow the trail.

"I'm actually boarding the jet now," Ryker stated. "I'll be heading to Chicago on a tip from McCormick's."

McCormick's. If the O'Sheas worried about rivals, McCormick's would be top of the list. But, Mac's family had been in the industry much longer and had far longer reaches into that world…both political and civilian. That, coupled with everything they had going on behind the scenes, definitely made them the most sought-out auction house in the world. They could get the job done, fly under the legal radar and have transactions completed quickly and efficiently. Their clients never knew the details of how things were handled, they only knew O'Shea's was discreet and got things done.

"Is this tip from a reliable source?" Mac asked.

"Reliable enough," Ryker said. "I'll keep you posted, but Braden was busy at some event with Zara and they couldn't be bothered, so I had to act fast. Where are you, anyway? Still in Barcelona?"

Mac came to his feet and glanced out the open doorway toward the inky water, shimmering only slightly from the moon peeking from behind the clouds. Bora Bora was one of the most beautiful places on the planet… it was also one of the most romantic. Not that he did the whole candlelight-on-the-beach kind of thing. He was more of a slam the bedroom door with his foot as he plastered a willing woman against the wall and claimed her type of guy.

"I'm in Bora Bora with Jenna. She had a family emergency." Sort of. "I'll be home in a week, but let me know as soon as you discover anything, no matter how minor."

"Will do."

Mac disconnected the call and gripped his cell in his hand. Every time there was another lead, he got anxious. After years of letdowns, Mac knew he shouldn't get his hopes up, but all of this searching had to pay off at some point, didn't it? Because none of them would stop until these scrolls were found. Unfortunately, Patrick O'Shea had passed before he could fulfill that vow. The heart attack that claimed his father was sudden. He'd gone in for surgery, knowing there was a risk, but it was his only option for survival. They'd lost him on the table.

Mac didn't know if he'd ever get used to the idea of his father not being around. Then again, he didn't want to get used to the loss. He wanted to remember his father for the powerful, loving family man he was. He may have been a hard-ass outside his inner circle, he may have had more blood on his hands than a corrupt politician, but Patrick O'Shea was loyal to those close to him. Mac missed that man every minute of every day and would continue to honor his father's legacy and work with his siblings to make the O'Shea name as reputable as ever.

With his mind spinning in so many directions, Mac was too wound up to go to bed. Well, he was too wound up to sleep. Getting between the sheets with Jenna right now wouldn't be wise. He wanted her so damn bad, with a fierceness he'd not allowed himself to feel before. She wasn't ready, though.

His priority for the next few days was to make Jenna smile, to make her life worry-free and to get her to see just how easy it would be to be intimate and still be friends. He wasn't looking for a lifetime commitment; they were already best friends and that was about as close to someone as he was willing to get.

Given the family business, he was used to keeping certain things close to his chest. He didn't want to get too involved with anyone because he doubted there was a woman in the world who would put up with his lies. And he would lie to Jenna—he *had* lied to her. He had no choice with his lifestyle, and he wasn't about to apologize for it.

He'd been born an O'Shea, born into a world that was glamorous, powerful and, more often than not, deceitful. He was proud of his name, dirty rumors be damned. Because, overall, the name O'Shea brought prestige and power. No one questioned them to their faces. And Mac would stop at nothing to help fulfill his father's dying wish in getting back the scrolls. At all costs. They'd been missing long enough and he wanted to be the one to bring them back to their rightful place.

Turning back around, Mac eyed the bedroom door once again. Was she asleep? Was she tossing and turning? Was she fantasizing about the offer he'd given? One way to find out. Stripping off his shirt, Mac tossed it to the sofa and padded toward the bedroom. No matter what she was doing, Mac was going in. He wasn't tired, but there was no sense in delaying the inevitable. A smile spread across his face as he unbuttoned his shorts, slid the zipper down and let them fall to the floor. He stepped out of them and slowly turned the knob.

Wearing only his black boxer briefs, Mac entered the darkened room, took in the curvy shape beneath the sheet and headed to the other side of the bed. After flipping his phone to silent, he placed it on the bedside table and sank onto the edge of the bed.

Behind him the sheets rustled and Mac had a hard time not letting his imagination run away with him. He'd never had a sleepover with Jenna before. Oh, she'd fallen asleep during a movie several times when he visited her or she came to his place. But Mac had never spent the night with her and she certainly hadn't been planning on him sleeping in her room, so had she packed adequate pajamas? Did she sleep in the nude? All those lush curves, begging to be touched...

Mac eased back onto his pillow, crossed his ankles, laced his hands over his bare abdomen and stared up at the ceiling. The blades of the fan whirled in a slow, steady circle, giving off just enough of a light breeze to make the sheer curtains billow in front of the open window. The perfect setting for relaxation. For seduction. If this were any other woman, Mac wouldn't put forth so much effort, but he knew full well that being with Jenna would be worth the wait and definitely worth the exercise in self-control.

A soft moan filled the silence of the room as Jenna shifted beneath the sheet again. Apparently she had fallen asleep, but she was restless. Good. Selfishly, he wanted her to be on edge, to be aching because he sure as hell was lying here in a state of...well, he couldn't quite put the proper term to it.

Another moan escaped Jenna, this one louder, longer. Mac clenched his fists at his side. She was dreaming. His ego liked to think she was dreaming of him, of his proposition. The thought of her with another man irritated him, but he had no permanent claim on Jenna. Wanting intimacy with someone was completely different than wanting a happily-ever-after.

His eyes adjusted even more to the darkened room as he rolled over to watch her. A sheen of sweat covered her face; her lips were parted just enough to be even sexier than usual. The sheet slid down as she shifted again. What the hell was she wearing? Was that…yeah, she was wearing some type of maxi dress. Why?

Mac eased the sheet the rest of the way down her body. No wonder she was sweating. As soon as that layer was off, he stood and reached for the fan control, to kick it up on high. When he turned back to the bed, that long dress had ridden up on Jenna's thighs. Mercy, the woman was killing him.

He knew she was insecure about her body. They'd never talked about it because he wouldn't give that negativity any attention. To him, Jenna was absolutely perfect. He didn't want her to believe her shape defined her. There had to be some way to make her see herself the way he did. To realize that she was a voluptuous, stunning siren and she was valuable to anyone who took the time to appreciate her.

Jenna rolled to her side, facing him. Mac watched the swell of her breast threaten to move over the boundary of the scoop neck of the dress. A tan line ran up around her neck—he resisted the urge to run his finger along the pale skin.

That damn kiss had completely messed with his mind. While he'd always found her sexy as hell, now that he'd fully tasted her, he could think of nothing but tasting her again. For years he'd thrown out one sexual innuendo after another, but he wasn't kidding any longer. That kiss had changed something in him and as soon as he knocked her guard down and made her his, he could eradicate her from his system and they could circle back to this friendship thing.

Before he could roll away, her lids fluttered open, her eyes locking on to his. She blinked as she licked her lips, her hand moving up to adjust the top of her dress.

"Why are you staring at me?" she asked, her voice husky.

"You were dreaming." He wasn't about to answer her question. "And moaning."

Her eyes widened, then closed briefly before she met his gaze once again. "Did I wake you up?"

Mac shifted on his side more, propping his elbow on the pillow, his head in his hand. "I just came in here. You're sweating and wearing a dress to bed. Care to tell me why?"

The second he mentioned the dress, she jerked and adjusted the material back down. "I didn't have proper pajamas for a bedmate and I certainly didn't plan on you being in my bedroom with me."

Mac swallowed and fisted the sheet in front of him. "What did you pack?"

"Doesn't matter."

Stubborn to a fault. No wonder they got along so well. The push-pull part of their relationship was half the fun.

"What were you dreaming about?" he asked.

When she hesitated, he knew. Good. He liked knowing he was in her thoughts when she wasn't fully in control.

"Nothing much," she replied, her eyes darting away.

"With moans like that? I'd say it was something pretty amazing."

Jenna rolled over the other way, threw her legs over the side and offered him her back. "Drop it, Mac."

Such emotion for someone who wasn't dreaming of anything major. He was getting to her, already she was thinking of them together. Seducing her would be a cinch. But he didn't want to just seduce her, he wanted her to come to him.

"Change your clothes." When she glanced over her shoulder, he added, "You're hot, you're uncomfortable and you need to rest. Whatever you brought to sleep in, I think I can handle it."

After a moment, she nodded. She went to the chest of drawers, got something out and disappeared into the bathroom. A sliver of light slid from beneath the door and Mac had to force himself not to march in there and take what they both wanted. He only had a week, but he'd give her another day to come to terms with the fact they would be sleeping together in every sense of the word. Lying beside her would be a new test in self-control, but this was his Jenna and she deserved to be treated with respect.

So he'd lie here and be the perfect gentleman…for now. This would be completely new territory for him, but he was willing to make the sacrifice for an epic end result.

When Jenna came back out, he couldn't tell what she'd put on until she passed by the open window and the soft moonlight flickered across her body. The image lasted only a second, but long enough that he was reevaluating this gentlemanly decision. She wore a silk chemise that hugged her every hollow and curve. The lace trim around the dip just above her backside teased him. What would she do if he ran his finger beneath that edge? If he slid one of those thin, silky straps off her shoulder and showed her how good he could make her feel? Would she prefer the real thing to her dreams?

As she slipped in beside him, Mac gritted his teeth and wished like hell he'd opted to sleep on the deck in the hammock. If he left now, though, she'd have the upper hand and he never gave up control that easily.

"Good night, Mac."

Facing the opposite direction, Jenna slid the sheet up and over her shoulders as if she wanted an extra layer of defense. A sheet and a piece of satin wouldn't keep him away, but the fact she was so special to him would. To-morrow was another day and all of this playing around in pretend-lovers' bliss would get to her. He'd make damn sure of it.

Okay, she'd done it. She'd made it through one night sleeping next to Mac and she'd even put on the chemise she'd packed. She loved barely there lingerie, it always made her feel sexy. Unfortunately, she'd risked putting silk and lace on with only one man, years ago…and that plan had backfired. She refused to make that mistake again.

Fortunately it had been dark last night and Mac hadn't seen her. This morning she'd gotten out of bed before him and could sneak off to shower and throw on another sun-dress before he got up. She'd thought for sure he'd sleep on the pull-out couch when she'd asked him to meet her here. Never would she have thought he'd use this situ-ation to get closer to her…she should've known better.

"Tell me we're going to have a huge lunch after this flower thing because I'm starving."

Jenna laughed and swatted Mac on the chest as they walked toward the lobby of the resort. She'd received a call that the flowers she'd custom ordered had arrived and were in the walk-in refrigerator in the kitchen. Jenna was so excited to see all the buds and blooms in various colors. Her sister had wanted a variety because she hadn't been able to narrow down her colors to just a few.

Being able to work with fresh flowers for a wedding was always a joy for Jenna, but to be doing it for her sister was even more thrilling.

Jenna passed through the open entryway to the lobby and glanced to Mac. "You're always hungry. How do you not weigh five hundred pounds?" Damn men and their flawless metabolism.

"If I'd had more than yogurt and fruit for breakfast I wouldn't be so hungry."

"You're hangry. It's okay. I get that way myself."

His brow lifted behind his dark shades. "Excuse me?"

"Hangry. When you're hungry and angry," she explained with a shrug as she reached the counter. "I forgive you and I promise to get you a nice meal when we're done here."

She patted his cheek with her free hand and directed her attention to the lady waiting to assist them. After they were escorted toward the kitchen, the woman directed them to the tubs of flowers that had been set outside the back doors for Jenna to sort through. The manager had made sure a workspace was set up for Jenna, and the employees were told to let her in and out as often as she needed while she crafted the various arrangements and bouquets.

The next hour flew by in a whirlwind of buds, greenery and tissue wrappings. Jenna meticulously sorted each bundle, leaving the lilacs off to the side. She'd be taking those back to her bungalow, along with a few other bundles, to start working on the smaller bouquets. Those would fit in the refrigerator in her own kitchen and that way she wouldn't be scrambling to do so much the day before the wedding.

Jenna glanced at Mac who was enthralled by something on his phone. With his dark eyes drawn in, the muscle ticking in his jaw and the death grip with which he held his phone, Jenna knew something was wrong.

She laid the flowers down and reached across to touch his forearm. "What's going on?"

Blinking, he looked up. "Just reading an email. I need to make a call."

Jenna removed her hand as he came to his feet and headed out toward the breathtaking garden area and gazebo, probably where the employees took their breaks. As she watched Mac's shoulders tighten and tense beneath his blue T-shirt, Jenna wondered what could be so pressing. He glanced to the sky and shook his head as if frustrated with the person on the other end of the line. Whatever it was, she had no doubt this call was work related.

Mac's work was definitely something she knew very little about. Oh, sure, everyone knew the O'Sheas of Boston—the family, with their auction houses around the globe, was infamous. Mac had actually just opened two more US-based locations in Atlanta and Miami—she may have asked him to open one in Miami so she could see him more often. She'd had no idea he would actually do it and move down there to oversee the office.

But as successful as his family was, Jenna still didn't know what all the secrets were about and Mac would never betray his family's trust. She'd never known a man to be so loyal.

Her father certainly hadn't been. Jenna knew people were responsible for their own actions, but she couldn't help but blame the man for running out and leaving her mother to turn to the bottle. Those years were pure hell, but with love and the unshakeable bond between a mother and her daughters, Jenna and Amy were able to turn their mother around.

Mac shoved his cell into his pocket and headed back her way.

"You okay?" she asked, bundling up the flower assortment she needed to take back to the bungalow.

"Just work." He caught a cluster of tissue-wrapped greenery that had started to slide off the table. "We hired a new manager at the main office in Boston. I just needed to get her into Miami to handle some issues concerning the upcoming auction."

Guilt slid through her. "If you need to go, it's fine, really."

Mac reached for her hand and squeezed. "I'm not going anywhere. This is nothing I can't fix with a couple of phone calls. Now, tell me where to take these so you can feed me that promised lunch."

Rolling her eyes, Jenna came to her feet and pointed to a pile of flowers. "Be careful with those or you'll get yogurt and fruit again."

He picked up the bundle and laughed. "Not many things scare me, but I know if I lose one petal you'll torture me."

Jenna carried her own stack and headed out. She informed the staff that they could put the rest away and she'd be back tomorrow to get more. With the flowers in hand, Jenna led Mac back toward their bungalow. The sun was already bright and it was still early. This would be a perfect day to lounge on her deck, fiddle with arrangements and continue working on her tan. Though she knew she wouldn't be more beautiful than the bride,

Jenna wanted to be at her best when she had to walk next to her cheating jerk ex.

As soon as she saw a familiar figure heading her way, Jenna froze. It was as though she'd conjured up the devil himself. She knew the moment was coming, but she was hoping her ex would avoid her for the sake of saving face. Apparently his ego had gotten the best of him.

"Martin's here," she muttered, clutching the stems of her bundles even tighter. "Let's turn around."

"Like hell."

Before she knew what was happening, Mac shifted his stash of flowers in the crook of one arm and wrapped his other arm around her. In the same instant, his lips crushed hers, forcing her to hold on to him with her free hand and enjoy the ride. Mac's mouth demanded more and she was all too willing to give it. This kiss, if something so powerful could have such a simple term, didn't feel like an act at all. This felt more like a stepping stone to something more private and intimate. And it certainly wasn't like the one from the other day. This kiss held…promise.

Jenna's entire body heated. Tingling started low in her belly and she had aches in places she'd never ached before. Mac's hold on her tightened and Jenna couldn't prevent the moan that slipped from her lips.

Martin cleared his throat and Mac pulled away. His lopsided grin and a naughty gleam in his eye told Jenna he was enjoying this. Just another reason she couldn't let her heart tumble into this charade. Mac was a professional player. This game was well within his comfort zone. That made one of them.

Once Mac stepped to her side, his free arm still draped around her shoulders, Jenna got a good look at her ex… and he was fuming.

"What the hell are you doing?" he demanded, staring at Jenna. "I told you I'd be here so we could talk and you're with this guy? He's more of a liar and a cheater than I ever thought of being."

Before she could respond, Mac spoke up. "Apologize to her now."

Martin's narrowed gaze darted to Mac. "Who the hell are you to tell me anything? Jenna belongs with me."

Mac pulled his arm away and stepped between her and Martin. "Not anymore. I'm her fiancé."

Four

"I cannot believe you just did that."

Mac watched as Jenna stormed through their bungalow. She'd carefully set the flowers on the kitchen island and then took off pacing, throwing her arms in the air and muttering words that would make his Irish mother, God rest her soul, blush.

"I only wanted you to pretend to be my boyfriend," she yelled as she turned to pace in the other direction. "Then you go and tell me you want to be my lover, you have my mother and sister thinking we're quite serious and you tell my ex we're engaged."

Finally, she turned to face him, her hands propped on her hips, her chest heaving. "Are you going to say anything?"

Mac shrugged and placed his flowers next to hers. "That guy is an ass. I'm not sorry for what I said."

"Are you sorry for the position you put me in?"

Maybe a little, but Mac hadn't liked this ex. He'd had *possessive* written all over him and nobody laid a claim on Jenna. Well, this week Mac did, but there was no way in hell Mac would let a guy like Martin have another chance with Jenna. Mac knew the type Martin was—a wealthy playboy who got whatever he wanted…damn it. Mac had just described himself.

But still, Mac worked hard for everything he had and he'd work just as hard to make sure Jenna never had to deal with that jerk again. The fact that Martin knew of the O'Sheas was helpful. Mac didn't purposely hide behind his name, but clearly Jenna had spoken of him and that only made Mac feel even more protective of her.

"You called me here to help." Slowly he closed the space between them and rested his hands on her shoulders, bending his knees so he could look her in the eyes. "The whole *engaged* thing slipped out, but now that it has, we'll deal with it the same way as before. Once this week is over, we just explain to your family that we decided we're better off as friends."

Jenna let out a heavy sigh. "You make this sound so easy."

He stared down into her mesmerizing eyes. She had a way of drawing him in before he even knew what was happening. Jenna was one of the most important people in his life and he wouldn't let her down.

"Trust me?" he asked, tipping his head to hold her gaze.

Her features softened as her shoulders relaxed beneath his touch. "You know I do. And it's not just my family I'm worried about. I've dragged you into this—"

"Do I look like I mind?" he asked, offering her a smile.

"You look like you're having the time of your life."

She laughed. "Don't get so caught up that you forget we're just acting."

Oh, no worries there. No matter how amazing Jenna was, he didn't want to be tied down to anyone for a lifetime commitment. And that was exactly how he viewed marriage.

"I think I can handle kissing you in public and still remember that we're just friends," he told her.

Something flashed across her face, but before he could analyze what it was, the emotion was gone. He wanted inside that head of hers, wanted to know what she truly thought about this entire arrangement…about him. But perhaps it was better to be in the dark. Maybe the truth would have him running in the other direction. Emotions were one area he tried not to venture into.

"Now, what are we doing for lunch?" he asked.

Jenna grunted as she laid her hands flat on his chest and gave him a shove. "You have a one-track mind."

He raked his eyes over her body, then threw her a wink and a grin. "I actually have a couple tracks, but I'm a whiz at multitasking."

"Let me put these flowers in the fridge and then we can go get a bite." She maneuvered around Mac and grabbed the flowers, carefully placing them on the shelf she'd emptied just for this reason. "While we're out we need to be holding hands. Maybe you can brush my hair back from my shoulders and look at me when I pretend not to notice. You know, do whatever people in love are supposed to do."

Silently, he closed the gap between them and came within a breath of her. She jumped at his nearness. "And what will you be doing?"

The cool air from the refrigerator did nothing to control the heat inside her. As she straightened and turned, he was literally right there.

"Um…" What was the question? Oh, right. "I guess I'll be smiling and nodding and hanging on your every word."

Mac brushed her hair over her shoulders, his fingertips trailing over her bare skin there, then up her neck to her jaw as he framed her face. "No, you're not that type of woman, Jenna."

Why was he looking at her like that? Did he give off that "I want to devour you" vibe to his other lovers?

"I'm not?" she whispered.

His thumb brushed along her bottom lip. "No. You're in control. You don't even realize it, but any man worth having you would fall under your spell. He'd hang on your every word and you would hold the power."

Jenna's breath caught in her throat. She held power? Over whom? Because she might not be experienced in relationships, but she knew she'd never held control over anyone.

"When we go out, I will be the one spellbound. We'll show this ex exactly what he threw away, because you are worth hanging on to."

Right. The ex. That's what all of this was about… right? Why was she having such a difficult time focusing? Oh, yeah. Because Mac had her backed up against an appliance. His body was practically molded against hers and he was looking at her as if she was the main course and dessert all wrapped up in one delectable package.

Jenna couldn't afford to get tangled up in her emotions. Mac wasn't good for her; they wanted two very different things in life. But now they were each playing a role and she had to remember it was only for a few more days. Getting swept away by the act of being Mac

O'Shea's lover was only asking for heartache…no matter how much her heart clenched when he looked at her with desire in his eyes.

Reaching up to grip his wrists, Jenna eased his hands away from her face. "There's a great restaurant here at the resort and normally you need a reservation, but our wedding party has been given full run of the place. They have some amazing local dishes. Let me change and we'll head out."

As she stepped aside, the fridge door shut. Just as soon as she moved, Mac blocked her path.

"Am I making you nervous, Jenna?"

Nervous? No. Achy, needy and ready to rip his clothes off? Yes.

"Not at all," she replied with a wide smile. "I'm worried about pulling this off, especially considering how angry Martin was earlier. He doesn't like to be told no."

"Yeah, well, I don't like the way he talked to you." Mac looked as if he wanted to say more, but he finally stepped aside and motioned toward the bedroom. "Go get ready. I'll wait on the deck."

Jenna rushed to the bedroom and closed the door at her back. They were on the second day of this charade and she only prayed she could make it the final five. Surely this would get easier…it had to, for the sake of her sanity and her heart.

Lunch was amazing and there were no additional run-ins with Martin the Jerk. Mac hadn't met the man before today, but just one look was enough to know he wasn't good enough for Jenna. Mac was actually looking forward to another encounter with him. He'd prefer the next one to be away from Jenna, but whenever the opportunity presented itself, Mac would be prepared. Martin seemed too full of himself to just let Jenna go and be happy. Mac would see to it that Martin would never be able to hurt her again.

"You're scowling," she muttered as she looped her arm through his. "People are going to think we're fighting."

He patted her hand as he led her down the narrow path toward the beach. "Then we'll have to kiss and make up in public. I'm fine with that."

"You just like to kiss."

Shrugging, he threw her a glance. "You have a great set of lips. Who wouldn't like to kiss them?"

Jenna reached out to push aside a tropical plant hanging over the walkway. "We're pretending, no need to start laying on the charm."

"I wouldn't lie about something like that," he replied. As they hit the edge of the sand, he turned to her. "You do believe me, right? I may have to keep secrets from you to protect you and my family but when it comes to other things between us, you'll only get the full truth from me."

Jenna stared at him as if he were crazy. "Yeah, sure."

Before he could stop himself, he snaked his arms around her and pulled her flush against his body. He captured her squeal when he covered her mouth with his.

Mac gripped the back of her dress, fighting the urge to lift it up and whisk it over her head. They were in public, but she was seriously doing a number on his emotions. Mac had originally set out to seduce her, but now he also wanted to dismantle any insecurities she had, so when she moved on to the next guy, she would know her self-worth.

Damn. The next guy. Mac didn't think any guy would be good enough for Jenna.

When she moaned, Mac lifted his head slightly, nipping at her lips a few more times before pulling back.

He'd always been able stay detached from any woman, but Jenna was becoming his drug of choice and he saw no way to break the addiction until he got her into his bed.

"Did you see someone?" she asked, her lids fluttering open.

"I thought I saw your mom down the way." Okay, so that was a lie and he'd just told her he wouldn't lie to her, but he wasn't sorry—he was selfish. Pretending to squint and look in the distance, Mac shrugged. "My mistake."

Lacing his fingers through hers, Mac guided her down the beach. Jenna leaned against his side and he wondered if she was as turned on as he was from that kiss. Each time he tasted her he wanted more, he wanted to take it to another level. Did she even have those thoughts? She couldn't moan like that, couldn't lean so perfectly against his body and not want more. His ego swelled, but more than that, hope filled him because now he knew she would reciprocate his need, this ache that kept bouncing between them.

"My sister asked if you and I were free to have dinner with her and Nathan."

Water lapping at their bare feet, they strolled down the shoreline. Mac decided he really didn't want to share his Jenna time with anyone else. This week was about seducing his best friend, finally getting her where he'd wanted her since propositioning her years ago at a party. She'd never let herself respond to him before.

"When did they want to get together?" he asked, stroking the delicate area between her thumb and index finger.

"Well, the only free night is tonight. We have a dinner tomorrow, a party the following night, Friday is the rehearsal and Saturday is the wedding."

Damn. He'd been warned of all the "outings" this week, but he didn't realize his time would be so monopolized by wedding events. On the other hand, he could totally play this to his advantage. If they were in public he would have to be in lover mode. Maybe there were some perks to these evening activities, after all. After making Jenna moan, who knew what else he could pull out of her during their remaining time on the island?

"I'll do whatever you want," he told her.

A mother and a father were splashing around at the edge of the water with their toddler son. Mac didn't miss the way Jenna stared at the family, the way her breath caught before a soft smile spread across her face. He'd bet she hadn't even noticed that she'd squeezed his hand a bit tighter. Mac knew this is what she wanted, a family, children. Everything he couldn't offer, yet everything she deserved. One of the many reasons this arrangement had to be a temporary thing only. After she was out of his system, he'd have to step aside and allow another man to come into her life.

Best friends. That was the highest relationship status he had to give. Jenna would meet the right man and start the family she wanted. The thought conjured up a whole host of images Mac didn't appreciate. No man would ever measure up, but that wasn't his decision to make. Shame, that.

Still, when she found a man and things started getting serious, Mac would do a complete background check and make sure the guy was squeaky clean because Jenna deserved a man on the right side of the law, a man with no secrets.

A man totally the opposite of Mac.

Not that Mac wanted that settled-down family lifestyle. The whole marriage thing was working for Braden and Zara, but Mac was just fine focusing on work, partying when he could and hooking up with women who were on the same playing field as he was. Life was good, so why mess it up?

Mac tugged on Jenna's hand to keep her moving. "Maybe going out tonight would be the best option," he told her. "That way Nathan can see us together as well and pass along to his best man that you're officially off the market and not interested in a reunion."

Jenna shoved her sunglasses up onto her head, pushing her dark strands back from her face. "Good idea. I'll let Amy know. You're too good to me, Mac."

With a laugh, he shook his head. "Nah. Remember, if you mess this act up, I get to cash in a favor at any time."

Jenna playfully nudged his side with her elbow. "I'm pulling this whole thing off beautifully so far, which means I'll get another favor. Don't get so cocky."

Up ahead, Mac caught sight of Martin talking with Nathan. Perfect opportunity to work this lover's angle and shove it right into Martin's face. Mac didn't just want to convince the guy that Jenna had moved on, Mac wanted to torture the man with what he'd let go.

"You ready to put those acting skills to the test again?" he asked, nodding straight ahead.

Her gaze followed his and she drew in a deep breath. "I'd rather just avoid him."

"You're not a coward."

Before she could protest further, he trudged forward. He told her a joke to get her laughing. Mission accomplished. Jenna's rich laughter had Martin's head whipping around in no time.

Game on, you sorry bastard.

Nathan waved with a smile, but his eyes were darting between Martin, Jenna and Mac. Mac figured he'd have to break the tension since he was the one who was adamant about this little meeting.

"Hey, Nathan." Mac greeted the man as if he'd known him forever. In actuality, he'd met him once when he and Amy had come to visit Jenna in Miami. "Jenna just told me we'll be going out tonight. Looking forward to it."

"Amy wasn't sure when you guys were free," Nathan replied. "I'll be sure to let her know. I hear congratulations are in order for the two of you, as well?"

Mac wrapped his arm around Jenna, pulling her closer to his side, ignoring the kick of just how comfortable he was playing the role of doting fiancé.

"Thanks. We didn't want to make a big deal of anything, since this is your week and I actually just surprised Jenna."

"Where's the ring?" Martin asked, his tone mocking, his gaze narrowed.

Without missing a beat, Jenna replied, "Mac is flying me to his favorite jeweler in Italy after the ceremony Saturday so I can choose the one I want."

Mac mentally high-fived her quick, clever response. She'd stiffened slightly against him, but she'd managed to squelch her nerves and fire back. Martin's expression was priceless and his silence was another win for Mac. Maybe Jenna could handle this role-playing just fine. His hand slipped to the curve of her hip. When he squeezed her there, she jumped slightly and attempted to shift. Mac held her right where he wanted her. Damn, those curves beneath his hand sent his mind into overdrive.

"If you'll excuse us, we were on our way back to our room. Haven't had enough alone time with my girl." Mac returned Martin's glare with a mocking wink before nodding to Nathan. "See you tonight."

Completely dismissing Martin, Mac guided Jenna back along a path that would take them toward the bungalows nestled on the water.

"Nice job," he muttered when they were far enough away. "I actually do have a jeweler in Italy."

"Where I'm sure your female entourage is well supplied," she tossed back.

Was that a hint of…jealousy? Interesting. Definitely useful information.

"It's okay, babe. I'll make it up to you. Do you prefer diamonds or emeralds? My jeweler made this gorgeous diamond necklace for me once. Personally, I think rubies because you get fired up sometimes and—"

Jenna jerked from his grasp. "This isn't real so don't lump me with your collection of arm candy."

Mac didn't even get to defend himself before she stomped off toward the bungalow. He followed her because if they were having a lover's spat in public, he sure as hell planned on making up in private.

But what the hell had gotten into her? He'd swear she was jealous, but she'd pointed out on numerous occasions that this situation was false. So why the narrowed gaze? Why the hurt lacing her tone?

Mac caught up to her just before she could slam the door. He was about to find out.

Five

This entire situation was getting out of hand and they were only on day two. Why had she thought this would ever work? For a split second, which was more than she could afford, she'd let her emotions take control, shoving aside common sense. When Mac had palmed her side, sliding his hand over her, she'd become fully engulfed in this charade. A charade she'd started.

Plus, her emotions were not getting the message to stay detached. When Mac had mentioned he actually had a jeweler, Jenna knew without a doubt he'd taken women there. Jealousy, table for one.

Gritting her teeth, Jenna tried to regain some control over her self-induced rage. This whole situation was her fault. Any hurt, anger or envy she had spearing through her was all brought on by her need to rid herself of Martin.

The door to the bungalow slammed behind her, but

Jenna kept her back turned. She'd let her control slip. In all the years she and Mac had been friends, she'd joked about his other women, but she'd never, ever shown him how much she hated his playboy lifestyle. The moment had literally swept her away.

Jenna actually hated the jet-setting, womanizing part of his life even more than the secrets surrounding the mafia rumors. She had to say no to him because of his excessive lifestyle. She wanted to be special to any man she was involved with and being with Mac in an exclusive way wasn't an option. He'd never made it a secret that he loved women, that he never wanted to settle down and find "the one."

"Jenna."

She stiffened at his demanding tone. Starting this second, she was back in control. This was her life and she needed to remember that Mac was her best friend. Always loyal, always willing to do anything for her…taking things any further would be a mistake. He'd come down here to help without hesitation and she wouldn't repay him by dragging him into the middle of this battle between her heart and her mind.

Jenna spun around and met his questioning gaze. "Sorry. I didn't mean to go all possessive girlfriend on you out there. I got caught up in the moment."

Shaking his head, Mac crossed his arms over his broad chest. "You don't like the idea of me buying jewelry for other women."

No point in lying. "Fine. I don't."

With a defiant tilt of her chin, Jenna adjusted her sundress and mimicked his stance as she crossed her arms. "You flaunt women all the time and doing it now is inappropriate."

There. That sounded convincing, didn't it? Those penetrating eyes of his raked over her, sending shivers racing through her body. How could the man be so potent from across the room? Did he have a clue as to the damage he could do to her? Did he have any idea how difficult it had been for her to even ask him to step in?

Jenna was starting to wonder if she'd made a mistake. Too late for hindsight now.

"I had the necklace made for Laney on her twenty-first birthday." The simple explanation made her feel utterly foolish…as she should because she had zero hold over this man.

"You were jealous," he stated.

Jenna quirked a brow. "I was not. I expect you to remember what we're doing this week and what your role is."

Like a panther to its prey, Mac stalked across the room, his eyes locked onto hers. "Oh, I remember exactly what I'm doing here this week. The question is, do you?"

He stopped within a breath of her. His hands came up, tugging her arms loose until they fell to her sides, then he closed that final sliver of space. She had to tip her head up to look at him.

"Do I what?"

A muscle ticked in his jaw as he slid his hand up her arm, curled his fingers over her shoulder and replied, "Do you remember what our roles are? Seems to me you may have slipped into the position of my lover a bit too easily. Makes me wonder if you really do want to take advantage of this situation."

Unable to think of some witty, snappy comeback, Jenna skirted around him and headed to the fridge. Grabbing the flowers, she unwrapped the layers of tissue and laid everything out on the kitchen table.

"We're not lovers, Mac." Her hands were shaking, but

hopefully if she kept them busy, Mac wouldn't notice. "We're friends. Don't read into this."

In a flash, Mac reached out and gripped her hand. "This? Are you referring to your shaky hands or the fact you can't look me in the eye when you lie? Or maybe you wonder what it would be like if we did sleep together and you're afraid to admit it out loud."

Without looking up, she jerked her hand back and attempted to separate the bundle of lilacs. "I've wondered," she admitted. "Of course I have, but that doesn't mean I'm going to let it happen."

When he said nothing, when silence filled the air like an unwanted third party, Jenna dropped the flowers and rested her palms flat on the table. With a heavy sigh, she dropped her head between her shoulders.

"Mac, after this week I still want you to be my best friend. No matter what you say, no matter what you may think is a good idea now, if we slept together we couldn't take it back."

Mac cupped her chin and turned her head. Jenna forced her eyes on his, because appearing weak was not an option.

"When I sleep with you, I won't want to take it back."

Jenna gasped at all the veiled promises in that statement. A reply was impossible as Mac slid his mouth over hers, but not in a demanding way like last time. No, this kiss was slower, seductive, yet more commanding.

The power she'd thought she possessed where Mac was concerned vanished the second his lips silently demanded all of her attention.

When he pressed his palm flat against her back, Jenna fell against his solid, defined chest. Instinctively, her arms looped around his neck, her fingers threaded through his coarse hair. Mac lifted his mouth from hers for the briefest of moments before changing the angle and going back in for more.

More urgent now, he reached behind her. Tissue paper rustled and a second later he gripped her waist with his hands, lifting her to the edge of the table. On every level she knew this was a mistake. Mac was used to this, to taking what he wanted when he wanted it. Jenna was more of a thinker, a planner…a dreamer. She couldn't afford to be selfish and live directly in the moment. There would be consequences for every single action.

But right now, with his lips covering hers, then roaming along her jaw, Jenna tipped her head back and arched her body, consequences be damned.

"You taste so damn good," he muttered against her skin.

Jenna continued to clutch the back of his shirt, battling herself as to whether she should push him away or let this glorious moment continue. How could she ignore this inferno raging between them? She'd never felt so alive, so out of control and on the verge of something utterly blissful.

The pounding on her bungalow door brought every tantalizing thought to a halt. Mac's lips froze on the hollow part of her neck.

"Expecting company?" he asked, his voice husky.

Unable to speak, Jenna loosened her grip and shook her head.

Mac's intense, dark gaze raked over her body as he slowly pulled away. Jenna realized her legs were spread wide to accommodate his body, her dress hiked up high on her thighs. Jenna jerked the hem down and hopped off the table. Mac moved across the room just as more pounding shook the door.

When he yanked the door open with more force than

necessary, Jenna caught Martin's angry gaze. His eyes darted from Jenna to Mac and back to her. Well, this is what she wanted...wasn't it? She wanted him to see that she and Mac were serious. There couldn't be any doubt as to what they'd been doing...or about to do. Her hair was tousled all around her shoulders, most likely her face was flushed and Mac was breathing a bit harder than usual. Her body was still very much tingling from the encounter.

Oh, mercy, had she honestly been about to have sex with her best friend on the kitchen table? *Keep it classy, Jenna.*

"Sorry, this is a party for two," Mac said as he started to close the door.

Martin put his hand up, blocking the action. "Jenna. I need to speak with you. Alone."

"You won't be seeing my fiancée alone. Ever." Mac's voice had taken on a deadly, menacing tone, quite different from the sexy rasp he'd delivered only moments ago.

"Get the hell out of the way."

Jenna stepped forward, placed a hand on Mac's back and glared at Martin. "Whatever you want to say, do it quick."

Mac tensed beneath her palm, but since this wasn't a real relationship, she wasn't about to let him ride to her rescue this time. Jenna could handle her own problems.

"Give me another chance. I know we can work this out." Martin's eyes seemed to implore her. "You don't want to marry this guy. He'll ruin you."

Before she could stop him, Mac launched forward and fisted Martin's shirt. "Get the hell out of here."

Mac shoved him back out onto the deck leading to the bungalow. Jenna knew enough about Mac to know this was not the time to step in. He was angry, he was taking charge and he wouldn't want her to intervene, even if this situation was all about her.

Martin knocked Mac's hands away and took another step back. "You'd rather take a shot with this criminal than give me a second chance?" Martin asked. "That's not the Jenna I know."

Normally, Jenna wouldn't side with a guy who was so aggressive, but she knew Mac. This was for show. He was only going along with her request to make their relationship look authentic. Wasn't he?

He wasn't about to unleash his rage here. Surely not. Mac definitely had a temper, but since none of this was real, perhaps he'd keep himself in check.

"You need to go," she told Martin.

Once again his eyes darted between her and Mac before settling on her. "I hope you come around before it's too late. The rumors surrounding his family are enough—"

Mac punched Martin in the face, sending Martin's head flying back. Martin stumbled as he reached up to feel his jaw. Jenna gasped, gripping the door. Clearly Mac's restraint had snapped.

"He just proved my point," Martin spat out before turning and stomping away. "This isn't what you need, Jenna."

Despite the heat, a shiver rippled through her. Mac had gone too far, in more ways than one. Her body still trembled from having his mouth and hands all over her. Their relationship had crossed the friendship line because there was no way she could erase that memory. Then he'd gone and assaulted Martin. Granted, Martin was goading Mac on purpose, but Mac had lost his temper…an O'Shea family trait.

The polar opposite personas of Mac had been revealed

within a span of five minutes. How could he be two completely different people?

Unsure of what to say, Jenna remained silent and went back inside. Her eyes immediately landed on the table, on the cleared-off spot where Mac had set her. The man could make her totally forget all common sense. But seeing him become so angry had snapped her back to reality.

"Jenna—"

Keeping her back to the door, she held up her hand. "No. I don't want your apology."

"I wasn't going to give you one," Mac retorted. "I'm not sorry I hit him. Nobody insults my family and nobody disrespects you. That bastard did both."

Something about the way he was so adamant about defending those he loved made him even more attractive. But still, she had to wonder just how far he planned on taking this charade, not to mention how often his anger got the better of him. She'd heard things, ugly things, but she'd never seen Mac get violent before.

Jenna spun around. "I asked you to play the part of my boyfriend. Maybe I should've made things clearer from the start." Gathering up the flowers on the table, she carefully repackaged them, wondering when she would ever find a moment's peace to actually do her sister's wedding arrangements. "I didn't want a fake fiancé, I didn't want you to punch my ex and I didn't want you to cross the boundaries of our friendship by kissing me."

Mac remained still, eerily so, as he locked his eyes on hers. "The fiancé reference slipped out. I will apologize for saying that, but I'll never apologize for hitting a man who cheated on you and put you second in his life. I'm not sorry he'll be wearing my fist impression on his face."

Now he moved closer, closing the gap between them in two strides. "Don't look at me like that, Jenna. It's still me. I'd never raise my hand to a woman. I protect what's mine and no matter what's going on here, fake or real, you're mine."

Jenna's breath caught.

"And I sure as hell will not apologize for kissing you," he went on. "You didn't say no. Far from it. I've wanted to for years and I plan on doing it again. This week, Jenna, you belong to me as more than my friend. You started this and I'm finishing it."

He glanced down to the watch on his wrist. "Better shower up. We have a double date in an hour."

With that, he stalked out the back door to the hammock and relaxed as if he didn't have a care in the world, as if he was oblivious to the turmoil that raged within her. He'd delivered that emotionally packed speech, got her hormones good and jumbled then just turned to leave?

And she was his for the week? As in...*his*?

Both fear and excitement coursed through her. What type of beast had she unleashed?

Six

Mac pulled out the chair for Jenna. Once she was seated, he moved her hair from her shoulder and placed a kiss on her bare, sun-kissed skin. Her familiar floral scent mocked him. He knew firsthand that she dabbed her favorite perfume beneath her ears and put a dot between her breasts. Not only had he seen her do it a time or two, but when he'd been making a path from her neck to her chest, he'd inhaled that scent and he'd wanted more.

"This is so exciting." Amy beamed from the other side of the table. "I'm so happy for you guys and I'm really glad we could carve out this time to spend together. After all, we'll all be family soon enough."

Family? No. His family was his brother, sister, Ryker and Jenna. That was all. Small, simple, effective in making his life complete.

"I finished one of the small bouquets today," Jenna stated, as if she wanted this conversation to take another path, too. "It's even more beautiful than I thought it would be."

Yeah, instead of taking hours to get ready like most women he knew, Jenna had opted to work on an arrangement, then had showered and transformed into evening-ready in minutes. She was stunning tonight with her bare shoulders exposed. Her dress hugged those curves he was dying to get back beneath his hands.

Amy reached across the table and patted Jenna's arm. "I didn't ask you to do the flowers because you're my sister. I asked because you're the best."

Settling back in his seat, Mac could relax a bit more now that the sisters had fallen into their easy chatter. The waitress popped over to their table to take their drink orders. Mac and Nathan ordered the local beer on tap, while the ladies ordered a house wine and slid right back into all things wedding.

"Don't look so glum," Nathan stated with a laugh. "It's not that bad. And if she's happy, then that's all that matters."

Mac grunted. "I think eloping would be the easiest."

Amy gasped, focusing her attention on Mac. "You don't mean that. Jenna has always dreamed of a big wedding. She even has our mother's wedding gown in storage because she wants that vintage feel."

Apparently word traveled fast and Jenna had already discussed the "engagement" with her sister. Mac glanced at Jenna who was waving her hand in the air. "I'll be happy with any wedding, Amy. So long as it's to the man I love. I'll get my happily-ever-after," she assured her sister.

Jenna didn't meet Mac's stare. When he reached beneath the table to slide his hand over her leg, she shifted away just enough so that no one could see, but her silent message delivered a blow.

He'd hurt her earlier. He'd hurt her with his own self-ishness and lack of control. But when that bastard Martin had spouted off about Mac's family…well, he'd been looking for an excuse to punch the guy since he found out Martin had cheated on Jenna.

The waitress brought their drinks and took their orders. The open restaurant provided a view of the crystalline ocean, which glowed even more in the moonlight, palm trees swaying in the gentle breeze and couples strolling around hand in hand. The carefree lifestyle here would be so easy to get lost in; it was the perfect romantic setting, but he wasn't here for romance and his plan of seduction was backfiring in a major way.

Jenna deserved more than a fling. Mac took a hard pull from his beer and realized he was no better than Martin—as difficult as that was to admit. Martin had used her and Mac was attempting to do the same. Oh, Mac could justify his means by saying he'd always wanted her physically, which was true, but after this week he would go back to his life and Jenna would be left with…what? She didn't have feelings for him beyond friendship, but she was the type of woman who wanted that fairy-tale ending. Hadn't her sister just stated as much?

The only role Mac would ever play in a fairytale would be a villain. The villain never got the princess.

"Mac?"

Blinking, he sat his glass back down and looked to Amy. "I'm sorry, what?"

"I asked what happened." She nodded toward his injured hand still curled around his frosted mug.

"He had a slight altercation," Jenna chimed in. "No big deal."

Oh, hell, no. She wasn't coming to his defense or making lame excuses for him.

"I punched Martin."

Jenna sighed and dropped her head. Amy jerked back in her seat and Nathan narrowed his eyes.

"Why?" Amy demanded in a whispered tone.

"He cheated on Jenna and—"

"And nothing," Jenna stated, her voice rising over his. "Let's just leave this conversation for another time."

"He cheated on you?" Amy asked, her wide eyes turning to her sister. "I knew you guys broke up, but you never said why. Oh, honey, I'm so sorry you have to walk with him during the ceremony."

Mac clenched his teeth. The thought of Martin getting close to Jenna only made him see red all over again.

Amy turned to Nathan. "Did you know about this?" she demanded.

Nathan held his hands up in his defense. "He's my best friend, but I had no clue. I'd say he didn't tell me for obvious reasons."

Jenna reached for her wineglass. "Seriously, it happened a few weeks ago and I didn't want to ruin the wedding, so let's forget this conversation ever happened."

As she sipped her wine, she turned just enough to glare at Mac. He wasn't going to apologize. Amy and Nathan needed to know what kind of asshat was in their wedding party posing as a friend and all-round good guy.

Mac couldn't help but smile at the thought of the jerk sporting a shiner for the ceremony. Probably not something Amy would find amusing, but Mac sure did. They should be thankful Mac hadn't broken the guy's jaw, or worse.

"Please, don't let this ruin anything," Jenna begged.

Amy studied her sister and finally nodded. "So, tell

me what you've decided on for your wedding. Surely you have a date in mind or some details."

Hell. He was going to need something stronger than beer to get through this.

"Actually, this is all still so new to us."

Yeah, like two days.

"I want to focus on your wedding before thinking about my own," Jenna went on. "Did the resort get with you on the time I can start setting up in the dining area for the reception?"

"They told me after the rehearsal would be fine. Does that give you enough time?"

"Of course." Jenna's tight smile implied the arrangement was anything but fine, but she'd never tell her sister anything different.

Nathan asked Mac about the auction business and Mac kept his answers vague. Though O'Shea's was thriving even more than usual, Mac's mind was on the scrolls and how Ryker was doing with his lead. Ryker wasn't one to just send random check-ins, though. He wouldn't contact anyone until he discovered something substantial.

When Mac's cell vibrated in his pocket, he slipped it out just enough to see his sister's name on the screen.

"Excuse me," he stated as he came to his feet. "I need to take this."

His sister wasn't one to chat on the phone for fun, so the fact that she was calling had him on alert. Shoving his chair back, he offered a smile in reply to Jenna's worried look.

"Laney." He answered the phone as he walked from the table and out onto a fairly empty dock.

"Would you tell the family Neanderthal to stop checking on me?" his sister demanded.

Mac flinched at the anger lacing her voice. Laney

wasn't an angry person, but there was one man who brought out such emotions in her and Mac didn't have to ask which Neanderthal she was referring to.

"What's going on now?" Mac asked, trying to keep his frustration from coming through.

"I started talking to Carter again—"

"Oh, Laney," Mac groaned. "Are you kidding me?"

"Anyway," she continued, ignoring his protest. "Suddenly Carter calls and tells me he can't see me anymore. You guys may not like him, but my personal life is not your concern. We had a rough patch and I was going to give him another chance."

Actually, it was very much their concern, but he wasn't getting into that now. Having Laney as a baby sister was exhausting at times, but they usually handled her by going behind her back to keep her safe. Mac wouldn't let any harm come to her as long as he was alive, and he knew full well Braden felt the same way, as did Ryker, even though he was only a friend of the family.

"And how does Ryker come into play?"

Laney laughed. "Seriously? He obviously called Carter and said something to him. We were supposed to go out tonight for the first time since we broke up and Carter was adamant he couldn't see me again."

Mac shrugged, even though she couldn't see him. If Carter was scared off that easily then he didn't deserve Laney. End of story and good riddance.

"Listen, Carter isn't a good fit for you," Mac started as he glanced back into the restaurant and met Jenna's eyes. "You deserve someone who will put you above everything else and be completely loyal."

"Maybe Carter was that person," she retorted.

Something flashed in Jenna's eyes before she turned her attention back to whatever her sister was saying. A punch of reality hit him in the gut. From here on out he had to do right by Jenna. She trusted him, only him, to come to her rescue. If someone ever set out to "help" his sister by means of seduction, Mac would rip him limb from limb.

How could he seduce her when she'd placed her heart, her protection in his hands? The answer was as simple as it was complex…he couldn't.

"We went to great lengths to get Carter out of your life when you needed us to step in," Mac went on as he took a few more steps down the dock and away from a couple who had just come outside. "Even if Ryker did call Carter to scare him off, then you need to realize he has your best interests at heart."

"He doesn't have a heart."

That was debatable, but still. Mac wasn't going to keep arguing. "You need to settle this with Ryker."

"He won't take my calls."

"He's working on a lead." He didn't need to say what for. They'd all been diligently searching for the scrolls since their father had made them promise to uncover them. "Don't take it personally."

"If you called him he'd answer," she muttered. "If that jackass thinks he can avoid me…"

Mac smiled. "I'm sure he'll return your call soon enough. I need to get back to dinner."

"Sorry. I know you're with Jenna. Tell her I said hi."

"Will do. Love you, Laney."

"Love you, brother."

Mac shoved the phone back in his pocket and made a mental note to contact Ryker tomorrow. Laney was an adult, yes, but she was beautiful, and as the only female O'Shea, some men saw her as a challenge. Like hell.

"Everything okay?"

Mac jerked around. "Yeah. My sister said to tell you hi."

Jenna's face softened. "I haven't seen her since she came down to Miami to visit you."

Mac slipped his arm around her shoulders. "Let's get back to dinner."

Jenna paused, her hand on his chest as she looked up at him. "If we could hurry and pretend we can't wait to get back to the room that would be great."

Mac swallowed at the thought of her in a rush to get him alone, but he quickly reminded himself he'd vowed to cool it and respect her during their charade. But he had a feeling that keeping that vow would test every ounce of his willpower and sanity.

"Martin just came in and sat at another table, but I want out of here before you blacken his other eye."

Mac kissed her forehead. "No more punching tonight, I promise."

Jenna patted his chest and laughed. "You're all heart. My sister is pressing for more wedding details, so we need to keep the conversation on something else."

"Not a problem." He'd discuss the damn weather before he got into a conversation about his impending nuptials. That day would never come and even in theory, the idea made him cringe.

As they neared the table again, Mac slid his hand along Jenna's neck, smoothing her hair aside. "I hope you're ready to put on a show to make this believable. We've still got that bet on the line."

Jenna froze beneath his touch, but quickly recovered enough to throw him a killer smile. "I think you need to get ready for my performance."

Mac nipped at her lips and pulled her close. "Baby, I'm always ready."

Seven

Amy was saying something about… Jenna honestly had no clue because Mac had scooted so close to her. His hand was traveling up her thigh, pulling the hem of her dress up, and he'd just whispered something so naughty in her ear, she wondered where he learned of such a thing.

If his intent was to get her flustered and squirming in her seat, mission accomplished.

Jenna tipped her head just slightly, suppressing a groan as Mac's fingertips made a pattern over her bare skin. If he moved his hand any higher she'd have a hard time remaining ladylike in public.

Damn that man. He was owning this role of fiancé/lover. No way would he win this bet, though.

Jenna smiled and nodded as Amy stated how their mother had found the most beautiful lilac dress for the wedding. But Mac's relentless touches had her shifting in her seat, spreading her legs slightly and letting out a low, soft sigh.

Mac froze a half second before he moved his hand to her inner thigh. Jenna's first thought was that he'd probably never felt a thick, bare leg like hers before. Her second thought was…she wished he could just go a little higher to relieve her ache.

"If you did a Christmas wedding, we could totally do a classy white theme," Amy went on, clearly oblivious to what was happening beneath the table.

Unable to help herself, Jenna leaned against Mac. She told herself she was just playing the part, but she was starting to think this part was playing her. He removed his hand from her thigh, and she nearly whimpered at the loss, but then he smoothed her hair away from her neck and started massaging the sensitive flesh there. Oh, yeah. He had some talented hands and she didn't want to think about how many women had groaned beneath his touch.

"No matter when Jenna decides to have the wedding, she'll be a beautiful bride."

Mac kissed her cheek and trailed his fingertips down her spine, sending an instant onslaught of goose bumps all over her body despite the heat.

"I hate to cut this dinner short," Mac went on. "But Martin is staring in this direction and I won't have him upsetting Jenna again. Besides, I want to have as much alone time with my gorgeous fiancée as I can. You understand, don't you, Nathan?"

Nathan nodded and lifted his nearly empty beer mug. "I do. I'll talk to Martin in a bit. I didn't know he was harassing you guys."

"He's not harassing us." Jenna refused to add fuel to the fire. The situation with Martin was bad enough. "He just thinks we're getting back together and I've had to tell him several times it's not happening. I'm sure now that he's seen how close Mac and I are, he'll back off."

Mac squeezed her shoulder. "Let's go, sweetheart. I'm done discussing your ex."

The endearment he delivered seemed so genuine, so perfect. Jenna didn't want to get so wrapped up in this that she forgot what was truly happening. Mac was simply playing a role. He wasn't a man she could ever tame and he wasn't looking for anything beyond this week. She knew him better than most, so to cling to any false hope would only leave her with a bruised heart.

Amy winked at Jenna. "See you tomorrow. Don't forget we have a bonfire on the beach at nine."

Jenna came to her feet when Mac pulled out her chair. "I'll be there," she promised. "See you guys tomorrow."

Mac rested his hand on the small of her back, his fingertips brushing her rear end, sending even more jolts of arousal through her. She didn't remember being so responsive before, but she'd also never been touched so intimately by Mac, either. Clearly the man had a special touch, one her body instantly loved.

As soon as they reached the doorway, Mac patted her bottom. "Go on ahead, sweetheart. I'm going to settle the bill and I'll be right there."

"There's no bill," she told him. "It's all part of the package my sister paid for."

"Go on, Jenna."

Something about the way his eyes seemed darker, his smile seemed tighter, had her wondering what he wasn't telling her, but Jenna nodded and headed back toward their bungalow. She needed a moment without Mac, a moment away from his touch, his powerful presence. Jenna pulled in deep breaths as she walked along the docks leading toward various areas of the resort. If she ever did get married, she'd seriously consider Bora Bora for her honeymoon.

If she ever found the one who made her heart kick up, who made her want to rip his clothes off, who made her want to reveal all her hopes and fears. Did that miracle man even exist?

Well, Mac did all those things, but he'd made it abundantly clear he couldn't be that man. As soon as she entered her bungalow, she slid out of her wedges and padded across the room and out onto her private deck. She sank down onto the hammock and carefully swiveled around to lie back. The gentle breeze had her swaying. Jenna laced her hands over her abdomen and closed her eyes. Yeah, she'd definitely bring her husband here.

She let the daydream of a faceless man flood her mind. Would they make love out here in the open, but where nobody could see them? Would they walk hand in hand along the shore and discuss their dreams for the future? Have a romantic dinner and come back to their bungalow and skinny-dip in the dark?

"That must be some daydream."

Jenna jerked at Mac's voice.

"That was the sexiest smile I've ever seen."

When Jenna started to sit up, Mac put a hand on her back. "Don't get up," he told her as he leaned against the side of the bungalow and propped his foot up.

"You look so relaxed, I hate to disturb you." His mouth spread into a wide, toe-curling grin. "Now, tell me what put that smile on your face. Or should I say who?"

"Nobody in particular," she replied with a shrug. Jenna settled back down onto the woven ropes of the hammock and sighed. "Just thinking of bringing my future husband back here for our honeymoon. It's too romantic and gorgeous not to."

When he didn't respond, Jenna risked a glance. His eyes held hers, a muscle ticking in his jaw as he crossed his arms over that broad chest.

"Do you really have your mother's dress in storage?" he asked.

Swallowing, Jenna nodded. "Yeah. It's satin with a simple lace overlay. Her marriage may have been a disaster, but I love the vintage dress and it was still my mother's. It's perfect for me if I ever find the right man."

Perfect because Jenna had inherited her mother's curves and the measurements were just right. Amy had a different father and got her athletic build from him... lucky girl.

"What else would you want in your dream wedding?" he asked.

Jenna stared at him for a second before she laughed, shook her head and turned back to focus on the water just beyond their private deck. "Does it matter? Or is this another ploy for you to seduce me?"

"If I wanted to seduce you, I'd have already succeeded," he told her. "You know I want you physically, any man would be blind and a fool not to. But you were right. We're best friends and at the end of the week, that's what we still need to be."

Great. She was right. He was finally seeing reason. So why did she feel like she'd lost out on a once-in-a-lifetime opportunity?

"I won't lie," he went on. "You're still one of the sexiest women I've ever known, but I respect you, respect what we have."

Wait a second. She was one of the sexiest women he knew? Now he was just being kind, but she wasn't about to say anything because she wasn't one of those women who went fishing for compliments.

"You talked to Martin after I walked away didn't you?" she asked, already knowing the answer.

"I'm done talking about your ex," Mac replied, which told her all she needed to know. "Are you going to work on those flowers tonight? I can go pack more in if you need me to."

Jenna smiled. "You want to help put together wedding arrangements? I knew you had a soft side."

Mac grumbled. "I'm just offering to do some grunt work. Don't read too much into it."

Jenna needed a breather and she had to get these arrangements made. "Fine. Go bring me the rest of the lilacs and half of the greenery."

With a mock bow, Mac gave her a wink. "Consider it done."

Even when he was being a sarcastic goof, he made her heart flutter. She couldn't afford the flutter, the bundle of nerves or the tingles from his kisses.

At dinner, Martin hadn't come over to speak, so perhaps they were making headway. Maybe seeing her with Mac over and over would get through to him—or maybe Mac's fist helped. As much as she wasn't a fan of violence, she also knew Mac was effective when he wanted to be.

She recalled a time he'd been more than forceful at a party when a guy had hit on her and she'd politely turned down his advances. Unfortunately that guy hadn't taken no for an answer and Mac intervened. A slam against the wall and a threat she hadn't been able to overhear sent that guy packing in the other direction.

Mac was definitely a man she wanted in her corner...
too bad she couldn't risk having him in her bed.

Mac's cell vibrated in his pocket just as he hit the entrance to the lobby of the resort. Glancing at the screen, he darted to the side of the building and slid his finger to answer the call.

"Ryker. What do you have?"

"Nothing yet on the scrolls, but we have a problem."

Not what Mac wanted to hear. He was having enough problems trying to remain on the strictly friend level with Jenna. Throwing in a dose of family issues wasn't going to help his mood.

"It's Shane," Ryker went on.

Shane, Braden's nemesis and all-round world-class ass. He'd tried to ruin their family years ago when a business deal had gone sour. He'd attempted to sic the authorities on Patrick, who'd still been running the show. Only Shane hadn't been smart enough to realize the commissioner, the police chief and the FBI director were in the O'Sheas' back pocket. Poor Shane, rookie mistake.

"What the hell is he doing now?"

"I have no clue who is feeding him information, but he's been following me for two days."

Mac glanced around to make sure nobody could hear him. "What the hell does he want?"

"No idea," Ryker stated. "He's trying to be sneaky, but I spotted him when I got to my hotel. I had Laney check into his travel arrangements, and he has an open-ended airline ticket. He's also staying in my hotel. Laney made things a bit difficult for him by hacking into his bank account and moving his funds around."

Mac ran a hand over his face. His sister, the computer hacker. She'd be dangerous if they gave her too much leeway.

"Did you call Braden?"

The cell rustled on the other end before Ryker's reply came through, his tone hushed as if he were worried about being overheard. "He texted me yesterday and said not to bother him unless I found the scrolls. Claimed something about a personal problem with Zara. I didn't ask any more."

Mac frowned. He'd gotten a text from Braden telling him there was a slight issue at home, but it was nothing for Mac to worry about. What was going on?

"That's not all," Ryker went on. "Laney received a threat from Shane through her email. He tried to encrypt it, but she was able to trace it back to him."

Mac gripped the phone. Nobody threatened his family and lived to follow through. "What did the message say?"

"She wouldn't tell me, but I could tell she was shaken up."

"It's not like her to be caught off guard," Mac stated. They'd never known any other way of life, so the contents of the email must have been pretty harsh.

"There's more," Ryker stated. "Someone tried to grab her as she went into a coffee shop two days ago. Luckily an off-duty cop was there and was able to stop it."

Mac's blood boiled. "Why the hell am I just now hearing about this?"

"Because I just heard about it," Ryker retorted. "Laney is smart. She's keeping low and staying home with her security alarm on, but she finally told me when I called her to check on another matter."

Braden may want this family to go legit, but there were times that extreme measures were called for.

"Shane has been a thorn in our side for years," Ryker

went on. "Now he's literally threatening one of our own. I know that was him who tried to grab her because she said the guy had a mask on, but it slipped. She saw the tattoo on his neck. I don't care that he's following me. I can handle him, but Laney is another matter. When are we going to end this once and for all?"

Mac rubbed a hand down his face and blew out a breath. Damn it, he hated making this call. Braden had been adamant about moving this family in a new direction since their father had passed. No more killings. That was Braden's main stance, but Shane had crossed the line by threatening Laney. "Wait," Mac stated. "Braden really wants O'Shea's to make a new start and I can't say as I blame him. He's got a fiancée to think of now and he's in charge. Let's try to get ahold of him again and see what he thinks. If we can't contact him, I'll make a decision."

Ryker sighed. "Fine. But if Shane gets in my way or tries to thwart my plans regarding the scrolls, I'm not backing down. And if I even think he's contacted Laney again, I won't ask for permission to proceed."

Mac gripped his phone tighter. "Make sure you call or text me before you do anything."

Ryker grunted and hung up. As Mac slid his phone back into his pocket, he thought back to all Shane had done. Braden had practiced serious restraint a few months ago when Shane had been harassing Zara. Apparently Zara and Shane had gone out a few times, and once Zara had showed interest in Braden, Shane took that as a personal slap in the face. His pathetic attempt at making their lives hell backfired, but Shane was lucky he was still on this side of the grave.

Mac tried Braden's cell, but got no answer. What on earth could be so dire at home that Braden had checked out? That wasn't like him, especially as the new head of the family. He took that role seriously. Worry slid through Mac as he shot off a quick text asking if everything was all right. Once he knew what Braden's status was, he'd delve into the mess with Shane because Laney's very life could be on the line.

Pulling in a breath and trying to focus on the task Jenna had sent him out for, Mac turned back toward the lobby. If Braden continued to be unreachable and Shane forced their hand, Mac wouldn't be able to hold Ryker back much longer.

And, in all honesty, Mac wasn't so sure he wanted to. Legitimacy be damned.

Eight

"I really need to get back to working on the flowers."

Not bothering to even slow down, Mac laced his fingers with Jenna's and kept walking down the beach. "You didn't come to bed until three this morning because you were working."

Well, that was true, but she'd also been avoiding going to bed because she was having a difficult time lying there beside such temptation. The fewer hours the better. The warmth of his body next to hers was something she could get used to and that was a major problem.

"I have yet to start on the largest arrangements and the wedding is in three days."

She risked a glance to see if he was going to respond, but he just kept walking in that sexy, I've-got-all-the-time-in-the-world kind of way. Without a shirt. With all those glorious, tanned muscles clenching with each step and strut.

And he was totally oblivious to the fact that he stole her breath and made her heart quicken.

Jenna blinked and focused on looking ahead. While Mac had all the confidence in the world, she tugged on her strapless cover-up once more to avoid a wardrobe malfunction. Mac had suggested they head to the beach to "be seen" so she'd thrown on the only bathing suit she'd packed, because it was the only one she owned. Clearly swimwear was designed by the devil and a host of supermodels.

The cover-up helped, though. As long as she kept her shield in place, she didn't feel so...exposed.

"Stop fidgeting," he commanded. "You look fine."

Great. She looked fine and he looked delicious.

"C'mon," he said, tugging her toward the water's edge. "Let's cool off."

Jenna pulled her hand free. "Go ahead. I'll just sit here."

She sank onto the sand, shoving her toes into the warmth. When Mac stood in front of her, blocking the sun, she eased back on her hands and stared up at him.

"Come in the water with me."

"I'm fine," she told him. "Go on ahead."

When he took a seat next to her, Jenna continued to stare out at the ocean through the tinted lenses of her sunglasses. They'd only seen one other couple walking along the beach. It was still early and the weather was perfect. Everything about Bora Bora, this wedding, the ambiance, was perfect. What wasn't perfect was the turmoil rolling inside her. Maybe Martin had gotten the hint and was going to leave her alone. Maybe she and Mac didn't have to be quite so touchy-feely in public.

Because her body still tingled from the table experience.

Mac's hand brushed along her shoulder, smoothing her hair away from her back and over the other shoulder. "Take off the cover-up, Jenna."

Stiffening beneath his touch, letting his husky words wash over her, Jenna's refusal was on the tip of her tongue.

"I know you're not comfortable," he went on, his tone low and soft. "But you're one sexy woman. You're made like women should be, Jen. All those curves."

He palmed her back as he leaned in closer. "You make a man think of things he shouldn't."

A shiver racked her body. "You're delusional."

"No, I'm honest."

Jenna glanced his way, her hair falling over her shoulder, the ends tickling her bare thigh. "You don't need to say pretty words, Mac. I only needed you to pretend."

Mac jerked off his sunglasses, then hers, and looked her dead in the eye. "You think I'm just saying this to make you feel good? I've always thought you were sexy, Jenna. That's never been a question."

Yeah, well, clothes could camouflage quite a bit.

Mac slid his hand down, his fingers curling around the elastic on the top of her cover-up. Jenna jerked.

"Don't," he ordered. "Let me."

Closing her eyes, she waited for him to pry her security blanket down. She hated this. Hated knowing she would be exposed in seconds. No, she'd never worn a swimsuit around him. She rarely put a suit on, period. Why was he doing this? To prove he could?

"Mac." Her plea came out as a whisper.

The material slid over her breasts and down her torso, and Jenna sat up, wrapping her arms around her waist in some vain attempt to keep herself covered.

"Lift your hips," he said, continuing to pull the material down.

In no time, he slid the cover-up down her bare legs and tossed it to the side. Jenna clenched her teeth, blinking back the burn of tears threatening to spill.

"Look at me."

Jenna pulled in a breath and turned to Mac. As he kept his eyes on hers, he gently eased her arms away from her body. "Hiding such beauty should be a crime."

When he said these things in such a convincing way, Jenna believed him. Mac kept secrets regarding his business at times, but he'd never flat-out lied to her face. Was he being sincere? Why did this tender moment feel so intimate, so raw and…real?

"I'm a heavy girl," she told him, still holding his gaze. "I know what I look like in a suit, Mac."

"If you know how stunning, sexy and intriguing you look, then we're on the same page." His smile nearly killed her. He wasn't mocking, he was flirting.

Mac. The good-time guy with a mysterious side.

When he smoothed his hand over her knee and up her thigh, Jenna tensed again.

"Wh-what are you doing?" she asked.

With a shrug, his eyes darted to where his hand traveled across her skin. "Being affectionate. What if someone is watching? What if someone can see us, but we can't see them?"

Right. The charade. But as his fingertips continued their path up and down her bare leg, Mac leaned in and kissed her shoulder.

"Mac—"

"Jenna," he murmured against her skin.

He kissed her again, higher on her shoulder this time, and Jenna couldn't stop the instinctive reaction as she tipped her head to the side, silently pleading for more of his touch.

Whatever he was doing felt absolutely amazing. For right now, she didn't care if someone was watching, she didn't care if she was sitting here in only her plain, old, black, one-piece suit. What she did care about was how Mac made her feel beautiful with his touch, with words that were from his heart.

When he slid his hand from her leg, up over her stomach, she stiffened slightly until he kept going. Continuing his trail over her breast, her collarbone and finally her jaw, Mac turned her face toward his and captured her mouth.

Jenna would never get used to this. Each time he kissed her, all three times now, seemed like the first. Nerves swirled around in her stomach, excitement and arousal kicked into high gear and she completely lost all touch with reality. Mac knew what he was doing and he knew he could kiss her anytime he wanted.

No, she didn't want to get hurt at the end of all of this, but she couldn't tell him no right now, either. Call her a masochist, she didn't care. How could she care about anything when Mac's hand slid into her hair, his other hand wrapping around her waist as he shifted his body and leaned into her?

Jenna laid a hand on his chest to steady herself. That hard muscle beneath her palm had her curling her fingertips into him, wanting more, greedily trying to take it.

Mac's lips slid over hers. There was so much power, so much dominance radiating from him. The complete and utter control on his part was a turn-on…something she never thought she'd be attracted to.

"Let me take you back to the bungalow," he muttered

against her lips. "Let's finish what we started the other night."

He tipped her head back, kissing a path along her jawline, then back toward her ear. That warm breath sent shivers racing all over her body.

"My word. You two are heating up the beach."

Jenna jerked away from Mac, but he kept his hold around her waist and threw a smile over her shoulder. Her mother's elated tone had Jenna cringing.

"Good morning, Mary."

Seriously? Did this not faze him at all? They'd been caught making out by her mother and he was acting as if they'd run into each other in the milk aisle at the grocery store.

Jenna twisted, eyed her cover-up mere feet away and glanced at her mother. "Morning, Mom."

Her mother's crooked grin spoke volumes.

"You two may want to head back to your bungalow," she said with a wink. "Young love can be a bit spontaneous, can't it?"

"That it can," Mac agreed.

He stood and extended a hand to help Jenna up. She grabbed her cover-up and let Mac pull her to her feet. Jenna held the material in front of her as she stared back at her still-smiling mother.

"I didn't get to see you yesterday," Jenna said, hoping this encounter wasn't as awkward as it was feeling.

"I heard you went to dinner with Amy and Nathan. I love that my girls have found two wonderful men who clearly make them so happy."

Jenna swallowed the lump of guilt as Mac slid his arm around her waist and pulled her closer to his side. The support he silently gave her was humbling. He was always giving, especially a few moments ago when he'd been ready to give her himself.

But that was not a thought she could entertain right now.

"Well, don't let me keep you two," Mary went on, waving her hand. "I need to finish my morning walk and then head to my massage. I may never leave this place."

Jenna instantly found herself wrapped in her mother's arms. "You look so happy, darling," her mom whispered in her ear before pulling away. Mary squeezed Jenna's shoulders and blinked back tears. "This is exactly the life I wanted for you. A strong man who will treat you right. Both of my girls are settling down."

Quickly, Jenna pasted a smile on her face, keeping up with the farce that had snowballed out of control.

After one more quick hug, Mary pulled away and patted Mac on the shoulder. "You're perfect for her."

As her mother made her way down the beach, Jenna wrestled into her cover-up, keeping her back to Mac who hadn't said a word. She suddenly felt awful. This wasn't right. None of it.

But as soon as she turned, that desire in Mac's eyes was still evident and she couldn't be strong enough for both of them because if he so much as touched her again, she didn't know that she could say no. She'd nearly proven that point moments ago.

Would she have gone back to the bungalow if her mother hadn't shown up? Would she and Mac be making love right now?

No. Because they weren't in love. He loved women in general and she refused to be just another proverbial notch.

"I need to get back to work," she said, skirting around

him. Making a quick, classy getaway on sand wasn't the easiest of moves, but Jenna forced herself to keep going.

As she made her way to the dock that led to the walkways to various bungalows, Jenna sensed Mac right behind her. She didn't slow down, couldn't turn and look at him right now. Honestly, she wanted to be left alone, but no doubt Mac would march right in behind her and make some argument for why they should give into their now-obvious desire for each other. Something about acting on emotions and consenting adults and such.

But his heart wasn't on the line. Jenna couldn't keep letting herself get close to Mac or she would find herself crushed at the end of the week, when they returned to Miami as friends.

As she entered the bungalow, she knew she had to put to the brakes on this. Just as she was able to catch her breath, Mac stepped through the door. Only a few feet from him, Jenna concentrated on his face and not the bare chest still exposed, still casting out too much temptation.

"This has to stop," she stated. "I can't do it anymore."

Mac crossed his arms, shifting his stance. "Don't be afraid of what happened, Jenna. I'm trying to keep my promise to you and play this part, but damn it, I'm having a difficult time keeping things G-rated."

Said the man who rotated women with the slightest shift in the wind's direction. To Jenna what they'd just shared was…special.

He'd gotten her out of her cover-up; he'd shown her how beautiful she was with very few words. She knew he wasn't just trying to seduce her. Mac cared for her and wouldn't hurt her like that, but he had no clue how fast she was falling for him. If he did, he would be on his jet before she could say "best friend."

"This isn't a game," she cried. "I thought I could distance myself from all of this emotionally. I thought I could pretend, but I can't. It's too much."

The muscle in his jaw clenched. "If you want me to leave, say the word."

His eyes held hers and Jenna saw a flash of hurt there. Jenna didn't want to think she had the power to hurt him. Mac was a force of nature, he was strong, much stronger than she was when it came to personal matters.

But he stared at her, waiting for her reply, and she only had one option.

"You should go."

Nine

"Honey, you're late."

Because I didn't want to come.

Jenna pasted on a smile and shrugged. "Sorry, Mom. I got caught up in the flower arrangements taking over my kitchen."

Mary glanced around and Jenna knew what was coming next. Cringing, she waited.

"Where's Mac?"

"He wasn't feeling well." The lie slid easily off her tongue. And it was that ease of lying to her mother's face that had Jenna needing this farce to come to an end. "Let's join the others."

Jenna slid her arm through her mother's and steered her toward the bonfire already in full swing. A beach party with music, laughter and what appeared to be enough food for a small village was exactly the distraction Jenna needed.

Spotting her, Martin immediately pulled one of the bridesmaids off to the side, no doubt to feed her some line of BS...poor girl. But if that meant he was leaving Jenna alone, who was she to complain?

It was a perfect evening. The warm breeze from the ocean felt amazing and a small band was playing some tropical tunes that blended romance and fun. Her sister had definitely gone all out with her budget, but Amy's defense had been that she only planned on marrying once so she was going big.

"The fresh pineapple is heaven," her mother commented. "You have to get a plate of food. Those kabobs with glazed chicken... I have no clue what the chef did, but I need that recipe."

Jenna half listened as her mother discussed the varieties of food available. She really wasn't in the mood to eat, wasn't in the mood to party. She'd been hoping that once she got here she would perk up, but all she kept seeing was Mac's face as he'd walked out of the bungalow. She'd hurt him. Knowing she even had that ability was crippling because she loved him. Loved the friend he always was, and was starting to love the man.

The shaky ground she walked on could crumble at any moment and where would that leave her? Falling face-first into a sea of humiliation and heartache.

"I'm actually not that hungry," she told her mother as she took a step back. "If you'll excuse me a minute, I want to find Amy and ask about the arrangements."

"Of course, dear. She was talking with Nathan and the caterer right before you got here, but I don't see her now."

Jenna patted her mother's arm. "I'll find her. Go dance and have fun. You look beautiful tonight."

Mary's smile widened. "You're sweet. Please, don't

feel you have to stay all evening. If Mac isn't feeling well, go back to him."

Go back to him. If he were actually hers, she never would have left his side.

"He'll be fine," Jenna assured her mom as she turned and headed in the other direction. At least she'd told her mom the truth. Mac would be fine. He was always fine.

But Jenna wondered where he'd gone. When he left he hadn't taken his stuff, but she hadn't seen him for several hours. Maybe he was waiting until she was gone to come get his things? She had no idea, but as soon as she got back, she was going to text him. She'd tried a few minutes ago and he hadn't responded yet. She couldn't handle this tension, the conflict she'd single-handedly placed between them.

Jenna smiled and said her hellos as she passed by the familiar faces from the wedding party. Amy's best friend from college, her best friend from grade school and her husband. Everyone was here for a good time and Jenna wasn't about to put a damper on her sister's big moment. The pity party could come later, when Jenna was back in her bungalow alone with the pint of ice cream she'd requested from the kitchen.

Jenna didn't care if sobbing into ice cream made her a cliché. She'd made her best friend pretend to be her lover and it had gone horribly wrong, so bring on the clichés and bring on the spoon because she was ready to dive into that container of Rocky Road.

"You look stunning tonight."

Jenna jerked around to see Martin standing way too close for her comfort. How had he sneaked up on her? Oh, yeah, she'd been busy plotting her evening of gluttony.

She resisted the urge to adjust her halter-style dress. "I'm looking for Amy."

Just as she turned to leave, Martin grabbed her arm. He didn't squeeze or use force, but she didn't want his hands on her.

Her eyes dropped to where he held her, then up to meet his gaze. "Let go."

"I just want a minute to talk now that your goon isn't around." He let his hand fall back to his side. "Can you give me two minutes?"

Jenna let out a laugh as she squared her shoulders and crossed her arms. "Two minutes? You think that will be enough time to undo the damage? Because I could give you two months to grovel and I still wouldn't forgive you or take you back."

Martin shook his head as he ran a hand through his blond hair. "I'm human, Jenna. I made a mistake."

"I'm human, too, but I wouldn't purposely hurt someone I care about."

And the second the words left her mouth, she realized she'd just told one more lie. What kind of person had she turned into? All to get Martin to stay away. How was that working out for her? Because Mac was gone and Martin was less than a foot away.

"Let me make it up to you," he pleaded. "You don't want to marry an O'Shea. You know what they say about that family. I put up with you being his friend, but I can't stand by and let you marry him."

Martin's eyes darted over her shoulder, then widened. Immediately Jenna knew who stood behind her. She tensed because Martin was still sporting the evidence of Mac's rage.

"Oh, don't let me stop you," Mac stated. Did he sound... amused? "I'd like to hear more of these rumors regarding my family and how you can't let Jenna marry me."

Standing directly between them, Jenna kept her back

to Mac. Hopefully she wouldn't have to become the human shield between these two.

"We're having a private conversation," Martin stated.

Mac's hands curled around Jenna's bare shoulders. "When you're talking to my girl, you're not allowed privacy. So, please, don't let me stop this speech because I'm sure you rehearsed it."

Tension seemed to envelop them, blocking them off from the cheerful party, the upbeat music and the laughter. It was more than Jenna could handle.

"Go, Martin. Before this gets worse. Just…go."

His eyes held hers, he opened his mouth as if he wanted to say something more, but finally wised up and turned away. Jenna remained still, waiting for Mac to say something, to remove his hands or…she didn't know what, but she didn't want to make the first move.

When he seemed content to stay just as he was, Jenna sighed. "What are you doing here?" she whispered.

"I told you I'd be here for you this week." He brushed her hair aside. Seconds later his lips grazed her ear. "I never go back on a promise, Jenna."

At the contact, chills covered her body. "I'm not sure I can keep this up."

"Are you saying I won the bet?" he asked, a hint of humor to his voice. "Because I'm ready to call in my favor."

Jenna shook her head and turned. "No. I'm not saying you won the bet. There's more to this than some silly bet we placed."

The humor vanished from his face. "For the next few minutes, we're in love. Whatever else we need to discuss can wait until we're alone. Deal?"

Jenna nodded and blew out a breath. "Deal."

Mac wrapped his arms around her, pulling her directly into his warm embrace. "I was never going to walk away," he whispered in her ear. "I only left to give you the space you needed. I would never desert you."

Tears pricked her eyes, emotions clogged her throat. Jenna nodded against his chest because words were not coming to her.

"Oh, you're feeling better."

Her mother's elated voice cut into the moment and Jenna cringed. Would Mac grasp the fact that Jenna had lied to cover for him?

"I wouldn't miss this party," he replied easily, sliding Jenna around to the crook of his side. "Sorry I'm late."

Mary waved a hand in the air. "Don't worry about it. I'm just so glad you could join us. Jenna looks happier than she did when I first saw her."

Mac threw Jenna a heavy-lidded glance. "I'll make sure she's always happy."

The promise in his eyes, the conviction in those words gave Jenna a false sense of hope. Once again. He couldn't possibly know what she was battling within. He couldn't have any idea how much she wanted him to be serious, to be saying these things as a man who was falling in love.

But Mac O'Shea didn't fall—in business or in love. He remained in charge, flitting from one moment to the next without a care in the world.

As if to solidify his statement, Mac kissed her. Nothing too intimate, just his lips to hers. A soft promise. A gentle understanding that he was a man of his word.

Yet, as plain and simple as his kiss was, Jenna felt as if she was twisted even tighter in his web. Despite her telling him to leave, he'd come back for her. He had nothing to gain by being here. Everything he'd done in the past three days was for her.

How could she not fall in love with a man who made

her feel so special, put her first in his life and made her toes curl with the simplest of touches?

Those were some very good questions. Too bad she had none of the answers.

Ten

Mac stood on the edge of the dock, staring out at the inky water. They'd stayed at the bonfire well past midnight. For the requisite toast, Jenna had opted to have a glass of wine. He'd never seen her drink because of her mother's past alcoholism. Mary had been clean for several years now and she'd not batted an eyelash when the wine was brought out. She was a strong woman; she'd raised strong daughters.

But the glass of wine on Jenna's empty stomach had made her woozy and she'd clung to him all the way home.

Home. Ridiculous to think of this little structure on stilts in the water as home. Even more ridiculous to think of living with Jenna as *home*.

Once they'd returned, Mac had showered quickly to rid himself of the bonfire's smoky scent. When he'd come out, Jenna had been pouring a glass of juice.

She'd downed that glass and headed to the shower.

Mac had waited outside the bathroom door until she was done. The last thing he needed was her falling and hitting her head because she wasn't used to alcohol.

Now he stood out on the deck, as far away from temptation as he could handle. Jenna was proving to be more of a problem than he'd originally thought. Well, she wasn't necessarily the problem, but his unwanted emotions were. Over and over he told himself to leave her alone, to stop all the touching and kissing, but then he got near her and all of that logic vanished, quickly replaced by hormones.

Bare feet shuffled behind him and he forced himself to remain still. She was tipsy, no doubt vulnerable, and the last thing she needed was flirty advances from him. When she'd sent him away earlier, he'd promised himself when he came back he'd be on his best behavior. That hadn't lasted long.

But he couldn't forget the image of Jenna's face when he'd arrived at the bonfire. She'd truly been shocked that he'd come back. Had she honestly thought he wouldn't be there for her? What type of men had she been dating?

"My father left my mother when Amy and I were younger."

Her soft words slid over him and he knew she was about to let him into that part of her world he'd never seen. After years of friendship, he truly knew nothing about her father…only that the man wasn't in the picture. Mac also knew Jenna and Amy had different fathers, but everything else he knew about Jenna was from events he'd been present for over the past decade.

"Apparently he'd been cheating on her for some time," Jenna went on. "Mom had no clue. She'd been so in love. She would have dinner ready when he came home from work. She'd iron his clothes and have them ready. She was always hugging him or laughing at his lame jokes. I saw the love in her eyes."

Mac didn't like the sorrow in Jenna's tone, but he wasn't about to stop her now. He needed to see inside her life in order to understand her better. But maybe she didn't want him to know all of this.

"Is this a drunk confession?" he asked, only half joking.

"I'm not drunk." Jenna laughed. "Okay, maybe a little tipsy, but I know full well what I'm telling you."

Mac turned to face her and an instant punch of lust hit him hard. She leaned against the door frame, casual as you please, wearing a short, strapless dress that clung to her damp skin. Her wet hair lay perfectly over one shoulder. The glistening droplets covering her body caught the moonlight with each breath she took and it was all Mac could do to stand still and not go touch her.

"My mother was devastated when my dad left." Jenna's arms came up, wrapping around her midsection. "She was completely blindsided and the bastard left her a note. He was such a coward. He left a note to a woman who was so in love with him she would've done anything he asked. He left two little girls who had to grow up too fast and learn the harsh realities of life and marriage."

The hitch in her voice gutted him. She'd dreamed of a wedding, she'd kept her mother's wedding dress. Clearly she believed she'd find "the one" despite all she'd witnessed as a young girl.

His Jenna had hopes and dreams, and he was riding a fine line of destroying everything. He knew she was getting attached. He could feel it in her touch, taste the emotion in her kisses.

"Amy and I had no clue how to help my mom," she went on, staring out into the night as if she were watching the events unfold before her. "She rarely got out of bed. When she did, it was to get a drink. Finally she started keeping the bottles by her bed. Amy would fix my hair for school and make sure to hold my hand as we went to the bus stop. Amy and I were pretty good at covering up the lack of parenting at our house until it came time for report cards and Amy forged my mom's signature."

Mac could easily see these two sisters looking after each other, and worrying for their mother who had been slapped in the face by fate's harsh hand.

"Long story short, our neighbors, who had kids our age, ended up taking us in while mom went to rehab." Jenna shook her head as if to clear her thoughts. "We don't talk about that time because it was so dark, so depressing and that's not who my mother is."

"That's why one glass of wine has you stumbling."

Jenna nodded. "I'll have a glass of wine every now and then, but I saw how it nearly destroyed my mother. I saw how falling for the wrong man crippled her to the point I didn't recognize her anymore."

And that's why she was fighting this attraction. Everything fell into place now. He'd vowed before not to touch her when he didn't have to, but now Mac knew he needed to be hands off unless they were in public and trying to keep up this charade.

Blowing out a frustrated breath, Mac moved to the hammock and eased down. Flipping his feet up, he reclined, lacing his hands behind his head.

"Go on to bed, Jenna. We've had a long day."

Silence filled the space, but she didn't move. He was hanging on by a thread here. As if he weren't physically attracted enough, now she went and threw vulnerability into the mix. He couldn't handle knowing she was hurting, but he only knew one way to console her. Having sex with her would be a temporary moment of happiness and once they were done, she'd hate him and he couldn't live with that.

Having Jenna hurt at his hands wasn't an option. This could never be just a fling for her and he should've accepted that from the beginning. Or, maybe in the back of his mind he *had* realized it, but didn't want to face the truth staring him in the face.

"Thank you for coming back," she murmured. "I thought you'd leave the island."

"I promised I'd be here for you, didn't I?"

"Yeah, but things are more intense than either of us intended."

Understatement of the year. And he was seriously rethinking his entire strategy.

"I'm sorry I hurt you earlier," she went on. "I'm not good at lying to people I love."

"A few more days and this will all be over."

"Will it?" she asked. "Because I'm not sure I can forget how you kissed me, how you've held me, touched me."

Shutting his eyes, he gritted his teeth and attempted to dig deep for willpower. If she'd told him this before her confession about her father, he would have been all over her. But now he knew why she was so leery and he knew he had to take a step back…even if it killed him.

"Can you forget?" she whispered.

"Leave it, Jenna. Go to bed."

"Where will you be?"

"Right here."

The second he heard her cross the deck, he froze. He opened his eyes to see her standing next to him, her gaze on his.

"You don't have to stay out here," she told him, her voice huskier than seconds ago. "Maybe I'm ready to give in. Maybe I'm ready to stop being so damn good all the time and holding out for the perfect man in my life."

"It's the wine," he told her. "In the morning you'll feel different."

He pulled his hands from behind his head and laid them on his abdomen. Those hands had done some ugly things, too many to even count, and he didn't deserve to have them on her body. He didn't deserve what she willingly offered.

"What if I don't feel different, Mac?" she asked. Those eyes of hers remained locked on to his and it was all he could do not to jerk her down on top of him and finish what she'd started.

"Go to bed, Jenna. Alone."

"Mac—"

"Damn it," he yelled, hating when she jumped. "You have no idea what you're saying. I don't do relationships, I do sex. That's it. I don't want more and I won't give more. We're friends. I shouldn't have taken it so far when we were alone, but you do things to me. I lost my head for a bit. I promise it won't happen again."

She bit down on her lip, crossing her arms in front of her chest. "You're a liar. You want me as much as I want you."

She was right. He was a liar. Millions of dollars rolled in from his ability to lie and cheat. He'd ordered killings and may again sooner rather than later. He didn't deserve this beautiful, sweet woman before him.

Mac eased up slightly on the swaying hammock and stared her straight in the eyes. "I can't want you. Not like that. Not anymore."

He heard her breath hitch, saw the shimmer in her eyes and he cursed himself. He'd never forgive himself if they were intimate and she fell for him. They'd go their separate ways in Miami and she'd be hurt. She couldn't be part of his life, not the ugly world he was born into. She'd be ruined and he hated like hell that Martin had been right.

With a tilt of her chin as she blinked back tears, Jenna took only a second to compose herself. "I never thought you'd turn into a coward."

"Coward?"

She leaned down, gripped the ropes on either side of him, sending the hammock swaying slightly. "You're afraid of wanting me for more than sex. You know it, and you're terrified because I know it."

Damn it, this was going too far. "Jenna—"

"Unless you're about to tell me I'm right, then save it." Her eyes narrowed as she licked her lips. Those lips he'd tasted, those same lips he craved when they weren't on his. "I'm going to bed alone. I don't care what you do anymore. If you can't be honest with me, then we have nothing more to say."

With a quick jerk he didn't see coming, she flipped the hammock and sent him plummeting face-first onto the deck. Mac turned his head just in time to see her bare feet disappear into the bungalow. The bedroom door slammed seconds later.

Mac couldn't help but laugh as he lay there on the hard floor. One glass of wine and his Jenna was aroused, angry and feisty.

Damn if that didn't make him want her more than ever.

Eleven

Jenna woke with a start when her pillow was jerked from beneath her head. Disoriented, she blinked against the bright sunlight streaming through her open blinds. Blinds she'd closed before bed.

Jenna turned her head to see Mac standing beside her bed, holding her beloved pillow.

"Whatever you're smirking about, go away and give me back my pillow."

His rich laughter flooded the room. "Get up, sunshine. Today we're getting back to Mac and Jenna. No wedding talk, no pretend relationship, just us."

Figuring she had no choice, and since she was already awake, Jenna sat up in her bed and rubbed her eyes. "What do you mean, back to us?"

He tossed her pillow behind her and took a seat on the edge of the bed, caging her legs in on either side with his hands. "I mean things have been too intense lately.

We need a break from this charade and I just want to be us again."

She couldn't agree more. One of them was going to break if they didn't step away from the emotional chaos that had been controlling them. But how could they just be themselves? They were on this island with a slew of wedding people, her mother and sister and Martin.

"What did you have in mind?" she asked.

"Just get dressed and meet me out front in five minutes."

Jenna laughed as Mac jumped off the bed and headed toward the door. "I'll need more than five minutes to throw clothes on and brush my teeth."

He gripped the edge of the door and threw her a look over his shoulder. "Fine. Seven minutes. No more."

Rolling her eyes, Jenna grabbed her pillow and tossed it across the room. Mac closed the door just in time.

Throwing her covers off, Jenna was out of bed in seconds flat. She got ready quicker than she would've liked, but with her hair up in a knot on her head, a simple tank sundress and clean teeth, this was as good as it was going to get. Who knew what Mac had planned? He was always acting on a whim, living from moment to moment.

Jenna was relieved he didn't bring up her blatant advances from last night. Perhaps whatever outing he had planned was a way to get them to move beyond this awkward, warped version of a fake engagement. She was too confused over what was going on, between what was real and what was completely fabricated, to keep up the pretense.

The bedroom door flew open just as she slid into her silver-sequined flip-flops.

"Oh, good. You're ready a minute early."

Jenna eyed her extremely anxious friend. "Am I going

to need a purse or my beach bag? A swimsuit? A little hint would be helpful."

"You look fine." He jerked his head. "Let's go."

With a shrug, she followed him out. She had no idea what he had planned, but she was more than ready for a break. Who knew she'd need a break from her fake boyfriend only a few days into the relationship? Perhaps she wasn't cut out for relationships of any kind.

Last night she'd nearly botched their friendship. How would this morning be playing out had Mac given in? Had they spent the night together, would he still be planning this surprise for her? Or would he have woken with regrets?

She shoved aside the what-ifs because, in reality, Mac was giving them a new start this morning. Maybe he was doing this so she didn't feel uncomfortable. Or maybe her throwing herself at him had meant nothing and this was just another day.

"You're frowning." Mac took her hand and led her down the dock. "Everything that happened before this morning has no place in your mind."

Jenna blinked against the sun. "Just tell me what we're doing."

He stopped, turned and offered her a smile that had her toes curling in her flip-flops. "We're going on a helicopter ride. We'll be away from the resort, nobody will be around, no cell phones, no fake relationships. Just Mac and Jenna."

"Sounds simple enough," she replied with a smile of her own. "I've never been in a helicopter."

Squeezing her hand, he headed to the end of the dock. "Then I'm happy to be your first."

Jenna leaned over and stared down at all the loveliness below. The lush, natural beauty, the sparkling water surrounding the small island. No buildings, no people. Absolutely breathtaking.

"I've never seen anything like this," she said into her headset. "I'm not sure I want to know how you managed to get a helicopter at your disposal. Not to mention the fact I didn't even know you could fly a helicopter."

Mac's rich laughter came through the earphones. "There's plenty you still don't know about me, Jenna. But you know the important stuff."

The important stuff. More like what he considered important. Still, she hadn't exactly opened up to him about her past…or the feelings that were overwhelming her now.

"Mac, look." She pointed to the breathtaking waterfall that came into view. "It's gorgeous."

Mac maneuvered the helicopter down closer. Jenna nearly plastered herself to the window as she watched the aqua water spill into a small, naturally made pool. The tropical plants surrounding the area seemed to invite only those who were lucky enough to find it.

As Mac took the helicopter even lower, Jenna turned to him. "I've never seen anything so stunning."

His eyes flickered to hers briefly. "I have," he murmured as he watched the controls. His words were so soft, so low, but she'd heard them loud and clear through the headset.

"What are you doing?" she asked as he hovered over the ground.

"Landing," he said matter-of-factly.

"Landing? Did you plan on bringing me here?"

With a shrug, he maneuvered the helicopter down on the ground and killed the engines. Finally, when he took off his own headphones, she did, too.

"Mac?"

A slow, easy smile slid over his face. "I knew this island was here. I wanted to show you, but I wasn't sure if we could land here or not."

Jenna squealed as she stepped from the chopper. "This is the coolest place ever."

Smoothing down her cotton dress, she tiptoed over the bright vegetation. The colors in all the blossoms and blooms were beyond overwhelming. She'd never seen anything like this.

Spinning in a circle, arms outstretched, she attempted to soak up all the beauty, to fully absorb everything all at once.

She caught Mac's smile as his eyes locked on to hers. "I knew you'd love this place," he told her. "I was hoping I could get you close enough because I found out there were plants and flowers here that are nearly nonexistent anywhere else in the world."

He knew her so well. He may buy jewels and fancy gifts for his arm candy, but Jenna knew their bond was too deep for such superficial things. When he wanted to surprise her, he went above and beyond.

"This is even better than the time you brought me a pint of Rocky Road and that terrible movie when I twisted my ankle."

She'd joined her local gym in an attempt to get healthier, but she'd tripped over the elliptical before she could even get on the darn thing. Jenna had taken that as a sign and never gone back.

"I'd say this surprise trumps that one," he agreed with a laugh. "Let's explore."

Mac held out his hand and as she placed her palm against his, she couldn't help but smile. The day was gorgeous, Mac was fighting to keep this relationship right where it should be. This is what they were. They were smiles and good times. They were surprises and last-minute planning. Well, he was last-minute; she preferred a spreadsheet.

"I can't believe you did this for me," she muttered as they walked toward the rushing sound of the waterfall.

"You needed a break. I wanted to take you somewhere where we could be ourselves, we didn't have to worry about pretending or cell phones or work."

"This is perfect."

Jenna's foot caught on a thick root, sending her tumbling against Mac. He caught her with his firm grip and held her tight. With her face right against his chest, she inhaled that familiar woodsy cologne and tried not to moan or close her eyes at the fact that just the smell of him turned her on. That's not what they were here for. He may have taken his flirty advances into another territory, but then he'd backed off. He'd wised up or given up, one of the two, and pushed her away.

So, whatever chance she may have had with her best friend, it was gone, and if she wanted to salvage the greatest friendship she'd ever had, she needed to cool it.

"Okay?" he asked, tipping her chin up.

With a nod, Jenna eased away. "I'm good. Just need to watch where I step."

He kept his hand in hers as he led her around the island. They discussed plants, flowers and he actually told her a few things she didn't know. Apparently the mysterious Mac O'Shea had done some homework before taking her out on this little excursion.

When he bent down to pluck a bright yellow flower, she halted her steps. He slid the blossom behind her ear, shoving her hair away, smoothing it on down past her shoulders. A shiver crept over her at the slightest touch and the way he seemed to be seducing her without even trying. Was he even aware of the effect he had on her?

"Don't look at me like that," he murmured, his fingertips trailing along her jawline before tapering off.

Jenna blinked and started walking ahead. Any response would only add fuel to the desire or start an argument, and at this point, they couldn't afford either.

The sound of the rushing water seemed to echo. Jenna walked on a few more steps then froze. She was at ground level with nature's pool, watching as the cascades fell over the edge of the cliff. The crystal water seemed so inviting, so refreshing. She'd worked up a slight sweat walking around, but she didn't mind one bit.

Slipping free of her flip-flops, Jenna tiptoed down to the water's edge. The coolness washed over her feet. She reached to the modest hem of her dress, and held it up as she waded in just a bit further.

Behind her, she heard Mac stepping in, as well. "This is perfect," he stated.

Keeping her back to him, she stopped when the water reached her knees. "I could stay here forever."

Only the sounds of a random bird chirping and the rushing of the waterfall enveloped them. Besides the beauty of their surroundings, there was nothing here that demanded their time or attention. Mac, Jenna and their own private island were all that existed in this world.

Jenna glanced over her shoulder and nearly gasped. Mac had taken his shirt off, those tanned muscles glistening in the sunshine. His board shorts were wet as he stepped in even further.

"If you want to take your dress off, there's no one else here," he told her.

Swallowing, Jenna kept her grip on the material bunched in her hand. "No, I'm…"

Mac stood only a few feet away, but he eased closer. "It's just me, Jenna. Don't be embarrassed."

"I only have on a bra and panties."

Mac quirked a brow. "And how is that different from a swimsuit?"

"I don't like wearing a suit, either."

"I know." He took her hand and opened her fingers, releasing the material. "You're beautifully made, no matter what you think or what you've been told. I'm not pressuring you, but if you want to swim in this once-in-a-lifetime place, then do it. Don't let insecurities rob you of this moment."

Why did he have to be so right? Why did he have to get inside her head and drive out all of the doubts? She'd justified each and every insecurity and felt she had a right to them. But when Mac talked to her, when he used that voice of reason, she listened. If she let her low self-esteem run her life, she'd miss out on some amazing things.

Turning away, she gripped the hem of her dress and slid it up over her head. Using the material as a shield, she moved closer to the shore and gave it a toss. Pulling in a deep breath, she rounded back and froze.

Mac's intense gaze was on hers, his hand extended, inviting her to join him.

Just friends.

Every now and then that reminder crept back into her head.

But there was something very intimate about being in a remote location with your friend, wearing nothing but your underwear.

No matter what happened today, this would be a memory she'd keep forever.

Twelve

What the hell was he thinking, inviting her to take that dress off? He'd slept in a damn hammock last night to avoid temptation and here he was begging for it to be rubbed in his face.

Jenna was absolutely breathtaking in her simple pink bra and panty set. Women threw themselves at him, purposely wore the sexiest of lingerie to entice him, but nothing got his attention more than a self-conscious Jenna wearing cotton. She moved him…so much that he had no idea what label to put on his emotions.

But he'd turned her away for a reason and he needed to keep in mind that, after this week, they both would return to Miami and the life they were used to. As friends.

Between thoughts of her in bed last night and texting Ryker, Mac hadn't gotten much sleep. Ryker was still playing cat and mouse with Shane. Unfortunately, Braden was still MIA and Mac was starting to worry.

He was also growing concerned he'd have to make a decision about Shane in short order.

Not something he wanted to think about while holding Jenna's hand in a place that could rival paradise.

"I know I keep saying it, but this place is so amazing."

She slid her hand free of his and ran her fingertips through the water. She dunked down so the water just skimmed the tops of her shoulders and Mac knew she was trying to keep her body hidden from him. He wasn't going to say anything. He didn't want to call her out or make her even more embarrassed. All he wanted was for her to see herself the way he did, the way any man with breath in his lungs would see a voluptuous woman.

"We probably shouldn't stay long, though."

Mac shook his head and slid onto his back to float.

"In a place like this, time doesn't exist."

"You're right. But I almost feel guilty for leaving and just—"

"Enjoying yourself?" he asked, coming back up to face her. "Don't feel guilty. The flowers are coming along so don't even think about those. And as for Martin, if I keep seeing him staring at you, I can't guarantee I'll hold myself back again."

Jenna laughed. "Hold yourself back? You punched him."

Mac nodded. "In my head I did more. He's lucky."

A sadness slipped over her features as she glanced away. "I wish you wouldn't be so cavalier about violence. You're too good of a man for that."

Mac clenched his teeth. He wasn't a good man. Moments ago he was contemplating making a call to end a life. There was evil in his family, though Braden was doing his damnedest to move away from that aspect of their activities. If Mac had to make the call, he would do so without a shadow of a doubt. He didn't make mistakes and he sure as hell wouldn't jump into a decision like this without fully analyzing every possible angle.

"You're my priority here," he told her. "You called me to help, and this is me helping. I don't like how he looks at you, how he treated you. He doesn't even deserve to be here, but that's not my call. I will protect you from getting hurt again, though. That much I can and will control."

Jenna's eyes widened; she bit down on her lower lip before turning away and diving into the water. She disappeared for a moment and popped up closer to the waterfall. With her dark hair slicked back, she looked like some type of dream rising from the waters. She was glorious, she was perfection…and for now she was his. He would resist temptation and give her this day of relaxation, no matter the cost to his feelings.

But taking his eyes off of her was not even a possibility. She floated easily on her back, her face tipped up to the sun, her mouth curved in a subtle smile that took his breath away.

Splashing water up onto his bare shoulders didn't help cool him off. Mac wasn't too certain anything would at this point. The sound of the rushing waterfall seemed to drown out everything else. Well, everything but his thoughts.

"You're frowning," Jenna stated as she waded closer to him. "How can anyone frown in a place like this?"

He blinked, attempting to will his demons away. "I didn't mean to."

As she neared him, her body lifted from the water as she threw her arms out to the side and closed her eyes. "I never want to leave. Ever."

He laughed at her childlike declaration, but as soon as she dropped her arms, the straps on her bra slid down over her shoulders. Without thinking, Mac reached out with both hands and pushed them back up. But instead of letting go and backing away, he curled his fingers around her wet, bare skin.

Those expressive eyes widened as she licked her bottom lip. Her heavy inhale pressed her chest out just enough to brush against his.

"Mac," she murmured.

"I know." Keeping his grip on her, he closed his eyes and told himself to pull away, but he couldn't. Not yet. "I didn't bring you here for this. But damn it, Jenna. I can't keep my hands off you."

With a tip of her chin, she reached up and held on to his wrists. "You know I won't be like all those other women in your life. That's not who I am."

Mac swallowed. "It's not who I want to be," he whispered. He had no idea if she heard him over the waterfall, but sleeping around wasn't something he'd set out to do. He'd never wanted a relationship, and being with women who were on the same page as him seemed to work. But right now, he felt…dirty. As if he wasn't good enough for her. He hated feeling like this.

Maybe he couldn't sleep with her, but that didn't mean he couldn't show her how much she meant to him.

With careful movements, and keeping his eyes on hers, he pushed the straps back down. Her hands remained around his wrists, but she didn't try to stop him. When he slid his fingertips over the flesh just above the lace trim of her bra, her body trembled beneath his touch.

When her hands tightened and she started to shake her head, Mac cut her off. "This isn't about me," he explained. "Let me show you."

Jenna remained silent, but held his gaze.

"Trust me," he added.

The slightest of nods gave him the green light he'd been waiting for. He hadn't even realized how monumental this was, but there was no way he could ever let her think she'd be like any other woman in his life. She was so much more.

She let go of his wrists, giving him complete control. Mac reached around and unfastened her bra, then removed the unwanted garment. Giving it a fling toward the shore, he allowed his eyes to rake over her exposed body. The water lapped just beneath her bare breasts and he could tell by the way she'd curled her body in and glanced away that she was vulnerable and doubting herself.

"You're the most beautiful woman, Jenna. Look at me," he commanded when she kept her eyes averted. "These perfect curves were made for a man's hands." *My hands.*

She didn't reply and he knew she didn't believe him. He was all too happy to show her exactly what he meant. Society had some warped idea of what a beautiful woman should look like, but in his opinion, a woman should be built like a woman. All curves and dips. A perfect layout to explore and enjoy.

Keeping his eyes locked on to hers, he wanted her to see every single emotion in his eyes. He wanted her to understand just how pivotal this moment was. And if he delved any more into that line of thinking, he'd terrify himself. But the last thing he wanted now was to pull away.

Mac cupped her face in his hands. "Don't take your eyes off me."

She didn't nod, didn't speak. She made no motion whatsoever. If Mac let his ego have control he'd think she was under his spell, but it was quite the opposite.

He cupped her breasts, loving how she quivered beneath his touch. When he moved his hands down her sides, she attempted to shift away.

"Never pull away from my touch."

Jenna froze. Keeping his eyes on hers, he let his palms travel over her soft skin beneath the water. Her stomach clenched, her hips tilted and he knew her body was reacting all on its own. Hooking his thumbs under the edge of her panties, he started pulling them down. A bit harder to do in the water, but he was a man with one goal in mind—to make Jenna feel like the beautiful, desirable woman she was.

"Brace your hands on my shoulders."

"Mac—"

"Do it."

Water trickled from her fingertips as she brought her hands from the water and placed them on his shoulders. Without another word, she lifted one foot at a time and let him remove the last of her clothing. Keeping one hand on her hip and the other between her thighs, he watched as her lids lowered halfway, desire completely consuming her. Her lips parted, a soft sigh escaped and Mac wanted more. Much more.

He wanted his name on her lips, he wanted her to know who was pleasuring her and why. He wanted Jenna to see this as much more than a quick release.

When he slid one finger over her center, her fingertips curled into his skin. Mac was barely hanging on by a thread because he couldn't wait to see her come undone. But Jenna was worth the wait.

As he moved his hand, she rocked her hips, never taking her eyes off him. There was something so intimate, so primal about watching her. He didn't think this much with other women, didn't analyze every detail. But he didn't want to mess up a single thing with Jenna.

Mac gripped her waist as his hand moved faster. Her body kept up with his rhythm and Mac watched as a pink tint crept over her face. A sheen of sweat covered her forehead and nose, but she never once took her eyes off him.

Her body jerked. "Mac, I'm—"

"Do it," he demanded.

When she tightened around him, his name slid off her lips like a whispered promise. Her eyes widened as if she wasn't expecting the onslaught. Mac held her close and kept pleasuring her until her body went lax.

Wrapping both hands around her waist, he pulled her against his chest. Her heartbeat seemed to be just as frantic as his own.

The sound of the rushing water, the occasional bird chirping and Jenna's panting were all music to his ears. Nothing else mattered but this moment, this woman. Words eluded him. Honestly, if he opened his mouth right now, he didn't know what he'd say. He was aching to be with her, but he wouldn't put her in that position. Beyond that, he wanted to say something sweet, something romantic…but that wasn't them. They weren't here for romance and he sure as hell didn't want her to get the wrong idea.

Jenna's hand slid over his board shorts, heading toward the one spot he needed her most. But he pulled away.

"No."

Jerking back, her brows drew in as she searched his face. "Why?"

Mac clenched his teeth. "This isn't about me or even us. This was all for you."

A slight grin tipped one corner of her mouth. "Hardly seems fair."

Taking her hands in his, he kissed her fingertips and placed her palms flat on his chest. "I don't want you to think you're like other women. This wasn't about sex, Jenna. I need you to know that."

She stared at him for a moment without saying a word. "I don't know what to think," she finally said. "You don't want anything in return?"

With a painful laugh, Mac shook his head. "You already know the answer to that, but you deserve more and I never want you to think that you're in a group with any other woman I've been with. You're completely different. I've never…"

Damn it. He didn't plan on confessing his doubts. He wanted to pleasure her, enjoy a little swim, have a few laughs and fly back to their bungalow. Why did this have to be so difficult?

"You've never what?" she prompted, moving closer to wrap her arms around his neck.

Swallowing any fear of opening up to her, Mac stated, "I've never just given without expecting something in return. I've never wanted to. A relationship has never been in the future for me so I always make sure to…"

Mercy. The more his thoughts started taking a stroll out of his mouth, the more he sounded like a jerk.

"I've been a bastard," he confessed, guilt slamming into his chest and squeezing like a vice. "I purposely find women who only want one thing and then I move on. I never set out to be that way, Jenna, and I don't know why I'm telling you this."

Mac dropped his head because the last thing he wanted was for Jenna to see him vulnerable or broken. Damn it, he hadn't even known how much this hurt him until he started saying the words out loud. He'd used his body in an attempt to ignore all the anxiety and fear that came with relationships. And maybe he hadn't even noticed until right now.

"You're telling me because you care." She tipped his chin up and he was rewarded with a megawatt smile that told him she completely understood and wasn't judging. "You're telling me because you value our friendship and you don't want to hurt me. And I never thought you were a bastard."

Mac reached up and framed her face. With her lush wet body plastered against his, he never wanted to leave this place, either. Why couldn't they just run away and be—

Wait. What the hell was he thinking? Run away? As in, together? He didn't have time or the emotional stability to attempt anything like a relationship and he sure as hell wouldn't make Jenna his guinea pig.

Just because he'd had some grand epiphany over his suppressed emotions like some damn woman didn't mean he wanted to explore boyfriend territory. He was still out for a good time…he just wanted that with Jenna and then he wanted to move on.

Damn it. He'd created a giant mess and plopped her right smack dab in the middle.

"What you did just now." She bit down on her lip before continuing. "Nobody has ever put my needs first. The way you look at me, the way you touch me…"

"What?" He wanted to hear her say it. Needed to hear her say it. And that made him not only a bastard, but a masochist, because he had nothing to offer her beyond the physical.

"You make me feel beautiful," she whispered.

Every part of Mac wanted to rejoice in the fact that

she'd finally seen herself as he did. "You are, Jenna. I've been trying to tell you that, and I needed to show you. It's been hell trying to keep my hands off you, but I didn't know another way. I wanted you to see how desirable you are, how much a man can completely break by being near you. You've got this power I don't even think you are aware of possessing."

Toying with the ends of his wet hair, Jenna held his gaze. "Things won't be weird between us, will they? Because I can't lose you."

"No," he vowed, praying he wasn't lying. "You won't lose me."

But he wouldn't, couldn't ignore this ache. No matter the internal battle he'd been waging with himself, Mac had gotten the briefest glimpse of Jenna's passion. He knew there was so much more to uncover and he planned on doing just that in the remaining days. He could figure out what to do for the long term later.

First things first. Jenna would be his.

Thirteen

The ride back in the helicopter was…strained. So much for things not getting weird. Of course, she couldn't even think about the tension that had settled between them because her body was still humming from that entire experience in the pool by the waterfall.

Oh, mercy, her best friend had skills. Why? Why did they have to be so compatible in the sexual department, too? Why did every part of her still ache for more, even after he'd satisfied her?

What did they talk about now? Seriously. Because no matter what subject they broached, she wasn't sure she could give up any of her mind space to mundane things.

So, silence it was, since he was apparently not up for a chat, either. Was he having regrets?

No. That was one thing she was pretty certain of. He'd made it a point to tell her she was different from other women. His raw honesty had surprised her. She'd never gotten a sense of any vulnerability from him whatso-ever. He'd always been so strong, so confident...so many things she wasn't.

But maybe they were more alike than she'd ever thought.

Once they were back on the main island, they walked to their bungalow. Silence still accompanied them and she worried just how they'd finish out these last few days.

As they headed down the dock toward their hut, Jenna slowed. "My sister and my mom—"

"I see them," he said, reaching for her hand and giving it a slight squeeze.

A sense of relief speared her. She didn't even know she'd been holding her breath, but with the simplest of touches, some of the tension left her in a long exhale.

Then she remembered the charade. He'd most likely taken her hand because her family was watching. That had to be it, because he'd not touched her and barely spoken a word since...the moment she didn't even have a name for.

"There you guys are," her mother exclaimed. "We just knocked and wondered where you went."

Jenna pasted on a smile, a bit relieved that others were here as a buffer. How ridiculous was that? Since when did she need a buffer between her and her best friend? This entire situation had gotten out of control and if she didn't do something to reverse this mess, she'd risk los-ing the best thing that had ever happened to her.

"I hope we can steal your woman away for a few hours," her mother went on, oblivious to the turmoil.

Mac stiffened at her side, she had to assume over the whole "your woman" comment. Jenna tried not to take it personally, though it was rather difficult. Everything about this week, this farce, had become personal.

"We thought with the rehearsal tomorrow and the wedding the next day, we'd take you out tonight." Amy beamed and clasped her hands. "Just us girls."

The thought of going into that bungalow alone with Mac, who may or may not be regretting what they'd just done, didn't exactly appeal to her. She may be a coward, but she needed time to think. Time away from his intense stare, time from his kisses, his touches...

"Give me a few minutes to wash up," she told them, pulling her hand from Mac's. "We found the most incredible waterfall and—"

Oh, no. Was she really going to start in on why she needed a quick shower? Her hair was clearly damp, her clothes were clinging to the wet parts of her body. It was obvious she hadn't just been out on a stroll.

"Go right ahead." Jenna's mom turned her smile toward Mac. "We'll keep him company. I want to hear all about what you've done today."

That's precisely what she was afraid of and why she had to get ready in record time.

"Make the call."

Mac sank down onto the leather sofa in the bungalow, rubbed his forehead and gripped his cell. Ryker's demand was simple, yet so difficult to act on.

"Shane isn't backing down," Ryker went on. "He actually intercepted a piece of art that's due for your auction in Miami in two weeks. It was a legitimate piece, not one we had to acquire, but he's showing his hand."

Which meant the O'Sheas needed to show theirs. Shane was ballsy, that was for damn sure. The man obviously didn't know who he was dealing with, or he was too stupid to care.

But to make the ultimate call on a death was not something Mac took lightly. Still, Shane had threatened Laney and now he was throwing his weight around like he could control the O'Shea family. Hell, no. That man had been a proverbial thorn in their side for years and the fact he thought he could use power against them was unacceptable. But trying to kidnap their sister was grounds for the ultimate punishment.

"I left a voicemail for Braden, but he hasn't returned my call."

Which meant the decision was Mac's to make. Obviously Ryker's choice was to end the conflict before it caused even more trouble. But Mac was starting to get even more concerned with Braden's silence. This wasn't like him and if Mac hadn't been so wrapped up in Jenna, he would've focused more on his own family than his hormones.

"Let me try to reach Braden one more time," Mac said. "I'll let you know."

"Make it fast. I'm done with this guy."

Mac hung up and eased forward, placing his elbows on his knees. Nothing kept Braden quiet for this long. Something was wrong and Mac couldn't tackle any other issue until he knew what it was.

He called Braden, not surprised when he got voicemail, too. After leaving an urgent message, Mac fired off a text. Maybe if he kept badgering him, Braden would answer.

Pushing off the couch, Mac stalked to the fridge to grab a bottle of water. Of course, he had to be careful of the blooms in there because Jenna would murder him in his sleep if he so much as touched a petal.

After grabbing a water, really wishing he had something stronger, he took his phone and the bottle to the deck. His mind was a jumbled mess, between the Shane situation, his brother's unexplained absence and the encounter with Jenna at the waterfall.

Standing on the edge of the deck, watching the orange sun settle on the horizon, Mac recalled the way Jenna had responded so perfectly to his touch. All that pent-up passion just waiting for the right man to come along and release it. For reasons he didn't even want to explain to himself, he wanted to be that man. He wanted nothing more than to...

What? He wanted her in his bed and beyond that he couldn't make plans. He'd be heading back to Miami as soon as this wedding was over because he had an auction that would be in the final stretch of preparations.

Mac took a long pull of his water and willed his phone to vibrate. After waiting another ten minutes, he shot off another text, demanding a reply of any kind or he'd be on the next flight to Boston.

After a few minutes, Braden's reply came.

Zara and I are dealing with something. Don't come home, but business is on you for the next few days. Will talk in person later.

Well, that answered one question but stirred up a whole host of others. What was going on with Braden and Zara? Surely not relationship issues. Those two were so in love it was almost sickening. Braden was so protective, so fierce about keeping Zara safe from their world. Surely nothing had happened to Zara. If so, Braden would've called in all forces to deal with the issue.

Then what was going on?

Mac finished off his water and sighed. At least Braden was safe, but the fact he'd passed all business decisions to Mac spoke volumes as to the severity of Braden's problem.

This also meant Mac would have to make a decision about Ryker's pressing matter.

Damn it.

Mac knew Braden wanted this family to take a less aggressive role in battling their enemies, but Shane had proven time and again that he was nothing more than a menace. He harassed Zara, he'd fought with their late father more than once and now he was getting too close to their main goal of retrieving the scrolls. Mac had to assume that's why he intercepted the recent art, just to prove he could get that close to their operation and slip beneath their noses unnoticed.

Unacceptable.

But, trying to take Laney was an act that could not be overlooked. The man was dead.

Gripping his empty bottle in one hand, Mac shot off a text to Ryker.

Finish it. Text me when you're done.

And with that weighty decision made, he went inside in search of something stronger than water.

Jenna walked back to her bungalow after an amazing dinner and laughs with her mom and sister, still anxious about being alone with Mac. They'd both had time to reevaluate everything and perhaps they could just ignore the fact that he'd given her the most intense sexual experience of her life. Well, maybe *he* could, but she wasn't so sure.

What would happen when she walked in that door? It was late, nearing midnight. Maybe he'd be asleep.

Jenna, Amy and their mom had eaten, gone for dessert, then ended up at their mother's bungalow where they'd discussed memories, good and bad, chatted weddings and even shed a few tears over the monumental day fast approaching.

Now here she was afraid to open the door to her own hut because she had no clue what waited on the other side.

Pulling in a deep breath, she adjusted her strapless sundress, gripped her purse and pushed the door open. Darkness greeted her, along with a sliver of disappointment. Part of her had wanted Mac to be waiting up for her. Going to bed with this sexual tension surrounding them would only cause another sleepless night.

"I didn't think you were coming back."

Jenna jumped and glanced toward the bedroom, where Mac's outline filled the doorway. His arms were braced on the frame above his head, and in the darkness the moonlight cast a soft glow into the hut, showcasing the perfection of his chiseled arms, his broad, bare chest and his narrow waist.

Jenna swallowed and dropped her clutch on the accent table beside the door. "We lost track of time. What did you do while I was gone?"

There. Keep the conversation friendly.

But when Mac pushed off the door and stalked toward her in that sexy, panther-like way, she had a feeling the friendly talk was finished.

"I don't want to talk about what I did." His growl washed over her body, sending shivers and goose bumps racing across her skin. "I don't want to talk at all."

"Mac—"

"No." With the gap closed between them, he placed his hands on either side of her head, caging her against the door. "We've danced around this attraction long enough. After today, I can't ignore it anymore."

Jenna licked her lips, aching with the desire to touch him, to be touched by him. "And what about tomorrow? Or when we get back to Miami?"

"We'll worry about it then."

His lips crushed hers as he gripped her dress and yanked it down, leaving the material to pool at her feet.

Well, that answered one question. She knew what to expect tonight and she wasn't about to put a stop to it, no matter what red flags were waving in her mind. For once, she was going to do what she wanted, damn the consequences.

Mac couldn't touch her enough. Between their excitement at the waterfall earlier and the business decision he'd had to make, Mac was strung way too tight. He needed Jenna, needed to feel her desire, her passion.

She pressed her lush body against his as he continued kissing her. Delicate hands gripped his shoulders. The bite of her nails into his skin only added to the pleasure.

Reaching behind her back, he unfastened her strapless bra and flung it to the side. Hooking his thumbs into her panties, he jerked those down, too. He wanted her completely naked, completely his.

"Mac." She pulled away, panting.

He trailed his lips down her throat and palmed her breasts in his hands. "I have to have you, Jenna."

She cupped the side of his face, pulling his attention up toward her heavy-lidded eyes. "Then have me."

Mac took her hands and put them on the waistband of his shorts. "Show me you want this."

Without hesitation, she removed his shorts, leaving him just as bare as she was. "I can't go slow," he warned. "I want you too much."

"I won't break, Mac. Do what you want."

Like a dam that had burst, he captured her lips once again. With one hand firmly gripping her waist, Mac slid his other hand between her legs. As she stepped apart, he touched her just enough to have her moaning into the kiss.

When he said he couldn't wait, he hadn't been lying. For days he'd been hanging on by a thread and today that thread finally snapped. He broke the kiss, reached down to his shorts and snagged the condom from the pocket.

"Looks like you planned this," she murmured, her chest heaving.

"I'm not sorry."

After covering himself, he stepped back against her and grabbed hold of her hips. "Wrap your legs around my waist."

"I'm too heavy," she argued, her eyes darting away.

"Do it," he commanded. "And never look away from me again."

The second her legs were wrapped around him, Mac slid into her. For a second, he didn't move, couldn't move. She was utterly, blissfully perfect, wrapped all around him in every way possible. Jenna held her breath; her eyes widened but remained on his.

He had no clue what emotions were lurking in his own eyes and he damn well didn't want to get into ana- lyzing them, especially when Jenna's curves were all his for the taking.

Her hips started moving as her body arched. Those pants and moans of hers were killing him. Finally, she was letting go of that control she clung so tightly to.

And Mac finally did what he'd been dying to do for years. He ran his hands all over the luscious dips and val- leys of her bare body. Each time he brushed the sides of her breasts, Jenna let out another moan.

When he feasted on them, she cried out his name.

Her body tightened, her fingertips curled deeper into his shoulders as her release swept over her. Mac pulled back, needing to see her face, wanting to watch as she came apart.

And he wasn't disappointed. Her eyes were locked on his, just as he'd demanded. A sheen of perspiration covered the bridge of her nose as she opened her mouth and cried out.

Mac couldn't hold back another second. He pumped harder, tumbling over the edge and clinging to Jenna as if she was his lifeline, as if she was every single thing he'd been waiting for his whole life.

His state of euphoria was overwhelming. Never before had so many emotions swept through him at once, and every single thing he was feeling was all because of Jenna.

And even though he'd told her to keep her eyes on him, he had to close his. He couldn't afford for her to see everything he was feeling…not when he wasn't ready to face the truth himself.

Fourteen

Mac lay in bed beside Jenna and watched her sleep. He couldn't shut his mind down even if he wanted to. After their intense encounter against the front door, Mac had carried her to bed where she'd promptly drifted off to sleep. Yet even in her sleep she kept a hand on him.

Swallowing his guilt, Mac stared at her delicate fingers on his abdomen. She'd given herself so completely, so honestly, and he wasn't worthy of any of it. He'd planned on taking her tonight. Had planned on making her his, when the last thing he deserved was sweet Jenna in his life, let alone his bed.

He'd ordered a kill only hours earlier and the reality still weighed heavily on his shoulders. He'd made the call in the past, but that was when his father had been alive and the situation called for such extremes.

Now his father was gone, Braden was incapacitated and Mac was in charge. Ryker had demanded over and over that Mac let him do his job and Mac knew Ryker didn't kill just for sport. The man may be their secret weapon, but he was also a professional. If there was another way, Ryker would've found it.

Still, Mac had made the final decision.

Delaying any longer could result in Laney getting hurt, even killed. Braden, Mac and Ryker preferred to keep Laney on the technical side of the family business and not in harm's way. But Shane was a ticking time bomb. Who's to say he wouldn't come for Zara—or even Jenna? The man was smart enough to know who mattered most in the lives of the men he was trying so hard to bring down.

Shane had to be stopped, permanently. Braden would understand.

Mac laid his hand over Jenna's as if to draw some of her innocence into his life. She was sweet, charmingly so, and completely the opposite of what his world entailed.

She arranged flowers for a living, for crying out loud. She literally made things around her beautiful while he dealt with lying, stealing…and murder.

His chest ached because no matter what he wanted, anything beyond a physical connection was impossible. But he hadn't been able to hold himself back any longer. Jenna had stirred something in him so primal, he needed her like nothing he'd ever known. And that fact scared the hell out of him.

Jenna shifted in her sleep and rolled toward him. Mac lifted his arm, allowing her to nestle deeper into his side. Call him a bastard, but he wasn't about to push her away. No, he didn't deserve her, but he wanted her. He was an O'Shea. They saw something they wanted and they took it. Simple as that.

For tonight, Jenna was his. She trusted him with her body and she'd given him full control. Only days ago they'd been friends pretending to be more. Could Jenna slip back into the friend role once this wedding was over?

The bigger question was, could he?

Jenna stood back and stared at the flower arrangements in the dining area where the reception would be held tomorrow. Everything was absolutely perfect. The purple from the lavender popped against the white tablecloths and the greenery. The fresh, yet simple arrangements were just what Amy had asked for.

The room was breathtaking anyway, with floor-to-ceiling windows encompassing the entire back wall. With the ocean view and the romantic ambiance inside, the small reception tomorrow would be absolutely stunning.

"Looks beautiful."

Jenna spun around to see Martin standing in the doorway. Great. The last person she wanted to be alone with.

Mac had gone back to the bungalow after he'd helped her carry the arrangements in. He'd stated he had some work to finish up, but she had the feeling something was bothering him so she let him go without question. After the sex they'd had, she was more confused than ever and perhaps he was, too.

"I'm not in the mood right now, Martin."

She had been given the okay to stay in the event space as late as she needed as long as she found a worker to lock up when she was done. This way no one would bother her…well, no one was supposed to bother her.

"I didn't come to argue," Martin told her. "I actually came to tell you that even though I think you're making a mistake, I'm not going to pursue you—us—any longer."

Jenna crossed her arms, not bothering to comment on the fact there was no "us" where she and Martin were concerned.

"What changed your mind?" she asked, her attention fixed on his bruised eye, compliments of Mac.

"Whatever you and O'Shea have going on is something beyond what you and I had." Martin shrugged and shoved his hands in the pockets of his shorts. "I saw how he looked at you during the rehearsal. He stayed on the sidelines, but his eyes never left you. He's intense, and I'm not getting in the way of what you have."

Jenna figured he didn't want to get in the way of Mac, period, but she kept her opinion to herself.

Had Mac been focused on her the entire time? She'd glanced his way more than once during the rehearsal and had seen him looking her way, but…the entire time? Maybe last night had switched something in him. Perhaps he was looking at her as more than every other woman who came before her. Maybe he'd been telling the truth when he told her she was special.

Jenna focused on Martin, still standing only a few feet away. "I'm glad you're moving on," she told him.

Martin nodded, then stared at her another minute as if he wanted to say something else, but finally he turned and walked away. Jenna blew out a breath and turned to survey the room one last time.

The lights went off and before she could fully react, a reflection in the windows caught her attention. Barely had she spun around when hands curled over her shoulders, lips feasted on the delicate spot beneath her ear.

"Stubborn man finally came to his senses," Mac growled. "And now you're done and all alone."

The veiled promise had Jenna shivering. "I thought you had work."

"I did."

He snaked an arm around her waist and drew her body

back against his. Her head fell against his shoulder as his lips continued to slide up and down her heated skin.

"You know what I've thought about all day?" he muttered against her neck.

"Wh-what?"

"Seeing if we can make last night's encounter seem tame."

Jenna gasped as Mac whirled her around in his arms, her body crushed against his as he slammed his mouth onto hers. Wrapping her arms around him, she opened, needing to feel that connection and anxiously wanting him to deliver on that promise.

"We can't do this here," she managed to mumble against his mouth.

"I locked the door after he left. Nothing to stop us."

Anticipation rolled through her as she threaded her fingers through his hair and tugged. "Then you better get to work because last night was pretty amazing."

His lips tilted into a grin. "Is that a dare?"

"Take it how you want."

"I'd rather take you how I want."

Mac smacked her bottom and grabbed hold of her as he walked her backward toward the dark corner away from the windows. She didn't want to analyze what it meant that he'd come to her and was so eager to have her. She only wanted Mac, wanted this experience that was unlike any other.

He kissed her lips, her neck, her bare shoulders. He eased the thin straps of her dress down, tugging until the scoop neckline fell below her breasts.

"You're so damn sexy, Jenna."

Pretty words could be said by anyone, but the way Mac showed her how he felt had Jenna believing every word. He did find her sexy, and because of that she had a confidence she'd never known before.

Feeling daring, she whispered, "Then stop talking and show me."

Mac sat her on the edge of a built-in bar and stepped between her spread legs. He grabbed a condom from his pocket, ever prepared, and rid himself of his shorts. Laying the foil packet beside her hip, he quirked a brow.

"You have on too many clothes."

Whipping the dress up and over her head, she tossed it to the floor. Were they really going to do this here? In the wide open room where anyone with the key could walk in and flip on the light?

Jenna had never thought herself staid, but this wasn't something she'd ever even imagined. Somehow sex always conjured up images of a bed, yet she and Mac had never even considered getting between the sheets.

After she wrestled out of her panties, Mac grabbed her hand and placed the condom in her palm. The silent command sent an even bigger charge of arousal shooting through her. She ripped open the packet and carefully covered him. She'd never done that with a lover before.

Mac cupped the back of her head with one hand and placed the other one on the small of her back, pulling her to the edge of the bar. Jenna slid her knees up his sides and locked her ankles behind him as he surged into her.

"Lean back."

Following his orders, she eased back slightly on her hand and watched as he took total control. With only the moonlight streaming in through the windows behind him, she had a sense of deja vu from the previous night. But this was better, far better. The nerves were gone, replaced by passion and need.

The desire that coiled low in her belly spread warmth

throughout her body as Mac gripped her hips and kept his eyes locked on to hers. She didn't know how he managed to make her feel so special and, dare she say, loved. She knew this wasn't love, not in the sense she'd like, but he cared for her, he wanted to be with her and she'd have to be content with the here and now.

Jenna tipped her head back, bowing her body when the pleasure became too much. Mac reached between them, touching her in the most intimate spot, sending Jenna spiraling out of control.

Bright light burst behind her lids as her entire body convulsed. Mac's body stilled against hers as he leaned forward and covered her mouth with his. She wrapped her arms around him as they tumbled into the abyss together.

Heavy breathing filled the silence of the room as reality settled back in. What would happen next? Would they go back to the bungalow and sleep together as they had done last night? Would she wake up in his arms again?

With the wedding tomorrow, she wondered just how far Mac intended to take this escapade. Only time would tell, but Jenna had another day to enjoy her best friend and she intended to do just that.

Fifteen

Mac watched as Jenna hugged the bride. The ceremony had been beautiful, if weddings were your thing. They were definitely not Mac's, but keeping his eyes on Jenna in her pale purple, figure-hugging dress was.

He didn't know how much longer he could handle being this close to Jenna and not touching her. And, lucky for Martin, he'd managed to keep his eyes averted for the most part.

Jenna crossed the outdoor seating area that had been set up specifically for this event. Even the way she glided through the white chairs had Mac's gut clenching. Everything about Jenna was getting to him. Her touch, her glances, the smile she'd thrown his way during the ceremony. No other woman had ever gotten beneath his skin and made him want more.

"Are you ready to escort me to the reception?" she asked as she neared.

Mac hooked his arm out and offered her a smile. "I don't think we'll be able to enjoy that room as much as we did last night."

She looped her arm through his and laughed. "No, I don't think we will."

Because he couldn't resist, Mac leaned down and whispered, "I plan on stripping you out of that dress when we get back and showing you exactly how sexy you looked today."

When her body trembled against his, Mac eased back and smiled. "Shall we?"

She turned her attention toward the rest of the wedding party filing into the dining area. "I may need a minute after that."

"Don't take too long or everyone is going to see just how hot I am for you."

"Come on," she stated, tugging him toward the open doors. "A toast, the cake and then we're out of here."

Mac laughed at her eager tone. They couldn't get out of this place fast enough. For once he wanted her in a bed, he wanted slow and he wanted to explore her the way she deserved.

Another first. He'd never once wanted to take his time. With every other woman he'd been there for one reason: release. With Jenna…he blew out a sigh. With Jenna, his life was completely different and he still had no idea how he was going to manage to let her go tomorrow.

But holding on to her would only prove to be a disaster in the long run. She didn't do secrets and lies. She didn't do dark and deceptive. Jenna was literally sunshine and flowers and happiness.

He may be a jerk for stealing some of her sweetness, but he had never been able to resist temptation and Jenna LeBlanc was temptation personified.

As they entered the bright room with the sun bursting through the wall of windows, he watched Jenna's eyes dart to the bar in the corner.

"Keep that in mind for later," he whispered.

He attempted to ignore the mental image of the two of them on that bar last night, but the force was too strong and the experience too fierce. Jenna had opened up so much over the past two days. Just the thought of exploring every inch of her when they returned to the bungalow was almost like foreplay.

"The place looks gorgeous."

Mac turned to see Mary smiling from ear to ear. Jenna released her hold on Mac and hugged her mother.

"It's a perfect day, isn't it?" Jenna asked.

Mac heard that wistfulness in her voice and wondered if she was thinking ahead to her own wedding…to some faceless bastard Mac already hated. But Jenna would, in fact, move on and she would marry because the whole family life was what she wanted. Who was he to prevent her from being happy and going after her dream with both hands?

That didn't mean he had to like it.

Mac excused himself as the two ladies chatted about the spectacular ceremony. He needed a drink. He'd prefer to hit something, but a drink would have to do, considering his location. When he returned to Miami, he and his punching bag were going to have some serious bonding time.

The bartender hooked Mac up with his favorite bourbon. Leaning one elbow on the edge of the bar, Mac swirled the amber liquid around and watched as the bride and groom came together in the middle of the floor for their first dance. That wasn't all he noticed. The soft, dreamy look in Jenna's eyes as she watched the couple was like a punch to Mac's gut.

Did she even know how radiant she was? How magnificent she looked when she was daydreaming? And there wasn't a doubt in his mind that the thoughts running through her head hinged on this beautiful day.

He watched her for the rest of the dance. But, when the music changed he couldn't wait another second. Without taking his eyes off her, Mac placed his glass on the bar and crossed the room. Her eyes met his, a ghost of a smile flirted around those kissable lips. He said nothing as he took her in his arms and started swaying to the subtle beat.

Her floral scent surrounded him, her delicate arms circled his waist as she laid her head on his chest. Why did holding her so intimately have his heart clenching? Everything in his life to this point had been simple regarding women. He saw what he wanted, he took it, he walked away.

But leaving Jenna seemed so cold, so harsh. And he wasn't referring to the physical leaving, but the mental form. Spending this week with Jenna had been…refreshing. He hadn't expected to be so relaxed in some ways and so worked up in others. This one woman managed to do what so many others had tried. She'd gotten under his skin and he didn't know what the hell to do.

Well, he knew what he wanted to do.

Mac's hands spread across her bare back, just above where the material draped low. He'd seen a confidence in her this week, almost a blossoming. She'd been so worried about her body, her very lush, sexy body, but he'd proven to her that she was built like every man's dream.

His dream.

Damn it. He didn't want to have a dream woman. There was no such thing in his world.

Mac closed his eyes and pushed every doubt and worry aside. For these next few moments, he just wanted to enjoy the feel of Jenna in his arms.

As the song ended, Jenna eased back and glanced up at him with desire burning in her eyes. Without a word, she took his hand and he gladly let her lead him out of the reception, out into the evening and toward their bungalow.

He fished the key from his pocket and unlocked the door. Jenna pulled him inside and when the door closed at his back, she turned and caged him in. With her body flush against his and her hands framing his face, she pulled him down and captured his lips.

Never in his life had an aggressive woman turned him on so much. He'd always thrived on control, on being in charge in his work and in the bedroom. But Jenna had fully come out of her shell and damn if he wasn't proud.

Mac gripped her waist, jerking her hips forcefully against his. As much as he wanted this fast and hard, he craved something different, something more. Jenna deserved more. Hadn't he said that all along?

While he couldn't give her a commitment, he could give her tonight. He wanted her to remember this, remember him…forever?

Forever wasn't a word he used.

Focusing on Jenna, Mac slid his hands up her bare back and reached for the thick straps on her shoulders. As he eased them aside, she frantically pushed her dress down and stepped back. The material pooled around her feet, leaving her in a strapless white bra and killer pair of panties.

Even though Mac intended to take things slow tonight, he wasn't about to stop her when she reached around and unhooked her bra. Only a few days ago she never would've done this in front of him. His heart quickened as she flung the garment aside and worked the lacy white panties down her shapely legs.

Jenna reached up, pulled a few pins from her hair and Mac's knees nearly buckled when that hair came tumbling down over her bare shoulders. He couldn't recall a more beautiful sight.

Cocking her head to the side, she quirked a brow. "Your move."

Damn, she was something else.

"What if I want to stand here and stare at you a bit longer?" he asked.

He heard her breath catch in her throat, watched as her eyes widened and her mouth froze in a perfect O.

Mac pushed off the door and, in one swift move, lifted her in his arms with one hand behind her back and the other beneath her knees.

"You can't—"

"I can," he stated, cutting off her protest. "And I am. I want you on the bed, our bed. All night."

She trembled against him as she laced her fingers behind his neck. She wanted him to make a move? Then this was it. He was spending the next several hours making her his, making this last impression of their time in Bora Bora absolutely unforgettable.

With the door to the private deck open, the sheers billowed in, the moon slashed a glow directly across the bed. And that's where Mac laid her. He wanted her wearing nothing but moonlight.

He eased back and Jenna started to get up.

"Don't move," he commanded. "I'm going to look at you while I undress."

Slowly, she lay back down, her eyes locked on his.

While he made quick work of the buttons on his dress shirt, he smiled as her gaze dipped down to his body. Having Jenna's eyes on him gave him a rush like nothing else. For the first time in, well, ever, he wanted approval from a lover. He wanted approval from Jenna.

Mac gave his shirt a toss to the side of the room and shed his tux pants and boxer briefs. He took a step toward the bed and ran his fingertips over the curve of her knee and up her thigh. The silkiness of her skin beneath his hands—hands that had done terrible things in his world—was a reminder of how different they were. But for now, they weren't Mac the Mafia Mogul and Jenna the Sweet Florist. They were a man and a woman who enjoyed each other, who wanted the same thing for tonight and didn't care what tomorrow would bring.

There was no tomorrow as far as he was concerned. The world could end right now and Mac would die a happy man. Then he wouldn't have to walk away and—

"What do you think about when you're looking at me like that?" she asked, breaking into thoughts that had no place in his mind.

Sliding in beside her, Mac continued exploring her body. "I'm thinking how lucky I am that you asked me here this week." He trailed his fingertips over her hip, across her quivering stomach. "I'm thinking that touching you is the single most important thing in my life right now."

Jenna reached up, running her hand along his jawline. "What are we doing here, Mac?"

He swallowed. He didn't want these questions, the ones he couldn't answer, settling between them in the bed. All he wanted was Jenna. He wanted to show her how magnificent she was and that nothing should ever bring her back down again. Not weight, not self-esteem and sure as hell not a man.

"We're about to have a memorable night," he whispered as he dipped his head toward her breast and slid his hand over the dip in her waist. "We're about to ignore the outside world and pretend nothing else exists."

She threaded her fingers through his hair. The slight tug had Mac smiling against her damp skin.

"You with me, Jen?"

Arching up to meet his lips, she replied, "I'm with you. I never want to be anywhere else."

Mac ignored the stab of guilt, the sliver of fear he felt at her statement. They were getting caught up in the moment. She knew where he stood and grasped that this was their last night together.

Mac focused on pleasuring her, on keeping his name on her lips each time she moaned or cried out. When he hovered over her, Jenna's hands trailed up his biceps as she looked him in the eye.

"I want nothing between us tonight," she whispered. "I'm on birth control and I'm clean."

Mac had never, ever been without protection. That was a major no-no. Most of the women he'd been with he'd just met and they didn't stick around long enough to earn his trust. But with Jenna, he trusted her completely and when her legs wrapped around his waist he said nothing as he pushed forward.

Gripping the comforter for some shred of control, Mac shut his eyes and willed his body to stay still. He wanted to savor this moment, being with Jenna in every single way possible. With absolutely nothing between them, Mac pulled in a deep breath and started to move. Jenna had literally wrapped herself around him.

"Look at me." He always wanted her eyes on him,

but right now, this second, was most important. "Only me, Jenna."

She tightened all around him and cried out, "Only you."

As Mac's release slammed into him, he captured her mouth. He couldn't get close enough to her and he wanted to make this moment last. Jenna's nails bit into his shoulders as she trembled and finally, her body went lax beneath his.

Mac eased to the side, tucking her against him. When her hand settled over his heart, the irony was not lost on him. She'd stolen it. The one thing in this world he swore he'd never give had been taken by his best friend.

None of this was okay. He didn't want to give her his heart, he didn't want Jenna in his world in every way possible. How could he protect her from all the questionable dealings he encountered? He'd just ordered a man killed, for pity's sake, so she obviously needed protection from the filthy life he led.

He'd never hurt her, though. Not physically, not emotionally. He'd kill anyone if they laid a finger on her.

Heaviness washed over Mac as Jenna's breathing softened. He laid his hand over hers, wanting to savor the moment a bit longer, but the flashing light from his phone on the dresser told him business was calling. His time in fairy-tale land was over.

Sixteen

Jenna rolled over, stretched and smiled as memories washed over her. Last night had been amazing.

Squinting against the sunlight streaming through the sheers, Jenna reached across the bed…encountering cool sheets. She sat up and glanced around the bedroom. The empty bedroom.

As she surveyed the area, she thought Mac could be in the living room or making breakfast to surprise her in bed, but she knew better. He was gone. There wasn't a stitch of his clothing in here, no bag, no shoes. Absolutely nothing.

With the rumpled sheets and the masculine scent of Mac still all around, Jenna might as well be mocked for her error in judgment. She'd been afraid to get this close, to let her defenses down where Mac was concerned, but she'd taken a risk. She'd known the consequences going in and she'd said to hell with it.

Well, now she sat here all alone in a bed where they'd been intimate only hours ago, which just proved she'd been right all along. Nothing and no one could change Mac O'Shea.

Even knowing all of this, even having her eyes wide open to the inevitable ending, didn't stop the hurt from spearing directly into her heart. Last night when they'd made love—and that's exactly what they did—he'd looked into her eyes, he'd held her like a man who was falling. She'd thought for sure they were feeling the same thing.

What they shared was so much more than physical closeness. They'd had a deep bond long before their clothes fell off.

Sinking back against the pillows, throat tight and eyes burning, Jenna scolded herself. What would crying do? Mac would still be gone and she'd still be here looking like a complete and utter fool.

Part of her wished he'd taken off because he was afraid. At least then she'd know he'd seen her as something more than just a friend or a casual romp. Nothing about this entire week had been casual, but Mac was done here. He'd fulfilled his obligation, his friendly duties, and he was off.

Jenna clutched the sheet to her chest and rolled over, away from the scent of Mac's pillow. The pain intensified the longer she lay there, but she couldn't bring herself to get out of bed. She knew Mac left because he told her he would, and Mac always kept his word.

Where was he now? On a flight back to Barcelona or wherever he'd come from before riding to her rescue? Was he going to meet up with one of his ladies, resume his life as though it was business as usual?

Jenna wished like hell she could be that blasé about

sex, but she just couldn't. She'd grown up dreaming of finding the love of her life, of being with the man who made her heart flip in her chest. From the second she'd seen Mac at the party of a mutual friend, her heart hadn't stopped flipping.

But they had completely different ideas regarding relationships…namely that he didn't want one and she did.

Jenna forced herself to get out of bed. The sooner she could start packing and get to the airport, the better. Her flight didn't even leave until later this afternoon, but she didn't want to stay in this bed, in this bungalow a moment longer than necessary. She couldn't handle the memories.

The past several days had been the best of her life. Her sister was happily married, her ex was off her back and Mac had set the new standard for any man who would enter her life next. He'd set the bar so high, in fact, she knew no other could ever reach it.

But wasn't the end goal to get Martin to go away? Well, mission accomplished. The cheater wouldn't attempt a reunion now.

As Jenna threw on a sundress and jerked her hair into a ponytail, she almost wished she'd just handled Martin on her own. Then she wouldn't be dealing with this ache in her heart and an overwhelming sense of emptiness.

But how could she regret asking Mac to come here? He'd not only dropped everything to help her, he'd made her feel beautiful and given her a self-confidence she'd never known before.

And it was that confidence that fueled Jenna now. The hurt wasn't going away, but a hefty dose of anger was settling deep alongside it. How dare he leave without a goodbye? Sure, he'd told her they were always going to be friends and, after the scam was up, that's what they would return to. But even friends said goodbye, right? So why

had he sneaked out of their bed as if he was ashamed of
what they'd done? Could he not face her anymore? Was
he in that big of a hurry to get where he was going, to
get away from her?

Jenna slammed her suitcase onto the messy bed and
started throwing stuff in. She wanted answers and she
wanted them now. Texting wasn't going to cut it. She intended to find Mac and demand he tell her why he just
left as if she was some cheap date or a one-night stand.
She deserved better, damn it.

And isn't that what he'd told her all along?

Mac stormed into the O'Shea family home in Beacon
Hill. Braden lived here with Zara. Well, the two went
back and forth because neither stubborn party would
sell their home. Understandably, Braden didn't want to
relinquish what was theirs and Zara didn't want to let
go of her late grandmother's house. Thus the stalemate.

The house seemed quiet. Too quiet. No staff? Someone was always milling about during the day.

Mac glanced from room to room and listened for evidence of any activity at all. Upstairs he heard a bedroom
door close so Mac made his way up the wide, curved
staircase.

When he reached the landing, Braden was heading
down the steps. His brother's eyes locked on to Mac's.

"This isn't a good time," Braden murmured as he
bounded down the stairs. "I didn't know you were coming."

Stunned at his brother's gruff, put-off tone, Mac
watched as Braden passed right by and went down to
the first floor. Something was terribly wrong and Mac
wasn't leaving until he had answers.

He had zero tolerance for games or for Braden's mood-

iness. Mac had his own host of issues. Namely the fact
he'd fallen for his best friend and now he had to figure
out how the hell to keep his distance. Crawling away from
her warm body that morning had been one of the hardest things he'd ever done. But as he'd lain there with her
body tucked against his, he knew he needed to move on
for her own good. He'd seen that look in her eyes, knew
that when she'd said "always" she meant it literally. She
hadn't just gotten swept away in the moment.

Mac pushed aside the confusion and fear over his emotions and followed Braden into the study on the first
floor. Braden circled the oversized mahogany desk and
sank into the leather chair behind it. Standing back, Mac
watched as Braden rested his elbows on the desktop and
held his head in his hands.

Whatever was going on was serious and personal.

"Braden—"

"We lost the baby."

Mac froze. The baby? What…oh, no. Zara had been
pregnant? And she'd lost the baby?

With slow, careful steps, Mac approached the desk.
No wonder Braden had been out of commission for days.
He'd been dealing with a new level of hell.

"I don't know what to do for her," Braden went on.
"She's upstairs sleeping now, but she just cries all the
time."

Mac rounded the desk and eased a hip on the edge.
Looking down at his always strong, always in charge
brother and seeing him so broken and miserable was
crushing.

"I had no idea, Braden. I'm sorry."

Braden pushed away from the desk and fell back
against the cushioned leather. "I didn't want to get into
this with a text or phone call. I didn't even know how to

cope or to say the words out loud. We'd just found out last week that she was pregnant, and were waiting to get everyone together to make an announcement."

In the span of a week Braden's entire life had changed. Mac completely understood how that worked. Suddenly Mac's issue seemed so insignificant in comparison.

"What can I do?" Mac asked.

Shaking his head, Braden finally met his gaze. "There's nothing. We'll get through this."

Mac had no idea what to say to make any of this easier for Braden. And Zara? He couldn't even imagine what she was going through.

"Tell me what happened with Ryker," Braden said, raking a hand over his face. The stubble beneath his palm rustled. "I hope you took care of whatever he needed."

Mac gritted his teeth and swallowed. Making that judgment call had never come easy, but he couldn't be sorry and he didn't do regrets. Regrets wouldn't change the facts and Mac never believed in looking back.

"We took care of things."

Braden's tired gaze narrowed. "What's that mean?"

Mac came to his feet and paced to the stained-glass window behind the desk. He shoved his hands into his pockets and debated how much he should tell Braden. Normally this would be a nonissue, but given all that Braden was dealing with, Mac worried the news would be too much.

"Ryker has a good lead on the scrolls," Mac started, keeping his back to Braden. "I haven't heard back from him regarding them, so he's still chasing that tip. If it was a dead end, we'd know."

"So what aren't you telling me?"

On a sigh, Mac glanced over his shoulder. "Shane attempted to toss his pathetic power around."

"How?" Braden asked, brows drawn in.

"He intercepted a package that's due for the auction I have coming up in Miami. Nothing we acquired for a client, but he did it to prove he could." Which still pissed Mac off. "He showed up in London and wasn't subtle about following Ryker around."

Braden slammed his hand down on the desk. "He's determined to keep coming at us. Does he think we see him as a threat? Maybe it's time I meet with him face-to-face. Settle this and let him know who exactly is in charge now."

Damn. This was the part he didn't want to tell Braden. "Shane won't be a problem anymore."

Braden's gaze held on to Mac's. Acknowledgment flashed through his eyes, the muscle in his jaw clenched. "Ryker made this call?"

Mac squared his shoulders. "I did."

Braden came to his feet, slowly, lethally. The leather chair creaked, anger rolled off Braden in waves.

"You did."

Mac nodded and fully braced himself for whatever rage Braden threw his way.

In one swift move, Braden gripped Mac's shirt and slammed him against the wall next to the window. "You made this call knowing I didn't want any more death on our hands?" Braden demanded.

"I made the call because we didn't know what was going on with you," Mac gritted out. "I did it because Shane has been a menace since Dad was in charge and I was damn tired of him getting in our way. And he threatened Laney."

The hold on Mac's shirt eased. "He what?"

Mac stared into his brother's eyes, so much like his own. "He sent an email threat to Laney. He tried to encrypt it, but she was able to trace it to him. He also tried to kidnap her."

Braden's eyes narrowed, the muscle in his jaw clenched. "What?"

"He tried to grab her off the street before he went to London to follow Ryker."

"Damn it." Braden's hands fell away, but he didn't move back. "Who the hell attempts to mess with my family and think their actions won't be dealt with?"

Raking his fingers through his hair, he muttered another curse. "That bastard. I should've killed him myself."

A gasp drew Mac's attention. Braden whirled around and in the doorway stood a very pale, very shocked-looking Zara with her hand over her mouth. Her wide eyes were red-rimmed and puffy, a clear sign she'd been crying for a lengthy amount of time.

"Zara…" Braden started across the study.

"Who?" she whispered.

"You should be sleeping," Braden said, ignoring her question.

When he went to reach for her, Zara held up a hand. "Who was killed?"

Braden threw Mac a look over his shoulder. Mac stepped forward. This was his mess, he'd take the blame.

"Shane."

Zara's eyes closed, she swayed on her feet and Braden quickly wrapped his arms around her waist and caught her.

"You promised no more."

Mac heard the whispered plea and the guilt consumed him. "The circumstances were different and Braden didn't make the call."

She glanced around Braden and eyed Mac. "But you knew he didn't want anymore…evil. Why did you do it?"

Mac wouldn't feel sorry for making a judgment call. He may hate taking lives, but sometimes there was no other choice…when it meant protecting your own. Just another life lesson from the late Patrick O'Shea.

"I'm sorry about your baby, Zara." He totally ignored her question to him, but he needed her to know he wasn't a complete monster. He was genuinely sorry for the child who was lost. Such innocence taken away. Mac knew how much family meant to Braden, knew his brother wanted a large family of his own.

Her chin quivered, moisture gathered in her eyes as she nodded and leaned farther into Braden.

"We'll talk later," Braden stated, glancing to Mac. "When are you leaving?"

Mac shrugged. "Whenever. My jet is waiting. I need to be home by tomorrow to sort out the last-minute details before the auction."

"Go on, then. Any word from Ryker or anything else business related comes directly to me."

When Braden turned to go, Mac stepped forward. "It was inevitable, you know. Just because you want to take this family in a new direction, doesn't mean you can. Too many outsiders won't let you. They're hiding, waiting to threaten us when we show a hint of weakness. We may want a different life, but change won't be easy."

Braden's shoulders stiffened and he froze for the slightest moment before finally ushering Zara out of the room without a word.

Mac blew out a breath he hadn't even realized he'd been holding. Braden was pissed, Zara was hurt and Jenna was…hell, he didn't know what she was because he'd run out of there the second he realized his feelings had taken a turn in a direction he didn't want to go.

So here he stood in the study of his childhood home,

all alone. In the span of twelve hours he'd managed to anger those closest to him. Now he just needed to throw Ryker and Laney into the mix to round out his crappy day.

Mac pulled out his cell and called his pilot. Might as well get back to Miami and concentrate on work. It was the one area of his life that hadn't fallen spectacularly apart...yet.

Seventeen

All Mac wanted was to crawl into bed and forget the world for a good eight hours. He'd flown from Bora Bora to Boston, then from there he'd come to Miami and gone straight to his new office. After working a few hours, he'd known if he didn't get home, he was going to do a face-plant on his desk.

He needed nothing but his king-sized bed and his phone on silent.

Mac started to unbutton his shirt as he made his way down the hall of his Miami condo. He'd chosen a penthouse with a killer beach view because he was so sick of the unpredictable weather in Boston. Miami was everything he loved: warmth, sunshine and attractive people. The art deco aesthetic in the city was also a great fit for his new offices and auction house. Considering O'Shea's pulled in art with every auction no matter the location, Miami was a no-brainer when it came to opening another branch and Mac had been all too eager to head it up. Not to mention Jenna had planted a bug in his ear about opening an office here since she'd arrived a couple of years back.

His gut clenched at the thought of her. So many times his mind just circled right back around to his best friend and he could do little to control it.

Mac jerked his shirt off and entered his bedroom. Before he could even tap the switch, that familiar floral aroma surrounded him.

"I thought you were never coming home."

Jenna.

Mac quickly flicked the switch, drenching the room in light and his gut clenched at the sight before him. Jenna in his bed. Jenna naked in his bed. Jenna naked in his bed with the sheets rumpled all around her.

She tipped her head to the side and held his gaze.

"I figure you didn't mean to leave me without saying goodbye, so I thought I'd give you that chance," she told him, as if this entire situation didn't warrant any questions.

"How did you know I was coming home?" he asked.

With a shrug, and clearly not concerned with her state of undress, Jenna let the sheets pool at her waist. "I used my key to get in and realized you weren't here. I called Braden, who told me you'd just left."

If he weren't so freaked out about his feelings, about hurting her, he'd be all over her in that bed. Damn, but she was the best accessory in the room.

"You seem to be uncomfortable," she went on. "Everything okay? I mean, I know we said we'd just play this week out, but even friends tell each other goodbye, right? Unless something else was bothering you and that's why you left me. Either way, I deserve an explanation."

Mac remained locked in place. If he took a step forward, he wouldn't be able to control himself. Suddenly sleeping was the last thing he wanted to do in that bed.

"I couldn't stay." At least that was the complete truth.

"Work?" she asked, quirking a brow as if she knew full well that wasn't what caused him to run.

He wadded his shirt up and tossed it toward the basket in the corner. "I can't get into this, Jenna."

As much as he hated to be the guy who was a jerk the morning after, he was going to have to make her leave. She needed to understand exactly what she was dealing with and how far apart their worlds truly were.

"Oh. What exactly can't you get into right now? Would that be your feelings or just the simple courtesy of letting me know you were leaving?"

She was understandably angry and he deserved every bit of backlash she threw his way.

"Are you going to get dressed?" he asked.

Jenna tilted her chin, shot a glare across the room and then slid from the bed. "I suppose now that the week is over you're done. I get it. I was even well aware of the plan going in, but I still thought something had changed."

She let out a laugh, void of any humor, as she scooped up her bra and panties. He watched as she slid into the bright red lingerie that was sure to make any man beg her to crawl back into that bed.

"I figured when you crept out of the room like a coward that you were scared of what had happened, so I was giving you the benefit of the doubt." She reached down and grabbed her red dress, sliding it over her head. "Apparently you felt nothing or you're still freaked out. Either way, I'm not begging. Coming here was a risk I was willing to take, but it looks like only one of us has a set big enough to admit what they want."

As she started to pass, Mac took one step and blocked the doorway. Jenna froze, staring into his eyes. She was clearly pissed, with her lips pressed into a thin line and the muscle ticking in her jaw. But it was the hurt, the vulnerability in her eyes that gutted him. He couldn't let her leave this room thinking she wasn't worth every single thing she wanted.

"I'm man enough to admit what I want, Jenna."

"Prove it."

There was no other way to do this. There was no happy ending between them unless they remained as friends, but was that even an option at this point? Could he honestly look her in the eye and lie about his feelings? He could if he wanted her to forget this notion that the two of them had any type of deeper relationship to build on.

"Wanting you physically has never been the issue," he told her, steeling himself against the fierce determination in her eyes. "But we're done. Not that I wouldn't mind another dose of what you were offering, but let's be honest. We're back home now, reality has settled back in and everything that happened in Bora Bora needs to stay there."

Those gorgeous eyes narrowed and Mac knew he'd struck a nerve, just as he'd intended. The knife he'd used to shred this bond was cutting into him and he was going to hate himself when she walked out of here. But at least she'd be safe, away from his lifestyle, and eventually move on with a man who had a completely legal job. Someone who didn't kill enemies who pissed him off one too many times. Someone who wasn't targeted by dangerous criminals dealing in death.

"You can't lie to me," she stated. "I know you. I know what we had in Bora Bora was real and I know there was something deeper there than just sex."

He said nothing. She was right, but he wasn't about to admit it. He admired her bravery. She'd come so far in such a short amount of time and he couldn't help but feel a swell of pride in knowing he helped her find her self-esteem.

"You can push me away, that's fine," she went on, taking a step back and crossing her arms over her chest. "But you'll be miserable and you'll always wonder what would've happened if you had taken a risk. Isn't that what you O'Sheas do? Take risks?"

She was on fire. The more she talked, the more intense her tone became. She didn't raise her voice, but kept it calm, controlled. Much more lethal that way.

Mac had never been drawn to a meek woman and Jenna LeBlanc was definitely not meek. She was strong, hard-headed, stubborn and determined. He wouldn't expect anything less than a fight because when Jenna wanted something, she went after it. So did he.

"You're more than welcome to stay, but I'm about one minute from falling face-first into bed."

Throwing her arms out to the side, she shook her head and sent him a mock laugh. "Go right ahead. Don't let me get in the way. But remember this, you're the one who let me walk out of here. You're the one who is throwing away something that could be amazing."

Yeah, that was adding salt to the wound. He was fully aware of the life he was throwing away. But the life she wanted, the life she deserved, wasn't the life he could offer her. Constantly keeping secrets, not opening up to her about his work, having to take private calls without her overhearing, would all be too much for a relationship to bear.

"It's for the best." He barely recognized his own voice.

She quirked a brow. "Really? Because you think you're

protecting me? Because you are afraid to fully let me in? Do you think I'm not aware that what your family does isn't completely on the up-and-up? I'm not naive, Mac. Did you ever stop to consider that I'm stronger than you think?"

Shoving his hands in his pockets in an attempt to prevent himself from touching her, Mac nodded. "I'm fully aware how strong you are, Jenna. You're one of the strongest people I know. But anything between us beyond friendship isn't possible."

"You think we can just return to being friends now?" Her eyes held his as if she truly thought he had a simple answer for such a complex question.

"That's our only option. You'll find someone you love and you'll spend the rest of your life with him. You'll wear your mother's wedding dress and get that fairy tale you want."

"You think that's what this is? Me looking for some fairy tale?" Jenna turned, paced his bedroom. "I didn't get swept into the moment on the island, Mac. I spent more time with you, I got to know more of you and I opened more of myself to you than I ever had before."

"Which will only make our friendship stronger," he stated, as if that justified her deep connection and let him off the hook from feeling any more for her.

Standing here before her, he knew full well he was being a jerk, but he literally saw no other way out of this. Making her unhappy now would help simplify her life and make her happier in the long run. He had to remain detached from that longing look in her eyes, that questioning stare full of the hope that he was shattering.

"This is ridiculous." Jenna shook her head and started for the door again. "Move."

Mac remained still. She glanced down to the floor, then back up, blinking against the unshed tears in her eyes.

Enough. Mac snapped and grabbed her arms, hauling her against his chest. He ignored her shocked gasp.

"You think this is ridiculous?" he demanded with a slight shake. "What's ridiculous is thinking a relationship can work between us. You need to trust me on this, Jenna. I'm pushing you away because I care about you, not because I don't want more."

Her eyes roamed his face as she blinked, taking in his statement. "You want more? As in…what?"

No. He wasn't taking the bait. Discussing things that could never happen was moot.

"It doesn't matter," he claimed. "What matters is our friendship. I need to keep you at a distance, to prevent you from getting in too deep. This way you're still in my life and you can have your own life without the stress that comes from living in mine."

"And you're making this decision for me?" she asked, quirking a brow.

He pushed her back and raked a hand through his hair. "Yes, damn it."

Jenna's mocking laugh had his gut clenching. She still didn't see that he was doing all of this because he cared so much…too much. And this was why he didn't do relationships. Too many ways to get hurt, both physically and emotionally. He wished she would see that remaining friends was their best option.

His cell vibrated in his pocket, but he ignored it for the time being. He'd check it once Jenna was gone.

"I'm not sure friendship is an area I want to go with you again," she told him, her defiant little chin lifted. "I've seen how much you care for me. I know it's in there and the fact that you're ignoring it only tells me how much you love me."

Mac jerked back. "I never said love."

In that moment a veil seemed to cover her face. Jenna's lips thinned, her lids lowered slightly as she gave a brief nod.

"That's all I needed to know. I'm sorry I made a fool of—"

"Hold on." He jerked the vibrating phone from his pocket. "I have to take this. Don't leave."

Her eyes widened as if she couldn't believe he'd cut her off.

The screen flashed Ryker's name.

"Hey, man."

"How soon can you meet me in London?" Ryker asked.

Mac's eyes darted to Jenna. "Did you find something?"

"I believe so. I called Braden and he said to see if you could come. He told me about Zara."

Mac swallowed his remorse. He hadn't told Jenna, hadn't wanted to pull the sympathy card.

With his eyes locked on Jenna, Mac replied, "I'll call my pilot and be in the air within the hour."

Mac listened as Ryker went on to explain where he was staying and how hopeful he was that this was the lead they'd been waiting for.

But all the while, Jenna was grabbing her purse from the dresser, pulling out her keys and brushing by him without a word or even a glance in his direction.

Before he could finish the call with Ryker, his front door opened and shut with an echoing click. He'd gotten his wish. He'd pushed her away and now Ryker had a lead on the scrolls the O'Sheas had been in search of for decades.

Now that everything seemed to be within his grasp, now that he was ready to go after his father's legacy, why did he feel such a void? Why did he have a gut-sinking feeling that the very best thing that would ever happen to him had just walked out that door? And she'd walked out because he'd told her to; he'd forced her hand and left her no choice.

No regrets. Isn't that the motto he'd always lived by?

For the first time in his life, Mac was second-guessing every action, every choice he'd made for the past week and wondering how the control had slipped from his grasp. Then he realized Jenna had always been the one with the control. As much as he thought himself so powerful and strong, Jenna was the force behind all of that.

Sliding the cell back into his pocket, the fact he hadn't slept for over a day didn't even register. All he knew was that as soon as he got back from London, as soon as this auction in Miami was wrapped up next week, he was focusing on Jenna. Somehow, he had to make this right.

Now he had to figure out exactly what he wanted from her because he couldn't keep hurting her. Their friendship was over, no doubt about that. Now he either needed to cut ties completely or fully submerge her in his world, where he could protect her and keep her safe from his enemies.

Mac grabbed his bag by the door and quickly exchanged some of his clothes as he rang his pilot. When he ended the call, his eyes went to the rumpled bed and he couldn't forget that image of coming home and seeing Jenna in his bed.

Just that act alone spoke volumes about the woman she'd become since last week. A woman he'd seen come out of her shell, a woman who willingly gave him everything he'd ever wanted and stood up to him. She'd shown no fear, had looked him full in the face and called him a coward. There wasn't a soul on Earth who had ever done that.

Which proved Jenna LeBlanc may just be the dynamic woman he'd never known he was looking for. He'd kept secrets from her for years, had kept his business separate from his personal life and she'd never questioned him. So how would being fully involved with her be any different?

A thread of hope slid through him at the possibilities. He had a few surprises in store for Jenna. In the end, he knew there was only one choice to make. There was no way he'd let her walk away from him again.

Eighteen

"Well, that went better than we hoped."

Mac sank into a vacant chair. The auction was over and the sales had been record-breaking. He considered this a good sign of things to come in Miami.

Too bad nothing had come of the whirlwind trip to London. In addition, the incident Mac had ordered Ryker to take care of was over and done. Braden hadn't said another word, but Mac was well aware of his brother's stance. There would be no more killings. They would have to find another way to protect their own.

Braden took a seat next to Mac and slapped his back. "You pulled it off. Dad would be proud."

Mac swallowed a lump of regret. That's what he wanted. He missed his dad, wanted him to be proud of the way he'd taken their business into another territory.

"I sent Zara to the condo to get some rest," Braden went on. "She was worn out."

Once Mac had opened a branch in Miami, Braden went ahead and bought a condo to have for visits. Smart move. Zara had looked dead on her feet. She was taking this miscarriage hard.

"How are you guys doing?" Mac asked.

With a shrug, Braden stared straight ahead to the now-empty stage. "We're getting better each day. As soon as the doctor says it's safe, we'll try again."

"I said I'm fine to drive," snapped a familiar voice.

Braden let out a sigh that matched Mac's. "Here we go again," Braden muttered.

Mac glanced over his shoulder to see Laney storming down the aisle, Ryker hot on her heels. Literally. The woman insisted on wearing sky-high shoes to every damn event.

"Tell the family bouncer that I'm fine to drive."

Mac nearly laughed at her childish attitude, complete with crossed arms and tapping foot, but he rather liked not having his head bitten off.

"She received another threat," Ryker stated in that low, controlled tone of his. "She won't tell you because she doesn't want anyone to worry."

"And if you hadn't been snooping in my things, you wouldn't know, either," Laney bit out.

Braden came to his feet. "What the hell is this about another threat? Who is it now?"

Mercy, would the threats ever end? Shouldn't taking their family in a safer direction ensure that those he loved would be secure?

What about Jenna? No matter the cost, he had to keep her safe. She was associated with his family and therefore automatically a mark.

Laney shrugged. "I don't know who this one came from and I'm not concerned. Just some hacker causing a slight problem. Nothing I can't handle and nothing like Shane."

Mac scrounged up the last bit of energy he had. "Let Ryker see you back to your condo. There's no reason not to."

"I'm a big girl," she said through gritted teeth. "Would you ask Ryker to hold your hand if someone threatened you?"

Mac and Braden exchanged a look. Ryker remained silent, shoving his hands in his pockets, but keeping his eyes on Laney.

"That's what I thought," she said. "I'm going back to my condo. Alone. I will gladly text each of you once I arrive so you know the big bad wolf didn't get me."

She leaned past Mac and hugged Braden. "Love you. Tell Zara I'll call her tomorrow and take her out for some girl time."

"She'd like that," Braden replied.

When Laney hugged Mac, he squeezed her back and said, "Don't be stubborn. Let him take you."

Laney eased back and smiled. "Good night, big brother."

She turned, squaring her shoulders and glaring at Ryker. "Your concern is noted, but not necessary. Good night."

And like the regal woman their mother always was, Laney took a chapter from Elizabeth O'Shea's book and walked out with head high and back straight.

Mac shot Ryker a look.

"I'm on it."

Ryker kept his distance, but slowly followed Laney out the door.

"Those two may end up in a fistfight before the night is over," Braden commented.

"Ryker's good, but my vote is on Laney. Mainly because she's pissed and Ryker would never hurt a woman."

"What about you?" Braden asked, leaning against the back of one plush chair. "You have dodged any topics concerning Jenna and I thought for sure she'd be here on your big night."

Mac snorted. "Don't ask."

"Let me focus on your problems for a while," Braden said. "We've had a successful night, Zara's resting and it's just you and me. Lay it on me."

Mac found himself pouring out the details of the last two weeks as if he were some damn woman chatting with her friends. But he needed Braden's advice and he was more than willing to offer his brother a distraction.

"So you pretended to be engaged and now…what? You want to actually be engaged?"

Mac raked a hand through his hair. "Hell, I don't know what I want. I know I want her back and as more than a friend, but to take it that far… I don't know."

"And you haven't seen her in a week?"

Mac shook his head. Not since he'd been on the phone with Ryker and she'd looked at him like he was a monster. He'd never get that image out of his head. He'd chosen work over her and he'd quite possibly destroyed her.

"I thought I'd have everything figured out by now, but it's been a week and I still don't know how to approach her."

Braden laughed. "On your knees, buddy. Plan on doing a lot of groveling. I've been there. It's hell on the ego and pride, but well worth it in the end."

Mac knew Jenna would be worth everything, but was he willing to risk her happiness for his selfish need to be with her? Would she get tired of all the secrets, all the sneaking around and him unable to answer the questions she was bound to have?

The scrolls were still out there somewhere and it tore him up that he had so little control over getting them back. But there was one thing that was still very much in his hands.

He was ready to fight for his girl.

Jenna rolled over in bed and froze. Why did she smell her mango tea? There was another scent that filtered in as well…some pastry? What?

Jenna jerked up in bed. She lived alone so any smell coming from the other room was a bit alarming.

She tossed the covers aside and tiptoed to the doorway. She opened the crack wider to peer out. From just the right angle she could see into the kitchen and what she saw stopped her cold.

Mac. He was bustling around in her kitchen as if he owned the place. She should've taken his key back the day she'd surprised him at his place, but she'd been too hurt and too angry. All she'd wanted to do was get out of his sight before she broke down and he saw exactly how much he affected her.

So after a week of nothing, what was he doing here?

Whatever it was, she wasn't going to give him an inch. She turned and headed into her master bath and went about her daily routine. She washed her face, pulled her hair back and brushed her teeth. Since this was Sunday, the flower shop was closed and she usually cleaned. But even if Mac weren't in the other room she still wouldn't feel like it.

In the past two weeks she'd gone from a beautiful state of euphoria to the lowest level of depression she could remember. No matter what she did, she was reminded of

Mac. They just had too many memories together. Movies, food, random little shops near her condo, countless places that held a piece of them, and she couldn't function.

How pathetic did that sound? Well, she could function, but she didn't want to. She wasn't quite finished with her moping just yet. He'd hurt her, hurt her badly, and she wondered if she'd every truly get over it.

In Bora Bora he'd been demanding, exhilarating and positively perfect. Then she'd seen him mask his feelings, hide behind work and force her to walk away. She wouldn't beg. She had too much respect for herself to ask a man to stick around. Mac may have wanted to ignore his feelings, but she wished he'd just come clean.

Which made her wonder, was that why he'd let himself in this morning? He was the only other person who knew her passcode for the security alarm, so he'd been quite stealthy about it.

But if he was in there making her breakfast, the least she could do was hear what he had to say. Then she'd have to decide what to do.

Perhaps he was just here because he thought they could get back to friend status. If that was the case, Jenna wasn't so sure she could handle that deal. She'd gotten too close to the man she wanted in her life forever. She'd seen a glimpse of the man who cared for her the way she deserved to be, and Jenna knew he loved her. He may not have admitted it to himself, but he did.

Her heart tumbled in her chest as she exited her bathroom and glanced down at her silky chemise. He'd seen her completely naked, so changing would be ridiculous. Besides, Mac was the only man she'd ever wanted to bare it all to. He made her feel beautiful and he showed her that she was sexy with curves, dips and a little extra weight.

And if he was here for the whole "let's be friends" spiel, maybe her state of dress—or undress—would make him suffer just a bit more.

Pulling in a deep breath, Jenna opened her bedroom door and padded down the tiled hallway. She stood in the open entryway to the kitchen and propped a hand on her hip. Or should she cross her arms? Maybe place both hands on her hips?

Jenna groaned inwardly. Maybe coming out here half naked wasn't the best option. It's not as if she had this whole seductress thing down, and why was she even trying? She wasn't the one who should be putting forth the effort now…right?

Rolling her eyes at herself, she started to turn when Mac glanced over his shoulder and his heavy-lidded, intense look froze her in place. So much emotion shone through those eyes: regret, desire, vulnerability.

"What are you doing here?" she asked, surprised her voice sounded stronger than she was actually feeling.

"Making your favorite breakfast."

She quirked a brow and slid her gaze to the box on the counter from their favorite bakery down the street. "Really?"

"I made mango tea to go with your Danish."

He turned around and leaned back against the counter, blocking the plate she'd gotten a glimpse of. His eyes raked over her body, and the effect was just as potent as if he'd touched her with his bare hands. But she didn't move any closer. She would keep her distance until she knew the full meaning of his visit. Her favorite breakfast was a nice start, though.

"I've missed you."

Jenna stilled, her breath catching in her throat. "Is that why I haven't seen or heard from you in a week?"

"I had to sort some things out. I was hoping you'd be at the auction."

Jenna lifted a shoulder. "I was hoping you wouldn't hurt me on purpose. I guess we're even."

Okay, that was petty, but damn it, she'd never been in this position before. She had no clue what the rules were when your heart was beaten and bruised.

"I'm sorry." Those bright eyes held her in place as the sincere apology wrapped around her. "I went about everything the wrong way."

Jenna crossed her arms. "Yes, you did."

A smile flirted around Mac's mouth. "You're not going to make this easy, are you?"

"Should I?"

"I wouldn't expect any less from the woman I love."

Taken aback by the sudden declaration, Jenna reached for the doorframe to steady herself. "What?"

"I love you," he announced, as if he'd said the words a million times before and was utterly comfortable with them. "As more than a friend. I wanted to keep you at arm's length, to keep you away from the ugliness that can sometimes surround my family."

Pulling her thoughts back together, Jenna stepped forward and gripped the back of a barstool at the center island. "We've danced around the topic for years now. I'm not judging you. I'm already in your life, so why not let me in a bit deeper?"

His gaze darted to the floor as he shook his head. With a heavy sigh, he glanced back to her. "I don't know how to answer that. I guess I thought keeping you as a friend but nothing more would be the best way to protect you. I could still have you in my life, but..."

Mac pushed off the counter and started pacing. Resembling a caged animal, he made a couple of laps before stopping on the other side of the island. He rested his palms on the countertop and let his head drop.

"I don't even know how to do this, Jen."

The brokenness in his tone nearly undid her, but she had to remain strong. Whatever internal battle he waged with himself was fierce. He needed to work through this in order to move forward. She desperately wanted to move forward with him and she hoped that was why he was here.

"I've done things," he whispered. "Things I never want you to know about. Not because I don't trust you, but because I don't want you to look at me with fear or hate."

Jenna gripped the back of the stool. "I would never look at you that way."

His eyes drilled into hers. "You did when you walked out last week."

Swallowing, Jenna pulled up every ounce of strength she could muster and circled the island. "I didn't fear or hate you, Mac. Never. I was disappointed, hurt and frustrated. I know the loyalty you have to your family and I admire you for it. I know there will be times you'll choose the business over me and I get that, too. But you were pushing me away, and to drive the point home you didn't even offer a goodbye. I was just like all the other women in your life and I won't be treated like that."

Mac reached for her, finally. His fingers curled around her bare arms. Jenna pulled in a deep breath, the tips of her breasts brushing against his T-shirt.

"You'll never be treated like just any other woman, Jenna. You're nothing like anyone I've ever been with before."

"Tell me again," she whispered, emotions clogging her throat. "Tell me you love me."

His hands slid down her sides and gripped her waist.

The strength of his touch warmed her entire body through the silk.

"I'd rather show you," he muttered against her lips. "But I do love you, Jenna. So much. More than I ever thought possible."

Wrapping her arms around him, she nipped at his lips. As if that set off some sort of spark in him, Mac lifted her up against him. Instinctively her legs went around his waist as he carried her from the room. She kissed his stubbled jawline as he made his way toward her bedroom.

"I need you now," he growled as they toppled onto the bed.

In a frenzy, he tore his clothes off and yanked her chemise down. Poised above her, he stared into her eyes. "Nothing between us," he told her.

Jenna nodded. She never wanted anything between them again. When Mac joined their bodies, Jenna wrapped herself around him, taking in all of his strength. This is what they were, a team, a force. They were lovers, best friends and so much more.

Mac's lips moved over hers, then down her throat as she arched into his touch. He whispered her name as she climbed and when she flew apart, he told her once again how much he loved her and then followed her over the edge.

Moments later, Jenna lay tucked against his side. There was so much that still needed to be said, so much that needed to be hashed out, but right now, she had all she needed.

When her stomach growled, she snuggled a bit deeper. "I'm starving. I worked up an appetite."

Mac slid his hand up her back and into her hair, which had fallen from the ponytail. "Stay here and I'll bring you breakfast."

When he got up, Jenna admired his perfect male form. And he was all hers.

"Look at me like that and I'll never make it out of this room," he told her.

"Bring me breakfast and I'll thank you properly."

He closed his eyes and groaned. "You're killing me. Don't move."

Moments later he had her tea and a plate of Danishes in hand.

"I'm pretty sure I could never get tired of you serving me breakfast in bed while naked."

He smiled as he placed the items on her bedside table. Mac sank down beside her, caging her in as he put a hand on either side of her hips. "Then marry me and I'll do this every day."

Jenna gasped. "What?"

"Marry me, Jenna. I don't want to be your fake fiancé or your pretend lover. I want it all."

Her mind spun in circles. Were they ready for this?

"Marriage is a big leap, Mac. Aren't we moving too fast?"

He laughed and smacked her lips with a kiss. "I've wanted you for years, Jen. I want to wake up with you every single morning and I want you to be legally mine. I can't get a ring on your finger fast enough."

Tears pricked her eyes. "Mac," she whispered.

"Before you say yes, I need to know something."

Blinking against the moisture, Jenna nodded. "Anything."

"Do you love me?"

Her heart swelled. As if there was ever any doubt as to her feelings, she threw her arms around his neck and kissed him. "I love you more than anything in this world.

I don't care what you do, I know you'll always keep me safe. I will marry you today, tomorrow, whenever."

He folded her into his chest and sighed against her neck. "I want you to have the wedding you've always dreamed of. I want you to wear your mother's dress."

Jenna smiled and pulled back. "I guess we can officially tell them we're getting married now?"

"Did they ever know any different?" he asked.

"No."

Mac shrugged. "Then let's not tell them. We're only moving forward. No regrets and no looking back."

"I couldn't agree more." She trailed her fingertip along the coarse hair covering his jaw. "But I want a honeymoon in Bora Bora."

"I want a honeymoon for the rest of our lives all over the world."

Mac laid Jenna back on the bed and proceeded to get started on that honeymoon…breakfast forgotten once again.

Epilogue

"We have a problem."

Words Mac never liked to hear, especially from Braden. They'd been riding life too easily lately...well, easily for them. Of course something had to land in their laps.

"What?" he asked, gripping the phone.

Jenna had gone shopping with her mother. Only a week ago he'd officially asked her to marry him and now the women were out planning. Mac didn't care what she planned, so long as she was his wife sooner rather than later.

"Laney called and said she's come across some chatter of an investigation being done on the down low."

"And we're the subject?"

"Yeah."

Damn it. "Do we know where the threat is coming from?" Mac asked, sinking into his leather office chair.

"Not yet. She just called me, but she's trying to hack into more databases," Braden explained. "She said this will take some time, so we need to keep things squeaky clean until we know where the real danger is."

Mac rested his elbows on his desk and eyed his shut door. He'd come into the office early but kept the door shut because he hadn't wanted to be disturbed when his assistant came in.

"Do you think it's someone who works for us or some unknown entity trying to get close to us?"

Braden blew out a frustrated breath. "I have no idea and I'm pissed. We don't know who set this into motion or how many are involved."

"We need to figure out who it is as soon as possible. We can't alert our allies in the FBI or local law enforcement until we know what we're up against."

"Trust me, Laney is on it and she's just as pissed as we are. Nobody comes at us like this."

And lives, Mac wanted to say. But he wasn't going to get into that hot debate again. As much as Braden wanted to move their family into a new, less violent territory, there had to be repercussions for such actions.

Still, it was a topic they could and would discuss once they knew more details.

"Does Ryker know?"

"I'm calling him next," Braden explained. "Just keep Jenna close until we know what we're up against. This may be someone out to harm us physically or attack our business. Damn it, I hate being in the dark."

Mac swallowed. This was one of the reasons he'd hesitated letting Jenna in so deep. But he realized that having her close was the best place for her. It was the only way to ensure her safety.

"I'll be sure to stay on high alert. We just need to keep Ryker in the background for now. Even the scroll hunt needs to be suspended. If he discovered where they were and went in—"

"Yeah. I know. I'll make sure he understands the severity of the situation."

"Any other bad news?" Mac asked.

"That's it. But I want you to be watching everything in your offices. This timing reeks and I don't believe in coincidences. We didn't have an issue until we opted to open new branches and I'm wondering if there's a plant in either the Miami or Atlanta location."

Mac came to his feet and rubbed the back of his neck. "I'll have Laney look deeper into the new employees' personal lives. I want texts, where they go on their time off, everything."

"Good idea."

Mac wondered if this would be too much to put on their sister, but she was just as strong and resilient as the rest of them...a point she often reminded them of. Still, she was their baby sister and they felt the need to shelter her.

"I need to get ahold of Ryker."

Mac stood at his floor-to-ceiling office windows and stared out onto the city. "I'll keep you posted if anything turns up."

Just as he disconnected the call, his office door flew open. Mac jerked in defense, but relaxed when he saw Jenna in the doorway loaded down with bags.

"I did some damage," she said as she breezed in. "Mom dropped me off on her way to the salon. I booked her an appointment and...what's wrong?"

She dumped the bags into the leather club chair by the

door and crossed to him. "Mac?" she asked, her brows drawn in.

He wrapped an arm around her and kissed the top of her head. "Nothing."

Jenna pulled back, her hand on his chest. "We're a team now, remember? If you can't give me details, I understand, but don't lie to my face."

"There's been a threat to the family. I don't know if it's personal or business. I really have no details but I can tell you that you're safe. I just need you to be vigilant when you're not with me."

She studied his face. "I know you'll protect me, but what about you? Who's going to protect you?"

"I'm fine." He squeezed her tighter against him as he stared out the window. "Everything will be fine, Jenna. I swear to you."

And that was a promise he'd never break. Regardless of his family's new direction, if anyone ever posed a threat to what belonged to Mac, he'd personally see to destroying that person with his bare hands.

"You believe you're safe, right? Promise me you're not going to worry about this."

Jenna looked up into his eyes. "I'm not worried one bit. I know you wouldn't lie to me about that."

"I love you, Jenna."

A smile spread across her face. "I love you. More than anything. Shall I lock the door and give you a sneak peek at what I purchased for our honeymoon?"

Arousal slammed into him. "Is that a rhetorical question?"

As he watched his fiancée close and lock the door, he knew he'd die before letting anything happen to her. This was the start of their life together and things may be rocky, but for now, having Jenna do some insanely erotic striptease in his office was all he needed. She was all he needed and they would face anything in the outside world together.

* * * * *

COLTON'S DEADLY
ENGAGEMENT

ADDISON FOX

For Aunt Bonnie

Godmother. Aunt. Friend. Cheerleader. You've always been that to me and so much more.

But would I be me if I didn't memorialise our oldest joke in your dedication?

Bonnie really IS a nickname for Angela. (Even if my 1st grade teacher still believes I'm wrong!)

I love you!

Chapter 1

Cold air pierced Finn Colton's lungs as he ran hell-for-leather beside his faithful and loyal partner, Lotte. Although she was trained specifically for attacking and guarding her quarry, the German shepherd was a mighty fine tracker and Finn followed in her wake as she pounded over the hills and valleys of Red Ridge, South Dakota.

In February.

Damn, it was cold.

As soon as the thought registered, Finn pushed it aside as he pressed on toward the fleeing figure about seventy-five yards ahead, weaving in and out of shadow. Was it possible they were this close to the suspect dubbed the "Groom Killer"?

Although he'd put little stock in the sensational and lurid depiction the local press had been dreaming up for nearly a month, he would cop to concern over the safety of his town. A police chief's duty was to his people and that was a mighty challenging job when everyone he spoke to admitted to walking around in fear.

Tonight's discovery of a second dead groom was going to turn subtle unease to full-on terror.

Lotte's bark pulled him from his dismal thoughts as she put on another burst of speed, leaping forward into the night. Finn ignored the cold air and kicked it up a notch, digging deep for the stamina to keep moving.

In an apparent burst of speed of his—or her—own, their quarry put on the juice and zagged out of view. Finn kept going, trailing Lotte so close he could feel her tail slapping against his thigh, but in moments it was clear they'd lost the trail.

Lotte whined as she slowed, running in a circle as she fought to pick up a fresh scent on the ground before letting out a sharp cry.

The distinct odor of bleach, especially piercing in the bitter cold, hit his nostrils as he narrowed the distance to his partner. He came to a solid halt and bent to settle his hands on his knees. He quickly stepped back, ordering Lotte with him, out of range of the harsh scent.

Years of consistent training and the deep love and affection they'd built had her backing up immediately and she moved to his side.

"We were set up, girl. That bleach was laid down only a little while ago. Bastard wasn't running from us. He was running to his own version of the finish line."

Finn cursed again and stood to his full height, willing his other senses into action as he searched the darkened night. A wash of stars lit up the sky, made even brighter by the thick halo of a nearly full moon, but revealed nothing. Whomever they'd chased was gone and the night held no clue as to where.

He toyed with following, anyway, heading in the last direction he'd seen his quarry, but knew it was a lost cause. If the killer was smart enough to put down the bleach in advance, he or she was smart enough to change direction once out of sight.

Lotte edged toward the chemical, backing away when the scent hit her nose once more.

"Clever," he muttered. *And dangerous*, he added to himself. Very dangerous if the killer had enough sense to prepare like that.

Red Ridge's K-9 unit was famous across the state and even farther on than the boundaries of the Black Hills and the South Dakota border. The killer would have known they'd use every resource at their disposal, including well-trained K-9 dogs who needed relatively little scent input to hunt their quarry.

He patted Lotte's head, burying his fingers into the thick pelt of her fur. She was lean and fit, but winter had brought her thicker fur and he loved the way his palm seemed to sink into the warmth. She was a beauty and he scratched behind her ears as he praised her, reassuring her of her successful tracking even if the perp did get away. Finn Colton loved his sweet girl and he always made sure she knew she was appreciated and important.

He also talked to her like a partner. While he harbored no delusion she understood the differences in the gauge sizes of guns or the headache of late-night paperwork, she understood her role in their partnership and always sat and listened, staring up at him with large, soulful eyes. They shared an amazing bond and he never took her or her training for granted.

His wealthy uncle, Fenwick Colton, had seen to it that his investment in the unit and its cofunded training center—one of the largest in South Dakota—was well publicized. His uncle was an old bastard, Finn thought, but a crafty one. Man could get three dollars out of one and was always looking for an angle. If there was an opportunity to put Colton Energy in the paper, on TV or splashed all over the internet, he leaped at the chance.

The K-9 unit and training facility had given Fenwick that and more. Not only did they receive more than their fair share of local news coverage and even the occasional spate of national attention, but the unit had been a tribute to Fenwick's late first wife. Dubbed "the only one he ever loved" by Fenwick's own admission, he'd continued the funding long after he'd assuaged his grief with a string of generously endowed younger women.

The training center was one of the few reasons Finn tolerated his uncle. While his appreciation had a solid core of selfish motivation for the continued support of his precinct, a small corner of his heart liked the fact that Fenwick might have been a decent human being once upon a time.

Since he'd gotten Lotte as well as his entire department from the deal, Finn could hardly complain. But it did mean his uncle came calling a bit too often at police headquarters. His recent rant over the need to catch the Groom Killer had been a world-class tirade. The fact that his uncle believed it was his niece and

Finn's cousin Demi Colton who was responsible, had added an uncomfortable edge to the proceedings. He knew how to deal with his uncle—he wasn't a man who backed down easily before anyone—but the determined rant that Demi had gone so far off the edge she'd started killing men was a tough pill to swallow.

If asked, Finn would have said it was ludicrous. But after finding her necklace at the first crime scene and her name drawn in blood beside the body, he could hardly ignore what was in front of his face. Given her strong motive—she'd been engaged to Bo Gage before he'd dumped her for another woman he'd quickly proposed to—and the circumstantial evidence, Demi was their prime suspect. Yet the man who'd known her since she was an infant wanted to believe in her innocence.

The police chief had to work every angle, run down every lead and needed a great deal of objectivity. Especially with Demi on the run and seeming uncomfortably guilty when he'd questioned her after Bo Gage's murder.

With their race toward answers lost, he gestured Lotte to follow him. It was time to head back to review the crime scene they'd abandoned—a celebration turned tragedy—to chase a murderer.

He still saw it in his mind—had already begun the mental walk through the details of the crime. The second groom lay outside the back door of the kitchen at the Circle T Steakhouse. The man had been murdered in the midst of his rehearsal dinner, his body discovered only when one of the line chefs had run outside for a quick break. The man's scream had been heard all the way inside the restaurant and it had taken the foresight of the head chef to keep everyone away from the body. There was no way anyone could have helped Michael Hayden, even had they tried.

Not with a bullet hole seared clear through his heart and a black cummerbund shoved deep into his mouth.

Darby Gage patted the cushion beside her and tried to coax Penny onto the couch. Darby had lived in the same house with the stubborn female for the past two weeks and had been unsuccessful in getting Penny to share any common space. She refused to share the couch, the bed or even a small chaise longue on the back porch.

Since it was February in South Dakota, the chaise experiment hadn't lasted long—it was too damn cold to sit waiting for a stubborn dog to join her on the rattan recliner—and Darby had taken some small measure of pride in the fact that she'd tried.

But enough was enough.

The German shepherd was the crown jewel in the dismal inheritance from her ex-husband and it was high time they came to some sort of grudging truce. Bo wasn't coming back courtesy of the bullet in his chest and Darby was in charge now.

Which seemed to have no impact on Penny. None whatsoever. Nor had it stopped striking Darby with that strange combination of surprise and sadness.

Bo was really gone. And the manner of his death…

She still shuddered when she thought about how he'd been discovered, shot and left for dead, a tuxedo cummerbund shoved into his mouth. It was dark and macabre. She'd tried to avoid thinking about it, but that was difficult when you considered how the *Red Ridge*

Gazette had run with a new story every day, each one more lurid than the last. Everything from Groom Killer on the Loose to Is the Groom Killer One of Red Ridge's Own? had graced the paper's headlines. More than that, it was as if a fever had gripped the town and no one could stop talking about it.

Was it a local like Demi Colton? The press had picked up on her as their favorite suspect and had been writing story after story on her background and her brief engagement to Bo before he'd dumped her for his new intended bride, Hayley Patton. Although she supposed anything was possible, as Bo's former wife Darby could hardly understand a woman committing a crime of passion over the man.

He was good-looking in his own way, but she'd learned too quickly that he'd also used those good looks to coast by in life. He'd carried little responsibility, preferring to dump his troubles on others. And other than his dogs, there was little he'd seemed to truly care about.

In the end, it had been his cheating that had killed their marriage. She'd come to realize that even had he been faithful, theirs wasn't a union that would have lasted. It had taken a while, but Darby had finally reached the point where she could accept that without the immense guilt that had initially accompanied the thought.

Which made her current circumstances all the more puzzling.

While she and Bo had ended things amicably enough two years ago, why had her ex seen fit to leave her his German shepherd breeding business? She knew and loved dogs—and she spent more than a few hours of each work week at the K-9 training center making a few extra dollars—but that didn't make her a fit breeder. Neither had her fourteen-month marriage to Bo. He was a responsible breeder—he loved his dogs and he took good care of them—but she hadn't involved herself in the business during their marriage.

Yet here she was. The new owner of Red Ridge's premier breeding business for the town and the county's K-9 units. They sold to assorted others besides the RRPD, but had a reputation to uphold with one of the state's primary K-9 departments.

The PD down in Spearfish had attempted a K-9 unit of their own a few years back and had trained a few of Penny's puppies. The cost of keeping the program had grown too much and they'd ultimately sold the dogs to a good security firm known for its excellent treatment and handling of their dogs.

Bo's other customers, the Larson brothers, were also good for a few puppies in each litter. A fact that settled uncomfortably on her shoulders. It was unfair of her—they doted on their dogs and treated them well—yet something creeped her out about the way the twins, Noel and Evan Larson, strutted around Red Ridge like they owned the town and everyone in it. They'd been raised by their kindly grandmother, Mae, after losing their parents, and Darby knew she should cut them a break.

But she never liked when the Larson boys came around.

Penny's light yip startled her and pulled Darby from her thoughts. The pretty German shepherd had dropped down to her belly, head on her front paws, and was even now staring at Darby.

"You don't like the Larsons, either, do you?"

Penny's dark eyes seemed to bore into hers. Even as she knew it was a silly thought, Darby could have sworn the dog agreed with her.

"You really can sit next to me. I won't bite and I'd like to get to know you better."

Penny's gaze never wavered as she considered her from her spot across the rug. The couch wasn't that comfortable, but Darby had to believe the threadbare carpet was even less so. She was still adjusting to her surroundings. She'd moved her few possessions in from the one-bedroom apartment she'd rented in town and the addition barely made a dent in Bo's small house.

It was so odd to be back in the house. Their marriage had been brief but she'd made some improvements when she'd lived here with Bo. She'd freshened up the curtains and had insisted they paint the living room and kitchen to brighten things up. Now those improvements simply looked garish, like the rest of the house had aged around them, an old woman wearing her years despite the heavy makeup she used to try to hide the lines.

Since the house was hers, she'd like to make a few changes, but the inheritance hadn't come without its challenges. One of which was a stifling mortgage that Bo had overextended himself on and a mountain of debt for the breeding business. She'd spent the past two weeks trying to get her arms wrapped around it all and was still puzzled by just how far into debt her ex-husband had gone. She didn't think he was in that deep when they were married, but in the end, who really knew.

All she knew now was that she had a hill of debt and very few options.

She was also worried about Penny. The dog had kept her distance but Darby wasn't blind to Penny's increasing age. She was the conduit to more puppies though Darby had real reservations about attempting to breed her again.

Which only made the problems she had since the reading of Bo's will grow even bigger.

Why had he chosen her? Was it punishment for a marriage gone bad instead of a gift?

Or was there something else at play?

Hayley Patton was his fiancée, yet she'd gotten nothing of his except the car they'd leased together and the rings they'd purchased in preparation for the wedding. She was flashing a mighty large rock on her left hand but Darby had no idea how Bo had paid for it. She could only be grateful the bill hadn't showed up on her list of debts on the property.

Whatever else he was, Bo Gage hadn't been a saver or a money manager. And now it was up to her to clean up his mess.

Lost in her thoughts, she was surprised to feel the heavy sway of the couch frame when Penny leaped up. The dog still kept her distance, curling at the opposite end of the three-cushion couch, but Darby smiled anyway.

Maybe they might figure their way out of this, after all.

Finn dropped into his desk chair and glanced at his watch: 4:00 a.m. It had taken them that long to secure the scene, interview the witnesses and take as much detail from the Circle T's property as they could. Only after they'd done that had they been able to move Michael Hayden's body.

The guy had snuck out the back of the kitchen to grab a smoke, his fiancée's legendary distaste for the practice sending him skulking out a rear exit to escape the rehearsal dinner festivities unnoticed.

Only someone *had* noticed.

They'd shot him.

Finn reviewed his notes, typing them into his report to ensure his thoughts were as fresh as possible. What he avoided including was the observation that sneaking cigarettes at your rehearsal dinner because your soon-to-be wife hated the practice likely wasn't the most auspicious start to happily-ever-after.

Not that he was exactly an expert.

His own marriage had crashed and burned in a fiery pile of ash after his ex-wife had grown fed up with his hours and the danger of his job. Mary was a good woman and he'd heard through the grapevine that she was remarrying. She'd left Red Ridge after their divorce, picking up work in Spearfish, about thirty miles away, as a digital designer for a local firm. He was happy that she had moved on with her life and wanted nothing but good things for her.

The fact that he'd felt nothing—not even the slightest tug—when he'd heard the news bothered him more than he could say. Wasn't a man supposed to be jealous if his ex moved on? Even a little bit? Yet here he was, content and maybe even a little relieved that she'd picked up her life and found someone new. He'd never worried much about his reputation as a cold, work-focused leader, but maybe it was time he started.

After, he promised himself. He'd worry about it all

after he got through these reports and the inquiries and found out just who was killing men in his town.

The report practically wrote itself. The men and women on his team were well trained and good at their jobs. Between their notes and work, as well as his own, he was able to paint a quick, succinct picture of the crime and Michael Hayden's unpleasant death.

Shutting down his laptop, he caught sight of a note scribbled by Carson Gage and left in the small wooden box he kept on the corner of his desk.

Carson was one of his best detectives on the force and the brother of the first victim, Bo Gage. Finn picked up the note, curious to see what, if any, details Carson had added to his already-robust case file.

Unsuccessful visit to Darby Gage. Persists in saying she had no idea why Bo left her the business and the house. Has alibi for Bo's murder but could have someone covering for her?

Despite the personal connection with his brother, Carson had been invaluable on the case. But that last question didn't sit well with Finn. He knew Carson had worked long and hard to find justice for his brother, but it wasn't like him—or anyone on Finn's team—to question a person's alibi simply for the sake of wrapping up a case and pinning a crime on a convenient suspect.

Was there something behind Carson's concern? Or was he so frustrated by the lack of leads that he'd begun grasping at straws?

Yes, it was suspicious that Bo had left his business to his ex-wife. But Finn had known Bo Gage and the man hadn't been the most responsible soul. It could be as simple as the fact that Bo had never had his will changed after his divorce.

Or there could be something else there.

He made a quick note to himself to go talk to Darby Gage. He'd spoken with her a few weeks before when suspicion had first landed on Bo Gage's ex-wife and hadn't come to any conclusions. Nevertheless, if something about the woman was nagging at Carson, then Finn would talk to her again.

His detective had a lot on his plate, including his own conflicted feelings about his brother's passing. Perhaps this case needed a bit more objectivity.

Up until their last meeting, Finn had known Darby Gage as he knew most of his constituents, by sight and a vague recollection of a conversation a time or two. She was pretty, with shoulder-length dark hair and vivid blue eyes, her figure petite and waifish. If he hadn't seen her at the K-9 training center a time or two, carrying pails of water to scrub out the dog facilities, he'd not have believed her capable of the work. The slender lines of her body belied a strong, capable woman.

One capable of murder?

He shook off the thought, unwilling to take the same leap as Carson simply for the sake of having a suspect besides Demi Colton.

Fifteen minutes later he was still thinking of her when he stepped into his ground-floor condo and peeled off his gun before climbing into bed.

Was it even remotely possible Darby Gage was the Groom Killer? She had a potential motive for killing her ex-husband—he'd left her the house and business, after all. But Michael Hayden had been killed with the same MO as Bo. And why would Darby kill Hayden?

The thought of her as the perp didn't sit well, but for some strange reason, just as he was fading off to sleep, he felt a shot of interest light up his nerve endings. There was something about her that caught a man's notice.

Something that had caught his notice, even as he'd been forced to remain professional and disinterested.

He hadn't given Darby Gage more than a passing thought over the past five years, but now that he *had* given her a passing thought, he couldn't deny his interest in talking to her.

So he'd go see her for himself.

And try not to notice if she was as pretty as he remembered.

Chapter 2

The hope that had carried Darby through the prior evening when Penny had opted to join her on the couch met an untimely end about ten minutes into breakfast. It had started with Penny's stubborn refusal to eat. Darby had tried to coax her with dry food and, when that hadn't worked, some wet food Bo had kept in the pantry. When neither met with success, she'd even gone so far as to cook the dog some rice and heat up some plain chicken she'd cooked for her lunchtime salads all week. All to no avail.

Penny wouldn't eat.

This had resulted in a call to the vet and a panicked round of "What did she eat the day before?" before the dog had shamed her into embarrassment by diving into her breakfast after fifteen shaky, fear-filled minutes. The only saving grace was that Darby hadn't called the vet out to the house, only to have paid for an unnecessary visit.

What the call *had* turned up as the vet probed on Penny's age and overall health was his concern that another litter would put Penny at serious risk. On some level, Darby had known it, but she'd told herself she needed a professional opinion.

And now she had it.

That dismal news and the breakfast battle of wills had been followed by the news of another murder in Red Ridge, this one eerily like Bo's. While the RRPD hadn't released all details of how Michael Hayden had been murdered, the fact that it was another groom-to-be—this one celebrating at his rehearsal dinner—was too coincidental for Darby's comfort.

After fielding three calls from concerned friends in town, along with two more she'd sent to voice mail, unwilling to engage in the expected idle gossip that would have resulted, Darby headed out to the back-yard and the property beyond.

The day was sharp and cold, but the winter sun was bright in a blue sky. Penny had reluctantly followed her outside and had skirted the property, seeming to take comfort in her perusal of the perimeter before settling on the rattan recliner on the porch, apparently content to watch her.

Darby shot the dog the gimlet eye but was pleased to see Penny's reluctant interest in her activities. "Chalk it up to a silent victory that she's interested enough to hang out here and move on," Darby muttered to herself before heading toward a large shed.

She dug out a bucket and some disinfectant and went to work on the large cage she'd pulled out of the garage the day before. The roomy nest served as Penny's private area when she was preparing for her litter and Darby wanted it clean and fresh.

Penny might not be able to use it any longer but the activity and the bracing air gave Darby purpose and something to do.

It also kept her mind away from the subject of just how far off the rails her life had traveled.

She'd believed her savings would be enough to carry her through the next litter of puppies. But the problems kept mounting and there was no way she could take care of the business, the house, the taxes and the need to purchase a new dog for the breeding program on the small amount she had in the bank.

Bo's once-thriving business with quite a few quality dogs was now down to Penny. Darby knew how much Bo had loved the dog and he'd obviously kept her even after he had to sell all the other German shepherds to keep things afloat.

Bo's father, Edson, had begged Darby to keep the business going in his son's memory, and she'd promised she would. It was only after seeing the degree of Bo's debt that she was fast coming to understand she shouldn't have made that promise.

What a mess.

Settling the thick padding from the base of the cage and the disinfectant on the porch, Darby headed inside to retrieve the water she'd left heating on the stove to mix with the cleaner. She'd nearly wrestled the heavy pot off the stove when the doorbell rang. Resetting the pot and narrowly avoiding the slosh of hot water against the edges, she headed for the front door. The house wasn't large, but she prayed with each footfall that one of the nosy voice mails still waiting on her phone hadn't decided to drive across town to strike up a conversation.

Offering up one more silent prayer, Darby pulled open the front door.

Just when she thought her day couldn't get any worse, she came face-to-face with Finn Colton, the Red Ridge chief of police.

Finn appreciated the authority that came with his position and he made it a point to behave in a way that earned him respect. He'd met a few cops over the years who'd forgotten that the trust the public imbued in them was as important as honoring that trust. He'd never wanted to behave in a manner that disregarded that bond.

His surprise visit to Darby Gage was both deliberate and purposeful. *Respectful*, but deliberate all the same. While not quite full-on disregard for her trust, he was doing a bit of bearding the lion in its den.

Aka surprising the pretty divorcée. On purpose.

"Mrs. Gage. I was hoping you could find a few minutes to speak with me."

"Chief Colton." She nodded but made no move to let him in. "What can I do for you?"

"I wanted to talk to you about Bo for a bit."

Resignation settled in her blue-violet gaze before she nodded her head. "Of course. Come in, please."

He followed her into the small house, surprised to see how run-down the place was. He'd grown up well aware of the long-standing Colton-Gage feud but had always believed the Gages lived well enough to afford the basics. Though he had little interest subscribing to something as antiquated—and decades old—as the town family feud, his reaction to the state of Bo Gage's home only reinforced that he'd never been particularly close with any of the Gages.

Fortunately, working with several members of the family on the force had changed that and he was grateful for it. Carson had his full respect, as did Carson's younger half sister, Elle. Although still a rookie on the K-9 team, Elle handled herself with poise beyond her years and had a keen ability to partner with her K-9 charge.

In Finn's estimation, the Gages weren't so bad, even if his uncles, Fenwick and Rusty, as well as his father, Judson, continued to perpetuate the ridiculous notion of a feud. He'd been called to more than one heated incident between members of the two families since joining the RRPD and knew it was only a matter of time before there'd be another.

Truth be told, he was surprised there hadn't been a skirmish yet, especially with a Gage murdered and a Colton as one of the suspects.

Even with his better understanding of the Gage family—or maybe because of it—Bo Gage's home was unexpected. He might have been a slacker, but Bo was still the son of one of Red Ridge's wealthier individuals, Edson Gage. Somehow Finn had expected Bo's fortunes to be a bit more robust than the shabby decor suggested. Even as his gaze roamed the place, Finn had to give Darby credit. The furniture might be worn and run-down, but it was clean. He didn't see dust on the end table or the TV and he could still see the outline of sweeper marks on the carpet.

Were murderesses that clean?

A quick scent memory of the bleach from the crime scene filled his nose and he struggled against the thought. Bo had been dead long enough that there would have been some accumulation of dust and dirt by now. Yet here she was, cleaning up and making the place her own.

"What would you like to discuss, Chief Colton?"

Darby's question pulled him from his musings, but Finn had to admit the angle wasn't one he'd considered. Perhaps it was time he started.

"You seem to be settling in."

"I didn't have much to move in with me."

"Clean, too." He stated it as an observation and was surprised when she just smiled back, her grin bright and proud.

"My mother raised me to believe cleanliness was next to godliness. Add on the fact that I'm keeping up with a seventy-pound German shepherd and my OCD kicks in hard."

"Does the dog hate the mess?"

"No, Chief. I do. And the endless piles of hair a dog sheds." She turned toward the kitchen. "Can I get you a cup of coffee?"

"That'd be nice."

Finn followed Darby into the back of the house, smiling when the purported mess maker—a German shepherd with the same coloring as Lotte—came through a doggie door and trotted toward him. He extended his hand, keeping an easy smile on his face. "Hey there, girl."

The dog slowed but continued forward, her tail wagging gently.

Finn kept his hand extended, pleased when she allowed him to pet her head. "Hi, sweetheart. What's your name?"

"This is Penny." The slightest grimace crossed Darby's face before she shot an indulgent smile at the dog. "She sure seems to like you."

He dropped to a knee and continued to level praise and affection on the dog. "Why do I sense that irritates you?"

"Let's just say Penny and I have come to a grudging truce since I moved in."

"How grudging?"

"I keep trying and Penny keeps her distance."

Finn stood to his full height. "She's a good girl. She's just had a lot of upheaval lately. Bo loved this dog."

"That he did. Which is why, when I was married to Bo, Penny and I had a reluctant truce, as well."

"She didn't like another woman in her territory?"

He saw the moment the idea struck, Darby's eyes widening. "I never thought about it that way, but I guess I can see that."

Finn had spent enough time with Lotte to know that she was deeply protective of him. And while that hadn't extended to the women he dated—mostly because Finn made a solid point not to bring them around his partner—he knew it was something he'd likely deal with should he ever get back in deep enough in a relationship.

An image of Lotte meeting Darby struck him, the thought out of place for the job he was there to do. He needed to talk to Darby Gage about her potential involvement in a murder, not imagine her making friends with his dog.

So why had the image struck?

Darby handed over a mug, oblivious to his wayward thoughts. "What would you like in your coffee? I have cream, milk and sugar."

"Cream would be fine."

She retrieved the small carton from the fridge and handed it over.

Penny watched her before backing away to take a seat beneath the kitchen table.

"Yep." Darby nodded as he handed back the carton. "She hates me."

"She's just trying to get used to you. Give her some time."

"I suppose."

Finn took a sip of his coffee and gestured to the table. "Mind if I take a seat?"

"Sure."

She fixed her own mug and took a seat opposite him.

"Do you know Michael Hayden?"

"No, I'm afraid I don't," Darby said. "But I've had several calls this morning telling me something terrible has happened to him."

"You could say that."

"Was he murdered like Bo?"

"It appears so."

She shook her head. "What makes people do such horrible things? I know Bo had his shortcomings, but to hurt him like that? It doesn't make sense to me."

Something weird bottomed in his stomach, fluttering beneath the caffeine hit, and Finn had to admit that he wanted to believe her. More than that, the sincerity in her eyes seemed legitimate. He had significant experience reading people—the wacky branches of his family ensured he had to be constantly on his toes—and he'd only further honed that skill with his job in law enforcement.

But the desire to believe her didn't change the fact that her alibi on record was a bit weak for the night of Bo's death. Nor did it keep him from having to ask where she was yesterday when Michael Hayden was murdered.

"Murder makes little sense."

"And here in Red Ridge, of all places. I know people deal with this in large cities. But here?" She shuddered. "It doesn't seem possible."

The fact that she still hadn't tracked to his line of thought was another checkmark in her favor, but none of it changed the point that she was one of the few who'd gained with Bo Gage's murder. "You've benefitted from Bo's death."

The distracted blue gaze, focused on the small circles she drew around the lip of her mug, snapped to attention, fire heating their depths. "This again?"

There she was. Defensive. Because she was guilty?

"This house. His business. Penny." Finn listed them all. "You're the one who profited by Bo's death."

"I was interrogated by your detective after the reading of Bo's will. I did not kill my ex-husband. But is that what you are suggesting, Chief Colton?"

"I'm just asking questions."

"No, you're not." She settled her mug on the table, her gaze direct when she next looked at him. "So I'd like to know if I'm a suspect before I ask you to leave."

Darby fought the waves of nerves that mixed her few sips of coffee into a dark sloshy brew in her stomach. Even with the subtle feeling that she was going to be sick, she refused to stand down.

How dare he come to her home and ask her questions like this?

She wasn't a murderer. More than that, she'd been so busy since Bo's death, she'd barely kept her head above water. What did he possibly think she was about?

And why?

Unbidden, images of the past few weeks' front pages of the *Red Ridge Gazette* filled her mind's eye.

Groom Killer on the Loose.

The Red Ridge Groom Killer—Crime of Passion or Premeditated Murder?

Love or Revenge? Does the Groom Killer Want Both?

One after the next, the headlines had grown more and more lurid as each day went by without any leads. The reporters at the *Gazette* had been having a field day with the biggest thing to hit Red Ridge since a four-month gold rush helped establish the town in the late nineteenth century. Now that a second groom had been killed, the headlines would only get worse.

Because it was worse, she reminded herself. There *was* a groom killer on the loose.

"You think I'm doing this? First Bo. Then this poor Michael Hayden, a man I didn't even know."

"I'm asking a few questions."

"No, Chief Colton. You're not."

When he said nothing, she continued. "Can you honestly sit there and tell me you think I murdered my ex-husband to get my hands on this?" She gestured to the kitchen at large, stopping when her gaze landed on

Penny. "Other than Penny, the man has left me with less than nothing."

He seemed to soften a bit at her mention of the dog, his hard gaze softening as it grew speculative. "I'm not sure his fiancée sees it the same way."

The comment was enough to respike her ire and Darby let out a heavy exhale. "Don't think Hayley hasn't been by a few times to make that very point."

"Miss Patton's been here?"

"Sure. She came to get her things. Made a point to prance out of the bedroom flaunting a small red negligee like it was going to hurt my feelings."

"You were married to Bo Gage," Chief Colton pointed out. He didn't even blink at the mention of a red slinky number. "Presumably she thought it would upset you?"

"Bo and I parted on amicable terms. The best thing I can say about the day I signed my divorce papers was the sense of relief."

"You weren't upset?"

"I spent the majority of my marriage upset. By the time I reached that day, I was just happy to be out, free to go about my life."

As the words settled between them, hovering somewhere over the sugar bowl in the middle of the table, Darby couldn't deny their truth. She'd had no desire to be a divorcée at the age of twenty-seven, but in the ensuing two years she'd come to accept the fact that ending her marriage to Bo had been the right thing to do.

She might not have found anyone to move on with, but she had moved on. There was strength in that, and a deep sense of pride that she'd been willing to make the tough decisions and stand up for herself.

It had also toughened her up and she knew she didn't have to sit there and answer Chief Colton's questions, no matter how attractive the questioner.

And darn her stupid feminine awareness for picking up on that fact.

Whatever she'd expected when he'd arrived, Finn Colton wasn't there to help her any more than any other gawkers who'd been by over the past few weeks. She was on her own.

Just like always.

But it was his next words that proved it.

"Would you be able to tell me your whereabouts for yesterday between the hours of seven and nine?"

Chapter 3

Finn poured himself another cup of precinct coffee, well aware the caffeine wasn't going to do any favors for the slick knot that still twisted his gut. His interview with Darby Gage hadn't gone well and after securing her unprovable alibi for Hayden's murder—an evening in with Penny—he'd left her in a fine pique.

Although he'd been hoping for confirmation that she'd been out with girlfriends or even on a date, her pronouncement that she'd spent the cold winter night in with her obstinate new roommate hadn't gotten him any nearer to removing Darby Gage from his suspect list.

He headed back to his desk from the small kitchenette the RRPD secretary, Lorelei Wong, maintained with the same ruthless efficiency with which she manned the front entrance. He'd deliberately used the single-cup brewer instead of making a pot so she wouldn't come in Monday morning and razz him for making a mess. She'd probably still find an infraction, but at least he wouldn't risk leaving a coffeemaker full of coffee grounds or stale coffee gone cold in the pot.

The case bothered him. He knew himself well enough to know that not only would it require his full concentration, but that that same concentration would likely reduce a few brain cells for the next few days.

Who was killing grooms-to-be in his town?

What makes people do such horrible things?

Darby's question haunted him, nagging at the back of his sleep-deprived mind. After his visit to Bo Gage's old residence, he'd headed back to the Circle T to review the latest crime scene with fresh eyes. The visit hadn't turned up much, other than the fact that the town was shaken. The restaurant had reported that nearly all their Saturday night reservations had been canceled before the owner was even able to make the calls that they would be closed that evening.

But it was the comments the proprietor, Gus Hanley, had fielded from those canceling guests that had Finn concerned.

"If someone's killing men who are about to get married, can I risk even going out on a date?"

"Big-city crime has come to Red Ridge. Maybe I need to try staying in for a while."

"Should we reconsider our spring wedding?"

Along with the canceled reservations, Gus had lost two events for early March—one for an engagement party and one for a rehearsal dinner.

No doubt about it, Red Ridge was in a panic. As a lifelong resident, Finn found that sad. As chief of police—it was unbearable. He'd become a cop because he'd wanted to make a difference. The fact that he was good at it was an added bonus that kept him focused, determined and dedicated. The *added* added bonus of working with Lotte had sealed the deal.

He hadn't always been a K-9 cop. His first few years on the force had been focused on learning the ropes and endless hours of traffic detail. But he'd showed promise and the old chief, Clancy Macintyre, had taken him under his wing. Chief Macintyre had been a good influence, balancing his innate ability to teach with the patience and care Finn's own father had never exhibited.

Judson Colton was a rancher and a damn fine one. But he'd never understood his oldest son, a quiet kid with an unerring eye for detail. That had always been true and, whether by choice or by habit, he and his father maintained a respectful distance. His father's second wife, Joanelle, had made that even easier to accomplish with her cold ways and dismissal of Judson's first child as a burden she was forced to carry.

But there was one thing ranch life had taught Finn and that was his love of animals. His opportunity to move in to the K-9 unit and work with a trained canine partner had taken his love of police work and made it his life's calling.

He was good at his job and he was good to the men and women who worked for him. They all kept Red Ridge safe and took pride in their role as protectors. And someone had come to their town and violated all they'd built.

Suddenly tired of it all, including the need to question petite women with silky hair and what read as determined—but innocent—eyes, Finn headed for his desk. The case weighed on him and he'd be no good to anyone if he didn't clear his head. It was time to wrap up the little paperwork he'd come in for, get his notes on the interview with Darby logged in and head home. Maybe he'd make a steak and a baked potato, the hearty meal a way to relax and recharge.

And then he'd eat it alone.

That thought hit harder than all the others that had bombarded him throughout the day.

He'd been alone since his divorce and had believed himself okay with it. He'd had dates from time to time. Had even progressed to something more like a relationship a few years back with a sweet teacher down in Black Hills City. But, ultimately, things hadn't worked out. She'd had visions of the future and in the end he simply couldn't get his head on the same page.

So why was he now imagining enjoying his steak and potato with a companion?

One who looked suspiciously like Darby Gage.

The squad room was quiet. His cousin Brayden, another K-9 cop on the team, was tapping away at his keyboard. He was nodding his head to whatever music pumped through his ears—classic rock, if Finn knew his cousin—but he did holler a "yo" as Finn passed.

Finn briefly toyed with inviting Brayden to join him for dinner, but for some reason the thought of sharing a steak and a beer with his cousin—whom he liked quite a bit—didn't entice the same way as images of dining with Darby.

Since his latest set of notes wouldn't write itself, Finn opted to ignore thoughts of dinner altogether as he sat down. His desk held what he considered a comfortable amount of clutter: stacks of files, a handful of notes, and a series of sticky notes that littered the top of his desk and the edges of his computer monitor. Shifting a stack of folders farther to the edge, he knocked over a dark box, the square packaging making a heavy thud as it hit the floor.

Finn bent to pick it up, quite sure the box hadn't been on his desk the night before. There was a small square card taped to the top and he flipped it open.

"'Chocolates for a cop with a big heart.'" The note was signed "an appreciative citizen" and had small hearts dotting the *i*'s in "citizen."

He wanted to think it was sweet—this wasn't the first anonymous gift he'd received over the past few weeks—but it was beginning to get out of hand. Red Ridge was a small town and he appreciated the proprietary way the citizens treated their local law enforcement. The holidays typically brought a steady stream of cookies and cakes for the staff and homemade treats for the canine members of the team. Summer often brought picnic baskets of fried chicken and endless vats of lemonade.

In all of those cases, the townsfolk enjoyed bringing in the gifts and thanking the staff in person. What Finn couldn't quite reconcile with the recent spate of gifts directed at him was why the giver felt the need to be anonymous.

Going with his gut, he dropped the chocolate into the trash can under his desk and went back to his report.

There really was no accounting for the wacky things people did. And since he had a killer to catch, he hardly had the time to worry about someone too shy to come in to the precinct to say hello.

Darby stared at her checkbook and tried desperately not to think about the debt that loomed once she got through the month of February.

"Welcome to Monday," she muttered to herself, well aware she'd have the same problem on a Tuesday, a Wednesday or any other day of the week. There simply wasn't any more money. And the vet's visit the day before—a courtesy visit he'd called it—had proved conclusively she couldn't breed Penny again. The risk to Penny's health was too great to support another litter, especially coming on the heels of the litter she'd had the previous fall.

He'd mentioned a sweet German shepherd he'd taken care of in a nearby town—one ready for breeding and whose owner would sell for a fair price assuming she could keep one of the litter as part of the arrangement. But Darby knew it was hopeless. She barely had enough to take care of herself and Penny. There was no way she could afford a new dog right now.

The breeding program would have to wait until she got back on her feet. A few more months of her regular jobs—waitressing at the diner and helping out at the K-9 training center—and she'd reassess. That was assuming the taxes on Bo's property didn't put her underwater before she could earn what she needed.

On a hard sigh, she slammed the checkbook cover closed and shoved it, along with several open bills, across the kitchen table. She'd worry about it later. The problem wasn't going anywhere and she had one more room to clean before she'd finally feel like she'd officially moved in to her own home.

When had Bo become such a slob?

While she hadn't lied to Chief Colton the other day—that she was pleased to be out of her marriage—Bo hadn't been a terrible guy. They weren't compatible in the least and once she'd gotten past the fact that she'd fallen in love with an image instead of an actual person, it had become far easier for her to assess her marriage through objective eyes.

Even his roving nature—undoubtedly the worst aspect of their relationship—had an odd sense of immaturity wrapped up in it. If Bo wanted something, he went after it. Like a child unable to leave a sweet on the counter or Penny snatching something from the trash. The item was taken because it was there.

Bo was the same with women.

What he hadn't been, if memory served, was a piggish man with a dirty home. Granted, he'd been a bachelor before she'd moved in the first time, and had spent more time out of the house than in, but she hadn't remembered the dirt.

Or maybe she'd simply had the blind gaze of a newlywed, determined to create a new life.

She crossed to the counter and picked up her scrub brush, soap and a large container of bleach. She'd nearly gone through the entire thing over the past week, scrubbing down anything and everything she could find. The small second bathroom at the back of the house was her last hurdle to conquer. She could then at least take comfort that she laid her head down each evening in a clean home.

An hour later, with the last section of shower tile

shining a gleaming white, a heavy pounding on the front door jarred Darby from her thoughts and the throbbing strains of pop music that played through her earbuds. The addition of Penny's barking had her peeling off her rubber gloves and dropping everything into the tub to go see who was at the door.

"Penny!" The dog had her nose pressed to the floor in front of the door, a low growl emanating from deep in her throat.

The pounding kicked up again and without the earbuds Darby had no trouble making out who was knocking. The high-pitched screech gave it away even before Darby pulled aside the small panel curtain that hid the glass beside the door.

Hayley Patton.

"Darby Gage, you let me in!"

Although it had been a few years since she'd lived with Bo and Penny, Darby hadn't forgotten her training skills or the way Bo had taught her to manage the dog. She used the required instructions to order Penny away from the door, satisfied when she took up her post a few feet back, blocking the small hallway entrance into the main living area of the house.

The uncontrolled barking was odd, but not unexpected. For all her skill with dogs as a trainer at the K-9 training center, Hayley had a worse relationship with Penny than Darby did. Whether there was something about the woman that disturbed Penny or just the pure knowledge that Hayley was a jerk, Darby didn't know. But nothing changed the fact that the two of them did not get along.

She didn't like another woman in her territory?

The conversation that had haunted her throughout

the weekend popped up once more, the chief's question ringing in her ears. Did Penny resent Hayley's place in Bo's life? Was that the root of her upset? Or was it possible there was something more?

Hayley had been playing the grieving fiancée to the hilt and while it pained Darby to think otherwise, was it possible the woman was responsible for Bo's death? She knew it was beyond unkind—the woman had lost her fiancée the night before the wedding—but something about Hayley had always run false to her.

Yet thinking Hayley had a hand in Bo's death seemed far-fetched. Especially now that there had been a second murder—one that had nothing to do with Hayley.

Dismissing the thought, Darby opened the door. Arm raised, Hayley had clearly been preparing to emit another round of pounding. The motion was enough to have her stumbling through the door on one high-heeled boot. Darby caught her, along with a whiff of heavy perfume and the knowledge that Bo had moved on to something bigger and better in the high, tight breasts that even now pressed against Darby's chest.

"Let go of me!" Hayley twisted out of the hold and quickly regained her feet. Penny let out another low growl, only to be on the receiving end of a trademark Hayley Patton eye roll. "Enough already! You know me!"

Penny dropped her head on her paws, as if acknowledging the truth of Hayley's statement, but kept her gaze firmly on her nemesis.

"What do you want, Hayley?"

"Nice welcome, Darb. You've gotten awful bossy since moving in to Bo's house."

"It's my house now."

"One you don't deserve," Hayley snapped.

Since the house was old and shabby and, up until the thorough cleaning had been as much of a physical mess as its meager finances, Darby toyed briefly with snapping a leash on Penny, tossing Hayley the keys and breezing right on out the door. Since that fantasy was easier than the reality of just walking out, Darby opted to play along to see what the woman wanted.

"Then maybe you and Bo should have talked about something important leading up to your wedding, like wills and finances."

"How dare you bring up something so crass and cold? I loved my Bow-tie."

Darby avoided making her mental eye roll a real one at the childish nickname and tried to summon up her cool. "I'm not suggesting you didn't. But you obviously didn't discuss your future if you're mad at me."

"I loved him and I thought he loved me. How did I even know he had a will? What twenty-nine-year-old has a will?"

A smart one, Darby thought. She'd made hers the moment she'd turned twenty-one and kept it in a lockbox with her other personal papers. "Well, Bo did."

"It's like tempting fate." Hayley shivered before her big blue eyes widened so far it was practically comical. "Do you think that's why he's dead?"

"I doubt it."

"Why not?"

"Bo's dead because someone put a bullet in his heart. I don't think a will had anything to do with it."

The sneer Hayley had carried through the door

faded at the harsh image Darby had painted. "I'm well aware of what happened to him."

"Are you also aware, then, that Michael Hayden was killed on Friday night?"

"The police have already been by to question me about it."

"They don't think you did it, do they?"

"Chief Colton says he's ruling out my involvement but I'm not so sure about that. He questioned me for a long time about Michael. Bo, too, on the night it happened."

Although Darby wanted to bite her tongue at the ready defense, it sprang to her lips all the same. "He's being thorough."

"Well, he should be looking at the real killer."

"You think you know who that is?" Darby didn't think anyone beside Demi Colton had been formally announced as a suspect, especially since the chief had visited on Saturday asking questions. She'd also been head down in trying to fix her life, so it was equally possible things had progressed and she was unaware.

"His cousin, of course. Demi Colton had a thing for my Bow-tie and I know she's the one who did it."

She'd heard the rumors about Demi Colton—that she'd been jilted by Bo for Hayley after only a one-week engagement, and had put her work as a bounty hunter to good use to go after the fickle man. But somehow Darby couldn't picture the woman as a murderess. Especially against Bo. She'd met Demi several times and the woman struck her as too smart, sharp and interesting to ever sacrifice her freedom over a man.

"I don't see it."

"Of course, you don't. You're too busy moving in to *my* house."

"Legal documents say otherwise."

"Which you're clearly milking to your advantage."

Patience at an end, Darby dropped the polite veneer. "What are you doing here?"

"I left a few things in Bow-tie's closet."

Darby had seen "Bow-tie's" closet and didn't recall anything that would have fit Hayley, but she gestured toward the bedroom. "Be my guest. I've packed up most of Bo's things to go to charity and I didn't see anything that looked overtly feminine, but have a go at it."

"You packed up his things?"

For the first time since the other woman's arrival Darby felt a shot of something. Not warmth, exactly, but something that smacked decidedly of compassion. "Well, sure. I'd rather see someone get use out of it."

The moment shifted and the screeching began before Darby could even process what was happening. "His things are mine! You can't have any of it!"

Finn heard the ruckus the moment he and Lotte got out of his police-issued SUV. The sound was a cross between a charging rhino and what he'd always imagined a "screaming banshee" actually sounded like. Since he already recognized Hayley Patton's cherry-red sports car in the small dirt driveway, Finn had some sense of what he was walking into.

And while he didn't anticipate violence, he did put his hand on his service weapon as he and Lotte approached the house.

When three heavy knocks and equally loud shouts

for "Ms. Gage" went unaddressed, Finn opened the door and let himself inside. Penny sat at full alert, staring at the two women who currently faced off in the hallway leading to the living room.

"My Bow-tie!" Hayley kept wailing the words over and over, pointing toward the door and intermittently screaming about Darby's cold heart, her grubby, grabbing hands and her temptress ways.

It didn't take long to piece together the root of the battle, especially when Hayley thrust her hands into a large black garbage bag, pulled out men's clothing and tossed it all over the small space.

Darby was calmer, but she didn't take the screaming laying down, either. She'd begun picking up the clothes, hollering back that she had every right to clean her home and deal with her ex-husband's old clothes.

"Ladies!"

Finn ordered Lotte to stay and moved forward, his focus on keeping the women apart and further separating Hayley from the bag of clothes.

"Miss Patton!" He pushed every ounce of authority into his tone and saw the moment when he finally got through. Hayley's gaze flicked past his on another dive toward the bag and it was only when she was about to throw a pair of shorts that his presence seemed to register.

Finn took his chance, moving in and taking hold of the shorts to still her movements. "Miss Patton?"

On a gulp of air, she tugged once before seeming to give up on a hard exhale of breath. Her shoulders dropped and her hands fell to her sides before she rushed into his arms. "Chief Colton. I'm so glad you're here."

Her arms tightened around his waist and tears immediately wet his button-down shirt as Hayley basically wiped her cheeks over his chest. Hands now full of another man's shorts, Finn tried a small "come now" as he patted her back. "It'll be okay."

Hayley only tightened her hold, the racking sobs growing harder as she shuddered against his body.

"Oh, for heaven's sake," Darby said as she marched toward the pile of clothes. In moments she had pieces bunched in her hands and was shoving them into the depleted garbage bag. "This is ridiculous."

Finn smiled at the muttered voice and had to agree. Hayley Patton had a reputation for making drama wherever she went. If the tableau playing out before his eyes was any indication, she'd brought a steaming-hot serving of drama to Darby Gage's new home.

"What seems to be the problem, Ms. Gage?" He congratulated himself on changing his salutation at the last moment, suspecting that calling Darby "Mrs. Gage" in front of Hayley would send the woman into another round of fits.

"She seems upset by my desire to give Bo's clothing to charity."

"It's so mean and cold," Hayley said against his chest before lifting her head, her eyes narrowing. "And why would an innocent person rush to throw away the clothes of a dead man? She planned this."

Finn's attention sharpened and he took a firm hold on Hayley's shoulders, pushing her an arm's length away. "Excuse me? Do you have relevant information in the death of Bo Gage or Michael Hayden?"

Hayley gulped, as if realizing she'd possibly overstepped. "I'm not talking about Michael Hayden."

"Then what are you talking about?"

"Her!" Hayley pointed to Darby, her expression murderous. "She's getting rid of Bo's clothes. What else has she gotten rid of?"

Although he wasn't ready to rule out anything, the mix of heightened emotions and melodrama wasn't something he could realistically take at face value.

"Why don't we move this into the living room and everyone can calm down for a few moments."

Without waiting for either woman's agreement, Finn directed Hayley into the living room. He gave Darby a quick nod, as well. "If you'd join us, please."

Darby reluctantly followed and waited, arms folded, as he settled Hayley on the couch. Lotte and Penny had remained in their places, but he could have sworn there was some silent communication going on between the two animals.

It took several long minutes for him to get to the bottom of the situation. After more rounds of tears, accusations and a moment when he thought things might come to blows, he finally had the details. And every last one of them centered on Hayley Patton resenting the hell out of the fact that her near-husband had left his home and his business to his ex-wife.

What wasn't quite so easy to gather was why Darby seemed on the verge of saying something, only to clamp her jaws tight each and every time, holding back whatever she'd been tempted to say. It was suspicious. More than that, it smacked of a secret that he couldn't understand.

Did she know something?

And why did her pretty blue gaze keep skipping around the room, landing at various points before settling on the dog and then racing around the room again?

After another tense fifteen minutes with Hayley persisting in her belief that she had some right to Bo's belongings, Darby finally gave in.

"Would you just take the clothes already? I want them out of the house. Give them to charity when you're ready."

"I'll never be ready to give up my Bow-tie's things."

Darby had remained stoic throughout the mix of sobbing tears and hard-edged rants, but something softened in her eyes when Hayley reached for the bag. Something that smacked quite a bit of compassion for the younger woman and all she'd lost.

On a hard cough, he excused himself from the couch and walked to the large bag that had been at the center of their tussle. "I can carry this out to the car for you, Miss Patton."

Hayley got off the couch and followed him, her sobs fading away to be replaced with a surprising amount of venom. "You're cold and heartless, Darby Gage. You stole a dead man's home and now want to erase all trace of him. Bo was right to leave you."

Whatever calm Finn had managed to inject into the room vanished at Hayley's parting shot. The compassion now gone, Darby pointed to where he stood holding the large bag of clothes. Her voice carried the slightest quaver, but her hand was firm and steady.

"Take what you came for and get out of my house."

Chapter 4

Darby walked down the hallway to collect her things from the bathroom. The lingering scent of bleach hit her nose as she cleared the bathroom doorway and, while harsh, it effectively removed the cloying scent of Hayley Patton's perfume.

What it couldn't erase quite as easily were the spiteful, hateful words.

Cold and heartless.

She supposed there were worse things to be called, but when tallied on top of a stressful weekend and a bleak future, Darby was close to shattering.

She wasn't cold. And she was far from heartless. If she were, she'd already have lined up Penny's next breeding session. Or worse, she'd have put the house and the business up for sale, effectively breaking Bo's father's heart.

Gathering up her cleaning supplies, she marched back down the hall, her arms overflowing with scrub brushes, chemicals and the now nearly empty container of bleach dangling from her index finger. It was only when she got to the living room that she realized her tactical mistake. The chief had returned and was even now pacing the living room, his large German shepherd blocking a path to the door.

"You're still here."

"I wanted to make sure Miss Patton was on her way. Now that she is, I can discuss why I'm here."

"That's not why you came?"

"No."

Short and succinct. Was the man a robot? Every time she saw him he was straitlaced and to the point.

And, of course, he wasn't here about Hayley Patton. How would he have even known the woman would come over today of all days? But it still didn't explain why Finn Colton had returned to her home.

"Do you have a lead on Bo and that poor Michael Hayden?"

Although she'd kept close to home that weekend, a few friends had called her in continued concern. Her true friends—the ones who hadn't been seeking a gossip session—had called each week since Bo's death, wanting to make sure she was doing well. But even without any intended gossip, the strange connection between Bo's murder and Michael's the Friday past had churned up conversation.

Finn's gaze dipped to her supplies, his eyes narrowing on her hands before working their way back up to her face. It was strange, the way his gaze went cold and flat. *Cop's eyes*, she thought to herself, and finally understood what that term meant. A chill ran up her spine like someone walked over her grave.

Why did the man always look at her in a way that made her feel like she'd done something wrong?

She appreciated his position and his dedication to his job. She'd always been someone who valued determination and hard work. Yet the fact that he kept looking in her direction for a crime not only that she hadn't committed but that wouldn't have even crossed her mind on her worst day, didn't sit well.

"If you have something to say to me, please just say it. I'd like to get back to my day and avoid thinking about the fact that I've somehow become the money-grubbing town whore." She turned away from the chief, determined to keep the lingering threat of tears out of his line of sight. "You'd think I'd be having a bit more fun if that was my angle."

She continued on to the kitchen, reordering her cleaning supplies in the plastic container she kept under the sink. She'd nearly finished lining up each item when heavy footsteps sounded behind her.

Would the man never leave? What did he want, anyway? A front-row seat to her public humiliation and shame?

"Can I see that bleach?"

She'd nearly shut the cabinet door when the chief's question registered. "I'm sorry?"

"The bleach. May I see it?"

Confused about the ask, but more than willing to hand over a two-dollar container of cleaning supply, she pulled the bleach out from the cabinet. "Here."

He took the bottle, seeming to weigh the heft before

lifting it in the air to look at the sides of the container. "How long have you had this?"

"The bleach?"

"Yes."

She wanted to laugh at the odd request but sensed there was something deeper underneath his questions. "A few days, I guess. I was out and needed it as part of my cleaning of the house."

"You've used a lot of it."

"Have you seen this house? It's shabby now but at least it's clean. When I moved in, it was shabby and filthy."

Since he seemed unconvinced, she pressed on. "What's this about, Chief Colton?"

"Nothing."

"Right. Because everyone's fascinated with cleaning products. I've got a really great glass cleaner I can share. And my steel wool is top-of-the-line. You want those, too?"

His expression never changed. If anything, it grew darker at her attempts at lightheartedness.

"Why are you asking me this?"

"It's police business. I would like to take this container."

"But why?" Darby pressed once more.

"I'll give you a receipt for it."

Something slick and oily settled like a large ball in the pit of her stomach. Hayley's visit had been unpleasant, but Darby had held her own. Yet something about the chief's visit—a person who should put her at ease instead of spiking her fight-or-flight response—had her in knots.

"Why are you really here? It obviously wasn't to

intercept Hayley Patton. And I'm quite sure it's not to talk cleaning supplies."

"I wanted to see if you remember anything from Friday night."

"I told you the other day. I stayed in that night. Penny and I are still acclimating to each other and I had hopes a quiet night in would help cement our new relationship."

And, she added silently to herself, *I have no money to go out so it was easy to pick a dog over my social life.*

"Can anyone prove that?"

"I spoke with my friend Karen around eight. You're welcome to call her and confirm."

"I did."

"And?"

"And she said the two of you spoke. But you could have called her from anywhere."

Darby fought the urge to roll her eyes and pointed in the direction of the living room toward the couch instead. "I was sitting right there all evening."

"Which can't be proven."

"It was about fifteen degrees on Friday night. I was bundled up in flannel pajamas, thick wool socks and that blanket right there."

Finn turned, his gaze settling on the area she'd pointed out. His deep voice grew husky, the tones low, as if he were talking to himself. "You could have snuck out. It would be easy enough to bundle up, drive across town, shoot Michael Hayden in the chest, then drive back here and fall right back into that cozy spot on the couch. It wasn't a big secret that he smoked. As a waitress in town, you'd know all about those secret habits Red Ridge's citizen's engage in. It would be easy enough to wait him out. Wait for his next nicotine hit."

The image that he painted so casually—like he saw it all in his mind's eye—had that ball of fear rising from her stomach to crawl up her throat. "What are you talking about?"

"Michael Hayden. Your ex-husband, Bo. Bo, I understand. Killing him gave you all this." He stuck out a hand to gesture toward the room at large before whirling around to stare her down. "But what about Hayden? Did you enjoy your first kill so much you had to go back for more?"

Demi Colton reached for the small tube of travel toothpaste off the bathroom sink and coated her toothbrush, then added a second swipe for good measure. She scrubbed at the layer of fuzz on her teeth, desperate to remove the sour, sick taste that had been a part of nearly every morning for the past four months.

Four months.

She stared at herself in the mirror as she brushed, still barely able to believe the truth. She was going to be a mother.

To a tiny, helpless baby who was going to be born fatherless.

The panic that had accompanied her at the news she was unexpectedly pregnant with Bo Gage's child had changed to fierce protection when it became evident Bo wasn't fit to be a parent. Heck, the man was barely fit to be an adult. His ethics were beyond shaky—a fact she'd discovered a few days before she was going to tell him about the baby. Instead of sharing the joy-

ful news, they'd had a wicked fight that had driven
Bo into Hayley Patton's arms.

Or, at least, that's what the town thought.

If anyone had bothered to ask her—and no one
had since they were all too busy thinking she'd gone
and offed the jerk—they'd have known that Bo had
already spent more than a few evenings in Hayley's
bed. All while Demi had still blithely believed them
to be a couple.

The lightest flutter rumbled in her belly and she
pressed a hand there, amazed by the feeling.

Life.

Bo's child.

Her child.

This baby was hers and there wasn't anything she
wouldn't do to protect him or her.

Which meant she had to stay on the run, continue
to lie low and figure out how to get away from the
roving eye of the law long enough to find out who
really had it in for Bo. Because the roving eye of the
law—one serious blue eye, in particular—certainly
had it in for her.

Chief Finn Colton.

She'd always had a strained relationship with the
various branches of her family. Her father, Rusty,
wasn't particularly tight with his two cousins, Fenwick
and Judson, but they'd all seen to it that the Colton
family populated Red Ridge in prolific fashion. Their
grudging acceptance of each other had further ensured
that their children hadn't formed particularly close at-
tachments to their cousins.

But even with that distance, it still hurt that Finn
had zeroed in on her as one of his prime suspects.

Yes, the evidence looked bad. And, yes, she did have motive against Bo if you counted the jilted-lover routine. And she'd even accept that her experience as a bounty hunter gave her exposure to some of the more unsavory ways to live a life.

But, damn it, she didn't kill Bo. Only now it was up to her to determine who did.

And why.

Finn Colton wasn't a man who intimidated women. But in that moment, the color leeching from Darby Gage's face as her blue eyes grew bigger and bigger, Finn knew he'd overstepped.

"You not only think I killed someone, but you think I enjoyed it? Enjoyed it so much I killed someone else?" Disbelief and a solid veneer of horror coated Darby's words, reinforcing what a bastard he was.

But what about that bleach? And the fact that she'd inherited Bo's home and business? She had no alibi he could verify for either murder and even less reason for inheriting the business.

None of which gave him the right to come into her home and intimidate her.

The near-empty container of bleach still hung from his fingers and he settled the bottle on a small end table at the edge of the couch. His gaze caught on Lotte's when he did and he could have sworn he saw serious disappointment in her eyes.

Which was ridiculous.

The last time he checked, all his knowledge of canine learning and understanding did not extend to castigating humans for unspoken thoughts.

He could manage that damn well all by himself.

"It's my job to consider all the angles."

"You call stomping in here and accusing me of unspeakable things angles?" Where he'd expected her to rant and rail, the stiff shoulders and steady voice suggested something else.

Darby Gage was a woman who could handle crisis. More, she'd obviously had to somewhere in her past. "Chief Colton, am I under suspicion for murder?"

"Do you want the truth?"

"Of course." Even though the color hadn't returned to her features, her voice was pure steel.

"You are a suspect in the murders of Bo Gage and Michael Hayden."

"Because I was in a will I had no clue I was a part of? And because I bought some cleaning supplies."

"You had motive."

"Not as far as I'm concerned. But even if I apply your logic to Bo, where do you get off accusing me of harming a man I never met?"

"There are any number of reasons."

"No, there aren't. Including the biggest, which is that I'm not a murderer."

"So you keep saying."

"If you think that, then I clearly need to get a lawyer."

"Suspicion isn't formal charges."

"Then why do you keep coming to my home?"

Once again, he had to give her credit. She held her own. She'd gone toe-to-toe with Hayley and was standing firm with him. Heck, she'd even settled in with the dog, determined to take care of Penny despite the animal's loyalty to Bo.

"I told you. I'm doing my job."

"Then go do your job. Get out on the streets of Red Ridge and find a killer."

Was he looking in the wrong place? Or was he so anxious to have some lead on the case he was willing to look anywhere? His gaze shot to the bleach once more before flicking back to Darby. "Why are you here?"

"Excuse me?"

"Bo's house. His dog. You had a life and, by your own admission the other day, you moved on from your marriage. So why come here and pick up your ex-husband's business?"

"Because there's no one else to do it," she snapped.

His interview with her on Saturday had nagged at him throughout the weekend. There was something about Darby Gage he couldn't define, but couldn't get out of his head. She was a combination of innocence and knowledge, and had become a complete puzzle to him.

"Hayley presumably would like the job."

"Hayley wants the house. There's the difference."

"And you don't?"

"I want stability and a future. And as of right now I don't have either."

The color had returned to her cheeks throughout their exchange, but at her last comment a flush crept up her neck. Was she embarrassed about something?

"I'd think moving out of your apartment into a home while also becoming a business owner would offer a considerable amount of stability and security."

"It might have if Bo Gage had possessed a lick of sense."

Although he wasn't proud of his behavior, Finn

was pleased to see that he'd made a dent in her armor. "That wasn't a particularly big secret around town."

"I suppose not." She took a seat at the small drop-leaf table that sat up against the kitchen window overlooking the backyard. The stiff set of her shoulders loosened, like a balloon deflating, as her gaze drifted toward the yard. "Other than a love for his dogs and a roving eye, I'm not sure the man had much to show for his life."

"He seemed to think it was a good life. I'd only met Bo a few times but I work with his brother and sister. Bo came around to visit them a few times and he was always a jovial sort."

"He lived life to the hilt." Darby pulled her gaze from the window, a sad haze dulling that bright blue. "And took whoever and whatever he wanted along on that ride with him."

Finn took a seat opposite her, softening his voice. Since she hadn't responded to his blunt approach, perhaps he'd get further if he slowed down a bit and actually listened to her. "Not a glowing testament to his personality or his life."

"Sadly, no. But it doesn't mean he deserved to die for it." That gaze lifted to his, a blaze of fire igniting. "I didn't kill my ex-husband. You have to believe me on that. I thought I was done with Bo Gage and have been living my life perfectly happy with that fact. How would I have possibly known the man left me in his will?"

"You were married to him."

"And the day I filed for divorce, I changed my will to remove any trace of him. I'd have expected he'd do the same."

"Well, he didn't."

"No, he didn't. And instead of leaving me some sort of fabulous inheritance, he left me with bills, a dog unable to continue breeding and a business I have no interest in owning."

Bills?

"I thought Bo's business was strong and solvent. Our K-9 unit buys several of his dogs. I know he's got others throughout the county who are on a waiting list for Penny's puppies."

"Then Bo expanded his business beyond what he could reasonably make." She shrugged. "Another sign of the Bo Gage mystique. Make people think you're successful and you are."

Reluctantly, Finn saw the picture she painted, of a man with too much charm and too little sense. Regardless of the destruction he'd wrought, it was Finn's job to do right by a murdered man. But that picture did point to someone who might have had more than a few enemies.

None of which explained why Darby needed to be stuck with her ex's mistakes.

"So why keep the business?" Finn asked.

"Because I made a promise to Bo's father that I'd try. And because I also feel a debt to Penny. She's gone through an awful lot and she deserves as much care and attention as I can give her."

For the first time since he'd seen the bleach bottle dangling from her hands did something ease inside Finn, tilting the scales from suspicion to sympathy. He wasn't ready to let her off the hook—not by a long shot—but he also wasn't entirely sure the woman who sat before him was guilty of murder.

Or even capable of it.

Which was when another thought struck him with even more force. It was so simple.

So easy.

And it would allow him to keep an eye on her while doing the necessary work to draw out the Groom Killer.

"What have you heard around town? About the murders."

"Same as everyone else. The killer seems to have a strange fixation on men who are about to get married. Bo and Michael Hayden were both shot in the chest." She hesitated the briefest moment before continuing on. "And rumors have been running high that your cousin Demi is responsible. Though I find that hard to believe."

It was a curious observation, especially as he didn't think Darby and Demi were particularly well acquainted, if at all. "Why's that?"

"I know her to say hello. I've waited on her several times at the Red Ridge diner. She's…well, she's—" Darby broke off before offering up a lift of her shoulders. "She's just so capable. Her reputation as a bounty hunter is rock solid."

"Which means she knows her way around weapons."

"Maybe." Although her comment seemed to acknowledge the thought, skepticism rode her features, narrowing her gaze.

"Maybe?" Finn asked.

"It's just that she's so cool and confident. Demi Colton is not the sort of woman who murders a guy who can't appreciate her. Especially if that guy was dumb enough to dump her for Hayley."

"So you think it's someone else?"

"Yes, I do. And that someone isn't me," she added in a rush.

That tempting idea snaked through his mind once more, sly in its promise of a solution to his current dilemma.

Catch a killer and keep an eye on Darby Gage. It's not exactly a hardship to spend time with her.

"Maybe you can help me, then."

"Help you how? I thought you were convinced I'm the town murderess."

"I'm neither judge nor jury. It's my job to find evidence to put away a killer and that's what I'm looking to do."

"Then what do you want with me?" The skepticism that had painted her features was further telegraphed in her words. Finn heard the clear notes of disbelief, but underneath them he heard something else.

Curiosity.

"Fingers pointing at my cousin isn't all that's going around town. What began as whispers has gotten louder with Michael Hayden's murder."

"What are people saying?"

Finn weighed his stupid idea, quickly racing through a mental list of pros and cons. Since the list was pretty evenly matched, it was only his desperation to find a killer that tipped the scales toward the pro.

With that goal in mind—closing this case and catching a killer as quickly as possible—he opted to go for broke.

"Bo Gage was killed the night of his bachelor party.

Michael Hayden was killed the night of his rehearsal dinner. One thing the victims had in common—they were grooms-to-be. And in a matter of weeks half the town has called off any and all plans to get married or host an engagement party."

"I still can't see what this has to do with me."

"If you're as innocent as you say you are, surely you'd be willing to help me."

"Help you do what?"

"Pretend to be my fiancée, Darby. Help me catch a killer."

Chapter 5

She was losing her mind. That was the only reason—*surely* it was the only reason—that Finn Colton stood in her living room proposing the most absurd thing she'd ever heard.

"Get engaged to you?"

"Pretend. Only pretend until we can lure out the killer."

"But you think I'm the killer," she pointed out.

The words chafed—more than she wanted to admit—but they needed to be said. Fifteen minutes ago he was looking at her like she belonged in the state penitentiary doing forty to life and now he was proposing they traipse around town like an engaged couple? Maybe he was the one out of his mind.

"I said you were a suspect."

"Careful, Chief. You might give me the warm fuzzies."

The problem was, the man did give her the warm fuzzies. Despite her better judgment—and she liked to think she had her fair share of it—Finn Colton did something to her. The man was too big, too in control, too...too everything.

And it bothered her more than she could say that the prospect of going on a date with him, even if it was fake from start to finish, warmed something way down deep inside her.

"Think of it as a win-win."

"How's that?"

"You can prove to me that you're innocent and I can catch myself a killer. Everyone ends up happy."

"You actually want to put yourself in the line of fire? The Groom Killer is actually killing the grooms."

"I'm a cop. I'll catch the killer before they can do any real harm."

She mentally added cocky to the attractive list. Bo had been cocky, too. It had been one of the things that had drawn her to him. That bright, shiny grin that smacked of sass and confidence. The swagger that went along with it.

She'd been hooked like a fish and let herself be reeled in by that smile, that confidence and a host of empty promises.

Even as she thought it, it felt wrong to lump Finn in the same category as Bo. The two men weren't the same, even if her hormones were having a difficult time parsing the differences.

"You're pretty sure of yourself."

"I'm pretty sure that this person needs to be stopped. And I'm also sure I need help to do it. Red Ridge is small. No one will believe it if I suddenly begin dating one of my employees at the station. People will believe you and I are for real."

Once again, those sly fingers of need wove around her spine, gripping hard. "Why do you think that?"

"You're an attractive woman. Presumably unattached right now?"

She ignored the sting of the presumption and gave him a quietly muttered "Yes."

"I'm equally unattached. We've seen each other around town and decided we each liked what we saw. We got to talking and quietly began dating. I've been so wrapped in the case, I haven't had a chance to take you out good and proper. So, now that it's the month of love, I've resolved to change that."

The month of love?

Was it possible she'd been so head down for the past few months she hadn't even realized it was almost Valentine's Day?

Even as Darby asked herself the question she knew the answer was a resounding yes. Not only had she forgotten it was nearly Valentine's Day, but she'd long stopped looking for a valentine. Or even a man to enjoy an occasional date. When had she stopped trying?

Or worse, stopped expecting that she could be part of another relationship?

For the longest time she'd convinced herself that she was well rid of Bo Gage. And while it pained her that he was dead, on a very real level, she *was* better off since their divorce. But had she somehow closed her heart off to believing that she could love again?

Even before the reading of Bo's will and the revelation of her inheritance, she'd been busy working.

She'd had the occasional date or two but when they hadn't turned into anything more, she hadn't worried about it. Instead she'd focused on keeping her head down and her meager bank account growing.

Funny how little she had to show for it.

Maybe it was that little spark of defiance. Or maybe it was simply the idea of going out for an evening with an attractive man, no matter the pretense. Whatever the cause, Darby found herself warming to the idea of fake dating Finn, even with the warning bells that jangled like sirens in her mind.

"You want to take me out?"

"Every night, and I want to be as public about it as possible. Dates in the front windows of all the restaurants on Main Street. Walks in Red Ridge park, snuggling with each other for warmth." He leaned in, his gaze direct. "We're going to make everyone in town think we're deeply in love and anxious to get married."

"No one's going to believe that."

"Why not?"

"Because—" Darby scrambled to find some answer but came up empty. "We're not in love. People can see the real thing."

"Bo certainly made people think the real thing. He had a string of girlfriends, an ex-wife and a soon-to-be wife, and everyone believed he was as deeply in love with the next woman as the one before."

"That's different."

"How?"

"Bo was…Bo. He was charming and a sweet talker. But none of it was real. There wasn't any substance beneath the veneer."

"Yet people believed it. Ate it up hook, line and sinker, best I can tell."

Finn made a convincing argument—people did see what they wanted to see—but could the two of them really pull it off? And while it was fine for him to brush off the danger of the situation, it *was* dangerous. He might be a big, bad cop, but he was also as vulnerable to a bullet as the next person.

"You really think this is a good idea?"

"I do."

"With me?" She pressed the point, unwilling to think too hard about the steady hum of desire that tightened her skin and tingled her nerve endings.

"Absolutely." That gaze never wavered, but Darby didn't miss the subtle calculation he couldn't fully bury. "But I'll do you one better."

His gaze shifted then, focusing on Penny before roaming over the kitchen. When he finally looked at her again, all hint of calculation was gone. "You help me with this and I'll pay off all your debts."

"You'll what?"

"Pay it off. All of them. I've got solid savings and I'm always open to an investment. You help me with this and I'll see to it that you're out from underneath whatever debt Bo Gage managed to run up in his twenty-nine years of living and then inconveniently deposited into your lap."

It wasn't possible. Whatever emotions had carried her to this moment, from anger to sadness to frustration, none of them compared to the sheer disbelief at his words.

"Why would you do that?"

"I consider it a fair exchange."

"But you can't pay for all of it. The house. The breeding business. I need a new dog because Penny can't breed another litter."

"Then I'll pay for a new dog. I'll pay for three of them if you want. Tell me what you need to get set up and I'll do it."

Three dogs? Not just fixing the business but an expansion, too? A real opportunity to go for it and make something of the business Bo had loved but clearly hadn't had a head for.

"But why?"

"Why not? It's my money. More, it's my town and I want to invest in it. You help me catch a killer and I'll help ensure Bo's business continues on under your ownership and management."

"But—"

"Consider it an offer you can't refuse."

That cocky smile was back, along with something warm and endearing that made her think of naughty little boys who swiped extra chocolate-chip cookies then tried to hide the chocolate stains on their fingers.

Only, Finn Colton wasn't a little boy.

And the stakes were far higher than a possible tummy ache from overeating sweets.

"You want to catch a killer so badly you'll put yourself in their sights?"

"Yes."

"That's the only reason?"

The smile faded, all trace of humor gone. In its place was a sincerity that nearly took her breath away.

"There is another reason. If I'm as wrong about you as you say—" He held up a hand before she could even protest her innocence. "Give me a chance to finish."

She nodded, willing him to continue. It hurt to hear how little he still thought of her, but she was willing to give him his due. "Okay."

"If I am wrong about you, and I'm perfectly willing to accept that truth, I'd like to see you end up in a better place. I've come to understand Bo Gage a bit better since his murder. It's abundantly clear he made life easy for one person. Bo."

It seemed mean to speak that ill of the dead but Darby could hardly argue with Finn's assessment. Bo had lived life for himself, the rest of the world be damned.

"But the one other thing I've learned is that Bo loved his dogs more than anything else in his life. He loved Penny and he loved the litters he ultimately sold to the K-9 unit and beyond. More than once he'd head over to the training center, catching up on how a pup was doing and seeing that he or she performed to their utmost potential."

"He did love the business. And Penny was as important to him as anyone in his life."

"Maybe he saddled you with all this because he believed you'd take care of it. That you'd handle it and make something of it all."

Darby's gaze drifted to Penny. The dog had eventually lost interest in their conversation and had stretched out near Lotte, her head on her paws and her eyes closed.

"You have no reason to take care of her," Finn continued. "Yet you're caring for that dog as if she were your own."

The compliment—and the glowing kindness—had caught her off guard. Where she'd come to accept the grudging acknowledgment that Finn believed her guilty, it was something else for him to extend such a kindhearted thought.

"She is now."

"Can you honestly tell me Hayley Patton would have done the same?"

"I try hard not to compare myself to her."

"That's wise." Even though he kept a straight face, there were distinct notes of humor lilting his voice. "You also know I'm right."

"Maybe I do."

"So, what do you say? Are you in? Are you willing to help me catch a killer?"

Darby had long known that choices made in desperation usually came out poorly. She needed Finn Colton's help and she was hardly in a position to say no him.

She should feel trapped. Caged. And thoroughly out of options.

So why was it that she couldn't feel anything but a clamoring sense of excitement?

"I'm in."

Finn took his first deep breath in a month as he walked to his SUV, Lotte at his side. It had taken some convincing, but Darby had agreed with his ploy.

The idea had seemed so right at the time, but now that he considered his actions in the bright winter sunlight, they struck him as reckless and stupid. He'd always prided himself on being neither, so it was a bit of a head slap to realize he might have misstepped.

His conversation with Darby replayed in his mind. He did his level best to recall when he'd suddenly veered off into the realm of stupid romantic comedy movies and TV shows that had been on for too many seasons.

A fake relationship and engagement.

Was he insane?

Putting aside his doubts about Darby—and the bleach bottle he'd just stuffed in the back of his SUV offered up a big one—he had no business dragging a civilian into a police investigation. Yes, the Groom Killer had targeted men so far, but who knew if the perp would add brides into the mix?

Was Finn putting Darby in danger, inadvertently making her a target?

Their county profiler had indicated the targets seemed deliberately male, with the method of death cold, impersonal and somehow masculine. But that didn't mean anything. Or it wouldn't mean anything if something happened to Darby under his watch…

Finn squelched the thought. Nothing was going to happen to her. He'd protect her and see to it that he caught a killer in the meantime.

The drive to the precinct was quick and he detoured through the lab with the bleach before heading toward his desk. The squad room was humming, his staff all in full swing with a busy start to their week. He was pleased to see Detective Gage at his desk, focused on his computer screen.

Carson had taken Bo's death hard. Despite the half brothers not being close, Carson had found Bo's body and was determined to see his killer behind bars. He'd worked so hard for the past month to uncover who was responsible. He was also on the way to becoming family, since he and Finn's younger half sister Serena, were a serious couple—on the down low.

He'd always enjoyed working with Carson, but their camaraderie was even stronger now and Finn wanted to update him on the latest. The work he'd managed over the weekend, his morning visit to Darby and the plan he'd hatched on the fly to bring out a killer. Shrugging out of his coat, he headed for his desk to drop it off when he saw the bouquet of roses laid over top of his piles.

A card, propped on the flowers, had his name written in bold scrawl on the envelope.

"You've been holding out on us, Chief!" another of Finn's cousins, Blake, ribbed him, his voice carrying across the sea of desks in the squad room. "Looks like you've got yourself a valentine."

An image of Darby filled his thoughts before he quickly brushed it off. She wasn't his valentine or anything else that suggested permanent girlfriend. She was a means to an end, nothing more.

Even as *more* tempted him with thoughts of heated kisses and even more heated moments wrapped up in each other.

He had no business thinking of her that way.

No business at all, Colton.

Which made it that much more unbelievable to realize that somewhere in the back of his mind, he *had* been thinking of her in that way.

Finn shot back a good-natured and off-color remark in Blake's general direction before picking up the card. The scent of the roses—expensive ones for the middle of winter in South Dakota—filled his nose and he fought the rising sense of unease that crept up his spine.

The card offered less-than-helpful details about

the sender, simply reading, "For a special cop, with love."

Unwilling to interrupt the laughter that still rumbled through the squad room at his exchange with Blake, Finn dropped the card into his top desk drawer and left the flowers where they lay. He needed to talk to Carson, anyway, and he didn't have time to deal with the mystery of who had suddenly developed a *tendresse* for the chief of police. He'd have Lorelei take them home if she really wanted them. Or, like the chocolates, he'd toss them.

The anonymous angle hadn't sat well the other day and he wasn't feeling any more comfortable with the increasing expense of the gifts. While he knew the flowers were pricey, he didn't feel honor bound to keep them if the sender couldn't be bothered to make a personal appearance.

Loping toward Carson's desk, Finn thought through his plan, the bouquet quickly forgotten. While it still nagged at him like a dull tooth ache that he might be putting Darby in danger, talking it all through with Carson should help to set his mind at ease. This was an op, nothing more. If they planned it well and put all the proper safety measures in place, including backup in shouting distance and advance recon of each of his proposed date sights, things would be fine.

She'd be safe.

"Who's the secret admirer, big guy?" Carson's grin was infectious as he stared up over the top of his computer monitor.

"Someone's just deeply grateful for the Red Ridge PD."

"Sure." Carson nodded. Finn didn't miss the clear

skepticism in his gaze or the quirk of his lips, but it vanished without Carson saying anything. "What can I do for you?"

"I've got an idea cooking and I want to talk it through with you."

"What sort of idea?"

"We're going to smoke out a killer."

Carson's smile faded in full as he sat straighter. "You have a new lead?"

"Not much more than we've been going off of, but I have an idea and a plan I think might work."

He walked Carson through the specifics. How he was going to put himself in the line of fire, pretending to be Red Ridge's latest, most smitten suitor. A date every night, public displays of affection, even a showy romantic dinner for Valentine's Day.

"Who'd you convince here to go in on this with you? You've got way too many cousins in this department not to make it seriously creepy, Colton."

While Carson spoke the truth—nearly half the department was a relative, including several of his female cousins—that was the exact reason he'd gone outside the precinct.

"Darby Gage has agreed to be my date for the month."

"Darby? My sister-in-law, Darby? You can't be serious."

Where Finn had expected support, or at least basic agreement, the immediate shuttering of Carson's gaze as he rose to his full height was a clear sign of his displeasure. It also had Finn forcing his point, unwilling to stand down. "Of course, I'm serious. And, last time I checked, she's your ex-sister-in-law."

"She's also one of the chief suspects in my brother's murder."

"Which makes this the perfect plan. She claims she's innocent, but I can keep a close watch on her. She can hardly act again if I'm glued to her side."

"This is insanity."

Carson wasn't convinced of the brilliance of Finn's plan and Finn was just stubborn enough to hold his ground on principle. He had a good relationship with all his cops and he had no interest in changing that, but he was also the boss and the weight of the department rested on his shoulders. He'd be damned if he'd sit around and let problems happen in his town when he could be out there doing something about it.

"Think of it as an undercover op."

"With one of the chief suspects on a damned short list."

An image of a nearly empty bottle of bleach flitted through his mind before Finn pushed it away. Carson was one of his lead detectives and he was good at his job, but the bleach was a line Finn was tugging on his own, nothing more. There was no need to poison the well against Darby any further in her former brother-in-law's mind, but the coincidence between her having a nearly empty bottle and the bleach that had been laid down to get him off the trail of Michael Hayden's killer was too timely for him to let it go.

But even if he chose to keep a few suspicions to himself, Finn wanted to better understand his detective's reservations. "What do you have against Darby?"

"Nothing until my brother's will said she got everything he had. That spells motive to me."

"What about Demi? Bo dumped her for Hayley and Demi's name was written in blood next to Bo's body. Bo pissed off a lot of people over the years."

At the mention of his cousin Demi and her connection to Bo, something flickered clearly in Carson's gaze. The words were nearly out of Finn's mouth to question the response when Carson pushed forward on his own. "You have other leads? Someone my brother pissed off?"

"Nothing concrete, but you know Bo wasn't a saint. I know he was your brother, and I'm not trying to speak ill of the dead, but we have to look at all the angles."

The comment about Bo—and it *was* speaking ill of the dead, no matter how Finn wanted to couch it— took the wind out of Carson's bluster. He dropped back into his seat, his dark eyes clouding with trouble. Finn had seen that look more than a few times over the past month and was glad that Carson now had a family to go home to.

Carson had made no secret of how unexpected his romance with Finn's half sister Serena had been. Her vulnerability—having had another man's child and navigating the waters of single parenthood—hadn't been easy, but they'd found their way. And now Carson had Serena and her daughter, Lora, to go home to.

The fact that Carson had found a way to chase those shadows with Finn's younger half sister and her baby girl had shifted the dynamic between the two men. He and his lead detective were still navigating all the nuances. Being on opposite sides of the issue when it came to Darby Gage looked like it was going to be one of those nuances.

"I know, Finn. Damn it, I do know. I've always cared for Darby. She's a good woman and I know my brother didn't do right by her. But I can't shake the fact that, of all the people in Bo's life, including a bright and shiny fiancée he was a day away from marrying, Darby is the one who ends up with my brother's life's work."

"For what it's worth, I think she's been wondering the same thing."

"She doesn't want the house or the business?" Carson asked, the conflicting anger over Bo's death that clouded his dark gaze fading, replaced by the hard, flinty edges that defined a cop.

Finn didn't miss the interest in the question, but kept his words carefully measured. "She's committed to the business and she's cleaned up that house like a whirling dervish. But I'm not sure it's the life she'd have chosen for herself."

He wasn't sure why he kept the issue of Bo's debt to himself but, like sharing the details on the bleach, something held him back. With the bleach it was respect for Darby as he waited for the lab to come back with some thoughts.

For the inheritance, it was respect for Carson.

The man had struggled enough knowing someone in Red Ridge had wanted his brother dead. The least he could do was allow Carson to hang on to one of the few illusions he might have possessed about his little brother.

Sometimes, Finn knew, illusions were all a person had.

* * *

The bouquet of bright red roses came through the front door of the police station first, visible for anyone who was looking. And she was looking.

And waiting.

She'd had them delivered earlier and had spent the afternoon waiting to see what Chief Colton would do with the gorgeous bouquet. She'd read up on the meaning of flowers and knew the blood-red blooms were the very definition of love, affection and desire.

The flowers came out first. Only, instead of seeing the object of that desire walking behind them, she saw the petite little secretary who manned the front desk like a pit bull.

A wave of fury filled her at the insult. How dare he? Those flowers were for Finn Colton. Why had he given them to the stupid little woman like they were some gift for her? Something white-hot began beating in her chest; a thick feeling that slammed blood through her veins even as she had an image of making Finn Colton pay for his unkindness.

She thought he was heroic. Perfect. Superior in every way.

More, she believed they shared something special and it would only take a few more gifts before he understood—no, before he *knew*—who was sending the gifts. Like a little game between them.

A lover's game.

That stupid little secretary carried the roses in her arms, juggling them as she dug for keys in her purse. Only, once she found them, she opened the back door and threw the roses onto the seat.

Threw them!

The white-hot anger that bubbled in her veins took on a new form as, suddenly, it all became clear. Finn Colton hadn't disregarded the blooms. That stupid little woman had kept them for herself.

The bitch thought she was so crafty, stealing what wasn't hers.

But the woman would know soon enough.

As she watched, she toyed briefly with going after the secretary, following the little hatchback through town and running her off the road. There were patches of black ice all over Red Ridge this time of year and no one would think twice about an untimely skid.

The thought tempted—sorely tempted—but she'd hold off for now. If she acted too hastily, she might attract Finn's attention in ways that weren't welcome.

And she couldn't afford to upset him. Not now. Not yet.

She had big plans for herself and Finn Colton.

The thought had the anger fading in her mind to be replaced with the sweetest anticipation. There'd be other bouquets. Other gifts. There was the one in particular that she couldn't wait to give him.

It wouldn't do to be hasty.

Oh, no. She needed to focus on her plans. If she kept to her schedule, they'd be laughing with each other and dreaming with each other and planning a future with each other. It was all coming together.

It was only a matter of time now.

Chapter 6

Be ready at seven sharp.

That was all the man had said that morning when he'd left. What had seemed like a simple set of instructions had grown maddeningly empty of information as the day wore on and the minutes ticked closer and closer to seven.

Should she dress up? Go casual? Were they going to dinner or dancing? Or both? Should she bundle up in her thickest coat or try to outmaneuver a frigid South Dakota night with nothing more than a wrap to get her from the car to the door of wherever it was they were going.

Wherever it was they were going.

Why hadn't she asked these things when she'd had the chance?

"Because I was too busy trying to keep my tongue

in my mouth at the instruction to be ready at seven sharp." The words came out in a disgusted rush to her partner in crime, Penny.

Although the dog hadn't warmed enough to allow even the most simple gesture of a pat on the head, she'd taken to following Darby around the house. Even now, she lay spread out on the bed, her eyes following as Darby paced a hole in the already-threadbare carpet.

"I don't even have anything to wear. Cinderella dressed better than I did and that was after her stepsisters got done with her." Darby muttered the words as she pawed through the meager line of clothes in the closet she used to share with Bo. Her work at the Red Ridge diner consisted of a uniform provided by the owner, and she would never dream of wearing anything dressier than jeans and a T-shirt or sweatshirt when working at the K-9 training center.

In the end, she opted for a black dress she'd bought for a wedding a million years ago and called it a day. It wasn't exactly dowdy but she wasn't going to set Red Ridge on fire this evening, either. But it did have a nice neckline and exposed enough cleavage that she might hope Finn Colton's eyes didn't stray to the unfashionable style as it wrapped around her hips and on down to her knees.

"Not that the man needs to be looking at my breasts."

Penny's eyebrows shot up but her gaze remained steady. Darby had the rueful thought that the dog had had sex more recently than she had.

Since that train of thought left her feeling worse than she'd have expected, Darby slipped into a pair of heels that were as old as the dress and marched out of the room. The clock read four minutes before seven and she'd barely cleared the hallway when a heavy knock sounded on the front door.

"Right on time." She didn't attempt to play coy by making him wait, nor was she willing to spend one more moment primping, so she skipped the hallway mirror.

Which made the funny little jump in her heartbeat that much odder when she opened the door to see Chief Finn Colton standing on the other side. Although she'd seen him around town without his uniform on, something about the black slacks, untucked gray shirt and leather jacket still caught her by the throat.

Oh, my, did the man look good.

Too good.

Confusingly good.

She ignored the rush of something a younger, more foolish Darby might have called lust and gestured him inside. "Come on in. I'll just get my things and we can get going."

"Take your time. I'm early."

"Bo was always twenty minutes late. Far be it from me to argue with a man who arrives when he says he will."

Finn's smile never wavered but something she couldn't define registered in his steady gaze. Was it the mention of Bo? This might not be a real date, but few men wanted to be compared to another man, even if that comparison was in their favor.

"Still, feel free to take your time."

Finn's smile lit up his face when he caught sight of her roommate.

Penny had followed her out to the hallway and was even now allowing Finn to rub and scratch at her ears and face, seeming to bask in the glow of male attention. Not that Darby could blame Penny. She wouldn't mind basking in the glow of Finn Colton's attention, either.

The man thinks you're a murder suspect. You've got plenty of his attention.

The practical little voice inside tossed that bucket of ice water, as cold as the Red Ridge River in…well, February. And while Darby tried momentarily to cling to the truth of that jarring thought, her hormones unfortunately won the battle and succeeded in shutting up her whiny voice of indignation.

Finn did look good. And watching the man pet and love on her dog thawed something deep inside her.

"Let me just get my coat."

Since he wore only his leather jacket, she opted for a thinner wool coat instead of the large puffy one she favored in winter that wrapped her from the bottom of her chin to the top of her ankles. It was the height of ugly, the puffy material giving her the fashion equivalent of round tires from her shoulders to her feet, but it kept her warm.

Which had her roundly cursing herself a few minutes later when Finn walked her to his SUV. Cold crept up her dress, freezing her legs on contact, and a series of shivers settled deep into her bones before he'd barely helped her up into the passenger seat of his large SUV. Finn rounded the vehicle and hopped in, but even with the sudden blast of warmth from the heater, she couldn't warm up.

"Penny seems to be warming up."

The choice of words—and the chattering that set in despite her best efforts—had a small burst of laughter bubbling in her throat. "She likes y-you m-more th-than she li-likes me."

"Darby?"

"So—sorry." A wave of chattering hit her again and she tried to bite back her words.

"Are you okay?"

"Ju-just got a ch-chill."

Finn turned the heater on even higher, then pulled to the side of the road. In seconds, he had his seat belt off and then his jacket. "Here. Put this on."

"I'm f-fine."

"Right."

Before she could register his actions, that big body simply seemed to envelop her. He twisted in his seat, his focus on her as he settled his large coat over her, tucking the sides up against her body, and then rubbing her arms to warm her. "It's a cold night."

"An-and now you're wi-without a c-coat." The chattering had already gotten better and Darby felt her jaw calming from the incessant rattling. "Aren't you cold?"

"I'm a furnace. Which does me well in the middle of winter and ensures I hate summer with a passion."

"Who h-hates summer?" The question came out almost normal but Darby had to hold back the stammer as he kept his focus on her. His eyes never left hers, even as he continued to rub at her arms through the warmth of his coat.

Between the layers of his jacket, her inadequate wool coat and the long sleeves of her dress, his touch should have felt impersonal. Or difficult to even distinguish.

But, oh, how she felt him.

The solid strokes of his hands. The long, capable fingers. And that penetrating, sloe-eyed gaze that did as much to increase her temperature as the body-warmed coat and steady movements to circulate her blood.

His hands slowed but he didn't break contact. "Better?"

"Yes." She nodded but didn't say anything else. The chattering teeth had faded completely but she couldn't be too sure her voice wouldn't crack under the scrutiny.

Finn didn't break contact but it was only after another long, tense moment that he seemed to catch himself. With a light pat on her shoulder, he repositioned himself in his seat and pulled on his seat belt. "South Dakota winters are nothing to mess with."

"No," she agreed, pleased when her voice came out steady. "They're not."

"Even when you do have a killer pair of legs."

The bright lights of the Red Ridge Trattoria beckoned them closer as Finn pulled up to the curb. The owner, Paolo, had worked in the competitive restaurant community of Los Angeles for nearly twenty years. He'd uprooted himself a decade ago, moved to Red Ridge and, in short order, had wooed—and won—the county beauty queen and opened up the Trattoria. Although Paolo had slowly adjusted to the slower pace of things in Red Ridge, he'd insisted on three things. Reservations. The highest quality meats flown in three times a week. And a valet that managed parking.

Finn handed over his keys to the young man who'd

clearly drawn the short straw to get parking duty on a night below freezing and mentally calculated an increased tip for the service. He then came around the SUV to help Darby out of the passenger seat.

He hadn't been joking about the legs. She was already starting to shift out of the vehicle, struggling beneath the extra weight of his coat, when he took her hand and pulled her out. Her legs came first, followed by the rest of her and, once again, he was struck by the sexy path from knee to ankle on display.

She was a looker. One that caught a man by surprise. She was pretty, in a simple sense, until you looked closer. Then you realized that what seemed cute on first glance had more depth and nuance that deserved a second look.

And a third.

What he couldn't quite get a grip on was why he hadn't looked closer before.

Her dark hair curled slightly, the light catching the swoops of her curls and setting off vibrant red undertones. Her eyes were large and round, that fascinating blue edging toward violet, and sat in a face carved with high cheekbones, a pert nose and a lush lower lip that drew his attention with the same fervor as her legs.

Although he'd certainly looked her over the past few days, as well as in the years he'd seen her peripherally around town, it surprised him to realize just how truly pretty she was.

And how small.

Strong, yes, but a petite little thing. Even in her heels she barely cleared his shoulder. Although he usually went for taller women—his ex-wife had been a statuesque brunette who was nearly eye level to him—he couldn't deny the surge of protectiveness that coursed through him as he took in the small frame beside him.

A fresh burst of cold air helped clear his head and he concentrated on walking her to the door. He hadn't been lying—he was warm-blooded—but the heat that suffused his limbs came from something else.

Something that struck him a lot like desire.

Once inside, Paolo himself greeted them, his proprietor's smile in place as he shook Finn's hand and fussed over Darby. Although he still took the reins in the kitchen from time to time, Paolo had firmly moved in to the role of restaurant owner and left most of the cooking to a young protégé from California who had figured out a lot sooner than Paolo had that he wanted a vibrant life away from the rat race.

Finn was still thinking about the kid as they were seated, a list of specials handed to him along with the wine list.

"That's an awfully enigmatic smile," Darby commented as she settled her napkin in her lap. "Care to let me in on the joke?"

Finn handed over the sheet of specials before opening his napkin. "Just thinking about the appeal of our small town."

"Oh?"

He tilted his head in the direction of the front door. "Paolo. The chef in the back that he hired from L.A. Both came here to change their lives and soak in the steady, easy pace we have here. Small-town life isn't all bad."

"Did someone say it was?"

"No. But there are times it can be, at the risk of sounding cliché, small."

She glanced out the window beside their table— the one front and center he'd specifically requested— her gaze roaming over Main Street. On a soft sigh she turned back to look at him. "I don't know. After the events of the past month, I sort of wish we could go back to small and quiet."

"We will. Soon."

"You seem awfully sure of that."

"Because I am."

The same searching glance she'd given the street transferred to him. "You can't know that."

"I know what I know. We're going to catch a killer. And we're going to figure out why they've done what they've done."

He just hoped he could do it before anyone else got hurt.

Or before the town's business owners went belly-up. It hadn't escaped his notice that there were few cars parked in the lot beside the restaurant when the valet had taken his car. Nor had he missed the number of empty tables. Even on a Monday, the Trattoria typically did more business than six scattered tables of diners.

Their waiter hurried over and reiterated the specials before asking for drink orders, gesturing to Darby to go first.

"I'll have a glass of your Chianti."

"And a club soda for me," Finn added.

"Oh. Well, then. I'll have an iced tea."

Finn reached over and laid a hand on hers. "Don't let me be the spoilsport, darling. Enjoy the glass of wine. It'll go well with whatever you order."

On immediate contact her hand stiffened beneath his, going positively rigid at the endearment before relaxing. "Okay, then. One glass."

She slipped her hand away once the waiter was out of view. "I don't need to drink."

"On the contrary. You should enjoy yourself. I can't drink because I'm technically on duty."

"Of course."

It was an op but Finn wasn't anxious to keep reminding Darby of that. He much preferred the wide eyes and small, supple body he'd wrapped up in his coat than the subtle defeat he saw in both now.

So act like it's a real date, Colton.

Although he couldn't afford to let his focus fade, it didn't mean he couldn't enjoy an evening with a beautiful woman. And while his dating skills were hardly legendary, he did know how to take a woman to dinner and give her an enjoyable evening.

Which took him right back to where they'd started the evening.

"I meant what I said in the car. Penny does seem to be warming up."

"I'm not sure. I mean, I see it in small ways. She's become my shadow, following me all over the house, but she still won't let me get near her."

"She'll come around. She knows you want to care for her and that'll win her over in the end."

"There's that Finn Colton confidence once more."

Before he could question the comment, the waiter arrived with their drinks and took their orders. Finn was pleased to see she'd ordered a hearty lasagna; he'd requested a Bolognese that was a particular favorite.

Picking up where they'd left off, he pressed his

point. "Dogs have amazing empathy. She knows you care for her. She's just working on building up her trust with you."

"Did you go through it with Lotte?"

"Not in the same way. I've worked with her since she was a puppy, so the trust has been different between us. But it did take us a while to get her on a service path."

"How do you mean?"

Their food arrived and after requested refills on their drinks, Finn took his mind back once again to his earliest days with Lotte. He hadn't thought of them in a long time, so it was funny to realize how much of that time he did remember.

"She showed a lot of promise as a puppy, picking up all the basic training exercises and obedience drills."

Darby nodded as she cut a piece of her lasagna. "Most of the work I do at the training center is centered on cleaning, but I also help out with the obedience trials since I have experience training puppies. Managing them around food and ensuring they can sit or move on command. The really little ones always break my heart. They're so wiggly and squirmy, I just want to pick them up and cuddle them."

"It gets harder for them after that, once they start learning how to track scents. Lotte made it through the early training really well but once we got together she wasn't able to keep her focus on tracking. I'd gotten so attached to her and had a rough month convinced she wasn't going to make it through the program."

"What was the breakthrough?"

"I had a really bad day at work. A domestic abuse case gone bad. I knew I shouldn't have gone to training but went anyway, and just couldn't keep my focus. We were using an old blanket soaked in something unmentionable here as we eat dinner and either I shoved it too hard in her face or I was just frustrated enough she wanted my attention."

He'd always judged himself for that moment, his selfish behavior toward Lotte an experience he was hardly proud of. So it was humbling when Darby's reaction was not only encouraging but innately kind, as well.

"She knew you needed something."

"I guess she did. I've always been sorry it took a bad moment to make the connection, but the pure empathy and her ability to read my emotions is something I've never forgotten. I knew I wanted K-9, but after that day I realized I wanted K-9 with Lotte."

"And she found the prize?"

"Then and every time since."

"Maybe it was a breakthrough for both of you."

In many ways it had been and he'd remembered the lesson in the ensuing years. "It's certainly made me a gentler handler and a better handler. When I finally understood how much she was taking in around her, I realized that all my actions had an impact on her."

"So Penny's just taking in what's around her?"

"She absolutely is. Her world has been upended and she's just trying to right herself again. She'll settle. And when she does, I predict you're going to have a beautiful friendship."

"I'll hang in there, then. I know she's worth it. And she's wonderful company." A mischievous light filled Darby's eyes as she laid her fork and knife on her plate. "She also functions incredibly well as a silent yet supportive girlfriend when nothing in the closet seems quite right for dinner."

"I'd say she did her job well, then. You look great."

A pretty blush filled her cheeks but she held his gaze. "I wasn't asking for a compliment, but maybe next time you can give me a clue where we're going."

"That takes all the fun out of it."

"Maybe yes, maybe no. Since I've proven I can't dress for winter weather to save my life, perhaps you can give me a clue."

While he wasn't crazy about her covering up those pretty legs, he had already planned out the week and the next night was straight-up-the-line casual. "Okay. Tomorrow night, jeans and a sweatshirt."

"We're staying in?"

"Hardly. You're joining me for bowling night."

All hints of mischief fled as she leaned forward over the table. "I'm horrible at bowling."

"Then you'll be an improvement over me."

"No, I'm really horrible. I throw gutter balls at least four frames per game."

"And I throw 'em at least five. Seriously, you can't imagine how much I stink at bowling. I believe my cousin Brayden calls it the height of suck-a-tude."

"Why do you play, then?"

"It's a league and it's the one place I can shame myself in front of my men and women and still hold my head high in the squad room. The RRPD fields three teams, along with one each from the fire department, the K-9 training center and the EMS squad, and two from the teachers at the high school."

"And you want me to come play?"

"We've been down a player since Carson has been

dating my sister Serena. Between a newborn and a budding romance, he hasn't been all that interested in bowling."

Finn knew it was also an opportunity for his team to review Darby and to get a sense of her for the investigation. His head was growing increasingly cloudy as he found it harder and harder to see the woman as a killer. It would do him good to have her reviewed by other seasoned professionals.

Having Carson distracted also gave him a chance to solicit an opinion from someone who *wasn't* Darby's ex-brother-in-law.

"I haven't been Carson's favorite person. Not since the reading of the will."

"He'll come around."

"First Penny. Now Carson. Is that how you deal with everyone who doesn't agree with you?"

"Most things reveal themselves in time. It just takes patience and a willingness to wait them out."

"Like a killer?"

Whatever tentative truce they'd built over the evening faded at the clear reminder in her words. He and Darby weren't out on a date. Nor were they building a relationship between the two of them.

They were hunting a killer.

He'd always had a legendary focus and commitment to his job. With a murderer on the loose, it was a damn poor time to suddenly lose his concentration.

Chapter 7

Darby ignored the cloudy skies and the threat of snow that had hovered since she'd woken that morning and worked her way through downtown Red Ridge, checking off her list of errands. The evening before hadn't been far from her thoughts, but the errands kept her busy and focused on more than Finn Colton's sky blue eyes, which reminded her of a pretty June day, or his broad shoulders, which were strong and oh, so capable.

They were a mirage. An oasis in the desert and she'd do well to remember that. Spending time with him was a job and nothing more.

The check in her hand that she was about to deposit at the Red Ridge Savings and Loan was tangible proof of that fact.

A job. That's all you are. And since it pays well and it's the path to get you off the suspect list and out of debt, you'd do well to remember that.

She kept up the mental pep talk as she walked into the bank, only to find a line of people gaping at a bellowing Fenwick Colton.

Red Ridge was a small town and everyone knew the owner of Colton Energy. Not only did the man employ half the town, but he was legendary for prancing through the streets like a proud peacock on display. Even his head bobbed in time to his own mental beat, Darby thought as she watched his small frame pace up and down in front of one of the desks used for conducting business.

Private business, she'd always thought.

"Half my investments in this town are sucking wind because of this damned Groom Killer!"

Darby tried not to listen, taking a place in line to wait her turn. But Fenwick's loud rant made that impossible.

"My daughter's supposed to get married at the end of the year. How's that going to happen if every wedding company in a fifty-mile radius is out of business?" Fenwick's voice echoed off the high marble walls.

"Mr. Colton." The bank manager did his best to calm him, but even those efforts were loud enough for everyone to hear. "If you'd like to take this to my office, I'm sure we can discuss this calmly and—"

"Don't you patronize me, Tommy Sanders. I remember when you were just a teller here." A loud thwap as Fenwick slapped a hand on the marble counter echoed off the ceiling before the distinct rustling of newspaper added to the din. "And we can just as easily discuss things here in front of the damn town.

We're all reading the same garbage each and every day in the *Red Ridge Gazette*."

"Yes, Mr. Colton, but if you'd—"

Again, Fenwick interrupted the poor, beleaguered Tommy, his voice straining as he read the headline Darby had already passed in a glass-fronted box out on the street. "Groom Killer Waiting to Make Next Kill. That's considered news?"

"Well, it's a big deal," Tommy said, his voice placating.

"It's salacious garbage and it's ruining this town day by day!"

While she didn't agree with his public display, Darby had to admit Fenwick had a point. The killings were awful enough and already had the entire town whispering, scared for its safety. Daily updates in the local paper, the front page screaming out all sorts of salacious innuendo, was hardly a way to keep everyone calm.

It also gave the killer what he or she wanted. If you were going to behave in such an awful way, wouldn't you want credit for it?

She wasn't a thrill seeker—she never had been—but she'd overheard enough conversations in the diner to know that when people did something out of the ordinary, they wanted credit for it.

Wouldn't killing someone be the height of that?

It was enough to bring a chill back to her bones, only, unlike the wind the night before, this chill went far deeper, settling into her soul.

Was it really possible they had someone walking the streets of Red Ridge who not only had killed her ex-husband and another man, but who was waiting to kill again? Someone who cared so little for another's life they felt it was theirs for the taking?

For the first time since learning of Bo's death, Darby felt something other than confusion or sadness or surprise. Something small flickered to life, burning away that veneer of cold.

Something a lot like anger.

She'd been so focused on her own problems the past few weeks she hadn't truly given thought to what was going on in her town. A remorseless killer, determined to snuff out a life as if it was no more than a fly to be swatted or an animal to be put down.

But it was more than that. People's lives were at stake. And, with sudden clarity, she realized that while the one who'd lost a life paid the highest price, those who loved them were paying a terrible toll, as well.

"Next!"

The call from the teller pulled Darby from her musings and she headed for the window. The transaction moved quickly, the money going into her account so quickly it was nearly anticlimactic. The hours and days of worry vanished as if they'd never been, Finn Colton's generosity now lining her bank account and her future along with it.

Which meant she had a choice. She could take what he offered and rebuild her life. Or she could fight back against the nameless, faceless injustice and help him catch a killer.

As Darby walked back out onto the street a few moments later, several large flakes dropped from the sky, coating her hair and coat immediately.

Instead of feeling the cold, all she felt was a fire in her belly that emanated outward, setting her entire being into motion.

Finn ran Lotte through a familiar series of drills at the training center, pleased for the chance to get outside and move a bit. Although he spent a fair amount of time away from his desk, his work taking him into town more often than not, the threat of snow had indicated a day that was likely to keep him in more than out. When the thought of sitting inside the precinct all day had left him with a stifling sense of claustrophobia, he'd opted for a trip to the training center.

The cold did a lot to clear his head as Lotte did a series of agility drills before they switched gears and worked on tracking some new scents. He'd read up recently on a dog who'd actually discovered electronics data and he was anxious to see what Lotte could do with scents that weren't innately natural in origin. So far she hadn't been nearly as successful as one of their other K-9 members—a large, lumbering basset hound named Goose—but he remained hopeful she'd get the hang of things.

In the meantime, they'd practice and he'd keep his focus on helping her learn.

By the time they'd finished an hour later, Lotte's tongue was lolling a bit and even Finn's warm blood had finally worn thin in the cold air. He took them both inside to warm up and came face-to-face with Hayley Patton.

"Chief." She had a puppy on a leash and was gently pulling him down the hallway toward the kennels.

"Miss Patton." Finn nodded, curious to watch her

retreat down the hall. The quiet moment gave him a chance to consider her and he was surprised to see how gentle and patient Hayley was with the puppy after the fireworks she'd put on at Darby's.

It had been more than obvious Penny didn't like the woman and Finn had always trusted a dog's sense about people as an important barometer. While not foolproof, there had been several occasions when Lotte had detected someone who was just "off." It was never the people who were afraid of dogs, but the ones who had a disdain that went beyond basic dislike or legitimate fear.

So what was up with Hayley Patton?

Was she the grieving bride-to-be she'd been playing around town? The raging shrew who expected everyone to bow and scrape now that she was practically widowed? Or was she really a gentle, misguided woman who channeled her energy and affection into dogs instead of the world around her? More questions without answers.

"Chief!"

He tucked away thoughts of Hayley and focused on the voice squawking through the portable radio clipped to his shirt. Answering the summons, he moved into a small conference room off the main hallway. "What's up, Lorelei?"

"Trouble brewing at the bank."

He'd known Lorelei long enough to take her statement as more gossip than danger, but held back the sigh at the unhelpful level of detail. "What kind of trouble?"

"Your uncle Fenwick was in there making a ruckus about the Groom Killer."

"What was he on about now?"

Lorelei clearly warmed to her story, her voice echoing from his radio with all the authority of a newscaster. He'd already gotten the gist of Fenwick's antics within in a few statements but let Lorelei keep on as he poured himself a cup of coffee from the steady supply kept on the conference room's banquette.

"He's claiming his daughter Layla's wedding is in jeopardy because of the Groom Killer, the headlines the paper keeps running and your ineptitude to find a killer."

Finn put his cup down, a streak of annoyance lighting up his limbs.

He tolerated his uncle on most days, but when the man insinuated he wasn't able to do his job, they had a problem. "I'll go see him now."

"Figured you'd want to know."

"You figured right."

As he disconnected with Lorelei, Finn drained the last of his coffee, fortifying himself for the conversation to come. Fenwick Colton saw himself as the king of Red Ridge and, normally, Finn was willing to let him have the crown.

But when the king started talking trash about Finn's hard work and the hard work of his department, he wasn't above taking action. It was mighty comfortable sitting on a throne, watching the world go by.

It was another matter entirely to take up a sword and battle the real monsters that lived in it.

Finn put little stock in legends and stories, especially when they gave people an excuse for bad behavior. The century-long feud between the Coltons and the Gages was one of those stories and he'd spent his life fighting the expectation that somehow his birth and his last name predisposed him to a set of choices.

He liked who he wanted to like. Disliked for the same reasons. And refused to believe that someone was bad simply because they'd been born into a family who lived across town.

Fortunately, his generation seemed to be the first in a hundred years that might truly trample the battleground that perpetually stretched between the Colton family homes on one end of town and the Gage family homes on the opposite end.

Carson and Serena had certainly trampled up everything in their path, finding each other despite the specter of a family feud. He'd also caught wind of another romance brewing between the youngest member of each family, his sister Valeria and the youngest Gage, Vincent. Word around town was that the smitten lovers had been caught kissing more than once and their parents were both determined to break them up. A position that had only grown stronger since fear had spread over the antilove-based motives of the Groom Killer.

He'd purposely stayed out of the teen love drama, even though his stepmother, Joanelle, had been haranguing him for a month to do something about the pair. Since he figured the kids had a right to their feelings, he'd left them alone, but had instructed his team to keep a watch on them. Fools might rush in but a well-trained police force should be able to keep an eye on two swoony teens.

No matter how easygoing Finn wanted to be about the teens, he had been forced to manage the Colton-

Gage situation a bit tighter with his cousin Demi. Nothing could change the fact that one of the lead suspects in the investigation into Bo Gage's death was a Colton. And that hadn't sat well with any member of the Gage family.

He and Carson had questioned his cousin, insisting she stay in Red Ridge until the whole situation quieted down, but she'd up and run at the first opportunity. Finn still wasn't sure if he'd want to throttle her or to hug her when they finally found her, but in the meantime Demi wasn't doing herself any favors in the "raising suspicions" department.

Which made Darby's assessment the day before that much more interesting. If Darby *was* the killer, wouldn't she grasp at any opportunity to deflect interest her way? And if she wasn't—and her assessment of Demi was right on—then maybe they were all looking in the wrong place.

It's just that she's so cool and confident. Demi Colton is not the sort of woman who murders a guy who can't appreciate her. Especially if that guy was dumb enough to dump her for Hayley.

With his thoughts racing through all the implications, Finn pulled off Bay Boulevard and into his uncle Fenwick's driveway. The large house sat on the very edge of Red Ridge, not far from one of the mountain passes that led up into the Black Hills. Fenwick's land was the farthest you could get from a Gage and still say you lived in Red Ridge, and Fenwick paid dearly to keep the mansion in pristine condition.

He also reveled in living on the edge of town along with the town's ritziest citizens, including the Larson twins. Evan and Noel had made quite a name for themselves in the past few years, their various investments including quite a few in tech, putting them on several lists of South Dakota's mavens under thirty.

Finn glanced down the street at the large, garish mansion the twins called home as he jumped out and rounded his SUV, not entirely convinced all their money was on the up-and-up. He'd put considerable focus on them before the Groom Killer situation had blown up but had very little to show for it.

Yet every time he saw either of the twins, something set off his radar. They were attractive and charming and played the "bright, shining citizen" roll to the hilt. Only, none of it could hide the fact that something mean seemed to live behind their eyes.

Finn sighed, again aware that the assessments he made of people didn't mean they were guilty of anything more than breathing air. The role of chief weighed heavy on his shoulders, but it didn't do to go looking for trouble where there wasn't any.

Even so, the Larsons bothered him.

Shrugging off the disdain, Finn climbed the steps to Fenwick's mansion, bracing himself for battle. He wasn't disappointed when his uncle greeted him with a sharp grunt a few minutes later after the butler led him to Fenwick's home office. The grunt was quickly followed up with Fenwick's play for the conversational upper hand. "Heard you had dinner last night with that Gage woman."

"Word travels fast."

"It does when my nephew is parading around town with a murder suspect."

"What would you know of my suspects?"

"I keep my ear to the ground."

The words carried quite a bit less bluster and Finn used the moment of quiet to press his advantage. "You messing around in my investigation?"

"Don't sass me, boy."

"Are you?"

Fenwick held Finn's stare, his lifelong success in business ensuring he wasn't going to back down. But the bluster didn't return to his tone, either, when he finally spoke. "I'm an interested citizen. Nothing more."

"Then why are you making things worse by carrying on at the Red Ridge Savings and Loan?"

Small and skinny, Fenwick Colton had spent his life with a chip on his shoulder. He'd used it to make something of himself, which Finn gave him considerable credit for, even if his methods were unorthodox and often annoying. The man ran his mouth, pushing his ornery attitude on anyone who would listen. He wasn't above engaging in a verbal battle of wills and he'd often reminded Finn of a Chihuahua.

Which was likely an insult to Chihuahuas.

But he'd be damned if he wanted his uncle mucking around in a murder investigation.

"Like I said, I'm an interested citizen."

"You're deliberately causing trouble and making a spectacle of yourself in front of the town."

The accusation was enough to have Fenwick dropping into his chair. "I'm trying to make a point, only no one's listening."

"What point would that be?"

"This killer out on the loose is ruining the town. Business is dropping. Half the couples getting married have ended their engagements. I'm a month away from Layla marrying Hamlin Harrington and the old coward's threatening to call it all off on account of this Groom Killer on the loose."

Finn feigned compassion, but was pleased he'd finally gotten to the bottom of Fenwick's real problem. Although he avoided family drama as much as possible, his avoidance didn't fully shield him from the goings-on of the Coltons. Just like his stepmother's insistence he interfere in Valeria's life, he was well aware of the sacrifices his cousin Layla was about to make on the altar of business by marrying the considerably older Harrington. Finn kept himself out of the gossip, but it wasn't a stretch to realize that the marriage of his cousin, a top VP at Colton Energy, to Hamlin Harrington, the long-time CEO of green energy company, Harrington Inc., was a front for a business merger.

Hamlin and Fenwick had a long-standing rivalry that would come to a lucrative end if the two entities united. A marriage of convenience between the Colton heir apparent and the old man would obviously see that through and create the largest combined energy company in the entire northwest.

Finn mentally shook his head and held in a sigh, unwilling to show even a moment's weakness in front of his uncle. But he couldn't deny this was the reason he liked dogs. They were far less complicated. And they sure as hell didn't marry their daughters off to smarmy old men to garner a big payday.

"I've told you before, the department is working as fast as it can to find out who's responsible."

"Well, work faster. Maybe if you quit roaming around town on dates, you'd make a bit more progress."

His patience at an end, Finn moved up to the edge of Fenwick's desk, more than willing to use his size to his advantage. "I suggest you focus on your own problems and off me."

"And what if I don't? I can't lose this deal, Finn."

"What does Layla say about all this?"

"She knows her role."

Finn had never been close with his cousin, but even he had a hard time seeing how she would want to bind her life to Hamlin Harrington.

Since he wasn't going to get an answer to that question any more than he was going to get his uncle to stand down and quit bullying everyone in town, Finn opted for retreat. But not before he got in his closing salvo.

"I'd suggest you understand your role, too. And stop making trouble in my town."

Pins clanged, the scent of beer permeated the air and a steady hum of conversation filled the bowling alley as the Tuesday night competition got under way. As Finn had promised, eight teams had showed up for the night's matchups, dominating the four lanes at the far end of the twenty-lane alley.

Finn's team—Large and In Charge—was up against Bad Teachers, and Darby was mentally reviewing everyone's name as she bent to tie her genuinely ugly green-and-gold bowling shoes.

"Be careful. They might see you in Montana," Finn teased her as he eased into the seat next to her.

"I was thinking eastern Washington, so Montana is a definite improvement." Darby lifted a foot, tilting right then left as she admired the truly heinous shoe.

Finn patted a hand on her thigh before pointing to his cousin two lanes over. "At least they're better than Blake's. We can only be thankful these shoes have no support and get no traction on the ground outside. He's threatened to wear those out in public."

Darby tried to ignore the warm outline of his palm that still imprinted her thigh as she looked down the lanes. True to Finn's word, the purple-and-orange monstrosities on Blake's feet were a sight to behold.

"Where did he get those?"

"Somewhere online that should be shut down for deliberately trying to blind people."

"Colton! You're up!" someone hollered from the direction of the ball machine.

"Which Colton?" a woman Darby recognized as Patience Colton from the K-9 training center hollered from her seat.

"Chief's up!"

Finn stood, his little-boy grin firmly in place. "This won't take long. I'll be back shortly."

"Convinced you'll strike out? That's not very forward thinking of you, Chief Colton."

Finn stilled, seeming to think about it. "You're right. Maybe a kiss for good luck will help me out."

Before she could register his words or the movements that matched them, Finn leaned in, caging her between his arms, his mouth on an unerring course for hers. *I should stop him* was the last coherent thought to enter her head before those gorgeous lips landed on hers, eradicating her ability to think.

All she could do was feel.

The hum of the bowling alley faded away, replaced by nothing but the slamming, insistent beat of her heart. Just like the night before in the SUV when he'd wrapped his jacket around her, the man seemed to envelop her. He effectively shut out the world around them and she quickly caught up to the kiss, unwilling to be a passive participant.

He gently coaxed her mouth open, his tongue seeking entrance, and she welcomed him in, glorying in the way he made her feel. Light and airy, even as a heavy weight suffused her limbs. Was it need? Want?

No, a quiet voice whispered in her mind. *Desire.*

This was what desire felt like, pure and simple. Only it wasn't simple at all.

And while her feelings might be pure, reality quickly diluted them with the fact that this was a game of pretend. An act. A pretense to draw out a murderer.

A piercing whistle pulled them both fully out of the moment and Finn ended the kiss, lifting his head and smiling down at her. The little-boy grin was gone, replaced with something more adult. Something that spoke of the knowledge of darkened bedrooms and heated sheets.

A smile that held promises if she was only brave enough to reach out and take them.

"You're up, Chief."

The smile faded and he held her gaze a moment longer before standing to his full height. "Looks like I am."

She watched him walk to the ball machine and pick up the large green ball he'd selected earlier. Unlike some of other players, he'd claimed that he was so bad at bowling he refused to invest in one of his own. Hefting the ball, he walked up to the lane and lined up his shot.

And threw a perfect strike.

Darby let out a cheer before she could stop herself, pleased to see his initial attempt produce a significantly better outcome than a gutter ball. She was still clapping when he walked back over to take the seat next to her.

"That was pretty lucky."

Finn shrugged. "Must have been the kiss."

"I don't know. I—" She broke off, awareness dawning like a sudden dousing. "You're good at this!"

"You give me too much credit."

She leaped up at that, whirling on him. "The whole gutter ball thing was just a big lie to get me to come. That's why you said you'd be quick. You're *really* good at this!"

"Look out, Chief." One of the men on the other team hollered the words before adding an eyebrow wiggle for effect. "Looks like you've been discovered."

"I'm not that good," Finn said.

Darby slammed her hands on her hips, staring him down. "When was the last time you threw a gutter ball?"

"I don't remember." He mumbled—actually mumbled—the words.

Darby turned to his teammates. "When was his last one?" She didn't even bother qualifying the question because she knew they'd all been listening.

"Oh, about never," Bo's sister, Elle, added.

Darby shot her former sister-in-law a grateful smile. "Finally. One truthful person on this team."

One of the other players smiled before adding, "He

just wanted to land a good one on ya. Come on, show him what you're made of. It's your turn."

She harrumphed before marching over to the machine and picking up the lavender ball she'd selected earlier. She inserted her fingers in the holes, testing the weight before marching up to the lane.

She'd show him. Finn Colton and his hot lips and crooked grin and *lying* ways.

Positioning herself a few steps from the small dots lining the floor, Darby pushed herself into motion, allowing the ball to fly from the end of her hand. It made a heavy thud as it hit the lane, but to her utter surprise, ran true down the center of the glossy wood. The thick sound of tumbling pins echoed back toward her and, while it wasn't a strike like her lying, fake date's, she managed to knock out six pins.

They were split straight down the middle, but at least it was points on the board.

She managed to get two more on her second roll before taking her seat once more. Finn, having obviously decided he was better off making himself scarce, was at the counter a few lanes down, ordering food.

"I'm glad you came out with us tonight." Elle took the seat next to her. Although they'd been friendly when she and Bo were married, Darby had lost regular touch with her former sister-in-law since the divorce.

"I'm glad I came, too."

"He's smitten."

"Excuse me?"

"The chief. The man doesn't bring dates to bowling. Heck, he doesn't bring dates anywhere."

Darby wanted to correct Elle but fought back the words. This wasn't a date. Nor was it the start of a major relationship for either of them. It was playacting, plain and simple. No one was smitten and her scrambled brain would do well to remember that.

Even as that thought struck a chord of sadness, Darby realized there was a silver lining. She'd conceded to herself that working with Finn was a chance to help keep Red Ridge safe. It was also a chance to do whatever she could to avenge Bo's death as well as Michael Hayden's. If she was doing a good enough job to fool a cop, then she had to take some solace in that.

Deftly ignoring Elle's words about Finn's dating history, she focused on the noisy alley. "I haven't been bowling in years."

"What have you been waiting for?"

Darby grinned. "I'm not sure."

"Well, I'm glad you're here." Elle jumped up to take her turn and Darby watched her go. Bo's sister was three years younger than her and there was a time when that had felt like an eternity. Now it just seemed like she'd missed the chance to make—and keep—a true friend.

How odd to realize now that she'd lost so many years by not keeping up with the other relationships in her life.

"Still mad at me?"

Finn took the seat next to her once more, his voice low as he leaned in to bump his shoulder against hers.

"I still think you're a liar, if that's what you're asking."

"You can't blame a man for trying."

"For trying what?"

"To kiss you."

The comment was so unexpected—and so at odds

with their fake situation—that Darby's mouth dropped open. "I don't need to be lied to in order to kiss a man."

Was that really her voice?

When had she turned into her mother? The prim-and-prissy attitude had been a staple of her mother's personality. Darby had believed herself free of the curse. Had she been operating under a delusion? Or had she simply grown old before her time?

"Then maybe I should try the honest way."

Once more, Finn Colton had the advantage as his hands tightened over her shoulders, pulling her close. His mouth clamped onto hers and, where the first kiss had been playful and exploratory, this one was all hot, lusty need. His lips traveled a familiar if more urgent path over hers and she opened as his tongue slipped inside.

The move was bold—the kiss even more so—and she lifted her hands to cling to his forearms as she kissed him back. A small moan caught in the back of her throat and she could only be glad the noise of the alley hid that verbal evidence of her need.

What she couldn't hide quite so easily was the warmth that filled her face or the sheer enjoyment she'd taken from the simple joining of their lips.

As Darby watched Finn get up to take his next roll—a second strike—she was forced to admit something to herself. Their situation might be fake, but that kiss had been 100 percent real.

The watcher had intended to enjoy an evening out at the bowling alley, nursing a few drinks at the bar while taking in the supreme moves of her most favorite cop. She looked forward to Tuesday nights and had been pleased when the long wait for bowling season to start up again after the holiday break had finally ended.

A month was too long to go without her Tuesday night watch party.

Only he'd brought *her*.

She had no idea who the woman was, but she'd been readily accepted by the other bowlers even though she played horribly. The first game had been unbearable to sit through. By the second, when the woman had kissed *her* cop yet again, the watcher had paid her bill and fled into the night.

Even now she sat in her car at the edge of the parking lot. Out of sight and far away from the powerful overhead lights, she watched the various league members head to their cars.

How oblivious they all were. Going about their days unaware of how boring and dull and *routine* their lives really were. It made her smile, a small giggle bubbling in her throat. They were all so boring and uninteresting and they didn't even know it.

Only Finn was different.

Only Finn understood her and would understand what life could be like between them.

Only Finn would take away this desperate clawing and craving that filled her chest, desperate to get out.

So she sat there in her car, waiting for Finn Colton to come out. As people filed out of the bowling alley, alone or in pairs, she knew none of them saw the woman watching them.

Chapter 8

Thick russet-colored fur bunched in Darby's hands as she smoothed her palms over the German shepherd her vet had recommended to her last Saturday. Doc Cooper had vouched for the dog and had helped set up Darby's meeting with the family selling her. Patience Colton, the vet at the K-9 center, had kindly offered them a backdrop for the meeting and had been more than willing to give a second opinion while also reinforcing the reputation of Darby's business.

Satisfied, Patience got up off the floor from where she'd sat, performing her checkup. "I'm pleased to say this girl looks amazing."

The owner, Mavis Whitley, smiled fondly as she looked down on the dog they called Lucy. "She's been such a sweet girl. We just want her to go to a loving home and I'd love for her to be part of such a good program. Dr. Cooper spoke highly of your business, Ms. Gage."

"I can promise you she'll be treated like a queen." Darby said.

"We're very impressed that you've decided not to breed your other dog. Care for her health is obviously your priority and it makes us feel that Lucy will be in good hands."

"Thank you." Darby appreciated the kindness, but she'd never questioned the rightness of her decision. Her first priority was Penny—the business had to be second. She could only be grateful Finn had ensured she'd still have a business. Bringing home Lucy was the next step in that process. Of course, taking that step was predicated on a match with Penny.

Darby had brought Penny along, as well, and gestured toward a windowed play area. "I would like to introduce her to my dog, if you don't mind?"

The Whitleys didn't mind. In moments they had Penny and Lucy meeting each other in supervised play. Darby let out her first easy breath of the morning when the dogs cautiously sniffed each other before raising their paws and swatting happily in play.

"I think they're on a path to being BFFs." Patience took a spot next to her, her arms crossed, a satisfied smile playing about her lips. They'd known one another for a while, Darby's work at the training center ensuring she'd spent time with nearly everyone there. Patience was one of her favorites, though.

"I'm just grateful we have a match. Lucy's so sweet, and I'm not sure what I'd have done if she and Penny didn't get along."

"You'd try again until you found the right one." Patience waved at the happily playing dogs, her love of animals clear in her smitten gaze. "You're strong and determined that way."

As compliments went, it was one of the nicest she'd ever received. "I'm not quite sure I agree, but thank you."

Patience laid a hand on Darby's arm, effectively pulling her attention from Penny and Lucy. "Don't underestimate yourself. I know you've had a rough go for the past few years, but you're strong and you're solid and you've got a big heart. The universe loves those traits and loves rewarding them."

The added compliment caught her so off guard, Darby could only goggle at the vet. Tall and pretty, Patience had an easy grace about her that was more boho than Red Ridge chic, despite being born with Fenwick Colton's silver spoon lodged firmly in her mouth.

It was the warmth in her dark brown eyes that was the real clincher.

"Thank you."

"You're welcome. Now—" Patience turned to watch the dogs at play but Darby couldn't help feeling the woman's attention hadn't wavered. "Tell me about these hot date nights you've been having with my cousin Finn."

Finn swung by the lab on his way into the precinct, the text he'd received earlier suggesting there was something that required his attention. The week had produced little news or evidence in the battle to find the Groom Killer. The fact that it was Friday—an entire week since Michael Hayden's death—and they had next to nothing to go on, had only ratcheted up the pressure on finding the killer.

Finn had kept up his dates with Darby, taking her to another showy dinner on Wednesday night and a movie Thursday, but so far they'd been unsuccessful in attracting any unsavory attention. Which was a major departure from everyone else in town who had suddenly become fixated on the chief of police's new love interest.

He'd gotten teasing comments from nearly every member of his family as well as several Gages. With the exception of Elle, his K-9 rookie, everyone in the Gage family had remained stubbornly skeptical, Carson's suspicion over Darby ensuring no one in Bo's family had mentally let her off the hook.

But adding on the general interest in town had become a bit much. That morning, in fact, he'd gotten questioned by Mae Larson while he'd waited for his coffee at Java Station. He'd always seen her as a sweet older member of the community, but her grandmotherly ways were surprisingly randy if the eyebrow wiggles she'd given him were any indication.

Did people really have nothing better to do?

Of course, their focus on his love life had helped some of the conversation die down over the Groom Killer. Even the *Gazette* had seemed to run out of headlines, taking a break and focusing on an impending snowstorm heading their way and threatening to dump over a foot and a half of snow.

While the snow was expected this time of year, it was only going to further ruin the crime scenes he and his team had run over and over throughout the week. The Groom Killer had chosen well, using the forests and thick covered ground that made up the edges of the town to an advantage.

The chase he and Lotte had given the week before over the terrain behind the Circle T Steakhouse had resulted in no discernible leads and they'd finally given the restaurant leave to reopen for business.

To further prove his commitment, Finn had booked a reservation for him and Darby that very night and the owner had agreed to give them the center table.

He was excited to see her again, the charade they'd kept up all week growing more and more intimate by the day. He knew he needed to keep his emotions in check, but he couldn't deny how much he enjoyed spending time with her. And while he hardly needed the public interest the two of them seemed to generate, he couldn't find too much fault since big and showy had been his intention from the start.

He wasn't so sure she felt the same.

It was subtle, but it was there. She'd yet to initiate anything intimate. That had been all him. And while he'd told himself the hand holding and the endearments and the kissing were all for show, in his quiet moments, he had to ask himself if that was the truth.

Mae Larson's eyebrow wiggles aside, he couldn't deny he enjoyed kissing Darby Gage.

A lot.

Brushing off the matter of Darby's kisses, Finn took the long hallway that led to the lab, willing himself to focus on the matter at hand. He did have a killer in his midst and no amount of time spent with a pretty woman with gorgeous legs and enticing lips was going to change that.

More, if he was going to keep his head and his

focus, he had to remind himself that dating Darby was all for show. The dates and the kisses were meant to draw out a killer, not allow him to forget he was hunting one.

He pushed through the heavy metal doors of the crime lab and found their resident lab geek, Charlie, outfitted head to toe in scrubs. Other than the four-inch heels she persistently wore, Dr. Charlotte "Charlie" Wallace looked like she was ready to march into a hazmat area.

"Doc."

"Finn." She turned from the microscope she peered into to face him. Dark eyes twinkled above a face mask and he looked down over his clothes before meeting her gaze once more. "I think I'm underdressed."

"Not at all. I swung out here because I knew you were coming. I'm dressed like this for some work in the other room." She pointed toward a door marked Do Not Enter and Finn wondered, not for the first time, what lived in the depths of Charlie's lab.

"Everything okay?"

"Of course. Just some necrotic tissue I want to handle with care."

Finn nodded "As one does."

"Your gallows humor is noted. And appreciated." Charlie waved to a point about halfway down the long counter that ran the length of her lab. "Come on over here."

He followed her, admiring her tall, capable form. What caught him off guard was the quick leap he made to imagining Darby's smaller, more petite curves in his mind. Instantly he recalled the feel of her beneath his palms and the fierce need that settled in his bones each time he kissed her.

"Finn?"

Charlie's question pulled him from his musings. "Hmm?"

"You okay? You look about a million miles away."

"Sure. Yeah, I'm good."

Charlie pointed to a setup on the counter. "Here's the bleach you brought me the other day and then the samples that were collected in the forest."

"You've kept this under wraps?"

"Of course." She tugged a pair of rubber gloves out of a box before handing the box to him to do the same. "I know how to manage an investigation and I've sent my notes to you only, as you requested. I'm not sure why Carson isn't updated on these developments, though, as one of the lead investigators."

"I want an unbiased opinion."

Charlie's dark eyes clouded. "You think he's biased in some way?"

"I think investigating the murder of his brother is a sensitive topic. Where I can take some of the load off or tug a few leads that may be inconsequential, I want to do that."

Her dark gaze remained sharp, but she finally nodded. "I'll defer to your wishes, but don't underestimate Gage. He's a good man and he wants justice."

"And I don't?"

Finn knew the question was steeped in his unusual secretive approach to the bleach, which was all the more reason he needed to recognize it was possible he was losing his objectivity, as well.

"That's not what I meant," Charlie said.

Finn slapped the gloves against his thigh. "I know it's not. And I know I'm not being fair."

Charlie hesitated for the briefest moment, as if weighing something, before pushing forward. "Would this have anything to do with your recent attentions toward Darby Gage?"

Finn understood the hesitation—and waited a few beats himself before ultimately opting for the truth. He'd had tough cases in his past and the duties of chief often meant he had to make hard choices, even between the members of his department. He did want Carson to assess the situation with the Groom Killer through a clear pair of eyes but he held himself to the same set of expectations.

None of it was a reason to keep the truth from Charlie.

"Yes, it does. Carson refuses to take her off his suspect list. Truth of the matter is, she's not fully off mine yet, either."

"And the bleach?"

"You've been analyzing the bleach found at the crime scene. The bottle I gave you was in Ms. Gage's possession as she cleaned Bo Gage's home. Which she inherited upon his death."

"I see."

Did she?

"I know it's a basic chemical compound, so I don't know if you can tell any differences, but the connection seemed suspicious."

"Did Ms. Gage act strange when you wanted the bottle?"

"She seemed confused that I wanted it, but otherwise didn't seem bothered by the request."

"What I can tell you is that the bleach you removed from her home isn't the same as what was laid down at the crime scene. The scene was highly compromised but the base chemicals and strength were different."

"You could tell that? From what I gave you?"

"What was at the crime scene was most likely a consumer brand. The strength level was high and had been liberally dumped on the ground. Even with the dilution of the snow cover, there was enough base product that I'd say the killer used at least two bottles, maybe a third."

"Wow."

"What Ms. Gage has is a generic brand. It's still potent, but the concentration was lower and likely cost her less. You're looking for someone who bought several bottles at once." She pointed to the setup on the counter. "Want to take a look?"

"Sure." Finn followed Charlie to the counter, taking her lead as she walked him through the various tests she'd run to assess the differences between samples.

As he left the lab fifteen minutes later, Finn took solace in the irrefutable proof that Darby hadn't doused the crime scene.

And struggled with the way he was going to tell Carson what he'd kept to himself since Monday.

Darby inhaled the savory aroma of her steak and breathed in deep. The filet was cooked perfectly, in just the way she preferred. Medium, with a side of mashed potatoes and creamed corn that would make the angels weep.

She'd only ever been to the Circle T once. She and Bo had come to the restaurant for their first anniversary. He'd wined and dined her, lavishing her with compliments. Three days later she'd discovered his cheating—and the fact that the woman he'd cheated with was the fourth since they'd married—and had moved out.

Aside from the matter that she couldn't afford it, she'd diligently avoided the Circle T and the role the restaurant played in the last good memory from her marriage.

"Is something wrong with your steak?"

Darby glanced up at Finn, his frown of concern a sweet rebuke against those memories. "It's fine. Better than fine, as a matter of fact."

"You sure?"

"Absolutely. In fact, I'm warning you now, I'm clearing my plate. No leftovers for me."

"Penny will be disappointed."

"Penny will survive." She cut into her steak, pleased when another delicious scent wafted up toward her. "And there's no way I'm feeding a dog a thirty-eight-dollar steak, no matter how much I care for her."

"There are many in this town who don't feel the same."

For all the time they'd spent together this week, she'd rarely heard Finn speak ill of anyone. Yet his comment—and the dry tone—had her considering that maybe the man did have enemies.

Or at least a few people who rubbed him the wrong way.

"You thinking of anyone in particular?"

"My uncle Fenwick, for starters. He's always enjoyed his role as the richest in the family. He'd think nothing of an expensive meal, or feeding it to the dogs."

Darby thought about the funny little man who'd bellowed his way around the bank on Tuesday. "I saw him. Tuesday morning, when I was depositing the check for the business. This word's highly inadequate, but he seemed to be in quite a snit."

The answering smile she received made her think it might be the perfect word. "I saw him shortly after that. I'd gotten a call that he was doing his level best to act like the town jerk, and headed over to see what was wrong."

"You find out?"

"He's upset about the Groom Killer. Claims it's ruining the wedding plans for his daughter. My cousin Layla," Finn added.

"Did something happen to her plans?"

"Her groom's crying off. Or threatening to. Claims he's at risk of getting killed if he goes through with it."

"That's an awful reason."

Darby understood what she and Finn were doing. The very real risks they were taking to draw out a killer. Even with that understanding, she hadn't given much thought to the fact that people who were actually in love would call off their plans.

"I'd say it makes Layla lucky," Finn said.

"What?"

"She's marrying Hamlin Harrington. The man's twice her age and it's basically a business merger. I'd think she had better things to do with her future than marry an old man."

Once again, Finn surprised her. He'd been so casual about them pretending to date each other, she'd internalized that to mean he had little interest in finding love himself. Yet to hear him talk about his cousin and his disgust at her marriage gave Darby an opportunity to probe a bit.

"I didn't realize you were so close to your extended family."

"I'm not."

"Yet you're upset that she's choosing to enter this marriage?"

Finn sawed at his T-bone, his movements deliberate and precise, as he removed the steak from the bone. "I don't understand people who don't get married for love. Marriage is hard enough. Why add that pressure on top?"

"People get married for a lot of reasons. Love isn't always at the top of the list. Or on the list at all."

His movements stopped abruptly. "Why did you get married?"

Images of that anniversary dinner flitted through her mind once again, followed quickly by the memory of the bunched-up panties she'd found three days later in Bo's car. "I was in love. Or thought I was."

"Would you do it again?"

"I don't know." In an abstract way, Darby had believed she would get married again, but in reality she hadn't been all that quick to go looking for it. "Would you?"

"I haven't given it much thought."

"What about your marriage, then? Were you in love?"

"Yes." His shoulders had grown more and more stiff as they spoke of their pasts, but it was like something broke. He laid down his fork and knife and looked at her. "But I might have been the same as you. I went into it with the best of intentions but somewhere along the way realized I wasn't really in love. And then, after a while, I began to question if I'd ever been in love at all."

"It's easy to armchair quarterback at the end. After all the bad things have been said, it's hard to remember there were ever good things."

"I suppose."

"It doesn't mean there wasn't anything good about the time you spent together. Which is why I need to thank you."

"Thank me? For what?"

"For this week. For however long this charade lasts. I've been existing these past few years but I haven't really been living. You've reminded me that I'm still young and still have something to give."

Finn stared at her, that firm jaw and penetrating gaze that had increasingly been occupying more and more of her thoughts holding her captive. In such a short time, he'd reminded her that she had a future. One she should work a bit harder for.

"Whoever is lucky enough to receive all you have to give, Darby Gage, will be a lucky man."

The sweet words hovered between them, as delicate as cotton candy at the state fair. She debated saying something, but hesitated to break the moment. And then the choice was taken out of her hands by the arrival of the Larson twins, with two equally vapid women on their arms.

"Look at this little party." Evan Larson spoke first. Or who she thought was Evan, but maybe it was his twin, Noel. She'd always had some trouble figuring out who was who. They were handsome men, but Darby had always steered clear of both of them. She'd waited on them from time to time at the diner, but in recent years when they'd lined their coffers with even more money from whatever interests they had going— real estate was the latest, she'd heard—they'd believed themselves above diner fare.

"Heard you're running Bo's business now." The one she believed was Noel spoke up, his eyes hazed with what she assumed was liquor.

"Yes, I inherited Bo's business."

"I want one of your puppies. Two, as a matter of fact." The woman at his side cooed when she heard the mention of puppies and he squeezed her waist in response.

"I don't know when my next litter will be ready."

The jovial smile on the man's face dropped. "Why the hell not? Bo said he was getting ready to breed his bitch."

"Penny's not ready to have more puppies." Darby held her ground but chaffed at the arrogance. And while she understood the technical term for Penny was *bitch*, somehow Noel's use of the word was more slur than descriptor.

"Well, get her ready. She's a damned dog."

The other Larson stepped up, laying a hand on his brother's free shoulder. "You'll have to excuse my brother's excitement. He's been looking forward to adding to his team of guard dogs. The training takes a while and he'd hoped to include some young blood into his team."

Finn stood then, his movements slow as he came to his full height. Although neither of the twins was a small man, Finn's tall form and broad shoulders had them backing up. "I'm sure Ms. Gage will be happy to let you know when she's ready for buyers."

Again, the one Darby she believed was Evan spoke up. "I'm sure she will."

He tightened his grip on his date and shot a smile to his brother that smacked of warning. "We'll let you get back to your dinner, then. Enjoy your evening."

The foursome walked to a private table in the back. Noel's tumble into his chair reinforced her belief he was drunk, though it didn't negate the dark look he shot her from across the room.

Finn took his seat after shooting a few dark looks of his own in the direction of the brothers.

"I guess your investment's already paying off." Darby tried to keep her attitude light and breezy, but the image of giving one of her puppies to Evan or Noel Larson stuck in her stomach and spoiled her appetite.

"What investment?"

"The money you've put into the business. I've already got buyers. Not the Larson brothers, of course. I'd never do business with them."

"That money's yours. I don't expect any of it back."

Although the past week hadn't been anything like she'd expected, Darby distinctly remembered their conversation when he'd offered to pay off her debts. "But you said the money was an investment."

"In you. In getting your help, yes. But I don't expect anything back from you."

"Why would you do that?"

"Because you needed help. And since I needed help, too, this was the quickest way to solve both our problems." Finn reached across the table and took her hand in his. Unlike the purposeful attempts at public displays of affection over the past week, there was something impulsive in the gesture. Like he meant it and wasn't trying to show off for anyone who might be watching.

"Thank you for the help, then." She turned her hand over beneath his, allowing his palm to rest against hers, and took solace in the simple gesture of affection.

Chapter 9

"Bring it to me! Come on, girl!" Finn hollered the words as he watched Darby's newest addition race toward the back fence surrounding the backyard. The property was larger than the fenced area, but the cordoned space provided lots of room to play and roam yet still kept the dogs near the house.

Lucy had picked up the game quickly, her transition to Darby's home seeming to go smoothly as he took her through several games and drills. Lotte and Penny were enjoying themselves, as well, racing around the backyard, chasing each other and generally rough-housing on the snow-covered ground.

"Do they ever get tired?"

Darby, bundled up in a thick coat, carried two travel mugs of coffee in her hands. She hip bumped the back door closed before crossing to him and extending one of the mugs. Finn took the offering and laughed as Lucy bounded back over the snow, racing close enough to kick up some powder as she skidded to a stop at his feet.

"Once again, the Finn Colton charm is taking down another one. What is your secret with my dogs?"

"I think they know I'm as big a kid as they are."

Darby cocked her head, the bold morning sun catching the red highlights in her hair. "The big, bad chief has a childish side?"

"One I pull out on rare occasions. Dogs are a safe space to do that."

"Have you had times in your life where you didn't feel you could be a kid? Where you needed a safe space?"

Finn heard the interest and knew he was the one who'd put the idea out there. What surprised him was how comfortable he felt continuing the conversation.

"It's a trait that started young and I guess I've kept it." He tossed the ball again, sending Lucy off on a race to catch it, her delighted barks filling the air.

"You're the oldest?" she asked.

"The oldest. And the only from my father's marriage to my mother. My half siblings are from my father's second marriage."

"I can see where that would be hard."

"It might have been easier with a different woman, but Joanelle is a tough woman on a good day."

"And on a bad one?" Darby asked, going to the heart of the matter.

"She made it perfectly clear she'd be perfectly happy if I hadn't been a part of her life most days.

Fortunately my siblings aren't the same. But I spent as much time out of the house as I could."

"You couldn't have been that old. I've met your sister Serena. She's not that much younger than you."

"Five years."

"So you could hardly run through town by yourself. Where did you go when you went out of the house?"

"The stables, mostly. I made friends with the ranch hands and they were good to me, but they kept their distance, too. Owner's kid and all that. The dogs, on the other hand—they were always good for long hours together."

He saw the concern in her eyes—saw the way the sympathy came over her like a wool blanket—and was positively suffocated by it. "It was no big deal. I survived. And I have a good relationship with Anders and Serena and Valeria. Joanelle couldn't mess that up, no matter how much she tried to poison the well."

Darby didn't say anything. Instead she turned and set her coffee down on a small table, then reached for his and did the same. The dog had bounded back during their conversation and before he could send her running again, Darby picked up the ball at his feet and tossed it, sending Lucy off like a shot in its wake.

She focused on him once more, the warmth in her gaze changing as he stared at her in the fresh morning air. Where Finn believed he'd seen sympathy only moments before, the light in her eyes had changed, reflecting something that looked a lot like want.

Then she proved him 100 percent correct by lifting up on her tiptoes and pressing her lips to his.

Finn caught her around the waist, boosting her up and crushing her to his chest at the same time. The tentative press of her lips on his picked up steam as she got into the moment with him, her tongue darting out to mate with his. In moments the kiss went from sweet and heated to wanton and erotic, a feast for the senses. He was beyond pleased she'd initiated the kiss—everything up to now had been all him—but he couldn't deny the need to touch her was overwhelming.

His hands roamed over her back, pulling her close and seeking the shape of her through the thick, heavy winter material. For the first time in his life, he wished for summer.

And wasn't that a kick?

A heavy paw swatted at his thigh before the distinct outline of a ball pressed into the same spot. He broke the kiss to stare down at Lucy, her eyes big and unrepentant as she stared up at him.

"She doesn't care she's interrupted something." The husky register of Darby's voice grabbed at him, a fist closing over the base of his spine as he kept one hand firmly wrapped around her. With the other, he took the ball and flung it as hard and as far as he could, not surprised when he heard a heavy thud where it met the fence line.

"That was some throw."

"That's because I want more time." Finn bent his head to hers once more, their breaths shooting puffs of steam into the cold morning air. He ignored all of it as he took her mouth, anxious to devour as much of her as he could.

Where had this come from?

A week ago he'd accused her of murder. When had he veered from thinking of her as a suspect to thinking of her as a lover?

Lucy's barks interrupted them once more and he sighed against Darby's lips.

"It's like a race against the clock," Darby said before a giggle spilled out.

"It's not funny."

"Yeah." She giggled again. "It sort of is. I've got one who won't let me pet her and one that won't let me kiss you. Maybe I should sell the business. I'm not sure I'm going to be very successful at it anyway."

Finn considered her in that moment—the big smile, the infectious laughter, and the clear love and commitment for the dogs—and knew it was time to tell her she was no longer a suspect. The bleach had provided proof, but the longer he spent with her, the less proof he needed.

She was a good woman. And she'd done right by Bo Gage's family and his business and his beloved dog. A killer would have run long before, but Darby had stuck around.

Their conversation about his childhood struck him once more. He'd pushed aside that time in his life, refusing to dwell too long on what it had meant to be an outsider in his own family. Yet she'd understood.

More, she'd taken an interest and asked.

Yes, it was definitely time to tell her she wasn't a suspect any longer. And it was time to give her a choice. He appreciated her help more than he could say, but she deserved a chance to get out of hunting a killer.

"There's something I need to tell you."

"About what?"

"Let's go inside. I'd like to update you on the case."

* * *

The watcher lifted the glass heart out of its velvet bed, turning the piece over and over in her hands. It was so delicate. Fragile.

Like the bonds she had with Finn Colton.

How was it he didn't see that?

She'd been to the precinct before. They'd spoken, for heaven's sake. *Connected.* How could he not know?

How could he not see how she felt about him?

But he obviously didn't. Not if the spectacle he'd made of himself this week was any indication. Dinner dates. Movies. The bowling Tuesday night. All week long she'd been forced to watch him squire around that woman. The murderer.

Oh, she knew what the town whispered about. And they'd been whispering long and low about Darby Gage, the Groom Killer. It wasn't a leap. She'd been married to the first victim. She was probably bitter and upset that he'd moved on. And then it had made her so mad, she'd killed another groom. Another man seeking his eternal happiness.

She traced her finger over the fragile heart, the glass so fine she could imagine it beating in her hand.

Like Finn Colton's heart. She'd have it someday, all to herself.

Soon, he'd be hers.

In the meantime, maybe she needed to help him out. Help make sure that woman, the murderer, wasn't able to kill again.

Darby set down refreshed water in three large bowls and heard the lapping before she'd even cleared the kitchen into the living room. With any luck the intense play session outside had tired out her charges. Of course, it wouldn't do Finn much good if his partner fell asleep on the job, but with it being Saturday, hopefully they wouldn't be called off to too much. In the relatively short time they'd spent together, she'd come to realize how dedicated he was to his job and his team. Even when he was technically off duty, he was always available to them.

Finn had poured fresh mugs of coffee for the two of them while she'd taken care of the dogs and had settled hers on the small coffee table in the living room.

He stood at the window that overlooked the backyard, his back to her when she walked into the room. The quiet moment gave her a chance to look him over and it struck her once again how big and strong he was.

Capable.

And very male.

It was funny, she'd never been a particular fan of big men. Bo had been physically well built but he'd been of average height. Most people didn't notice it because his personality had been so oversize, but he hadn't come anywhere near to clearing six feet. The few men she'd dated before getting married had all been average size, as well.

She'd liked it that way. While she'd never been afraid of men, growing up with a single mother, her life had revolved around being careful and being a good girl. Dating a large, overbearing man had always seemed like the antithesis of that.

Sunlight framed Finn's body, backlighting him and showing off the gold in his thick dark blond hair. Once again, she could see traces of the little boy she imagined in her mind every time he smiled. Only, now she had a different picture. One he'd painted of lonely days with only the farm animals for company.

It explained his innate sense and easy comfort with the dogs. It also explained his unconditional love for them. While having a pet was a responsibility—running a business with them even more so—there was also an ease there. They genuinely craved care and affection and, if given, gave back far more than asked for.

It was that belief that had her hanging in there with Penny, persistent and steady as she worked to build a trusting relationship between them. And it was that same belief that had her so excited Lucy was now a part of their lives.

Finn turned from the window, catching her staring. She knew she should be embarrassed—it wasn't like she'd acted shy that morning, either—yet she couldn't see her way to even a blush. She enjoyed his company. And while things were confusing between them, especially with Bo's death still unsolved, it wasn't like he'd pushed her away.

Was it possible he considered things between them, as well?

The thought warmed her until a second followed on its heels. He'd said more than once that he'd wanted to keep their romance front and center to catch a killer. And he'd told her that he'd had a development in the case.

Had she only imagined a relationship building in her mind? She hadn't dated in quite a while. And she had reveled in the affection he'd lavished on her over the past week. Maybe she'd fantasized this all out of control and turned it into something it wasn't.

Something ugly and sick began to swirl in her veins, clouding her vision with memories of that morning when she'd thrown herself at him.

"Darby? You okay?"

"Sure. Fine. Of course." She crossed the small space to the oversize chair that sat at the corner of the couch. "I know you have something you wanted to discuss. I'm sure I've taken up way too much of your time this morning and here I am lollygagging."

"You're not—"

She patted the arm of the couch, a gesture to call him over. "What was it you wanted to discuss?"

A strange expression passed over his face and he looked about to say something, but opted not to at the last minute and took the seat she'd suggested. He stared at her for a few more moments before taking a sip of his coffee.

"What is it, Finn?"

That intense gaze didn't let up and the sinking feeling that had carried her to her seat grew more intense. *Oh, no, you really did misread the situation. Smooth move, Darbs.*

"I need to update you on the investigation."

"You're allowed to do that?"

"I'd say so, since I've pulled you into it. I also need to talk to Carson and I thought you might like to go with me."

Whatever she'd been expecting him to say, inviting her to a meeting with her ex-brother-in-law wasn't it. "On official police business?"

"Yes and no. Technically you've been helping out on official police business, so I'm not quite sure I should get uppity about it all of a sudden."

"Oo-kay." She nearly smiled at the image of Finn getting uppity about anything, but his serious expression had her reconsidering. Something had him bothered and he was making her crazy as she waited to hear what it was. "Why don't you tell me what's going on?"

"You're no longer a suspect."

A weight she hadn't even realized she'd carried lifted off her. Like the deal he'd struck the past week, releasing her from the bonds of debt Bo had left her in, yet different at the same time. That had simply been money. While difficult, it was something she knew she would find her way past.

This was her life.

And she had no idea how she'd worried that her freedom and her choices would be taken away.

"What changed your mind?" she asked.

"Several things. But the bleach was a big one."

Bleach? What was he talking about? "I'm afraid you've lost me."

"The bleach last Monday. The bottle I took from you."

"Right." She nodded, puzzling through the odd change in conversation. "I figured you needed to clean something up."

"That's all you thought?"

"Yeah, sure." She shrugged, trying to recall the situation. He'd seemed fixated on the bottle when he'd seen it in her hand. When he'd finally asked for it, she'd handed it over. "You do have a dog in your car. I can't say I gave it much thought."

"I needed to take it to the lab."

"And you've lost me again."

The jangling of dog tags pulled her attention from Finn as Penny, Lucy and Lotte all trotted into the living room in single file, Penny in front. They lined themselves up on the floor and Darby was fascinated to watch how they positioned themselves with Lotte closest to Finn and Penny nearest to Darby. Lucy had taken the middle, as if she understood where she fit in the pecking order.

Simple. Understood.

Unlike the conversation she was having with Finn. "Why don't you take this one apart for me? I really don't understand what you're talking about or what it has to do with deciding I'm no longer a suspect."

"That's what I'm trying to tell you. I was doing my job."

"What did you think I was doing with the bleach besides cleaning?"

"There was bleach discovered as part of the Hayden crime scene. I thought maybe you'd put it there."

That strange, inscrutable expression on his face when he'd stared at her cleaning supplies suddenly made sense. She had noticed it then, even if she hadn't understood why. "That's why you looked at the bottle like it was a coiled snake?"

"Yes."

"And you thought I used bleach to commit a murder?" She quickly cycled through the headlines she'd read over the past month on the town paper. "But the killer has used a gun. Bo and the other man were shot and killed. What does bleach have to do with it?"

"Why don't you come with me to see Carson? I'll explain everything."

Finn turned into the entrance of the Double C Ranch, his childhood home. He visited as little as possible, taking part in only the basic requirements of family life. Since his stepmother liked it that way, preferring to ignore the fact that her husband had a family before they'd met, it was a mutually agreeable situation.

Despite the active avoidance, he'd been here several times in the past few months. His sister Serena had just had a baby and Lora was the apple of everyone's eye, including her uncle Finn's.

Serena had also been at the heart of the mystery surrounding Bo's death and their cousin Demi's possible involvement. Although Serena had defended Demi, claiming she couldn't possibly be involved in Bo's murder, she hadn't been able to give any good reason why Demi's necklace had been found at the murder scene. Nor could she explain why Bo Gage, with his last breath, would have written "Demi C" in his own blood.

It had been one of the most grisly things Finn had ever witnessed. While he wanted to believe his sister, he simply couldn't remove their cousin off the suspects list because Serena thought she was being framed. The fact Demi had jumped town hadn't helped her case one bit.

"We're not going in the front door?" Darby asked after they parked at the side of the house.

"I'd prefer to avoid my stepmother. Serena has a private entrance and it's just easier."

"Of course."

She seemed to take his comments in stride, but surprised him when she took his hand as they walked toward the entrance to Serena's wing of the ranch.

He surprised himself even more by how good it felt

to have her support. He squeezed her fingers before dropping her hand to knock on the door.

As expected, Carson was there with his fiancée and soon-to-be adopted daughter and was the one to answer the door. His normally impassive gaze—known for giving away nothing—widened when he saw Darby. "Finn. Darb. What can I do for you?"

"Can we come in? I have news."

Carson backed up immediately. "You have a breakthrough on the case?"

Finn laid a hand on Carson's shoulder, stilling him. "No breakthroughs, but an update you should know about."

His top detective seemed to consider things for a moment before nodding. "Since Darby is here, I presume Serena can hear the details?"

"Of course." Finn nodded.

"Let's go get Serena, then, and we'll sit down."

Since he'd been there a few weeks before, Finn was surprised by the additional changes that had taken place in such a short time. Although there had been blankets and bottles scattered around, on the walk from the door through the living area, he passed a cradle, a stack of toys there was no way Lora was big enough to play with and a large colorful mat that had what looked like a bridge arcing above it.

"It sure does look different in here."

Carson grinned, the weight of the investigation fading in his excitement. "We're baby central around here. Lora's so close to rolling over, it's going to be any day."

Finn had no idea why that was important but began to nod at the news when Darby spoke up. "Already? She's still so young. She must be a fast learner."

"She's a champ," Carson agreed, gesturing them to the kitchen table before excusing himself to go find Serena.

Finn waited until Carson was out of earshot to question Darby. "What just happened?"

"What just happened?"

"Since Bo's death, he's been convinced you're a hardened criminal and now you make one comment about Lora and he's ready to be your best friend?"

"For starters, I don't think Carson really thinks I'm guilty. I think he wants to think I'm guilty so he can catch his brother's killer. Second, every parent wants to talk about their child's achievements and milestones."

"But he's not—" Finn broke off, realization dawning. He'd certainly not minded when his sister had hooked up with Carson. The detective was not only one of his best members of the force, he was a good man with a good head on his shoulders. But to realize that he loved Lora as much as he loved Serena...

"He's her father in every way that counts," Darby said, her voice gentle.

Finn was prevented from saying anything as his sister walked into the kitchen, Carson trailing behind her. Unable to stop himself, Finn gathered her up for a huge hug, lifting her off her feet and spinning her around.

"Finn! What's going on with you?"

"I'm happy to see you. And I assume she's sleeping, but I expect to see Lora before I leave, too."

"We can make that happen. And since my daughter has decided to eat with the timing and precision of a train conductor, she should be up in about—" Serena glanced at the clock over the stove "—thirty minutes."

Carson got them all settled at the table with coffee.

Recognizing they were under a ticking clock before his niece woke up, Finn started in with his story.

Carson and Serena listened to his overview of the chase he and Lotte had given the night of Michael Hayden's death, the bleach finish line that had stopped them and the bottle he'd discovered at Darby's house. They nodded throughout, seeming to understand the implications, of both the killer's craftiness and the possible connection to Darby. When Finn explained his initial thoughts about the bottle Darby had used to clean her home, Serena had reached over and laid a comforting hand on Darby's arm.

But it was when he'd explained the results of the lab tests that Carson got up and went around the table, pulling Darby to her feet.

"I'm sorry. I'm so sorry I doubted you."

Finn had known relief when Charlie had cleared Darby's involvement via the bleach lab testing. But as he watched Darby cling to Carson, for the first time since Bo Gage's body had been discovered, Finn had hope they'd all come out the other side of this.

They'd stop the Groom Killer and allow the residents of Red Ridge to sleep safe at night once again.

Chapter 10

Darby brushed away tears, shocked at how deeply she felt Carson's forgiveness. They'd always gotten along and from the first time they met she'd enjoyed and cared for Bo's oldest brother. She'd often thought that Carson was the type of brother she'd have loved to have if she'd had any siblings. Strong, sure of himself and deeply committed to his family.

While she'd understood on a visceral level how much it hurt to lose that approval, it was only now that she had it back that she understood how much his doubt had truly pained her.

And though she'd meant what she'd told Finn—on some level she had believed that Carson had found her to be an easy scapegoat for Bo's murder—it was freeing to move past all of it.

Carson and Serena held hands, their simple joining evidence of their support for one another. Carson directed his attention to Finn, yet it was clear he had remained focused on Serena, especially when he squeezed her hand. "I'd like to be mad at you, Colton, for not telling me about the bleach and the lab work, but I've got something I've been holding on to, as well."

"Me, too." Serena added.

"Serena?"

His sister nodded, before seeming to take strength in a subtle head nod from Carson. "You know Demi and I got close over the past year. Since I got pregnant with Lora. I was alone and scared, and Mom hasn't exactly been a pillar of support."

Darby registered the comment about Finn's stepmother and, when added to the story he'd told of his own childhood loneliness, she couldn't quite hold back her judgment of Joanelle Colton.

Had the woman really abandoned her daughter—even if only emotionally—when she'd gotten pregnant? She vaguely knew the circumstances of Serena's pregnancy—a one-night stand gone wrong—but even if they hadn't been ideal, the joy and celebration of a baby was something to treasure. Thankfully Carson had seen the beauty and the joy and was clearly smitten with both Serena *and* her daughter.

It was unfair and unkind to judge, but Joanelle's treatment of her children was unfeeling and cold, and Darby fully understood why Finn had favored the side entrance to the house. Although her thoughts were uncharitable and judgmental, Finn said nothing against Joanelle, and instead pressed his sister to continue.

"Demi has been a good friend to me. The best friend. Which is why I've not wanted to share this."

"It's okay, Serena," Carson coaxed. "Tell them."

Serena gathered herself, coming to some sort of conclusion in her mind. "Demi took a pregnancy test the same week Bo was murdered. She believed she was pregnant with his child."

Demi Colton pregnant? With Bo's baby?

Everything stilled inside Darby, seeming to slow as she sat at the table with the others. Bo was going to be a father?

Somewhere inside, Darby figured she should be upset. She had never been lucky enough to start a family with Bo. Yet even as she thought it, she could only find relief that a child had never resulted from their union.

Bo had been careless with others' emotions and if Demi was that recently pregnant and Bo was still planning to marry Hayley, the situation only reinforced his negligence. He jumped from woman to woman, with little thought to feelings or, obviously, consequences.

"Is Demi pregnant?" Darby asked.

"I think so." Serena nodded. "But I don't know for sure. I know she bought the pregnancy test but I don't know the results."

"Even with that news, you don't think she killed Bo in a crime of passion, do you?" Finn spoke up, but his question to his sister had a gentleness that touched Darby's heart.

Whatever the situation—and certainly it was increasingly convoluted—Serena's certainty was evident. "Demi's a tough woman and she doesn't take lip from anyone. Bo was a charming man and I know she had a time when they first began dating that she was smitten with him. But she's also not one to pine for someone who couldn't be committed to her. Nor would she kill a man just because her feelings were hurt."

Darby was surprised by how much Serena's assessment matched her own impressions of Demi Colton. She was well aware people could act in any number of unexpected ways, but Finn's cousin didn't come off like a woman who'd give a man who scorned her the time of day, let alone put her personal freedom at risk. If she did carry Bo's baby, those risks would be even higher.

But if Demi wasn't the killer, what was Bo trying to say with the words he'd written in blood? Did he know his killer? Or had someone tried to frame Demi? So far, there was nothing to connect Demi to the murder of Michael Hayden. But Demi Colton was their only real suspect in Bo's murder—and the MO for both crimes was the same.

Grooms-to-be shot in the heart of the night of wedding festivities, a black cummerbund stuffed in their mouths.

So were they back to square one?

No suspects and an unnamed, unsuspected murderer still on the loose in Red Ridge. If they had no idea who the killer could be, then they were all at risk with no idea when he or she might strike again.

The distinct cry of a hungry baby filled the air, breaking the tension at the table and acting as an odd punctuation to the discussion of pregnancy tests.

"Someone's hungry." Serena smiled, her immediate concern for her child taking priority. She got up and quickly left the kitchen.

Darby watched her go and was surprised to again find herself thinking of children. What if she and Bo had found themselves pregnant? Her child would be a toddler by now, running around, likely chasing after Penny and adding a dimension to her life Darby had never really imagined.

She'd always wanted children, but in a sort of abstract way. A "someday" thought instead of something that was concrete and defined in her mind. Just like her love life, since her divorce she'd allowed the idea of children to remain an unformed thought instead of an active need. Was it self-preservation? A way of keeping her heart safe from wanting something she wasn't in a position to have?

Or was it another example of living her life in a haze, grinding through day by day instead of really living?

Carson and Finn continued their discussion of the case, talking through angles, lab results and strategy. Their discussion—and topics she didn't fully understand—gave Darby a new insight into what Finn did every day. She wasn't a big fan of crime shows and had never given much thought to police work. It was fascinating to realize how complex it was, as well as how scientific much of it had become. From the lab results on the bleach to their continued discussion of scientific reports on everything from the bullets that had killed the two men to the forensics details secured at each crime scene, Darby was amazed to realize how detailed Finn's job was.

And how small details were so key to police work.

She'd just gotten up to fix herself a fresh cup of coffee when Serena came out of the bedroom, Lora in her arms. Darby put down her mug, her attention immediately drawn by the baby. "She's beautiful."

A crop of dark hair covered her head like a cap and vivid brown eyes stared out of a sweet little face, alert and taking in her surroundings. Darby had never understood the term "cherubic" but one look at those cheeks and she had a good idea.

"Would you like to hold her?"

Serena was already handing over the baby before Darby could say otherwise and she suddenly had that sweet little bundle in her arms.

My, how long had it been since she'd held a baby? She'd babysat steadily throughout high school but since then she wasn't sure she could name a single time. She and Bo had never had children, nor had there been any babies born in his family during their marriage. Her own family was basically nonexistent, being an only child of an only child.

Which meant it had been over a decade since she'd felt that sweet heaviness in her arms or smelled that lovely scent that bespoke baby powder and innocence.

A shot of longing filled her and Darby couldn't quite hold back the streak of melancholy that had her thinking of her own empty future. When everything with the Groom Killer was over—and it needed to be over, she knew and believed that—she would go back to her home and her new business and her quiet life and all this would vanish. The companionship of others. The connectedness of spending time with others.

And Finn.

When this was all over, they'd each go back to their lives, like boxers returning to their separate corners.

Even with the beauty of new life in her arms, Darby couldn't deny just how bleak her future appeared.

Finn spent the remainder of the day actively avoiding the image of Darby Gage with a baby in her arms. He'd been excited to see his niece again, Lora's arrival bringing a sense of familial bond he'd never fully known. He loved his siblings, but he had no idea what fierce protective instincts would be—or even could be—generated by the arrival of his sister's child.

One look at the baby and it was easy to understand why. She was so small and helpless, the natural urge was to protect. The fact she was family made that need infinitely stronger.

Yet the sight of Darby holding her had been off the charts. It made no sense, but he couldn't shake the image of the protective cradle of her arms securing Lora or the sweet cooing noises she made to his niece as she'd held her.

Which only made him imagine her with a baby of her own in her arms.

His baby.

The thought was so jarring he must have tensed up because Lotte barked beside him, the slightest whine edging her communication. She nudged his hand where he still held her favorite ball, her eyes full of question. He brushed her cheek with his crooked finger before tossing it once more.

The light touch and toss of her favorite rubber ball sent her off, barking all the way, down a long stretch of cleared path in the park by his apartment. The Red Ridge parks department had cleared the walking paths after the snowfall earlier that week and since the park

was relatively empty he didn't mind using the areas
for Lotte's exercise. The snow piles on either side of
the path didn't deter her enthusiasm and she skittered
toward the ball, tumbling over her quarry and landing
with half her body in the snowbank.

Leaping up, she shook it off and raced back toward
him, her tail wagging all the way.

This, he understood. Quiet moments with his dog,
the one entity in the entire world he trusted more than
himself. He didn't even trust Darby. Heck, up until
the day before, he'd been half convinced she was a
murderess.

But what about the other half?

All along he'd questioned if it was even possible
she'd murdered anyone. His half-cocked plan to roust
out a killer by pretending to be a couple was putting
himself directly in the line of fire if she had been
guilty. Yet it had never crossed his mind that Darby
would hurt him or that he was in any sort of danger
from her at all.

He tossed the ball again, watching it bounce down
the path, with Lotte racing after it, and wondered when
things had become so unexpected. Wondered even
more when he had he begun thinking of Darby on
such personal terms.

And where had that strange thought of children
come from?

He'd accepted a long time ago that the family life
that worked for so many wasn't meant for him. He'd
gone into his marriage with good intentions and had
realized fairly quickly that it wasn't for him. The commitment part he valued—even loved—but he'd never
expected that the same level of fidelity extended to

sharing his work or the requirements on his time that came with it.

Mary had quickly tired of the demands on his time and he'd tired of her frustration. He couldn't account for a bad day at work or the need to deal with a criminal problem over the weekend. And she was hardly at fault for wanting her husband around for family events or uninterrupted hours together. It had been the biggest revelation of his marriage. His calling to police work—one of the things that had attracted her to him—had been the same thing that had broken them apart.

He'd been divorced for five years and he still wasn't sure who he resented more for that fact.

As the thought lingered, Finn suddenly realized Lotte hadn't bounded back. He started down the path, surprised at how far the last toss had gone that he managed to send her around the bend in the path, only to stumble upon his sister Valeria.

And the boy she'd become inseparable from.

"Finn!" Valeria stared up from where she crouched, petting Lotte into a state of ecstasy.

"What are you doing here?" he asked before shifting his gaze to her companion. "Vincent."

"Sir."

Finn had to give Vincent credit. The youngest Gage held his ground, his hand already extended to say hello.

He shook the kid's hand, the grip firm. He was a solid young man, which made his stepmother's upset he was dating her youngest even more ridiculous. The kids were a couple. A seriously besotted one, if the looks the two passed each other—hot enough to melt an acre of snow—were any indication.

"What are you two doing here?" Finn asked. "Park's pretty deserted."

"Same as you. Getting a bit of fresh air." Valeria held his gaze, her stare direct, before her eyes dropped. "You're not gonna tell Mom, are you?"

"I'm not telling Joanelle anything." He owed his stepmother nothing and he wasn't going to be a hypocrite about that fact.

But he did love his baby sister. And he was determined to keep her safe, even if she wasn't thinking straight in the midst of her grand love affair.

"She's convinced something will happen to us because of this Groom Killer thing. As if." Valeria rolled her eyes.

"You don't think there's anything to worry about?" Finn shot a dark look at his sister before turning it on Vincent. "Because I have two dead bodies that say otherwise."

The eyes so like his own widened as Valeria reached for Vincent's hand. "You really think there's something to this? Something to worry about? Mom's such a drama queen about everything, I figured she was making it up."

Finn's assessment of Joanelle was less charitable, but the underlying message was the same. His father's second wife excelled at creating drama and seemed to enjoy living in a state of over-the-top panic about everything. She'd done it for so long, no one took her seriously when it truly counted.

"Valeria. Two men have been killed. Both were shot the night before their wedding. I'm not trying to start a full-on panic in Red Ridge, but I'm not going to sit here and blow smoke at you that nothing's wrong."

"We've been keeping a low profile. That's why we're here," Vincent said.

"If by 'low profile' you mean you don't know it's going around that you're planning a Christmas wedding?"

Once again, his sister's eyes grew round and Finn had the grim satisfaction that he still had his ear on the pulse of things in his town. The fact those "things" involved fear of a killer and raining on his baby sister's parade sucked.

Vincent spoke up and, once again, Finn had to give credit where it was due. The kid was respectful, but there was a distinct note of defiance in his words. "We are being careful, Chief Colton. But we're not going to live in fear, either."

"I don't want you to do that. But I do want you to be careful. Avoid making a splash of things. Stay closer to home. There are plenty of places to hide out on the ranch." Finn knew better than most, since he'd spent so much of his childhood hiding away.

"Mom's got all the ranch hands looking out for us."

"Come on, Val. Put all your sweetness and charm to good use. The hands love you way more than Joanelle. They'll go to bat for you."

"Cal is always winking at me and knows I always save the biggest pieces of cornbread for him on the days we make chili."

"There ya go." Finn pulled his sister close for a hug. "Just be careful."

She squeezed him back and it struck Finn that somewhere along the way his baby sister had grown up. She was still young—nineteen fell clearly in the innocent column—but she wasn't a child any longer.

And if she had her way, she'd be married before the year was out.

One sister had a baby. Another was getting married.

How was it that the people in his life had moved on and all he seemed to do was stand still?

His visits with his sisters still weighed heavy on Finn's mind when he climbed the front steps of Darby's house. He'd planned an elaborate evening out—something flashy and showy for anyone watching—and he tried to keep his focus on his plans instead of the weird thoughts that kept intruding. Yet, try as he might, he hadn't shaken the dark cloud that had accompanied him all day.

He should be happy for his sisters. Serena was a new mother and soon-to-be-wife, happy and as serene as her name implied. Valeria, while headstrong and a bit foolish with it, was in love with Vincent. After their meeting in the park, he'd dropped Lotte back at his condo and taken the lovebirds to lunch, pleased to see how innately kind and genuine they were to each other. From Vincent's quiet request to their waitress for a refill on Valeria's iced tea to his sister's excitement over Vincent's recent accomplishment in one of his college courses, they loved each other. More than that, they had a mutual care for each other that was tangible and the compatibility to make a real go of marriage.

The porch light on Darby's front door had been replaced and he stood in its warm glow as he knocked. She opened the door, gesturing him in out of the cold.

"Hurry up, get in here. It's freezing." She waved him in, a thick set of curlers covering her head. She had a blanket wrapped around her shoulders and he could see a silky robe peeking out from underneath. That flash of red silk had his body going on high alert, but it was the match of fuzzy shark slippers capping off those gorgeous legs that sent him over the edge.

Oblivious to his anguish, she shook her head as she closed the door. "What am I saying? It's South Dakota in February. Of course it's freezing. But it's extra cold tonight. Which is why I'm running so late. I couldn't get Penny and Lucy out of the backyard as they romped their way through the snow."

Alert to their names, Penny and Lucy raced over to greet him. Their tails wagged in unison as he lavished praise on them, their pleasure in seeing him going a long way toward assuaging the roiling thoughts that had accompanied him to Darby's.

"I'm almost done. Promise!"

Finn watched Darby race off down the hall before refocusing on Penny and Lucy. And didn't miss the speculative look in Penny's eyes as she stared up at him.

"Don't go getting any ideas."

Penny just wagged her tail and kept up that close scrutiny. He was tempted to argue with her but recognized his sanity was on the line. So he maintained the steady combing of his fingers through her fur and ignored the thought that even the dog had a better sense of how he needed to live his life than he did.

Rather than stand in the entryway, Finn led the dogs over to the couch. With one eye on them and another on the room, he could see the progress Darby had made. The furniture and carpet were still threadbare, but she'd strategically placed a few blankets over the worst parts of the furniture and had added some colorful throw pillows to fool the eye. She'd spruced up the place and she'd done it with light and color.

Maybe it was that thought, still so vivid in his mind, that had him turning at the sound of her heels on the hallway floor. Or maybe it was the strange melancholy that had accompanied him all day. Or maybe it was simply being in the presence of a beautiful woman.

Finn didn't know and as he caught sight of Darby, clad in a colorful sheath that draped her body like a second skin, he didn't care. He wanted her. And in that moment, she was all he could see.

Before he could even process the move as rational thought, he was off the couch and headed for her, pulling her close and into his arms, his mouth on a determined path to hers. He caught the slightest sense of surprise in the widened O of her mouth and the light squeak of her voice as she said his name.

And then there were no words.

Or questions.

Or nagging thoughts that seemed to have no place to land.

There was only Darby. Sweet and sexy Darby. The woman did things to his good sense and he was fast losing his ability to keep his head around her.

But as her lips met his, her arms wrapping around his neck in warm welcome and acceptance, Finn didn't care. He was lost to her and the kiss.

Chapter 11

Hot. Liquid. Needy.

A run of abstract thoughts crisscrossed Darby's mind as she fought to keep up with Finn. Or fought to keep up with his mouth, which was more accurate at the moment.

Want—elemental and desperate—coursed through her body, tightening her nerve endings and making her skin feel as if it were on fire. Everywhere he touched seemed to explode with feeling. Every place his fingers settled lit from within.

She wasn't sure what had happened. One moment she was still fussing over a twisted curl that wouldn't lay straight and the next she was wrapped up in Finn's arms, being positively devoured. Thoughts of that errant curl fled as she got into the moment. After all, how often did a gal get devoured by a big, handsome man in her own living room?

And, oh, it was glorious.

Large hands covered her hips, pulling her flush against the hard planes of his body while his mouth maintained a steady pressure on hers, dragging sensation after sensation from somewhere inside her she hadn't even realized existed. Some deep well of feeling and emotion and need she'd never known—or even comprehended—was there.

Yet Finn knew. And he'd unerringly found it, with his kind eyes and his sexy lips and his determination to give his town peace and calm once more.

She'd bought the brightly colored dress on sale earlier in the week and even at a steep discount, she'd berated herself a bit for the extravagance. Now, feeling his hands over the thin fabric, Darby knew it had been the right call.

His mouth slanted over hers once more, greedily, and she amended her thought.

The *exact* right call.

"Finn?" His name bubbled to her lips, her questions in all she didn't say.

"Darby." He pressed his forehead to hers, a smile forming on his lips. "Did I mention you look beautiful tonight?"

"I'm pretty good at reading between the lines."

"So you don't have to, let me say it again. You look beautiful."

"Thank you." She nipped his lips for one more kiss before stepping back. Before stepping away from a man who could not only make her lose all rational thought but, if he only asked her, could likely convince her to stay in all evening. When the image of making love with him accompanied the mental invitation, she took another step back, putting solid distance between them.

"Let me just put down food for Penny and Lucy, and we can get going." She puttered nervously into the kitchen, her heels tapping against the linoleum as she crossed back and forth from the sink to the pantry for their water and food.

What had she been thinking?

More, what had he been thinking?

This was platonic. They'd had their moments, of course. Those fleeting kisses meant to fool anyone watching them from afar.

But this? In her house? It was so fierce. So *needy*.

Darby fought the small shudder that raced down her spine and finished preparing dinner for the dogs.

With that small moment of distraction over, there was no reason to remain in the kitchen. As she tap-tap-tapped her way toward the living room, she prayed for strength.

Strength to resist the most amazing man she'd ever met.

Finn pulled Darby's chair out and fought the urge to tug at one of the loose curls that covered her head. They'd kept up a veneer of vague conversation in the car—their earlier visit with baby Lora had provided an excellent subject to distract them both—and he'd grasped at the conversational lifeline like a drowning man.

The chatter had kept them both from discussing what had happened in her living room.

What *had* happened in her living room? And when had he lost his focus?

He was running a murder investigation—the worst that had ever hit Red Ridge. He had no business stealing kisses from a woman who was only helping him do his job. More than that, he had no business wanting kisses from her.

"Smile, Finn."

"Hmm?" He still stood beside Darby's chair and it was only her pointed gaze and the lift of her hand to his cheek that had him refocusing.

"Smile, darling. We're the focus of the entire restaurant. It would hardly do to make people think I was dating a grizzly bear."

The grizzly bear comment was a funny one and he suddenly had the image of sprouting hair all over his body and roaring down Main Street. With a smile, he lifted her hand and pressed his lips to her palm. Whether it was the indulgent smile she gave him or the heat from earlier he couldn't quite shake, Finn wasn't sure, but he used his position to run his tongue lightly along the seam of her palm.

Indulgence shifted to desire in a heartbeat as her eyes went a smoky gray.

"Finn?" Her voice was as smoky as her eyes and as equally powerful.

Again, she used only his name. And again, that same impulse that pushed him earlier had him in its thrall once more, rushing through his body and forcing his ardor higher and higher.

Satisfied he'd made his point—and well aware he'd tempted himself equally—he squeezed her hand before gently settling it back on the table and taking his seat.

Their waiter, who'd hovered a discreet distance

away, rushed over, menus in hand. The restaurant specialized in seafood, crafting dishes each night that could be inspired from anywhere. From the Pacific Rim to West Coast cuisine to the Mediterranean, the chef was whimsical and eclectic and had created a place with good buzz and consistently satisfied patrons.

Although he saw relatively few young couples—the lifeblood of a hip, happening place—Finn was pleased to see the restaurant was full. Maybe this was one place people still felt comfortable coming out for the night.

"Welcome to Pesce this evening," their waiter gushed. "We're so glad to have you."

The specials were duly noted and drink orders taken—wine for Darby and another one of the endless club sodas for Finn—before their waiter disappeared once more.

"I've heard good things about this place but haven't been here. Red Ridge has certainly improved its restaurant game in the past few years."

As conversation topics went, it was an easy one, empty of land mines. But Finn realized it gave him an opening he'd been curious about.

"Red Ridge is small, but between Colton Energy and Harrington Incorporated, there's enough business to keep things hopping in town. And enough people on their payroll who can afford to eat like this all the time."

"I suppose." She nodded and sipped the wine the waiter had set down. "It's progress and it's good to see. But it does make me think of what it was like when I was a kid. I couldn't have imagined a place like this, let alone expected to dine in one."

"You didn't go out much?"

"I had a single mother on a limited income. A place like this was so far out of our reach it was laughable."

Darby's gaze was distracted by the large mosaic mural of a mermaid hovering over undersea treasure. He waited until she returned her attention from the wall to him. "You don't say much about her."

"My mother?" When he only nodded, she continued. "There's not much to say. My father ran out when I was young and she blamed him and me until the day she died."

"When was that?"

"About five years ago. She worked two jobs until the very end and was found crumpled up against the Dumpster behind the diner."

Darby's words formed an image and Finn realized he remembered that day.

Vividly.

The small, slender woman found victim of a heart attack out behind the diner. She'd taken a large bag of trash outside and hadn't come back. It had only been when another waitress had gone out for a coffee break that she'd found Darby's mother.

"I'm sorry."

Darby's blue gaze remained direct and devoid of tears. "I am, too. I'm sorry she saw the world through such disillusioned eyes. And I'm sorry that her life ended as miserably as the rest of it. But I'm not sorry she's gone."

"That's understandable."

"Is it? She was my mother."

"Is it fair I can barely think of my stepmother without adding a mental string of curses to go with it?" Finn knew their situations weren't the same but also knew they weren't entirely different, either. Joanelle's behavior—and her inability to love a small boy—belonged solely to her.

On some level, he'd always known that. But after seeing how Carson had bonded with his niece, Lora—a child he would adopt through marriage—Finn knew Joanelle's rejection had been that of a bitter and cold woman.

Carson had accepted Lora as his own and would never treat her as less than because she wasn't biologically his. It was a gift they'd both share—and a love that would grow through the years.

"She's earned every one of those curses, Finn. She emotionally mistreated a little boy. That's terrible."

Darby's ready defense touched him, but it also reinforced the point he was making to her. "And what your mother did was any better?"

"No." She shook her head. "I suppose not."

He reached out and ran the tip of his finger over her cheek, catching a lone tear that had finally surfaced. "I'm sorry to make you cry."

"It's okay. I've had a long time to come to grips with how I feel. Most of the time I'm okay with it. Every now and again, I'm not."

"I feel the same. Most days I don't give Joanelle Colton a second thought. For some reason, she's been front and center in my thoughts lately."

The waiter came back and took their orders, the small reprieve enough to give Finn an opportunity to collect his thoughts. Once they'd ordered, he picked up where they'd left off. "I saw my younger sister Valeria today."

He filled Darby in on the impromptu visit with Valeria and Vincent and their naive dismissal of the danger in town from the Groom Killer.

Darby's already pale skin grew even more so in the muted lighting of the restaurant. "You don't think someone would hurt them? They're just children."

"I don't know what to think. And since we can't seem to get a handle on motive or anyone who might be a suspect aside from my cousin Demi, I told them to be careful."

"Do you think they'll listen?"

Finn thought about the subtle defiance in both of them to be together, but was also reminded of how innately kind they were to each other. There was something genuine and loving between them. He had to hope that underlying concern would override any youthful impulses to tempt fate.

"I think so. I'll keep an eye on them. The staff will watch out for them, too."

"Youth." She smiled before shrugging her shoulders. "I know it's been a decade since I was that age, but it feels like a lifetime ago."

"Would you go back if you could?"

"Never." A warm smile filled her face and, once again, he was caught. Captured by whatever it was that lit her up from the inside. "You?"

"Go back to being that young and dumb? No way."

She reached over and took his hand, lifting her glass with the other. "To adulting. Some days it stinks but at other times it's not so bad."

"Like now?" he asked, daring to hope she agreed.

"Like right now."

He clinked his club soda against her wineglass, the light tinkle rising between them. "To adulting."

The muted lights of the restaurant didn't hide a clear picture of the diners inside. Table after table filled with people having a good time and enjoying their expensive meals.

Expensive and wasteful.

Who spent that kind of money on something you could pull out of the river yourself? It was indulgent. And greedy.

And hurtful.

Once again, the chief was parading around town with that woman. She pranced beside him, a colorful whore in the dress that wrapped tight around her body and the hair teased out to draw a man's eye.

She'd believed the chief above such trickery.

Yet here he was, kissing the woman's hand and holding the chair for her and staring at her as if she'd walked out of a movie set. Actresses were whores, too, which only reinforced the point.

It was illusion.

Yet the chief's adoration looked very, very real.

Oh, how it burned.

She'd watched and waited…and for what? To be ignored and discarded in favor of some scantily dressed woman who lured him to her bed? Did the chief not understand? Had he not received her gifts?

An image of the fragile glass still nestled in its box in her closet drifted through her thoughts. She'd meant to save it for Valentine's Day. That was less than a week away. Could she wait? Or did she need to send it sooner?

Thoughts drifting as she sat in her car and stared into the restaurant, she imagined that glass heart beating in its box. Beating with love for her.

Beating the way her own heart pulsed and throbbed for Chief Colton.

If he only knew.

They had a connection. And once he understood that, the rest would fade away. The whore in the colorful dress meant nothing. Would mean nothing.

She'd make sure of it.

Darby snuggled deeper into her coat as she and Finn walked to the SUV. The air was cold and clear, the stars shining above them like glittering diamonds. It was cliché, but as she watched them shine from afar, she knew it was the only description that fit.

Red Ridge *had* grown since she was a child. It had prosperous businesses and a population of busy, industrious people. But it was still small enough to feel isolated and free, somehow. The Black Hills National Forest provided the perfect backdrop—wilderness for miles on end—and the Spearfish River added another natural border.

She'd not traveled much in her life, but she'd been to Seattle and Portland and had liked both. Had even enjoyed her time away. But neither had felt like home. The steady stream of strangers who had passed her on the street had seemed foreign and, while not threatening, just *separate* from her. The thought of trying to make a life in that throng of humanity hadn't appealed and she'd welcomed the flights home with open arms.

Maybe she wasn't so different from her mother, but she liked to think she'd channeled her needs and wants a bit differently. She stayed in Red Ridge because she chose to, not because she lacked options.

Which might have been laughable when she'd stared down a mountain of debt and an uncertain future. Yet even then, she'd been focused on doing right. By Bo. By Penny. And by the business that had meant so much to her ex-husband.

Never once had she felt trapped.

Without warning, the thought shifted and strangled, her adrenaline spiking as her gaze shifted toward the dark night that surrounded the parking lot. She reached for Finn's hand, so close to her own, and came to a tottering halt on her heels.

"What is it?"

"Someone's out there."

She kept her voice low, turning into his body to keep up the charade of closeness and to shroud her voice in the clear night air. Rising on her tiptoes, she pressed her lips to his ear. "Out there. I can feel it. Someone's watching us."

Finn's demeanor shifted immediately, his arm tightening around her waist as he held her in place. "Do you see anyone?"

"No. I feel them, but that's the best I can tell you."

He wrapped himself around her, shielding the majority of her body with his own. "I want you to get in the car and call for backup."

"Where are you going?"

"To check it out."

"What?" The screech edged out the whisper in her

voice as she tried to slow his steady march toward the SUV. "You can't go out there by yourself."

"I have a gun."

"Maybe they do, too."

"It might be nothing."

"And it might be something." She tried standing still, pressing the back of her forearm against his flat, muscled stomach, but he continued to move them forward.

"In the car, Darby. Now."

Arguing with him was impossible and she almost wished she hadn't said anything when the throb of an engine roared to life.

"In the car. Now!" Finn had the door open and was shoving her inside, before slamming the door after her. She saw the glint of his gun reflected in the overhead lights of the parking lot and watched him race off.

What had she done?

Scrambling for her cell phone, she called in the situation, speaking as calmly as possible with her heart throbbing in her throat. She gave their location and the details as best as she could, stressing over and over that the chief needed backup.

"Where are you, ma'am?" The disembodied voice echoed through the phone, the urgency there suddenly penetrating her fear for Finn.

"I'm in the chief's car."

"Is a dangerous threat nearby?"

Threat?

Darby had ignored the parking lot, so focused on Finn's retreating back and on calling for help. Now she looked around. The parking lot was well lit, but the dark night beyond seemed to close in around that light, leaving lurking shadows at the edges.

"Ma'am?"

"Yes."

"Is there an immediate danger to you?"

"I don't think so," she said, her voice sounding foreign to her own ears.

"I've dispatched backup but I need you to stay on the line with me."

"Okay."

"My name is Frank. Frank Lanelli. I need you to stay where you are and lock your doors."

Darby fumbled the lock switch, the snick a small comfort in the creeping quiet.

"Did you do that?"

Frank's voice was kind yet firm and she found herself nodding, even if he couldn't see her. "Yes."

"Our chief's a fine man. I've got backup on the way. You can probably hear the sirens already."

At Frank's words, the distinct notes that screamed emergency came in muted through the SUV's windows. "Yes, I hear them."

"Now, who am I talking to?"

"Darby, sir. Darby Gage."

"Why, Ms. Gage, I had a feeling it was you." Frank's kind voice calmed her and she listened to him rattle on, securing information as he went.

"I heard you and the chief were headed out for the evening. Small towns and all. Took you to Pesce, did he?"

"Yes."

"Our chief is a sucker for a good meal and a pretty lady."

Darby smiled in spite of herself and the situation. "Frank, are you flirting with me?"

"Only to stay young. I'm a happily married man with five children of my own."

"Your wife is a lucky woman."

"She's the love of my life, Ms. Darby. Don't think there's a day that goes by that I don't know I'm the lucky one."

As she sat there huddled in the SUV, the flash of red and blue growing clearer through the front window, Darby figured Mrs. Lanelli was one lucky woman. And she was deeply grateful to her for sharing her husband for the evening to calm a frightened woman shivering inside an empty SUV.

One who waited for confirmation that the man who protected her would come back safe.

Chapter 12

Finn raced over the edge of the parking lot, heading as far into the woods as he dared before retreating and retracing his steps. He missed Lotte's keen nose and ears desperately, but did his best to keep watch for any telltale signs.

Footprints. Creaking branches as someone stepped. Any hint at all of movement.

Over and over again, he entered the shadows, then retreated, seeking some sense of who was there. Or who had been there. When nothing materialized, he backtracked to the parking lot, the flash of red and blue lights warring with the fluorescent overheads.

He'd hated leaving Darby but couldn't risk losing his potential quarry by waiting in the SUV. The order to lock the doors and call for backup had seemed like a good idea at the time, but as he thought about it now, he felt as if he'd let her down somehow, leaving her to fend for herself.

Without warning, Mary's voice came back to him, one of their last great fights drifting through his mind.

You leave me day in and day out, that damned job of yours more important than our marriage. More important than me!

You knew what I did when we got married. I have a responsibility. A duty.

You have a duty to me. To us.

Anger had filled her words, yet unlike their prior fights, he'd heard something hollow and empty echo beneath.

I know what my duties are. Devotion to my job doesn't make me a bad husband.

No. She'd shaken her head. *But my resentment of it all makes me a bad wife. Which is why I want out.*

Out?

He'd wanted to rant and rail at her in that moment. On some level he'd wanted to beg her to stay. To fight for their marriage. To fight for him.

That's what a good husband would have done.

But he'd only nodded and said okay. Agreed that he wanted out, too.

The life they'd built had dissolved quickly, their divorce making it well and truly final six months later. He should have been upset about that. Even now, five years later, he wondered at the lack of anger that had accompanied the dissolution of his marriage. Had he given up?

Or had he simply accepted that he wasn't fit for marriage? For the requirements of being devoted and committed to another person.

Two cruisers were parked next to his vehicle and he could see Darby in the front seat of the SUV, her door slightly open as she spoke with Elle Gage. Elle's bulldog partner, Merlin, stood by her side, sniffing around the SUV as his rookie officer kept Darby company. Merlin always looked a bit funny next to the larger dogs of the K-9 squad, but his smushed-up face hid a warrior. Finn had seen the dog sniff out any number of objects, beating the rest of the K-9 squad in nearly any trial involving retrieval by scent alone. His persistence had even turned up a small fragment of cloth six months ago that had led them to a robbery suspect.

He loped over to the vehicles, his cousin Brayden already out of his cruiser and scanning the parking lot.

Brayden started in the moment Finn was within earshot. "You always take off unaccompanied by backup, Chief?"

"I had a chance and I took it."

"You went in blind and you know it. Why didn't you wait?"

"There wasn't any time to wait. Darby sensed she was being watched."

Brayden shook his head but refrained from saying anything else. Finn knew he was right. He knew even better that haring off alone was the fast track to unexpected injury or even death. Every cop entered their job knowing they put their life on the line, but following protocol upped the odds of personal safety.

He'd disregarded all of it to chase after a faceless nemesis Darby hadn't even seen.

But, damn it, she'd felt something. He didn't take that sort of certainty—or sheer gut instinct—lightly.

Brayden handed him one of the heavy lined jackets they all kept in their SUVs and Finn pulled it on over his coat. The chase had heated him up but the frosty air was quickly clawing at the line of sweat at the back of his neck. Darby was already bundled in one from Elle's cruiser, her gaze on him even as she remained by his vehicle.

"Not a stellar way to end a hot date," Brayden teased him. "But sure is a way to get some attention."

Several diners at Pesce had paused at their cars to watch the proceedings. He could also see several members of the staff hanging around the back entrance, presumably on break, their attention laser focused on the parking lot.

Since attention was the very thing he was going for, Finn decided to use it to his advantage. If it also assuaged the trembling in his limbs and the raw, edgy fear that coated his stomach, then so be it. He crossed the remaining distance to Darby, pulled her from the SUV and into his arms. He pressed his lips to hers in a move meant to offer comfort and reassurance.

But as her sweet lips met his, warm, open and welcoming, Finn knew the truth.

She provided the comfort. He was simply using the opportunity to bask in the warmth.

"Take us through it again, if you don't mind?" Carson asked the question, but from the grim look on Finn's face, she could tell he was as eager for the answer as his top detective.

Darby sighed and wrapped her hands around the mug of tea Serena had pressed on her shortly after she and Finn had arrived at the ranch. "We were walking out of the restaurant and talking casually. Without warning, all I could feel were eyes on me."

As silly as it sounded, even now Darby could feel the way her blood had run cold. Her heart had leaped, her pulse ringing in her ears, and the only rational thought in her head had been to run for safety.

Only, Finn had done the running.

Straight into danger.

"You're staying here tonight." Serena walked into the kitchen with a heap of pillows and blankets in her arms. "I don't want any arguing."

The order had Darby leaping up. "Thank you. Really, thank you, but I can't leave the dogs all night. Penny and Lucy are good but they can't go that long."

Finn laid a hand on her arm. "I'll go get them. I'll get Lotte, too."

"I'll go with you." Carson was already up and out of his chair. "No time like the present."

She'd barely blinked and both men were gone. Which left her and Finn's sister all alone in the kitchen, the muted lighting and quiet calm in direct opposition to her roiling thoughts about Finn Colton.

"My brother is a force of nature." Serena smiled before crossing to the stove to make her own cup of tea.

"He certainly is sure of himself."

"Always."

While she had no interest in spying on him, this glimpse into the life of Finn Colton was too juicy to resist. "He's always been like this?"

"As long as I can remember. He's calm and capable, logical, and slow to anger. It drives my mother crazy."

"Your mother is Joanelle?"

"The one and only." Serena rolled her eyes. "She's

a difficult woman on the best of days. On the worst…
well, let's just say Finn got more than his fair share
of those."

"It's a shame."

Serena nodded. "More than I can say."

Silence descended between them. While she had
her definite opinions of Finn's stepmother, the woman
was also Serena's mother. She, of all people, knew how
complicated mother-daughter relationships could be
and figured silence was best.

"You care for my brother."

"I—" Darby broke off, not sure what to say.

Serena was a kind woman but Darby hardly felt
comfortable enough to spill her guts about her feelings toward Finn.

Did she actually have feelings about Finn?

Even as the question drifted through her thoughts,
Darby knew the truth. Despite her best intentions—
and every rational thought she possessed—she had
come to care for him.

She was attracted to him, but attraction was the
easy part. He was good-looking and competent, with
a finely tuned moral compass and a need to protect the
town. What wasn't there to be attracted to?

But to care for him? That was a different level of
commitment entirely. That suggested sticking around
and spending time with each other after the Groom
Killer was caught. It was something she wanted, but
did Finn?

Whether he did or not, it hardly changed her feelings. On a soft exhale, she looked Serena in the eye.
"I guess I do."

"He cares for you, too."

"I don't think—"

Serena cut her off this time, laying a soft hand over hers. "Don't think. That's usually where we end up going wrong. I know I did with Carson and that was nearly the end of our relationship. Fortunately he had enough faith for the both of us."

Darby latched on to the lifeline and hung on for all she was worth. "You and Carson had a tough go of it?"

"He's a Gage and I'm a Colton. That's usually more than enough to cause problems. But as someone who married into the family, I'm sure you already knew that."

Although Darby knew of the Colton-Gage feud— most people who'd spent any time in Red Ridge knew of the history between the two families—Bo had seemed somewhat oblivious to it. On the few occasions he'd mentioned it, it was usually laced with humor at how old-fashioned and "Wild Wild West" his family loved to act about their century-long feud with the family across town.

"Is this family feud really that big an issue?"

"For the older generation it is. That includes my difficult mother," Serena added. "And since my father follows along with anything she says, it was a problem for him when Carson and I got together."

"What else caused problems?"

"I'd just had a baby. That was quite a hurdle."

It was Darby's turn to offer comfort and she laid her free hand over Serena's. "It looks like Carson has more than embraced his role as father."

"That he has." Whatever shadows clouded Serena's gaze lifted immediately. "He really has. He's a wonderful father. Lora and I are so lucky."

"I think Carson's pretty lucky, too."

Serena smiled at that, her dark brown eyes warm and inviting. "I suppose he is."

Their conversation shifted and Darby was grateful that Serena didn't push again on the subject of her feelings for Finn. They were enough of a surprise to her as it was. Instead they seemed to find an endless series of topics from the baby to Darby's K-9 business until they finally ventured back around to the Groom Killer.

"It's a scary time in Red Ridge. I know we have crime now and again. People seem to find ways to do bad things no matter where they're put. But a killer?" Serena shivered. "It's hard to imagine."

Darby was prevented from saying anything when headlights reflected through the window and slamming car doors echoed from outside.

Something settled inside her when Carson came in the door, a trail of dogs in his wake, followed by Finn in the rear. The events of the night had unsettled her more than she'd realized and it was humbling to realize how good it was to see Finn back, safe and sound.

He carried a small gym bag she recognized from her bedroom closet as well as her pillow. "I wasn't sure if you were one of those people who preferred their own pillow so I grabbed it along with your toothbrush and the PJs on the edge of the bed."

"Thank you."

"It's the least I could do." He set the bag near the couch and put her pillow down, as well. "I'm sorry you're stuck with me tonight."

"It's okay." Carson had disappeared with Serena and it was just her and Finn and their combined pack, who'd positioned themselves in an arc around the front door. "More than okay, actually. I can't say I'm anxious to spend the night by myself."

"Then it's good we're here. The Colton Ranch is pretty well fortified, but we'll batten down the hatches, anyway. Nothing wrong with settling in for the night."

"Thank you."

He pulled her close, wrapping her in his arms before his chin pressed down on the top of her head.

On a hard exhale she hadn't even realized she was holding in, all the fear she'd bottled up since the parking lot came tumbling out. "I was so afraid. So scared that you'd run into the killer. Or worse, that they were waiting for you."

"It's okay."

"No, it's not. What's out there, lurking and waiting? Who is so determined to kill and to ruin the lives of others?"

"I wish I knew."

"It's sick and twisted. And evil." Another shudder ripped through her and Darby fought the creeping sense of hopelessness that threatened to swamp her.

"We're going to figure this out. I know we are."

She wanted to believe him. With all her heart she wanted to believe Finn could hunt down a killer and put him away.

But what happened if he couldn't?

That question still haunted her twenty minutes later as she settled into the couch. Serena had apologized profusely that there wasn't a spare room in her wing of the mansion now that Lora was here, but both Darby and Finn had brushed it off. He'd had no desire to move in to the main house and she could easily live with sleeping on the oversize sectional for the night.

Finn was still huddled with Carson at the kitchen table, their voices low as they worked through various scenarios over coffee.

She listened to the murmur of their voices and took solace in their presence even as she drifted toward sleep. Images filled her twilight moments, thoughts of a killer invading her mind. Bo, a hole in the center of his chest, reaching out to her from a shallow grave in the backyard, his arms stretching toward her. Penny racing around the hole, barking. But when Darby finally walked over, all she saw was Finn in the shallow grave, a gunshot wound spreading blood over his chest.

She came wide-awake on a harsh breath, narrowly holding back the scream that crawled up her throat.

Dropping back against the pillow, Darby fought to catch her breath. The image of Finn, his chest bloody, refused to leave her mind, lingering like a dark stain in her thoughts. A small whine echoed from beneath her and she turned onto her side to find Penny beside the couch, her gaze focused on hers.

"Hey, sweet girl. It's okay." She nearly reached out but held back, aware the dog wasn't keen on her ministrations.

Penny whined once more before coming to a fully seated position and resting her head beside Darby on the couch. She reached out and pressed a hand to Penny's head, her fingers sinking into the thick fur. Penny edged forward a few steps, coming closer for Darby's touch, before burying her nose against her side.

The fear that had pulled her from sleep faded slowly,

the soft, soothing strokes on Penny's head going a long way toward calming her. But it was Penny's light sigh several long minutes later that fully pushed the toxic images from Darby's mind. Seemingly satisfied she'd done her job, Penny jumped up onto the couch and curled up at her feet.

With the steady weight of her dog settled in against her, Darby allowed herself to drift off once more. Only this time, there were no dreams waiting for her.

Just the soft, gentle weight of Penny's body pressed against hers.

Finn rolled over on the thick air mattress to find a large, furry body sprawled next to him. The sprawl was accompanied by a steady snore and he fought the urge to poke Lotte until she cleared the mattress. He didn't allow her into his bed, having trained her to use the large, fluffy dog bed in the corner of his room, but the unusual setting and the presence of Penny and Lucy had clearly tossed all his good training out the window.

He scanned the living room, his suspicions confirmed when he saw Penny curled up at Darby's feet and Lucy a few feet beyond, also curled up on his sister's well-stuffed and oversize sectional.

"I think this place has gone to the dogs," Darby whispered before punctuating the comment with a throaty giggle.

"My sister is going to kill me."

"I'll vacuum once we're all up. No one will know we were here."

Finn couldn't resist teasing her. "The Queen of Clean rides to the rescue once again."

"I told you my mother thought cleanliness was next to godliness. When I'm done with the couch and the carpet, you'll never know there was a dog in here, let alone three."

"I won't stand in your way."

"In the meantime, since we're here, the least we can do is be good houseguests. I'll put the coffee on."

Finn glanced at his wrist, his watch flashing back the time. "It's 6:00 a.m."

"Which means it's time to get up."

She was already off the couch, navigating the small space between it and his air mattress. She'd nearly cleared the space when inspiration hit and he reached for her ankle, tugging her close. The move was enough to unbalance her and he used her tumble to his advantage, pulling her neatly into his arms.

Semineatly, he had to admit as he underestimated the landing. He'd kept her from falling onto Lotte but caught the full weight of her body. She was small, but falling as a dead weight still hit him square in the stomach.

"Finn!" She breathed his name and struggled out of his arms. "What are you doing?"

"Kissing you good morning."

"It's—"

He cut her off, making his point more than clear as their lips met. She might have gotten off the couch with a distinct goal, but he was pleased to see she could be swayed to a new activity. Her body was still warm with sleep and he pulled her close, nestling her body against his. The desire that had been touched off the night before in her living room when he'd picked her up flared to life once again.

Had it ever really died?

As his hands roamed over her body, Finn knew it hadn't. And based on the light, eager moans that emanated from the back of her throat, he knew it hadn't for Darby, either.

His fingers drifted over her stomach, finding flesh where her pajama top rode up over her yoga pants. He teased the tip of his finger over the seam of her pants and was rewarded by a light shiver.

"Cold?" he whispered against her lips.

"Not at all."

As if to prove it—or, knowing Darby, not to be outdone—her hands drifted over his hips before moving up to mold to the lines of his chest. He normally slept naked, but in deference to a house full of people, he'd left a T-shirt on with a pair of K-9 team sweatpants that had grown threadbare from so many washes. The heat of her palms warmed him through the cotton T-shirt, but it was the slim body pressed against his that had his eyes crossing.

His erection strained against the thin material of his sweatpants, pressing into the slim vee of her thighs, and Finn suddenly wasn't sure of his own sanity. What had possessed him to start something with Darby this morning?

And when had he begun channeling his inner fifteen-year-old, convinced he'd die if they stopped?

Cosmic proof that he was wrong came in the form of his baby niece's early morning cries, breaking the thin threads that had woven around them both this morning.

"That's a baby crying," Darby said before pressing one last kiss to his lips. "Which means the house will be up shortly."

He reached for her, desperate for one more kiss, but she'd already backed away, stumbling over the edge of the air mattress before righting herself as she padded out of the living room. He was fool enough to enjoy watching her go, the sweet curve of her butt shown to perfection in the black yoga pants that sculpted her curves.

Lotte eyed him from the edge of the mattress where she'd moved at some point during his morning romp with Darby and even now wore a speculative gaze.

"I suppose you want to go out?"

Her eyebrows shot up, but her gaze remained steady.

"Do I take that to mean you're irritated we woke you? You were sleeping like the dead."

When Lucy trotted over, followed by Penny, seating themselves beside the mattress, he took in their steady attention. "I'll be. I guess there were a few more in this house watching the show this morning."

Since his witnesses would never tell, he figured he and Darby could continue to fly under the radar. That was assuming his niece kept his sister busy enough for him to get the dogs out and to take a quick—and cold—shower.

Satisfied his witnesses were well occupied outside, romping through the light coating of snow that had come overnight, Finn headed off to the bathroom. He made his escape without anyone seeing him and was in the shower in moments. But try as he might, even standing underneath a shower as cold as the snow outside, he couldn't quite get his body to calm.

Nor could he shake the heated images of what might have happened if his family hadn't been twenty feet down the hall.

* * *

More than a few days had begun with the vague thought that coffee was the elixir of life, but Darby had to admit to herself that the almighty coffee bean had nothing on the glorious, mind-blowing powers of Finn Colton.

Oh, the man was fine. And waking up to slow kisses and lazy caresses over her body was something she could definitely get used to.

Since she needed to battle such fanciful thoughts, Darby threw herself into playing the perfect houseguest and had coffee on and muffins baking when Serena, Carson and Lora came into the kitchen a half hour later. The baby's sweet smile reached out and wrapped around her heart and Darby couldn't resist smiling in return.

Only to get an even bigger smile and a giggle to sweeten the deal.

"She loves the morning." Serena stopped by the stove and peeked in the front glass at the muffins even now rising with the heat. "You made breakfast."

"It's just muffins."

Serena turned to her, tears shining in her eyes. "You baked something."

Carson reached around Serena, easily plucking the baby from her grip and cuddling Lora into one elbow while comforting Serena with his free arm. "I promise you we'll get past eating all our meals as takeout soon. Lora needs your attention much more now than I need a home-cooked meal. And since my cooking is the equivalent of eating rocks, you really want me keeping up my dialing skills."

"But I don't cook anymore." Serena sniffed. "I had no idea it would upset me so badly."

Darby bent to take the muffins out. She briefly toyed with apologizing but decided that new-mom hormones had way more to do with Serena's reaction than any real upset over breakfast. Her faith was rewarded a few minutes later as they all sat around the table, digging in to the muffins.

"I'm so sorry." Serena waved the freshly buttered half of her muffin. "I'm not sure why I reacted like I did. These are amazing and I'm happy you made them."

"You're welcome." Darby finished slathering butter on her muffin top and broke off a piece. She was pleased with the outcome and slowly munched her breakfast when a vague thought struck her. "If Demi is pregnant, how is she eating?"

Finn paused, his muffin partway to his mouth. "How's she what?"

"Demi. If she really is pregnant, how is she getting by? She'd need food under any circumstances, but if she's an expectant mother she needs to take care of herself. How's she doing that in hiding?"

Carson looked up from where he helped soothe Lora with a pacifier. "Do you think that would pull her out of hiding?"

"It might. Or it might mean she's gone even farther to ground," Darby said.

"Why would it make her go into hiding?" Finn had stopped eating his muffin, his attention fully focused on her.

"Well, it wouldn't be too hard to stock up at one of those big stores that sells in bulk. She'd need perishables like milk and eggs on an ongoing basis but she could get by for a while if she stocked up on food and maybe protein drinks?"

"All this is predicated on assuming she's pregnant," Finn added, voicing his thoughts out loud.

"Even if she isn't, she needs food."

Finn turned to Serena. "How sure are you that she's pregnant?"

"I don't really know. But—" Serena considered "—it's not like Demi to make things up, either. If she thought she was pregnant, she likely had a good reason."

"I don't know why I didn't think about this when you brought up the pregnancy." Finn was already on his feet. He headed for the stove, snagging two more muffins and wrapping them in a napkin.

"Where are you going?" Serena demanded.

"I need to get Lotte and go over Demi's apartment. See what we might find."

"You'll need a warrant," Carson pointed out.

The rational, reasonable note didn't deter Finn in the least. In fact, as she watched him stride around the kitchen, Darby wondered where the man who'd pressed sexy morning kisses on her had gone.

Hot, sexy Finn was nowhere in sight.

Cold, focused Chief Colton had taken his place.

As she watched him rally his resources, calling in orders to his team at the precinct and then putting in a call to the D.A.'s office to request a warrant, she had to give him credit. The man she'd made out with an hour before may have vanished, but the sharp-eyed, focused cop who'd taken his place looked more than capable of catching a killer.

Chapter 13

Finn made his pitch to the D.A.'s office and, in a matter of hours, a warrant was making its way through the system to allow him to enter his cousin's home.

While he'd waited, he'd run Lotte through several pieces of Demi's clothing and had also purchased a few pregnancy tests on the way on the off chance Lotte could process the plastic scent and chemicals in the test strip to make a match somewhere in the apartment.

It was a long shot, but since he'd been sitting on this damn case for nearly a month without a lead, he'd take what he could get.

Carson was with him. Darby and Serena had wanted to join, as well. He'd ultimately won the battle, arguing they couldn't enter a suspect's house, but it was a close thing. His sister had clearly had some half-cocked idea that insulting him might change his mind. Since "close-minded stick-in-the-mud" hurt less than a paper cut, he'd won the round and left them with the baby, the remaining muffins, and a solemn promise that he and Carson would come back and tell them everything.

"Serena pressed me again before we left, trying to convince me Demi is innocent," Carson said to break the silence. "Evidence is evidence, but my gut says she's innocent."

"I hope she is." Finn wanted that, he realized, more than he'd understood. He *wanted* his cousin to be innocent. Wanted there to be an answer to why she was on the run and hiding from them and the help they could provide. But he couldn't run from the facts, either.

That knowledge was sobering, but it kept him focused on their problem. "Look, we can't keep going on instinct with this. We need proof. There's a killer on the loose, and if Demi is carrying Bo Gage's child, she had some degree of motive."

"I know," Carson said. "Damn it, I know."

"So what has you hesitant all of a sudden?"

Carson was probably his best detective, so the fact that the man seemed so at odds with the investigation was a surprise. He couldn't dismiss the fact that it was Carson's brother who'd been murdered. Yet, somehow, it seemed bigger than that. And ran deeper, too.

"It's just that I can't think of a pregnant woman without thinking of Serena and Lora. It's messing with my head."

And there it was.

Finn considered and then tried to play devil's advocate. "Not every pregnant woman is as gloriously happy as my sister."

"No, but rarely, if ever, are pregnant women driven to murder."

Finn couldn't fully fault Carson's logic. Hormones might be at play—and he knew from his sister's behavior the past few months that they could be intense at times—but the leap to murder was a big one. Even if Demi was a tough woman, her ability to handle herself as a bounty hunter didn't mean she'd suddenly turned to murder to take care of men who pissed her off.

"That's pretty amazing how Darby came up with the food angle." Even though he couldn't see it for driving, it was hard to miss Carson's smile as it imprinted in his words. "The woman can cook some seriously delicious muffins and she's a pretty solid detective. She's a keeper, Chief."

Since his own thoughts hadn't been too far off the mark, Finn could hardly argue with Carson's assessment. So he ignored it, pulling into the small parking lot fronting Demi's apartment complex. "Let's get to work."

Finn retrieved the key from the super before circling back to the SUV to pick up Lotte and Carson.

They headed straight to Demi's apartment and let themselves in, the stale air proof no one had been there in a few weeks.

"She's pretty neat," Carson said, pulling on a pair of rubber gloves from his pocket as he walked the perimeter of the apartment. "I hate to say it, but for that reason alone I can't see her putting up with my brother."

Since Finn had seen Bo's clutter firsthand—and Darby's compulsive need to clean up after him—

he had to agree with the assessment. He headed for the apartment's single bedroom, pulling on a pair of gloves of his own before riffling through Demi's closet. Several hangers were empty, giving more credence to the fact that she'd run. Opting for something with an even stronger scent, Finn went to the bed and pulled off several pillows.

He called Lotte to him, using the pillow to instruct her on what he was looking for. He then opened one of the pregnancy test kits, holding the small stick and walking her through his instructions once more.

Pillow. Test. Pillow. Test.

He gave her a few minutes to adjust to his intentions and, before he could instruct her further, she was off. She retraced Carson's walk around the perimeter of the living room before working her way into the center of the apartment in slowly narrowing circles. It took a little less than two minutes before she found her spot. On a deep bark, she sat, her tail thumping on the hardwood floor.

"Damn," Carson muttered. "That was fast. She'd give Merlin a run for his money."

"She *does* give Merlin a run for his money." Finn shot him a grin, exceedingly proud of his girl. "And she's a heck of a lot cuter."

"Don't let Elle hear you say that. She loves that bulldog more than life itself."

"Our secret," Finn muttered as he dropped beside Lotte and began feeling around the wooden planks of the floorboards. He ran his fingers over the smooth wood, satisfied when he felt the slightest give beneath his fingertips. He pulled a small knife out of his all-purpose kit and used it to pry at the board.

"You find something?"

"Looks like." The board came loose with minimal tugging and, in moments, Finn was staring down into a hidey-hole.

One that contained a pregnancy test that read positive, a stack of letters, and a photo of Demi and Bo during better times. There was a large red X over Bo's face and the word *liar* was scrawled across the photo.

Carson dropped to his knees beside Finn and let out a long, low whistle. "Wow. This does not look good."

"You can say that again."

Unwilling to simply sit and stare at the incriminating evidence, Finn began the careful work of removing Demi's belongings.

And another layer of proof that she had a vendetta against Bo Gage.

Darby bundled up against the cold in the oversize puffy coat Serena had lent her and gave Penny and Lucy a chance to stretch their legs. They'd stared longingly when Lotte had gone out earlier with Finn and Carson, and she'd finally taken pity on the two of them and taken them out for some exercise. The morning air was brisk but gave her a chance to clear her head as the dogs went off to sniff around on uncharted territory.

She'd made out with Finn this morning. It had caught her off guard at just how good it had felt to have a man's body pressed to hers after so long. Even now, she could still feel the imprint of his solid form against her skin. Which shouldn't have been a surprise, but was a reminder of just how much had been missing from her life.

Of course, none of it changed the fact that they were

in a tense situation and it was natural to seek comfort where available. It didn't mean there was truly something there. They could enjoy each other's company—could even move things forward and satisfy the physical—but that wouldn't guarantee something long-term.

When had she begun thinking of him in that way?

A week ago he was her enemy, his suspicions that she could be a murderess a massive gaping hole between them. And now here she was thinking about having a relationship with the man. Was she mad?

Or had she come to see him in a new light?

He was a good cop. She'd seen his dedication firsthand, including his willingness to put himself in the line of fire as they hunted a killer. She'd also seen him with his niece, making funny faces and sticking out his tongue to get a smile as he'd held her safely in the crook of his arm.

And then there was Lotte. His dedication and devotion to the dog indicated respect and affection as well as a dedication to the animal's well-being. There was a kinship there and absolute trust.

Was it really so silly to look at each of those things and tally them in the good column?

"What is with all that racket?"

The imperial voice interrupted her thoughts, seeming to float out of the ether behind her.

Darby whirled and came face to face with Joanelle Colton. "Mrs. Colton."

"Do I know you?"

"I'm Darby Gage. I'm a friend of Serena's."

"A Gage?"

Darby could have sworn the woman actually stared

down her nose at Darby's introduction but she held her ground. "Yes. By marriage."

"One of Carson's people, then?"

"I should have been clear. My former marriage. I kept the name Gage."

Something lit in Joanelle's gaze, dark and calculating. "You're the ex-wife. The one who inherited the dead man's possessions."

Other than Penny, there'd been minimal possessions to possess but Darby chose not to point that out. "I used to be married to Bo Gage, yes. I'm sorry for his death and for Carson's loss."

She could have sworn the woman muttered something about one less Gage in the world but couldn't be entirely sure. Joanelle's reputation preceded her, but was she truly that cold?

"What are you doing here, Ms. Gage? And why are you letting those dogs roam over my property?"

"They're getting some morning exercise. And I know how to clean up after my pets."

"Mama!" Serena slipped from the house, a large blanket wrapped around her shoulders as she quickly crossed the yard. "What are you doing out in the cold?"

"I saw this woman on our property and I came to investigate."

"Darby is my friend. And last evening she was my houseguest. Surely you could be a bit more welcoming."

Joanelle let out a small huff before plastering on a smile. "What brings you out to the ranch, Darby?"

"She stayed here with Finn last night. It wasn't safe to go back to her home."

Joanelle's eyes grew round and her already stiff frame seemed to go positively brittle. "Why ever not?"

"They were out for the evening and had an issue. Someone lurking in the shadows. Finn felt it best to stay here."

"He's the chief of police. While he may have trouble catching a killer, surely he can manage to keep one woman's home safe from harm?" Joanelle pressed on. "And whatever possessed you to allow them to stay here? You have an infant in the house and you're welcoming in a woman who's drawn the attention of our town's criminal element after everything that happened here last month? I must go speak to your father about this."

Joanelle huffed off without a backward glance and Darby wasn't sure if she should be grateful or prepare to suit up for round two.

"And that would be my mother." Serena waved a hand in the general direction of Joanelle's departure. "The very definition of hospitality."

"I don't know. She may have a point." Although the delivery was designed to belittle and demean, Darby couldn't argue with Joanelle's underlying meaning. "You do have a baby. You don't need the sort of trouble that's been hovering around me in your home."

Serena closed the short distance between them and wrapped Darby in a tight hug. "It's fine. And the ranch is now one of the safest places in Red Ridge. You don't need to give it another thought. Nor do you need to worry about being here."

"But what about Lora?"

"No buts." Serena silenced her before she could protest further. "Come on. Let's go inside. It's cold and I've got hot coffee and a cute baby to distract us from my mother's unpleasant welcome."

Darby followed Serena into the house but couldn't shake the melancholy Joanelle had managed to impart in their short meeting. Nor could she fully shake the sadness that lingered when she thought of Finn growing up under the cold and unfeeling presence of Joanelle Colton.

"You okay?" Finn glanced over at Darby, seated in his passenger seat, when he pulled to a stop a few streets away from the police station. He and Carson had already been there to secure the evidence, then had headed back to the ranch to provide the promised updates on what they found to Serena and Darby.

After an elaborate game Finn had mentally dubbed "you'll stay with me no I won't" had finally ended to his satisfaction, he and Darby had run Penny and Lucy back to her house and were now on their way to the precinct.

"I'm fine," Darby said.

"You're mad at me, but that's okay. I know you'd rather have your day back and time to yourself, but I'm not comfortable having you stay at home alone just yet."

"What is possibly going to happen to me? And while I have absolute faith in you that you will catch the Groom Killer, do you expect to babysit me until he or she is caught?"

"Any number of things could happen to you."

"In my own home? With two German shepherds to protect me?"

"Could you humor me for a few hours? Something

has had me itchy since last night and I'd rather know you're okay."

She didn't agree but, for the first time since leaving Serena's, she didn't argue, either, so he figured that was progress.

The precinct was quiet for a Sunday but busier than usual. The Groom Killer murders had everyone on high alert and every member of his staff was pulling extra time to try to stop the killer from striking again. The evidence he'd discovered at Demi's had been logged in and the team had been eager to begin a review of the forensics.

Although the evidence was heavily weighted to the circumstantial, coupled with Bo's bloody handwriting at the scene of his murder, it didn't paint a good picture of Demi's involvement.

Darby stared at the items in the evidence bags spread out on a table in the conference room, but didn't touch anything. "These are the items you and Carson found at Demi's apartment?"

"Yes."

"Where'd you find them?"

"Lotte sniffed them out in the floorboards."

Darby leaned closer, but still didn't make any attempt to touch anything before standing to question him. "She found a pregnancy test?"

"She's sensitive to a lot of scents."

"Including plastic?"

Finn considered all the tests they'd run on the various members of the K-9 team. "The dogs can find natural scents the easiest, but you'd be amazed what they can detect. Most recently we've been running trials on electronics equipment."

"Lotte can smell metal and plastic?"

"Yep. So can the other K-9 squad. Merlin's shown some of the strongest aptitude on that front, but I'm hopeful we can work on all the dogs over time."

"That's amazing. I wonder if we can breed them for that." Lost in her thoughts, she bent back over the table, focused on the items.

Finn watched her, that mix of curiosity and keen interest keeping her attention off him and on the evidence items as she worked her way down the table. Her hair fell in soft waves along the curve of her jaw and he could see reddish tones shining in the light that came in through the conference room's high overhead windows. The same fierce need that had gripped him that morning was back, only this time it was layered with an ice-cold veneer of rawboned fear.

What if something happened to her?

He'd spent this op convinced he could make himself the target, but what if he'd miscalculated?

"Finn?"

He was so lost in his thoughts she neatly turned the tables, her attention now fully focused on him. And in that moment he had an overwhelming sense of remorse mixed in with the bone-numbing fear.

"I'm sorry. I'm so sorry."

"For what?"

"For dragging you into this. For coming up with this stupid scheme in the first place."

"But you needed help and—"

He reached for her hands, effectively cutting her off. "I had no right to drag you into this or to ask you to put your life on the line for this dumb idea."

"But I agreed."

"Only after I held your personal situation over your head."

"That's not true. You offered me a way out."

If only.

Something dark and bitter coated his throat as he thought about what he'd really done. He'd used a sweet, kind, generous woman to meet his own ends. Even worse, he used her financial situation against her, putting her in a position where she could hardly say no. "I used you to meet my own ends and it's wrong."

"But I want to help. I may have fallen out of love a long time ago with Bo Gage, but I was married to him. I also loved him once. I want justice for him and for the other poor soul who was gunned down so horrifically. No one deserves that and they certainly don't deserve it on the eve of one of the happiest days of their life."

"But I didn't give you a choice."

"Of course you did."

"That's not true and you know it. The one thing you needed was money and that's what I dangled in front of you to do what I wanted."

The sweet, quiet woman who'd snuggled in his arms that morning was nowhere in evidence as she shoved at a chair. The thick metal made a heavy clanging sound as it hit the floor as she whirled on him, her voice rising with each syllable.

"You may have steamrolled over me to get me out of my house today but you're not going to steamroll me on this, Finn Colton. I had a choice! I could have easily let go of it all except for Penny. I could have kept her and gone back to my life."

"You would have done that?"

"Of course, I'd have done it. I was going to do my very best by Bo, but if I couldn't handle it or couldn't find a way out of the financial situation, I'd have explained all that to Bo's dad, sold off what was left of the business and gone back to my life. It's as simple as that. So stop talking about my choices and how you took them away. You offered me a chance to keep what I wanted *and* to clear my name *and* to help you end this evilness that has put a level of fear into this town I've never seen before."

Heat still flared high in her gaze, but along with it he saw something else.

Satisfaction.

Where he'd mistaken her for a woman with little choice or opportunity, he suddenly realized just how wrong he'd been. The situation Bo had put her in—a nearly broke business and a barely functioning home—had actually made it easy for her. She could have walked away from all of it with minimal loss and still taken care of the one thing Bo had valued above all else. Penny.

He'd believed himself holding the upper hand, but all he'd done was provide an opportunity. To fix all Bo had done wrong but also to provide an avenue for her to see that Bo hadn't died in vain.

If the steely look in her gaze was any indication, he'd have a damn time convincing her otherwise. "It's too dangerous. I can see that now."

"Then we face it together."

He tried once more, bringing back recent events in the hope of deterring her. "No. Absolutely not. We're done parading around town. Last night's chase through the parking lot proved that to me."

"We've come too far to back out now."

Where had this stubbornness come from? And why was he even considering—for one small nanosecond considering—going along with what she demanded?

"You can't do this. There are other ways, but we're not setting ourselves up as bait for a killer."

"Cold feet, Finn?"

"That's ridiculous."

"Is it?" She cocked her head, seeming to consider the situation. "Or are you backing out now that we're finally making progress? If that was the Groom Killer last night, hiding out in the parking lot, that means we got his attention. We're too close to stop."

"We're too close to danger."

"So what's the alternative?"

She moved closer and placed a hand on his chest. His pulse was already racing, but the press of her warm palm did the oddest thing. Both calming and exhilarating, the beat picked up even harder, even as he felt a strange sense of peace descend over him.

He'd worked so hard over the past month to keep his spirits up, but he'd be lying if he didn't admit to the fraying he'd begun to feel around the edges. Bo's death—still unsolved—and then a second murder had put a black mark over his department and the men and women who worked so hard to keep the peace in Red Ridge. Add on the general sense of panic in town and the loss of business experienced by so many of Red Ridge's merchants and the murders were taking their toll.

Finn laid a hand over Darby's, the support he felt there going a long way toward reinforcing those flagging spirits. Yet even with her support, he questioned the wisdom of continuing to flaunt their relationship in the hope a killer would pay attention.

"What is the alternative?" Darby asked again.

"We end this now and go back to our lives. If the killer is looking for couples, there will be no need to look at us any longer."

"And what if that makes them go after a different target? One who isn't able to handle himself against a threat like that?"

Unbidden, an image of Michael Hayden lying in a pool of blood at the Circle T filled his mind's eye, his fiancée crying softly inside the restaurant.

"That's not fair."

"None of it is fair. That's why we have to do what is right."

Darby moved even closer, the hand on his chest tracing a path up over his collarbone before settling behind his neck. She placed her other free hand around his waist and pulled him close. "We have to see this through. It's *ours* to see through."

Protest after protest rose to his lips but Finn discarded each and every one. They'd started this and, even if it had begun as a scheme to draw out a killer, it had become a mission for both of them. The time to change course had passed.

So had the time to bail.

They were in this. And while he wished he could go back in time and change the unbelievable hubris that had dragged him down this path in the first place, he had no choice but to play the hand.

The one he'd dealt all on his own.

Chapter 14

Darby took her first easy breath when Finn nodded his agreement. She still wasn't sure when the conversation had shifted—or when she'd begun thinking of the help she was providing Finn as a sort of personal mission—but she couldn't deny the urgent need that now drove her to see this through.

She did have a choice.

He might not see it, but she saw it clearly.

All her choices, both the one she'd made to join Finn in this work and all the ones that had come before, had led her here. She could no more walk away than he could.

Pressing her slight advantage, she leaned into him and took comfort and strength from their connection. Her earlier thoughts—wondering where they were going and if they had a future—seemed distant and unimportant. Instead she would focus on the moment and take what was here.

In this, too, she had a choice. And she chose Finn.

His lips met hers in a warm welcome and Darby sunk into him. Into the strong arms that reached up and wrapped her in their strength. Into the sexy shift of his mouth over hers. Into the maelstrom of need and want and raw desire that seemed to grip her every time they both got out of their heads long enough to enjoy each other.

This was choice, too.

And for as long as he'd have her, she'd choose Finn Colton.

Darby looked around the squad room, fascinated with the hum of activity. She could only envision it during the week—each desk full, conversation, laughter and likely an insult here or there tossing back and forth across the open space.

Finn's office had been turned into a "war room" of sorts—a place where they could set up their murder boards and hunt for the Groom Killer. He could easily have kept the office for himself, yet he chose to sit in among his men and women.

As one of them.

Did he realize how special he was? She'd watched him as he'd worked with Carson back at the ranch, going over the problem of the killer as well as the questions both had had about Demi. Finn had listened to Carson, probed when he'd wanted to know more and asked for additional clarification as the man argued his points. Finn had then posed his own thoughts and ideas, yet it in a way that was both collaborative and complementary, even when they'd differed. Darby knew she had gotten an inside sneak peek most civilians didn't ever see because of her involvement in "dating" Finn, but it had been fascinating to watch all the same.

Her experience with men, while not nonexistent, had consisted mostly of the years she'd spent with Bo and a few other pockets of dating that hadn't lasted all that long. She and Bo had rarely argued but she'd always had this vague sense that he was humoring her whenever they disagreed on a subject. Almost as if he were hearing her yet not truly listening to what she'd had to say.

She'd had friends at the time who'd expressed similar frustrations about their husbands and she'd chalked it up to one of those things about marriage people forgot to mention. After the vows and the champagne and the cake were done—after you went home and tried to make a life—you had to figure out how to communicate with each other.

And if you got a dud?

Well, that was marriage.

It had seemed terribly unfair. More, it had been a frustration to realize that someone she was trying to make a life with and find middle ground with seemed content to sit on his own personal high ground instead. Worse, Bo Gage had been loathe to share it with her.

"It's sort of a mess right now. We do a massive cleanup twice a year and we're definitely due for it."

"Hmm?" Keying into Finn's words, she shifted her focus to him. "What's that?"

"The squad room. We're a bit of a mess right now.

I know how much you like cleanliness and order, and we're a bit short on both at the moment."

She might like order but she liked closed cases better. "I'd rather know you had a messy precinct where everyone worked on shutting down crime than waste one minute worrying about where everything was filed."

"You surprise me. You got so quiet, I figured it was a creeping sense of horror and a desperate urge to flee out the door."

There it was again. That reality that Finn paid attention to her.

"I was actually thinking about marriage," she offered. "Which, if we're being fair, sends some people fleeing for the door, too."

"What made you think about marriage?"

"I was thinking about how you are with your staff. How you listen to them. Take their thoughts into consideration. It's an amazing trait and one not everyone has."

A dull flush crept up his neck. "It's my job."

"No, I don't think so. Your job is running the precinct and carrying the weight of Red Ridge on your shoulders. That would make anyone think their way was the right way. Yet you bring others into the process."

"I may carry the weight of expectation but the men and women of my squad are out there every day, putting their lives on the line. It would hardly do to forget they have eyes and ears, too. They see things I never will because I'm stuck in here so often. And they're never going to hone their instincts or their ability to think through a problem if I shut them down all the time."

Did he have any idea how rare he was?

Putting Bo and their relationship aside, she'd known a lot of people in her life and few were as emotionally evolved as Finn. From her fussy boss at the diner to the way Hayley Patton had pranced around the K-9 training center, hollering out orders to the staff even though she had no real authority, Darby had observed far too many people who just wanted it done their way.

Without checking the impulse, she tugged on his shirt, pulling him close for a kiss. Every time felt fresh, but something had changed. She saw Finn Colton through a different light than before and it changed everything. The kiss was deeper. More intimate.

And while all that had come before hadn't been even remotely cold or unfeeling, this one was hot.

A loud hoot interrupted their kiss and Darby pulled back, a big grin on her face. "Sorry. You are at work."

"They'll survive."

"Still." She backed away, bumping into the edge of the desk he'd set up at here in the squad room. The move was enough to have a stack of papers and folders tumbling off the edge along with a loud thud.

"Oh! Oh! I'm so sorry." She hunkered down, reaching for the folders, and saw a small package nestled among the mess of papers. Darby picked up the box, surprised at how heavy it was. A small card was stuck to the top with "Chief Finn Colton" printed in neat script. "This looks like it's for you."

"Where did you find that?"

"It was here. Among the folder and papers. I must have knocked it off along with your files."

"Was it on top?"

She'd seen any number of emotions flicker through his gaze over the past week, which made what she saw now that much more startling.

Traces of fear.

"Finn? Are you okay?"

"Sure. I'm fine."

He took the box from her and shoved it into his pocket.

"What is that?"

"Nothing, I'm sure."

"It looks like something. And, wrapped in red paper, it suggests you have a valentine."

The idea that Finn actually did have a valentine stabbed at her. He'd told her last week when they'd started their fake relationship that he was unattached. How silly of her to believe him.

And how easy it was to fall back into the same pattern. An attractive man showed interest and in a little more than a week she was right back to the same place she'd been in her marriage. A trusting fool.

"I don't have a valentine."

"It appears otherwise." She kept her tone low and even, praying the quaver she felt tickling her throat didn't come through.

"I really don't. These—" He broke off, a grimace turning his mouth into a straight line. "These gifts keep showing up. They're all anonymous and they suggest I have a secret admirer here in town."

A secret admirer? Was this 1952?

"No one knows who's sending them?" she asked.

"I didn't pay attention at first. And the last few that I did question were brought in by a delivery service."

"Do they know who it is?"

"Someone paid cash."

She wanted to press and probe him as to why he wasn't taking the situation seriously, especially because it was at direct odds with the behavior she'd seen with his staff. Where he focused on them and encouraged their work, his reaction to these so-called gifts to himself seemed to be dismissive.

As if he sensed what she was thinking, he rushed on. "It was a box of candy, some flowers and a few dopey cards. What am I supposed to do about it?"

"For starters, maybe take it more seriously. Finn, you've been trying for the past week to entice a killer. Maybe you've succeeded."

Finn ignored the discomfort that tightened the back of his throat. "It can't be the Groom Killer. The gifts came before you and I began parading around town."

"That doesn't mean it's not. He or she may be courting a new victim. Did Bo or Michael Hayden receive any presents or trinkets?"

"No. Not that we've found."

"So what if it's some sort of escalation?"

"Darby—" He stilled, her comments sinking in. "You're not half bad at this, you know."

"I watch cop shows."

He frowned at that. "Most of which are loosely based on the truth and dramatized in most parts to highlight a sense of danger. I mean the way you've quickly processed this."

It was just like earlier, when she'd posed the question of breeding her dogs to better detect materials. She was whip quick and, with sudden clarity, he saw a reality of her life.

She'd spent most of it sorely underestimated.

First by her mother and later by her husband.

He thought about Bo's business, his beloved Penny and the future of the dogs he loved so much. The man might have been a poor husband and unskilled business owner, but the one thing he'd loved without reservation had been his dog. Finn had to wonder that maybe Bo had known exactly what Darby was capable of and known all along what he was doing. It certainly gave credence to why Gage had never changed his will.

The dead man's faith had been rewarded. Darby was devoted to Penny's welfare and, even without his help or her earlier comments to the contrary, Finn believed she'd have found a way to keep the business afloat even if he hadn't given her the money.

"So why won't you open the gift? See what it is?" Darby asked.

Thoughts of Bo's motivations toward Darby faded as Finn reached for the small package he'd shoved into his pocket. It had a weight to it, whether from what was inside or what his imagination had already created. Setting it on the desk, the small present drew their collective focus as if it were a coiled cobra waiting to strike.

He opened the card first, the neat, precise script just as it had been with the other packages. Only, where the comments in the past had all suggested a concerned citizen or a shy admirer, this one was different. The tone was darker and the message, in Darby's words, had escalated.

Roses are red, so is blood.
Mine's true. Is yours?

Finn ripped open the package, only to find a small pewter rose inside. He picked it up, the detail intricate and precise. It was only when he changed hands, attempting to turn it over to get a better look, that one of the lifelike thorns pricked his finger.

"Ow!"

"What is it?"

Finn was careful to handle the piece by the leafy portion to hold it up to the light. A small, sharp needle stuck from the edge of the thorn, sharpening the point that was crafted in pewter.

"You're bleeding."

A small trail of blood ran down his finger and over his palm, and the pad still stung where he'd been pricked.

Darby dug out a tissue from her purse and handed it over, then pulled out another one and wadded it up so she could gently take the rose from his hand.

He wiped up the blood, then kept pressure on to staunch the flow. It stopped quickly, but still stung.

"This is more than just a pointy thorn." Darby twisted the rose in the air, shifting it so he could see what she did. "This looks like it was built to purposely cause pain. Look at that thorn. The third one down."

Finn saw immediately what she meant. The rose had obviously been crafted to do harm, the thorn she pointed to as sharp as a needle. "I wonder if some-one had this made. Putting aside how dangerous it is, it's a beautiful piece. The work is so detailed, it could easily be custom."

"Do you have a way of finding that out? And you should have it checked to make sure there wasn't any-thing on the thorn, like poison."

"I feel okay."

"But have it checked out."

Her concern was touching and while he didn't feel different, he'd make sure the forensics team checked out the rose.

What he was more focused on was finding out who might have sold the flower.

"Fortunately, we do have ways. Believe it or not, tracking something like this is easier than a box of store chocolate or real flowers. The fact that it's so unique makes it an easier find."

"This may be a real break toward finding the Groom Killer. Something that proves Demi didn't do it," Darby said.

"Now you sound like Serena."

"You think Demi did do it?"

Finn considered his cousin and the evidence they'd secured to date. "I don't think we can rule her out."

"But if she is the Groom Killer, why would she send her cousin love notes?"

That was where IDing the person sending the gifts fell apart. If the Groom Killer was his cousin, the like-lihood she and Anonymous were the same was highly unlikely. He wasn't close with the other branches of his family but he knew them. In his entire life, there had never been anything but a sort of grudging respect between him and Demi.

Certainly not unrequited love between first cousins. Heck, his family barely did affection.

Which only added to the knot that had settled in his gut the night they'd discovered Bo Gage's body. Was he dealing with two faceless criminals? The Groom Killer and Anonymous? Or, if they were one and the same, was there someone running around Red Ridge who wasn't even on their radar?

He could put out an alert on a known suspect. They could watch for them and put others on alert to do the same. But the not knowing was another matter entirely. Not knowing meant the person could strike again.

And a third strike meant they were well and truly dealing with a serial killer.

"Is it wrong to have a glass of wine?" Serena looked up from her menu, indecision playing around the edges of her eyes.

"One glass?" Darby asked. "I can't see how it will hurt. I'm not your doctor, but you can just dispose of that breast milk, right?"

"You're absolutely right and my doctor told me I could do this." Serena nodded as if decided. "I've been pumping to have extra and so Carson can feed Lora now and again. Which means Mama gets her first glass of wine in a year."

Darby nearly laughed at the look of anticipation and avarice that filled Serena's dark gaze. "Isn't it funny how much more interesting something becomes when you can't have it."

"You know it. I wasn't a big drinker before having a baby, yet at this moment I'm more excited than I can describe. And I get a night out. I love Lora more than I could have ever imagined but I'm looking forward to an adult activity."

Serena's comment only reinforced the earlier thought. Darby suspected Serena had never worried about adult outings before. Yet now that they were scarce, they seemed more exciting.

Sort of like Finn.

She'd been without male company for so long, each time she was with him felt heightened. Special. It had to be the only reason she was so giddy to be out with him. And so determined to make the most of every moment.

Since the reality that their charade would soon be over had begun to fill her with an odd sinking feeling in her stomach, Darby focused on Serena instead. "Who's watching Lora tonight?"

"Finn and Carson made Valeria and Vincent do it. Part of Finn's plans to keep the kids close to home and out of sight."

"Valeria's your sister?"

"Yes, my baby sister. She's madly in love with Vincent, Carson's youngest brother."

Darby remembered Vincent. He'd been a young teen when she and Bo had started dating. She'd always found him sweet, but could hardly imagine him getting married. "They're only nineteen, right?"

"Yes, and know their own minds. I'm hoping a night with a fussy baby makes them both rethink their marriage plans."

"But Lora's a happy baby."

"Most of the time. Since I think her first tooth is threatening an appearance, tonight is likely not going to be one of those times."

Suddenly, Serena's excitement for the wine and the evening out made even more sense. "You're diabolical!"

"I'm a concerned sister. I love Valeria and Vincent, too. And while I have no hesitation believing they have a love that will last, I'm a bit in my mother's camp on this one. Until this Groom Killer situation is solved, I want them safe. Running around town mooning over each other is the surest way to get on the wrong person's radar."

Sadly, Darby had to admit Serena was right. There were so many unknowns right now, but flaunting a relationship wasn't ideal. And since youth rarely saw itself as anything but invincible, they likely hadn't put the Groom Killer and their own romance in the same category.

Finn and Carson chose that moment to come back to their table. Finn looked so handsome and Darby sent up a silent prayer of thanks he'd run her back to her house earlier to get a fresh change of clothes and to drop off the dogs. It might be silly, but she wanted to look pretty for him.

"Everything go okay?" Serena asked Carson as he took his seat.

"Yep. Backup's positioned just where we planned."

Although it felt like another escalation, Darby knew the precautions were wise. She and Finn had been going out without backup since their charade began and the night before she'd been forced to call 9-1-1 while he'd raced off after a suspect. Between last night's scare and the anonymous present that had arrived for him, it seemed better to be prepared and to put police presence in place.

Finn took her hand, the move a match for Carson and Serena, and Darby was suddenly struck by how hollow his touch really was. Carson and Serena had a future. They were now parents and they were deeply in love. All she and Finn had was that charade.

The endlessly roiling emotions every time she was with him had been manageable up to now. But suddenly, faced with a couple who had not only weathered a personal storm but who had truly found their forever, Darby couldn't deny the overwhelming sadness.

No matter how she spun a fantasy in her mind, she and Finn Colton had nothing.

Finn sensed the change immediately yet couldn't place the reason. Darby's hand beneath his had stiffened when he'd touched her, at complete odds with their time together up to now. He'd gotten used to touching her. To the warmth of her skin and the easy connection they made whenever they were together.

Their waiter arrived to take their orders but it wasn't enough to dislodge the sense that something was wrong. Had Serena said something while he and Carson were securing the kitchen and back entrance?

Or had something else happened?

His sister was normally on point with others, sensitive to their needs and emotions, so he struggled to think she would have said anything that was overtly unkind or hurtful. But what else could it be?

He did a quick scan of the Trattoria, almost convinced he'd find Hayley Patton lurking at one of the tables, but the woman was nowhere to be found among the scattered groups of diners.

"And for you, sir?"

Distracted, Finn hadn't realized it was his turn and he hadn't even looked at his menu. He ordered one of the specials that had sounded vaguely interesting and went back to brooding.

Had he done something? While he'd enjoyed their evenings out alone, the idea to have Carson and Serena join them had seemed like a good one after the arrival of the rose and that clear sense of escalation from Anonymous. It also gave them the chance to flaunt the expansion of their relationship; two happy couples out for the night.

And it had sounded like fun.

Genuine, personal fun.

Finn wasn't sure when he'd begun thinking like that, yet he could hardly deny it. Somewhere along the way, his pretend relationship with Darby had become real. He thought about her when they weren't together and he anticipated getting back to her when they were apart.

And he liked her, damn it. In both the deeply attracted and interested sense as well as the genuine enjoyment and affection for another person.

"Can you believe the winter festival is next Saturday?" Serena asked. She shot him a small wink across the table, only reinforcing his earlier thought that she was on point and aware of others with her deft change to an innocuous subject.

Or a seemingly innocuous one.

"Don't remind me," Carson groaned. "It's all Lorelei has been talking about for two weeks."

"The sweet woman at the front desk?" Serena asked.

"Sweet?" Carson and Finn asked the question at the same time. It was enough to break whatever tension had settled in and Finn relaxed a bit when he heard Darby's light laughter.

"She is sweet," Serena argued. "She's been nothing but lovely to me the few times I've met her."

Carson shot his hands up in a gesture of innocence. "I'm going to choose to believe you. I'd just say my experience with her has been a bit different."

"How so?" Serena challenged.

"She yelled at me at least three times a week the entire first year I worked for the RRPD."

"Finn?" Serena demanded. "Did she do the same to you?"

"Yep. And three a week sounds about right."

"What did she yell at you for?" Darby asked.

"All depends on the day," Carson said. "Some days it was because my lunch smelled. Some days it was because I didn't put paper in the copier despite the fact that I hadn't even used the copier. Other days it was because my shoes squeaked on the floor."

"And after a year?" Darby said it first but Serena had leaned forward, clearly prepared to ask the same.

"She stops yelling," Finn said. "And then she loves you. Elle's about done her penance. Her rookie year's nearly over."

"But she seemed so sweet," Serena said. "She fussed over Lora and was so nice."

"Why do you think she acts that way?"

"Who knows, Darby? Some say it's because she has teenagers, but I started before her kids were that big." Carson sighed. "Once I got over being scared of her, I finally asked her why she does it. She claims it's a test."

Carson was right. Finn might joke about Lorelei—and done his year-one rounds with her himself—but he also respected her instincts. The woman knew the tenacity required to be a cop. Inside and outside the precinct. "If you ask Lorelei, she says it's because she's trying to weed out the cops who won't make it."

"That's her job?" Darby asked, genuinely surprised.

"She's made it her job. And since we're an important department with a K-9 unit, I've hardly argued with her." Finn couldn't resist the smile, an image of Lorelei sending his cousin Brayden off in tears in his first year. "I like to think she not only keeps the place in line, but she adds her own HR services for free."

"Is it working?" Serena asked.

"Without question." Finn said. "And, all joking aside, Red Ridge is better for having her on that desk."

Finn thought about the men and women currently stationed outside the Trattoria, two in the back and two in the front. He trusted all of them with his life. Knew they trusted him with the same. He'd say Lorelei's brand of personnel evaluation was working just fine.

"We're all better for having her on that desk." Carson lifted his glass of soda, gesturing them all forward for a toast. "Adversity makes for determination in those who have the patience to push past it."

As the glasses clinked, Finn couldn't help but take Carson's words to heart. Adversity did make people stronger. If a goal meant enough, hard times assured you'd keep reaching for that goal with even more determination. He'd proved that to himself more times in his life than he could count. So had Darby.

What he couldn't quite shake was the sense that the Groom Killer possessed the same sort of determination.

Chapter 15

As he walked Darby to her front door, Finn still couldn't shake the sense that she was upset. Their conversation over dinner had ebbed and flowed with ease, but something had remained off. She'd smiled and laughed, and the stories about Lorelei had seemed to break whatever tension had gripped the table initially. In the end, though, it hadn't been enough.

Their quiet ride to her house had only reinforced that.

"I'll just get Lotte outside quickly. I want to check the house."

"Of course," she said as she unlocked the front door and pushed it open, then flipped on the hall light.

He hated to leave her but could hardly force her to allow him to stay. The threat that she'd sensed the night before in the restaurant parking lot hadn't manifested into anything and their evening at the Trattoria had been uneventful, as well. He'd confirmed his team would do patrols through her neighborhood but other than taking some sense of calm from that small task, he had no right to tell her what to do.

Three sleepy dogs, their tails thumping in unison when he and Darby walked through the door, only reinforced the sense of safety. He made a fuss over them all as the wagging turned to excitement that they were home. Once they were up and moving, he quickly ushered them all outside to relieve themselves.

The winter sky sparkled overhead as crisp air shocked his lungs, his exhales making thick puffs in the glow of the house lights. The house wasn't deserted but it was set off from the road, the acreage big enough to ensure privacy. Lotte and Lucy had trotted to the far edge of the property, sniffing around as if to check out whether anything had changed.

Only Penny stayed by his side, those big eyes of hers solemn.

"You are a sweet girl." Finn bent to rub at her fur, pleased when she pressed her head against his thigh. "You watch out for her."

He'd always believed that animals communicated. Their inability to speak was only a limitation if you wanted it to be. Their expressiveness and their loyalty told an entire story if you only paid attention.

Penny's tail wagged as he patted her, light and steady, and he knew she understood him. He also knew that steady movement, back and forth, was her agreement that yes, she'd watch out for Darby. That she was committed to keeping Darby safe.

Just like the patrols, he'd have to take that as enough.

He called Lucy and Lotte to him, the two dogs bounding over the hard-packed snow that covered the lawn. They would happily stay out longer if he'd let them, but it was late and he needed to head home before he made an ass out of himself.

Because he didn't want to leave.

He didn't want to leave Darby alone. And he wanted more.

The sort of more that he had no right to want or to ask for. They had no commitment to each other and he had to own the fact that he'd not asked for one. Yet, as each day went by, Finn couldn't shake the idea that he did want a commitment. He wanted to go out with her in a way that moved past their pretense and toward something deeper.

Toward something more.

He followed the dogs to the door, stomping his feet on the front mat to remove any excess snow. He grabbed the towel Darby kept near the door to rub down the dogs and wipe the snow off their feet, and was instantly aware of her as her light scent and the warmth of her body brushed up against his. "I'll help you do that."

She had an extra towel and worked over Lucy's paws while Finn did Lotte. Lucy bounded off and Darby had already turned to Penny, praising the dog as she rubbed her down. "You were much better than your sister. Only a little bit to dry off."

"She stayed close. Lucy and Lotte took off exploring."

Darby kneeled, coming face to face with Penny. "Not feel like a romp tonight, sweet girl?"

Whatever distance had been between them had

vanished and Penny leaned into Darby much in the same way she'd accepted his gentle affection outside. She laid her head against Darby's shoulder and stood still as Darby offered praise and affection.

"Looks like you two have officially bonded."

"Finally." Darby smiled her first real smile of the night as she looked up at him. "You were absolutely right. She did come around."

"She just needed a bit of time to get used to her new reality. To grieve her loss of Bo and to accept that she's safe and loved by her new owner."

Darby ran a tender hand over Penny's soft head. "That she is."

Finn knew he should leave. Knew he should call Lotte over and give Darby space. Yet something kept him rooted to the spot. "Did something upset you tonight?"

"When?"

"At dinner. You seemed—" He stopped, well aware that he was crossing an invisible threshold. Whatever pretense they'd kept up between themselves, if he pressed what was on his mind, there'd be nowhere to hide.

"I seemed what?"

"Upset."

"I was laughing and having a good time."

"I know. But underneath." He sighed, knowing he was making a mess as he fumbled his way through what he suddenly needed to say. "You just seemed upset when Carson and I came back to the table. You were lovely as you always are, but I can't shake the fact that something is bothering you."

"We're not a couple."

"Oh?"

"That was what was bothering me."

When he only stood there dumbfounded, Darby gave Penny a final pat on her head and then stood.

"You and me. It dawned on me as I listened to Serena that she has a real relationship. She has a child. She also has a man who loves her and her daughter without limits. I don't have anything close to that. And now I realize that I've been deluding myself that a fake relationship is somehow a replacement for going out and finding those things in my life."

She took a deep breath, fire burning in her blue eyes as she kept her gaze level with his. "I've become lazy in my personal life since I got divorced and I'm sick of settling. Settling for living a half life, all by myself. So I have you to thank for that. Whatever else this experience has been, it's given me a push I've sorely needed."

Finn took in her words but struggled to understand what she was saying. She wanted to go out and find a relationship? Here he was, hoping to find something with her, and she was ready to look elsewhere?

"I see."

"Do you?"

"I think I do. You have a bright future in front of you and I'm standing in your way."

"No, Finn. You've cleared the path."

It was silly and small, but as he stood there staring right back at her, refusing to let his gaze drop, he had a revelation. Or more a solidification of all he hadn't been able to admit to himself.

She might want a future for herself but he wanted one with her. Or at least a shot at one. And the only way he was going to get that shot was if he put his balls on the line and told her.

"What if I told you I wasn't ready to step off the path?"

"Excuse me?"

"Maybe you're standing in my way." He moved in closer and laid a hand at her waist. "And maybe I like it."

"Me?"

"Yes."

His answer was final, a resounding welcome to everything he'd been running from in his life. He did want a shot at things with her. At something that went beyond a fake relationship and a hunt for a killer.

But he knew he needed to be gentle. Darby wasn't a woman to toy with. She'd been honest with where she was coming from and what she wanted in her life. "That's what I want. A chance to find out what's between us. I feel a spark. Do you?"

"Yes." She nodded before a small line crinkled her brow. "But I was afraid I was making it up."

"I can assure you, you weren't." That line smoothed out as a small smile edged the corners of her mouth. "So now it's up to you. What do you want, Darby?"

"I'd like a chance, too."

Before he could answer, she closed the distance between them, assuring him she was as on board as he was. "I'd like that chance with you."

They both moved at the same time, her arms around his waist as his wrapped around her shoulders. He'd spent the past week taking kisses wherever he could and all had been delicious, but this was different. The pretense was gone, replaced with the woman who had come to mean so much to him in so short a time.

Her tongue dueled with his, a merging of mouths that would be the precursor to the joining of their bodies. Despite the cold evening air that still lingered in the hallway from the open front door, they quickly generated more than enough heat to battle the lingering chill. But it was the firm actions of her hands that confirmed all they'd still not said.

She dragged his coat off, leaving it to pool at their feet with a thud. Her quick fingers then moved to his waist, tugging the hem of his shirt from his slacks. As her fingers met flesh, Finn sucked in a hard breath at so simple a touch.

It was sweet and seeking and intimate, all at once. And in that moment he wanted her more than he could have ever imagined.

He walked her backward into the hallway, on toward her bedroom. He heard the light tinkle of dog tags and stopped, turning to three witnesses who'd suddenly decided to trail them to the bedroom. With firm command, he stared down Lotte, Penny and Lucy.

"Out there for you three. Keep watch."

He saw the slightest hesitation before acceptance filled three sets of eyes. But it was the wag of Penny's tail as she followed the other two to take up a spot in the living room that suggested she approved.

And that she was more than happy to give them some privacy.

Darby watched three tails disappear around the corner of the hall into the living room and couldn't hold back a giggle. "That's impressive, Colton. It would have taken me considerable cajoling and likely half a box of treats to accomplish the same thing."

He shrugged. "I'm alpha dog."

The funny thing was just how true that statement was. Finn Colton was the quintessential alpha dog. At work and throughout Red Ridge, the man was in charge. In return, he protected everyone in his role as pack leader. Even more than that, he took his role as protector seriously. It was more than a job for him. As she'd come to observe him, she knew it was also his calling.

"I guess you are."

"You guess?"

"No." She shook her head. "I know. You're a protector to your core."

He stilled, his blue gaze crystal in the muted light of the bedside lamp. "You have the same qualities, you know."

Her? "I'm not a protector."

"I think you are. Your commitment and devotion to Penny suggests it, but so does your focus on helping me with the Groom Killer. Your immediate attention and upset earlier over that pewter rose showed it again. Even the way you hold Lora, so close and safe against you. You're a protector, too."

The process of getting to know Finn had been a revelation and it was both humbling and shocking to realize that much of what had been revealed were things about herself. Areas of her personality or the way she was observed by others that she'd never thought of or even considered.

"I want you to know something. Before we—" She

broke off, her glance drifting toward the bed. "I want to be with you, but I want you to know that I have no expectations. Of us."

"I do."

His declaration, so swift and immediate, caught her off guard once more. "You do?"

"For starters—" he pulled her close again, nuzzling her neck "—I expect we're going to have a great time."

She arched her head to allow him better access, her voice going breathy. "I sort of expected the same."

"Good." He pressed a long, lingering kiss there, his tongue finding a pulse point and shooting sensation through her that made her knees weak. "But that's not all."

She tried to focus on his words but the strokes of his tongue against the column of her throat were making it hard to concentrate. "There was something else?"

"Oh, yeah." The hands that had held her in place as he kissed her neck began to move, drifting over her stomach in light strokes. His fingers glided higher, coming to rest beneath her breasts before he cupped her fully with each hand.

And when he did—when his hands settled over her—Darby saw stars. Sparks seemed to flash beneath her skin as all her awareness settled in the glorious way he made her feel and the private cocoon that wove around their bodies.

Here, it was just the two of them. The outside world and all that was wrong with it had no place between them. For a few short hours, Darby knew, they could both shut it out and the responsibilities they'd both go back to. For now, their only obligation was to each other.

"I also expect that you're going to surprise me. Because you've done it every day since we met and I've found that I like it."

"I'm not very surprising."

"Then I'll be all smug and point it out when you do it again."

His thumbs flicked over the peaks of her nipples and pleasure shot through her with all the force of a rocket. The time for talking and thinking and even dreaming had ended. It was time to take advantage of her chance to be with Finn.

Reaching for the hem of his shirt, she pulled on it, lifting it over his head. The strength she'd already felt through the fabric was on full display, his skin golden in the soft light. A dusting of hair covered his chest, tapering down over his stomach into the waistline of his slacks. She traced the path, pleased when his already impressive stomach muscles tightened beneath her fingers.

Taking full advantage of the moment, she traced the path in reverse, flattening her hands so that she could cover as much area as possible.

Strong and solid.

The muscles that quivered beneath her hands spoke of both and seemed to be the outward sign of what she'd observed in his personality. In his choices and in his life, he was so strong and solid. He had the will to chase after killers and to spend each and every day working to keep Red Ridge safe. He also did it from a position of inclusion, as focused on the work as the men and women of his team. As much a part of things, working with Lotte to catch criminals, as what he asked of his squad.

There was nothing soft about Finn Colton. And as she felt that strength wrap around her, pulling her against the solid length of his body, she gave thanks for that.

In moments, interwoven with long, mind-bending kisses, Finn stripped her clothes from her. As each piece fell, that steady sense that there was nothing but the two of them grew. And once they were both naked, he pulled her down on the bed and covered her body with his.

The intimate press of his body—and the urgency that had built steadily between them—had a streak of shyness weaving through her. Turning her head, she stared at the wall, suddenly embarrassed about what was to come.

"Darby?"

"Hmm?"

"What is it? Do you want to stop?"

Stopping was the furthest thing from her mind, but the sudden embarrassment of just how long it had been since she'd been intimate with a man clawed at her. She wanted this to be good between the two of them and she hardly had a great track record of setting the sheets on fire. Even her marriage hadn't produced a particularly Olympian-like sex experience. Bo's infidelity had put a stop to things relatively early on and other than the first halcyon days of their relationship, her experience was woefully lacking.

All of which only made the moment worse—that she was bringing Bo Gage into bed with her and Finn.

She pressed at Finn's shoulders, struggling to sit up. He moved immediately, giving her the room she needed.

"What is it?" His voice was soft, his touch full of concern where it rested against her back.

"I…um…oh, um, well…" She stopped, the embarrassment growing at the fact that not only had she interrupted what was building between them but she now fumbled over her words. "It's been a while since I did this."

"Okay."

When he said nothing else, she turned to face him. Where she'd have expected frustration or even anger filling his gaze, all she saw in the blue was concern. True, genuine concern.

"It's embarrassing."

"Why?"

"Seriously? Here I am with a sexy man and I'm the shy woman who hasn't exactly been setting the town on fire. Heck, I was so sexy even my husband got tired of me faster than you can say *newlywed*."

As the words spilled out, Darby recognized the truth. She saw it reflecting back in Finn's gaze, but didn't need that reinforcement to know what had truly been festering inside all this time.

Bo's infidelity and casual dismissal of their marriage had done damage. She'd understood it on some level, but believed herself past it. How humbling to realize that it not only still lived inside her, coiled and waiting to strike, but just how little she'd dealt with those feelings.

"I'm sorry. I'm ruining something wonderful and special."

"No, you're not. But can I say something?"

"Sure."

"Bo Gage was an ass."

A giggle bubbled to her lips before she could stop it. "It's not nice to speak ill of the dead."

"Why?"

Her laughter stopped abruptly, cut off by that simple question.

"I'm serious, Darby. Why is it wrong? I'll do right by Bo Gage in solving his murder. He's one of mine and I will see that he gets my very best. But why should I suddenly decide to think well of him because he's dead?"

"I don't know. It's just because you're supposed to do that. We're still alive and he's not. It seems unfair to speak ill of him."

"Sorry, but I don't buy it. Especially from where I'm sitting. You're a beautiful, vibrant, compelling woman who is nothing short of amazing which, to my mind, is the exact reason Bo left you the business. Shame he couldn't have found a way to tell you that, especially because the man has left you feeling less than and alone. If that's not worth speaking ill of, I'm not sure what is."

A sense of joy unlike anything she'd ever known unfurled in her chest. It was warm and sweet and freeing.

So very, very freeing.

With a smile she couldn't hide, she gave him the side eye. "You're not just saying this to get me into bed, Colton?"

"News flash, Gage. I have you in bed."

She looked down at their naked bodies, whatever sense of embarrassment or shame that had stopped her fading. She wanted Finn. And if she truly did believe life was for living, she'd be foolish to let the moment pass them by. "I guess you do."

They turned to each other in unison, their mutual intent clear. And as her lips met Finn's once more, her joy burst through in a big welcoming smile.

Finn lowered Darby onto the bed, his mouth never leaving hers. While he'd not have called their prior moments passionless by any means, something had shifted in their conversation over Darby's past.

The kisses with her were sweeter. Hotter. And considerably more heartfelt. She was an amazing woman and he was determined to make her feel that in every single second they spent together.

With one final press of his lips to hers, he shifted, moving down her body. He spent some time in that sensitive hollow at her neck, enjoying the way her hands grew more urgent at his back, one more point of evidence to how good things were between them. Continuing the journey, he traced a path with his tongue, pressing kisses over her collarbone before coming to her breasts.

She was a small, petite woman, but her curves were lush and gorgeous and absolutely perfect. He plied those curves, pleased when his touch elicited a small moan from the back of her throat before he closed his mouth around one pert nipple. Her moan deepened and Finn felt himself groan as he sank into the moment.

Time passed. Minutes or hours, he had no idea. All he knew was a sense of urgency matched with an unwillingness to rush things. He wanted her—wanted to awaken her to true passion—and his only focus was Darby.

Where had this attraction been lurking, he wondered as he shifted to her other breast, determined to pleasure her for as long as he could before giving in to the demands of his body.

He'd seen her around town. Known who she was. How had he never before noticed how beautiful she was? Or how well they fit together?

Finn pressed on in his sensuous journey. His lips pressed against her belly button before he dipped his tongue to lightly tickle her. The quiver of flesh beneath his lips let him know he'd done what he'd set out to do. But it was the long, low moan and arch of her hips when he fastened his mouth at the very center of her that had his flesh quivering. He would make this last. Would see that she found pleasure with him, over and over. Even as his body demanded release.

"Finn!"

His name had never sounded sweeter—nor had a woman ever tasted better—as he pleasured her. Long, lush strokes with his tongue. A hot tease of his breath against sensitive flesh. And the addition of his fingers to send her over the edge of pleasure.

He watched her, gratified at the amazing responsiveness, before she pulled him close for a hot, carnal kiss, clutching at his shoulders as she found her release.

But it was the whisper that followed against his ear—half moan, half plea—that let him know he'd not last much longer.

"Now, Finn. I need you. Want you—" she practically purred against his throat "—now."

The sudden realization he'd left protection halfway across the room had him pulling back, determined to reach his pants when she stopped him. "The drawer. I…um…" A blush stained her cheeks, adding to the already pretty flush that painted her skin. "I wanted to be prepared."

Despite the demands of his body or perhaps because of them, laughter bubbled up, swift and immediate. "What was that I mentioned earlier?"

"About?"

"You, Darby Gage." He leaned in and pressed a hard kiss to her lips before reaching for the drawer. "I told you that you were full of surprises. How happy I am to prove you right."

Her smile was bright enough to power half of Red Ridge as he tore open the condom packet and made quick work of putting it on. "I told you I wanted to be prepared."

"Far be it from me to argue with a woman who knows her own mind."

"Good." She reached down to stroke the length of him, guiding him toward her body. As he found her sweet warmth, he sank in deep, shocked anew by how good she felt.

But it was as they began to move, at first tentative then faster as they picked up on each other's rhythm, did the pleasure expand. Build. Grow.

As Darby's release built, his own was nearly upon him. Harder, faster, he thrust, welcomed each and every time by the amazing woman in his arms. His body tightened, his ability to hold on nearly giving out when he heard the change in her breathing. Her arms tightened and her back arched, and Finn felt the telltale muscles intimately sheathing him pull him in, ready to drown him in her body.

Finn gave in then, his release coming on him fast as the crack of a whip and doubly powerful.

All he'd imagined earlier paled in comparison to the real thing and as his body emptied into hers, Finn knew the truth.

He didn't just have more. He had everything.

Chapter 16

Finn ran his hands over her skin as he held Darby close and desperately tried to bury the sense of anger that washed through him. The sensation was foreign and had no place in bed with them, especially after the warm, deep sense of satisfaction that still filled him from their lovemaking. But, damn, if he could let go of the ire or the upset that anyone had caused her a moment of pain or self-doubt.

She was perfect and the fact that Bo Gage had been such an ass to her bothered him more than he could say.

He'd never been happy for a crime committed against one of his constituents—and he certainly wasn't going to start with murder—but it was damn hard to feel any sense of sympathy for a jerk who'd used people and discarded them when he was done. Which was exactly what Bo had done to Darby.

Marriage took two—he knew that better than anyone—but when one behaved in a way that was pure betrayal, it was hard to see the injured party as equally at fault. He and Mary might have had their issues, but he'd remained faithful to her for the duration of their marriage, including the time before their divorce was finalized. He'd made a commitment of fidelity to her and he'd honored it.

"Who are you mad at right now?"

"What?"

Darby's voice was sleepy but her eyes were sharp as she lifted her head to look at him. "I can practically hear the anger in your head. It's got your chest all tight and your arms keep tensing up."

"I'm not mad."

"You are, and you're a crummy liar to boot." She sat up, her hair framing her face in a messy tumble. "What has you bothered?"

"I don't want to upset you."

"Okay. Then I promise not to get upset."

"You will."

"No, I won't."

Finn knew the conversation was too far gone to pull back so he gave himself a moment to prepare his thoughts and hopefully say things in a way that would minimize the pain.

"I'm mad at Bo."

"Why?"

"Before. The way you felt. You're amazing and incredible and beautiful, and the idea that anyone made you question that… It upsets me."

"You're right."

Where he expected something—even if it was a

raised voice or a lone tear—nothing manifested. All he saw was complete and absolute agreement.

"And you're not upset?"

"I was before. But right now I feel stupidly happy." She patted him on the cheek, her wry smile loopy around the edges. "Don't worry. It won't last. But while it does, I refuse to ruin it."

And there it was again. Surprise.

"Remember what I said before?" he asked her.

"About?"

"About being full of surprises." When she only nodded, he added, "Look at my smug face and count this as one of those times."

"I'd rather kiss your smug face."

He pulled her down on top of his chest, his hand at the back of her head to guide her to his mouth. He thought that she had a rather smug smile of her own.

"By all means, Ms. Gage. Don't let me stop you."

Finn made a few stops on his way to work on Monday, the memories of the night before going a long way to battle the lack of sleep. Darby had been a revelation and making love to her was more than he could have ever imagined. Better than his most elaborate fantasies, and he'd had more than a few.

Which made the shift in headspace from a gorgeous, responsive woman in his arms to a hunt for a cold-blooded killer that much more jarring.

But no matter how wonderful it was to escape for a few hours with nothing to focus on except Darby, there was still a killer on the loose in Red Ridge.

He and his team had split up all the tips that had come in and he'd followed up on several, canvassing

Red Ridge and the surrounding county, none of which had paid dividends. The first two had some merit, suggesting his cousin Demi, had been sighted a few towns over. The next one had been a fishing expedition on the part of a tipper, hungry for information about the case. By the fourth, he hadn't even gotten past the front door, the woman who called it in one of the precinct's "regulars." The woman wasn't a menace, but she was a pest, calling the police out for everything from what she believed was the scent of gas to a perceived slight from a neighbor.

Finn kept his tone stern, even as pity filled him for the slight woman on the other side of her front door. She wasn't that old—a recent check of her license had her in her midthirties—yet she'd developed a strange addiction to calling the precinct. "What was it you wanted to share with us, Lydia?"

"Hello, Chief. I know you've been keeping watch out for Demi Colton. I wanted to tell you I think she's guilty."

This was a new one. Lydia typically complained about neighbors and frequently told him she was prepared to make a citizen's arrest for noise violations. "Oh? Why is that?"

"Please. It's cold out. You're welcome to come in."

He nodded his head but stayed firmly put. "That's very kind of you, ma'am, but I don't want to take up too much of your time. But if you do have information on Demi Colton, I'd like to know about it."

The woman seemed flustered by his kindness and a slight flush crept up her neck. "It's a sense, really. I'd seen her around town before she fled and she's a hard woman, Chief. It would be so easy to see her killing men for sport."

"So you don't actually have information?"

Lydia seemed affronted. "Why, that's information. I'm a concerned citizen making sure I'm keeping the police up-to-date."

"Of course." Finn pulled out his notebook and made a show of writing down what she'd told him. He also made a note to flag the slightly daffy Lydia in Lorelei's files. They'd always respond to a citizen's needs—he refused to ignore someone simply because he or she was a bit off—but his officers needed to go into a situation with their eyes wide open.

He was ready to go when Lydia spoke up again. "Well, I might have something else."

For the briefest moment he could have sworn something sly flickered in her hazel gaze, but the sense was gone as quickly as it had come.

"Your help would be very appreciated."

"I've also seen that Darby Gage around town. Word is that she hated that her ex-husband was getting remarried. It wouldn't be too hard to think she wanted revenge."

Patience at an end, Finn nearly said something, holding back only at the last moment. It was only because of Lydia's long history of contact and the sheer sadness that he felt for her that he held his ground. "Ms. Gage has grieved the loss of her ex-husband. Regardless and based on police work, the precinct has ruled her out as a suspect."

"Oh."

"Thank you for your time, Lydia."

Her hand snaked out and, for a second, Finn

thought she was going to take his hand, but she pulled hers back at the last moment. "I know you'll catch the killer, Chief Colton. I have faith in you. From the bottom of my heart, I do."

"Thank you, ma'am." Finn smiled at the odd woman before heading out to continue his work for the day. It didn't take long for the annoying exchange to become a distant memory in his mind.

Darby checked the food in the oven with a meat thermometer, pleased to see her pot roast coming along nicely. She'd spent the past few days in a haze and it felt good to do something in her own house. With no one around to notice the small hearts and cupids floating around her head in circles.

"Or the dopey smile that's likely been riding your face," she added to herself before shooting a look at Penny and Lucy. The dogs had taken up sentinel duty in the kitchen, no doubt praying a fervent canine prayer the oven would open of its own accord and spew its contents in their direction.

"Yeah, you'll get some, too. I can't feel this goofy and happy and not share with you both. Lotte, too, when she and Finn get here."

She'd already anticipated the quiet dinner she and Finn would share. The public dates and show they'd kept up for all of Red Ridge had served its purpose—and she knew they'd be back at it tomorrow night—but she'd made the decision to keep Valentine's Day all to themselves. The mention of a home-cooked meal had Finn quickly agreeing.

Not that going out with the man was a hardship. She'd been cognizant of their pretense in the past, but now all she could feel was the sheer joy of being with him. And of the desire to shout to the rooftops that she was with this man, in every hour either of them could possibly drag free.

Their days were spent focused on their jobs. Hers on Lucy's breeding schedule and making contact with Bo's former clients to see who might be interested in her first litter. Finn's on the continued hunt for the Groom Killer. The lack of clues remained a problem, as did the continued disappearance of Finn's cousin Demi.

But he'd find her. He had to.

Even if it got harder and harder to believe as one day rolled into the next. What was Demi hiding? And if she really were innocent, why didn't she believe the RRPD could protect her?

Darby questioned the woman's motives as she finished up a few website updates at the kitchen table. She wasn't the world's best web designer, but she'd played around with a few programs and had given the site for the breeding business a nice makeover. That and the pot roast and she'd call it a damn productive day.

Both had also kept her mind running in the background with thoughts of how to help Finn.

She'd lived in Red Ridge all her life. Surely she had enough knowledge of her fellow citizens to be of some use beyond the public ruse of dating Finn. But because of knowing the townsfolk all her life—or maybe in spite of it—she couldn't shake the mystery of Demi Colton, no matter how many ways she twisted and turned the puzzle over in her mind.

Darby knew firsthand how infuriating Bo Gage

could be. And while she hadn't been pregnant with his child, she had been married to him. So if you compared life choices, she and Demi had at least a common frame of reference. Even if she mentally added the even deeper importance of a child to the mix, she simply couldn't see being mad enough to kill the man. Angry, yes. Disappointed, absolutely.

But murder?

Even with time to think about it and consider Demi as the one who'd put a bullet into Bo, the woman just didn't seem like a match for the crime. That only became more true when you considered the second victim. Demi might have a personal motive against Bo, but that flew out the window when Michael Hayden was added to the mix.

Killing Bo would be personal. Killing Michael would be twisted and sick. Had Demi just snapped and was going around killing grooms on the nights before their weddings? All because Bo had broken their engagement after a week? When they'd only been together a few months anyway?

But they hadn't discovered anyone else with motive, obvious or otherwise. Two dead bodies and next to nothing to go on. Even with the new direction Darby and Finn's relationship had taken, and the enjoyment of their time together, the endless questions haunted him. She saw it in his eyes and knew it kept him awake long after she'd fallen asleep in his arms.

Which was why she'd demanded that Valentine's Day be private and just for the two of them. The meat-and-potatoes meal she'd crafted—pot roast and Idaho reds—was as down-the-line "man food" as you could get. The appreciative smile he gave her a few hours later when he and Lotte walked into the kitchen reinforced his interest in the food—a sure sign she'd selected correctly on the meal.

"That smells amazing."

"Thanks. Penny and Lucy have lain around the kitchen all afternoon, basking in the smell."

"I don't blame them." He kissed her, a sound, smacking smooch on the lips, before he bent to pet both dogs. Their immediate offering of their bellies suggested the pot roast wasn't the only thing in the kitchen that had them happy and she enjoyed watching the ease with which he won over the ladies of the house.

Worn circles filled the creases beneath his eyes and Darby considered asking him about the case. Since it was his time to relax and take a break, she filed it away, promising herself she'd find a way to bring it up later.

He pulled her close for another kiss, long and lingering this time, and she let the thought flit away, content to sink into him and the quiet moment between them. It had been like that since Sunday, the easy, generous lover she'd taken showing his affection and consideration in a million different ways.

It was humbling to realize how quickly she'd come to crave that. The soft, yet deliberate, touches and the easy way of being together.

She'd already set the small, drop-leaf table for dinner and pointed toward the wine on the counter. "You still on duty or would you like a glass of wine?"

"We're in for the night. I'll open it up."

Finn focused on the wine and she pulled dinner

from the oven, their domesticity yet another element that was easy. Companionable.

And with that realization came another.

She was in love with Finn Colton.

The pan tilted in her hands as she bobbled the pot roast, nearly answering the dogs' prayers.

"Easy there, Darby. Do you have it?" He'd moved next to her, his hands nearly to hers before she sidestepped him.

"Yes!" she squeaked before gripping the pan harder. "Don't touch."

"You okay?"

"Of course. I just don't want you to get burned."

He snagged a few hand towels off the counter and helped her settle the pan on the stove top. "I'm fine. Are you sure you're okay?"

"Of course." Her heart pounded in her throat and she could have sworn they heard her heartbeat three towns over. "I'm fine. Just a bad grip. It's fine."

"The pack over here is disappointed your hands are so steady." He pointed to Penny, Lucy and Lotte, all intently focused on the stove.

Darby fought for some sense of equilibrium and grabbed at the silly conversation about the dogs. That was normal. Simple. And had nothing at all to do with love or feelings or an inappropriately needy response to the man you'd been sleeping with. "They've been hoping for a taste since before I put it in."

Oblivious to her upset, Finn snagged a roll she'd left covered on the counter. "Our opportunistic roommates. It must be hell not to have opposable thumbs."

The silly comment was enough to have her laughing and she vowed to push the thoughts of love from her mind. She'd pull them out later, when Finn wasn't around and she could truly analyze them. It was Valentine's Day, after all. She was feeling fanciful and silly.

That was it.

It had to be.

Finn finished loading the dishwasher at Darby's insistence that no one cleaned dishes in the sink on a holiday. And since he'd equally insisted the one who cooked the meal wasn't stuck cleaning it up, he'd sent her into the living room while he worked. His stomach was full and the meal, shared with an amazing woman, had been one of the best of his life.

So why was he still so riled up? Was he giving off vibes?

Whatever weird moment had gripped her earlier, when he'd first gotten to her place, had passed. Their meal had been fun and lighthearted, with both of them talking about some of the funny and lovable dogs who hadn't made it through K-9 training.

There was Buster the black Lab, who was even now enjoying life on a farm two counties over. And Sinclair, one of the rare German shepherds not to graduate from the program. He'd been adopted by a teacher at the high school and, through a random act of leash twisting, wrapped her up during lunch one day in the park with one of the mechanics from the Red Ridge Tire and Lube. The three of them now lived happily ever after in an apartment over the garage.

It had been fun and silly and had conjured up memories of Buster and Sinclair and a host of other dogs he'd been happy to see adopted so they could go on to a future that was exactly right for them.

It had also been the antidote to the bad mood he'd walked in with. The gift that had come to the precinct that afternoon had gotten to him and he hadn't fully shaken it off. He'd own it and admit that, finally, his anonymous gift giver had rattled him. Finn knew he should tell Darby about it, but he hadn't wanted to spoil the evening.

But now that dinner was done and he wasn't a liar—or even an omitter—on principle, something urgent nagged at him to tell her.

"Dishwasher is on." He walked into the living room, amused to see Penny curled up next to her on the couch, the dog's head in Darby's lap. "What was that you were saying about her coming around?"

"I guess she has."

Sheer delight filled Darby's face at Penny's closeness. Her smile was warm and inviting, and he felt himself being drawn even deeper into the living room.

Finn didn't want to break the spell with something ugly and unpleasant, but he also wanted to share it with her. Wanted her opinion and her thoughts.

Wanted her comfort.

"Can I show you something?"

"Of course."

He crossed to his bag and pulled the heavy box from where he'd buried it in the bottom. The inside of the box was coated with fabric over a layer of protective foam and from it he pulled out the glass heart.

"That's beautiful." Her smile vanished, replaced

with a frown. "But it's another gift from Anonymous, isn't it?"

"Yes." He handed her the heart—the lab had already done a quick overview and confirmed no prints—so he'd felt comfortable taking it with him.

Darby shifted Penny slightly before taking the heart and turning it over in her hands. "It's not as dangerous as the rose. Nothing sharp or out of the ordinary." She ran a fingertip over the glass. "It's smooth. Heavy, too. And expensive, by the looks of it."

"That was the lab's assessment when I ran it over."

"Did they say anything else?"

"Only that there weren't any prints they could find. One of the techs is going to look into the manufacturer to see if they can find anything. It is Valentine's Day. Any number of stores could be selling something like this."

She held it up to the light, turning it back and forth before shifting her gaze once again. "Did a card come with it?"

"Yes."

He pulled that out of his bag, as well, and held it up. Just like the other gifts, it followed a pattern. The writing was neat and it had been anonymously sent. But, like the rose, there was a sense of escalation in the message on the card.

A heart is fragile, take care with it.

Finn handed over the card.

"How do you take care with something, or someone, in this case, if you don't know who they are?"

"That's been the mystery from the first."

"It doesn't make sense. If the Groom Killer wanted to taunt you, you'd think there would be a better way. There's no ownership or bragging over the murders."

Yet again, her sharp intelligence shone through and he was caught up in the wonder of Darby. He and Carson had discussed the situation, and as trained professionals had come up with the same conclusion.

"It also doesn't make a lot of sense that my cousin Demi would be sending something like this." He wasn't ready to rule Demi out, but it was one more point of incongruity in trying to pin the Groom Killer details on her.

Assuming the two were related.

"No one's seen the delivery person?"

"Lorelei's been on the lookout but this was delivered in a stack of packages and it wasn't until after the delivery man had gone that she even realized it was addressed to me. She followed up with the service but they had nothing."

"That's even weirder." Her hand shook slightly as she handed back the card. "This doesn't feel right."

"I know."

"Do you really?" She gently moved Penny's head from her lap and resettled the dog on the couch before standing and coming to his side. "Does this scare you as much as it scares me?"

"I'm a big manly man. I don't scare easily." When the bad joke failed to make her smile, he went with the truth. "Yeah, it does. More than I want to admit."

"What are you going to do about it?"

"Keep doing what I've been doing. While it may not be related to the Groom Killer at all, I need to follow this lead. Demi is still a suspect and we're chasing down whatever we can, but she's poofed. These gifts are from someone who's actively taunting the chief of police. I need to work with that."

"And continue putting yourself out there as bait."

"Yes."

It was both statement and agreement. And right now, it looked like his only chance to catch a killer.

The watcher moved through the center of Red Ridge like a wraith. That's how she'd always seen herself. Neither here nor there, just a spirit that most people weren't even aware of.

All her life, that's how it had always been.

Until she'd met police chief Finn Colton.

He was so magnificent. He kept the town safe—kept *her* safe—and she owed him a debt of gratitude for pulling her from the abyss. No longer did she lie alone at night in bed, afraid of what lurked in the shadows. Her mom had taught her to be afraid of what hid there but the chief had slowly helped her come into the light.

There was a big world and if the right man was there protecting it, everything would be okay.

He was even going to catch the Groom Killer. He might be short on clues now but she'd been keeping watch for him. She'd pay attention for any changes in town and she would tell him. A concerned citizen.

The only problem was that Gage woman. She put the chief at risk. Made him turn his head away from his responsibilities, and it had to stop.

The watcher drifted to the edge of the town square. Work had already started on the booths and stages for the winter festival. She usually hated the festival. It came right on the heels of Valentine's Day—a holiday that never favored her—and was always a celebration full of happy families, sappy couples and people out in groups enjoying themselves.

Her mother had called them heathens and it was a term that had stuck. The Red Ridge Heathens. It happened every year, a beacon the town looked forward to in the middle of winter. Because what it really was, after all, was a chance to drink in public and make a lot of noise and ruckus.

Images of those people enjoying themselves made her think again about the chief. He'd been squiring that Gage woman around town and she knew she had to expect he'd come there with her.

Didn't he care there was someone out there who only wanted his happiness? Who loved him? She'd sent the heart to show him how much she cared. Maybe that would be enough to make him think twice about Darby Gage.

She hoped so.

She continued on down Main Street, the lights from the restaurant windows spilling out onto the street. They weren't all crowded for Valentine's Day—another side effect of having a killer on the loose—but there were people out. Couples staring at each other across the table. A few families out enjoying being together.

If the chief would only pay attention to her gifts, they could be sitting there, staring at each other, too. If he only knew how much he mattered to her.

She'd put herself squarely in the Groom Killer's sights for a date with the chief.

Her gaze caught on the town square once more and she considered what she'd do. The festival would be the place to make her move. To let him know how important he was. To show him they should be together.

She could do it. She could be a heathen, too. Her mother might not approve, but Mother wasn't here any longer.

It was time to step into the light.

Chapter 17

Darby came awake, the angle of the light shining in the window a surprise. This wasn't her room.

Where was she?

Before the question could register, a large male arm tightened around her stomach, a lethargic groan emanating from the back of his throat as he pulled her close in his sleep. And then she remembered.

She and Finn had put on their love show for all of Red Ridge since Valentine's Day. Big, flashy outings around town including a snowball fight he'd initiated at the edge of the town square the night before that had ultimately gotten what seemed like half of Red Ridge involved. By the end, they'd had a laughing pile of people, tired from tossing snowballs and melting snow dripping off their winter caps. Finn had used the moment to his advantage, tackling her in front of everyone and kissing her senseless in the middle of the town square.

Which should have made her embarrassed but had only left a warm, rosy flush to her skin every time she thought about it.

After last night's snowball fight and dinner at the diner with the rest of the snow battalion, they'd come back to his place and made love.

Which only made her more rosy and even more flushed as she thought about sex with Finn.

He was amazing. He'd unlocked something inside her that she knew she had been missing, but hadn't realized quite how much. Yet now that he was here, in her life every day, she couldn't deny how welcome he was.

Which took her right back to being in love with him.

She'd managed to put it out of her mind since Valentine's Day, but like those erotic flashes of making love with Finn that kept her company off and on throughout the day, her feelings popped in and out, as well. A few days to consider how she felt and let it sink in hadn't changed her mind. Nor had it gotten much easier to digest.

She glanced down at the large forearm that rested over her stomach, tracing the length of corded muscle with her gaze. He was a powerful man—impressively so. But his strength came not only in the physical but in his ability to practice restraint in equal measure.

He was unfailingly kind to his constituents. Any number of people had stopped him over the past few days and he'd been cordial to all of them. Even his family members who clearly believed it was wrong of him to keep looking toward Demi as a suspect had earned his kindness and respectful, affable conversation. Even his ranting uncle Fenwick—an unexpected visitor to their table the other night as they'd shared a steak dinner—had been met with Finn's easy manner and efficient competence.

Which only shows how far gone you are, Darbs.

Willing her gaze off the sexy length of his forearm—and, seriously, obsessing over his forearm?—she forced herself to look around his bedroom to distract herself from her thoughts. The warmth spreading through her chest, reinforcing all she'd eagerly observed, needed to be squashed.

Or, at minimum, contained.

For all the time they'd spent together he hadn't indicated he had any thoughts about something longer term. He said he wanted to try a real relationship, which had been wonderful so far, but what did that really mean? Would he still be with her by spring? Or summer? And what happened once he caught the Groom Killer?

She'd heard stories of how heightened danger could make a person feel intense feelings that couldn't possibly last. What if that was true for Finn? While she knew her feelings were genuine, what if his were of the moment? How would she ever survive what would no doubt be a major heartache if what was between them suddenly vanished once the lingering threat of a killer was contained? Ignoring the hitch in her throat the thought induced, she focused on his bedroom instead.

Like the rest of his condo, it was small but comfortable, with more than enough room for a single man. He lived in a complex near downtown Red Ridge, which he'd mentioned he'd chosen for the easy access to work.

The warm, overstuffed furniture in his living room was welcoming and lived in, and his condominium felt like a home. A bachelor pad, evidenced by the limited supplies in the fridge and the layer of dust on his bookshelves, but a comfortable home all the same.

"And you accuse me of being a loud thinker." Finn punctuated his sleepy comment by shifting onto his side and tightening his hold at her waist. He pulled her close in one smooth move, his mouth finding a particularly sensitive spot on her collarbone.

"Good morning."

"That it is." He smiled against her skin. "The sun is shining and I've got a beautiful woman in my arms."

"You sweet talker, you."

He lifted his head, a wry smile tilting his lips. "Is it sweet talk if it's true?"

She snuggled closer. "I don't see why not."

They spent several quiet moments, kissing and touching, wrapped up in each other, when Finn let out a quiet curse.

"What is it?"

"I've got an urgent paw in my back that doesn't care about our make-out session. She wants to go out."

Darby sighed, knowing Penny and Lucy would need to do the same. Finn rolled out of bed and as she stared at his incredibly attractive—and entirely naked—backside, she acknowledged how morning routines worked at his place. "I guess it's a bit different having a dog in a condo than letting them out into the backyard."

That smile was back, deeper and naughtier this

time. "My neighbors prefer I wear pants. Since I feel the same way about them, it works nicely. But, yeah, it's not as easy as just opening the door."

"I'll let you get to it, then, and I'll put coffee on."

"Deal."

He dressed quickly and Darby couldn't quite persuade herself to get out of bed. She watched him pull on an old sweatshirt and gym pants, fascinated by the stretch of muscles before that magnificent chest disappeared under thick cotton. Finn shot her a wink before rounding up the dogs, and she realized he'd been well aware of the show he'd put on.

Their quiet interlude at an end, she sighed and got out of bed. Dragging on the sweater and jeans she'd worn the night before, she padded out to the kitchen in the wake of Finn and three dogs. It didn't take her long to find coffee in his fridge and filters in a drawer. In short order the pot on his counter was up and running.

Her gaze caught on his workbag, nestled in one of the kitchen chairs. The box holding the glass heart peeked out of the top and she considered it from where she stood. Like a coiled snake, it became her sole focal point as she stared at it across the kitchen.

Although she had nothing to go on, the entire situation suggested a woman. Which was irrational and likely territorial, she acknowledged to herself, but there it was.

The anonymous notes, the deliveries and even the types of gifts. Whatever Finn might be dealing with, Darby instinctively believed Anonymous was female.

She was also certain the sender wasn't Finn's cousin Demi. Not only did the presents have an underlying sense of something sexual, which would be odd from a family member, but all Finn's comments up to now suggested that he and Demi weren't close. And if they did follow the supposition that Demi had killed Bo in some sort of lover's rage, why would she suddenly become attracted to her cousin?

Which was when it all clicked.

Hard.

The presents hadn't seemed to have anything to do with the Groom Killer because they *weren't* about the Groom Killer at all. They were about Finn.

If the escalating notes and gifts were any indication, he was possibly in more trouble than either of them had suspected. Finn and his team were on the lookout for a killer with a gun and a grudge.

But what if the real threat came at him from a direction he'd never even considered?

Finn laughed as he coaxed Penny into the hallway of his building. Although he had a small fenced patio off his first-floor unit, which he allowed Lotte to use in a pinch during bad weather, he believed it was his responsibility to get her outside to deal with her needs every day. Penny and Lucy deserved no less.

Lotte had long gotten used to a common entryway, but Penny seemed overly intrigued with the setup. Between the smells entering the hallway from his neighbors—including the tantalizing scent of Saturday morning bacon—and the perpetual layer of noise from the elevator, she hovered in a confused haze of activity. She'd raced inside as soon as they'd all finished their outside business, sniffing everywhere she could find and then trotting back and forth from the elevator bank to the hallway and right back again.

"Come on, girl. Let's go see what Darby has."

Penny reluctantly followed, her training and obedience taking over, but he didn't miss the look she shot the hallway over her shoulder.

"Poor thing. Pot roast on Wednesday. Bacon on Saturday. It's a crazy world." Those soulful eyes looked up at him in agreement as they walked into his condo.

Penny's attention shifted immediately and she barked as she ran over to Darby. The swift change in behavior had him following on the dog's heels into the kitchen. "What's wrong?"

She leaned against the counter, her arms folded over her stomach, her face pale.

"Darby?"

"The heart. I think I get it."

"Get what?"

He followed her gaze and saw the box holding the glass heart. He'd been carrying it around, hoping he'd find out where it had come from. But his canvassing of Red Ridge stores, the closest mall in the county and an outdoor shopping district in Spearfish hadn't turned up a single clue.

Or anyone who even recognized the glass piece.

Several shop owners had commented on its quality and one had even suggested a few possible manufacturers, but other than that, he had nothing.

Except an object that made his bag far heavier than its weight suggested.

"What do you get?"

Darby pushed off the counter. Her skin was still pale, but determination rode her gaze. "You've been targeted."

"By the Groom Killer?"

"What if the Groom Killer is a convenient distraction? What if there's someone else who wants to do you harm and all this chaos in the midst of the murders has given them a chance to strike?"

He knew she spoke from concern, but couldn't fully keep that in the forefront of his thoughts as anger shot through him. "You're telling me I've got another problem on the loose in my town? 'Cuz I'm having a hard enough time keeping up with one."

"Face facts, Finn. These 'gifts' and messages have escalated. What if this person is looking to do you harm?"

Face facts? Wasn't that what he did every damn day? "Then we catch them. It's that simple."

"But they're on the loose."

"A fact I'm well aware of." He crossed the short distance to the table and pulled the box from his bag, shifting it from hand to hand. "You think I don't understand what this means? Or that I'm oblivious to the danger?"

"Are you? Because you seem to think you can handle this all, but how are you going to go up against a crazy person with a gun? Or possibly two?"

He had no right to be upset in the face of her concern, but all he'd wanted was a quiet morning with her and the dogs. A chance to shut out the world and the noise and focus on something other than blood and death. Yet, here she was, pushing it in his face and suggesting he didn't understand what was really going on in Red Ridge.

Or, more to the point, what he'd somehow ignored as it had built and grown and *seethed* beneath the surface of his quiet little bucolic town.

He owned that.

Was responsible for it.

And since Bo Gage's death, he'd been forced to accept that his ability to keep law and order was waning at best.

"I know what I can handle."

He saw recognition fill her eyes. Saw the moment she understood that her pushing had gone from a discussion about a killer to a discussion about him. And he hated himself for it.

"This isn't about you, Finn. Surely you can see that? It's about people with problems. With an inability to see or understand that harming others is wrong."

"And there you go again. We should consider hiring you for the force. Your detective skills are bar none. Should I now add psychology to the list?"

Her pale skin and wide eyes had vanished, heat flushing her cheeks and blue fire sparking in her gaze. "Be mad at me if you want. Take it out on me, even. I won't shatter like that glass heart. But don't tell me you're oblivious to the danger."

"I'm not oblivious to anything."

"Could have fooled me."

She pushed off the counter and stomped out of the kitchen. As he stood there and watched her go, he made no move to stop her.

Laughing, happy people surrounded her as Darby worked her way through the Red Ridge town square. The winter festival was in high gear, in spite of the biting cold and the snowstorm that threatened to end things early. Space heaters had been set up at varying intervals to ensure people could warm up; adding those to thick coats, heavy mittens and hands full of cups of hot chocolate, the hearty residents of her town seemed fairly good at staying warm.

She and Finn had reached a tentative truce as the day had worn on and he'd finally acquiesced and let her go home for a few hours to get a few things done. The time away had done her good and had given her a chance to clear her head a bit.

When Finn had met up with his team, she'd told him she was going to wander off to explore and say hi to a few people. He'd attempted to argue but broke off at her protests that she'd be fine at four in the afternoon in and around several hundred fellow residents.

She loved him. All her inward protests and mental gymnastics couldn't change that. Or, more to the point, wouldn't change it. But she also wasn't his punching bag, willing to sit around while he brooded over his job and his town and the problems that lay beneath.

Finn was a good cop. But being a good cop meant that he was going to run up against people who defied logic or understanding. That wasn't his fault, or his doing, and the reality that he'd begun to think that the presence of a killer in his town was evidence he wasn't doing his job was a puzzle.

She headed for the hot-chocolate table to pick up a cup and got in line behind a family. A child of about five stood with her parents, her hand wrapped in her mother's. She chattered happily about a booth where she could win a stuffed dog and how she was going to sink a golf ball into a bowl to win.

Darby had passed the booth earlier and knew the

game was rigged to ensure every child got a prize, even if it wasn't the large stuffed toy that hung from the top of the booth, drawing the eye and beckoning people over. She thought about Lora and how in a few short years she'd be here, ready to do her own ball toss.

As she waited, her thoughts tumbling one over the other, Darby let her gaze roam the crowd. Was a criminal here? Whether it was the Groom Killer or the sly, swirling threat from Anonymous, she filtered each person she saw through the lens of potential criminal.

And realized that it was considerably more interesting to look at the excited five-year-old and contemplate her happiness at winning a stuffed dog.

What changed people? How did one go from happy at five to disillusioned at thirty-five? Forty-five? Older? And how had she been lucky enough to escape that?

Her mother had spent her life disillusioned. Convinced the only thing the world gave was drudgery and misery, her mother had toiled away without ever finding joy in anything. While not as outwardly dangerous as the Groom Killer, it wasn't a way to spend a life.

Why could she see it yet Finn couldn't? He felt responsible for his town, which she understood. But he couldn't take any responsibility for the choices his townspeople made.

She stepped up to get her cup of hot chocolate and wondered at the sudden chill that whipped through her. Tension ran the length of her spine and she turned at the sudden awareness of being watched. Taking her cup, she stepped to the side of the table and made a show of blowing on the hot liquid as her eyes scanned the crowd.

More families. A few couples; one that she recognized from the diner. And a few of Finn's deputies spanned the perimeter, watching the proceedings. Darby continued her scan, running over the same set of faces again, slowing as she got to a lone woman, standing at the edge of the festival square. She didn't know why she stopped—or why the woman drew her attention—but as Darby stood there she caught the woman's hard glare.

Was the woman watching her?

And why did she look so weird, standing there alone?

It was an unfair thought, Darby knew. She was alone. She'd spent the past hour contentedly walking around the grounds and didn't think twice that she didn't belong or that she should leave.

Yet something was odd about the woman.

She'd just begun to walk over when large arms wrapped around her from behind, warm lips quickly finding the sensitive spot beneath her ear. "You look better than that hot chocolate."

She whirled in Finn's arms, the menace of that quietly stoic figure fading in her mind at his arrival. "It's delicious and I'm not sure I'm sharing."

His arms widened enough to allow her to turn, but he didn't break his hold. "I deserve that."

"You do not—"

He squeezed her and pressed a quick kiss to her lips, effectively cutting her off before he lifted his head. "I do. I was a jerk and, worse, I was a jerk to you."

"I don't fault you for caring about your community. For being frustrated over your work. But I don't understand blaming yourself."

"Funny. Carson said something similar a few

minutes ago. I believe his words were a bit different though. More pragmatic, too."

"Oh?"

"He told me to get my head out of my ass."

"Sound advice." She handed over her hot chocolate, offering him a sip. "Have some hot chocolate. It'll give you a head start."

Pain, white-hot and sharp, stabbed at her. As forceful as knives, Lydia nearly doubled over in pain as she watched Finn Colton wrap his arms around that Gage woman.

She'd seen him earlier. Had even gotten up her courage to pass by him and brush her arm against his. He'd been distracted by his meeting with his officers, but she knew he'd sensed it.

Had known he'd felt her love.

Yet here he was, flaunting his relationship with that woman in front of her. In front of the whole damn town.

She slapped a hand over her mouth, holding back the rising bile as the chief bent his head to kiss that woman. That should be her. He should know how she felt. He should be with her.

Only, he didn't. He wasn't. He'd ignored her gifts and had brushed off her attempts to draw his attention with her information about the Groom Killer.

As she stood and stared at him, watching how he wrapped his arm around Darby Gage's shoulders, Lydia knew the devastating truth. Finn Colton would never be hers.

But as she stood there, gathering herself in the cold, Lydia made a vow. Her chief wouldn't be anyone else's, either.

* * *

Finn carried a small stuffed dog under his arm as he and Darby crossed the last block to his condo. The winter festival had been a success, the townsfolk seeming to enjoy themselves through another cold February night. He'd waited through shift rotation, when a new set of deputies came on duty and, after making one last turn around the grounds, had left the last hour of the festival to them.

"I can't believe you got the dog in one try."

"I'm a good shot."

"No, you let that little girl win the big dog." She reached over and ran a fingertip over the head of the small toy. "And you got me the little one instead. Very heroic of you."

"All in a day's work."

"For you, maybe." She stood on her tiptoes and pressed a kiss to his cheek. Finn wasn't sure if it was relief that they'd moved past their argument or just the joy of being with her, but her words and her kiss made him feel ten feet tall.

He let them into his unit and took his first deep breath since they'd left. The festival was a success and no one had been lurking in the shadows, waiting to cause trouble. To add to it, he'd had a chance to make up for his earlier crappy behavior and was satisfied to see a smile once again curve Darby's lips.

The dogs greeted them with a few barks and three rapidly wagging tails. He gestured them out the door. "We'll be back in a few minutes."

Darby surprised him by pressing another kiss on him, this one hard and urgent against his lips. "I'll wait for you."

The kiss and the promise of the woman waiting

inside carried him back down the common hallway and out the door. The lightest strains of music echoed in the distance, his condo close enough to the town square that he could still hear the festivities. He smiled again and would have whistled if he could, considering how much better he felt.

He'd hated fighting with Darby. Worse, he hated the fact that he'd attacked her when all she'd tried to do was help. It didn't speak well of him, but it was a revelation to realize that she hadn't held it against him.

And very different from his experience when married.

For as gentle as she seemed, Mary had been more than willing to fight dirty. An argument between the two of them, regardless of who started it, usually resulted in a few days of deliberate silence, even if he apologized. Which had made it that much more surprising when Darby had not only forgiven him but had welcomed him back with a warm kiss and a sexy smile.

Nothing had lingered. She'd been her bright, beautiful self and if he hadn't been a part of the fight, he'd never have known they'd had one.

It was funny how his marriage had been on his mind lately. For something he'd managed to bury for the past five years, it had been quick to surface with the reality of Darby in his life. It had been an even shorter leap to compare her to Mary. And, with it all, he found Darby a wonder at every turn.

Whether it was the thought of his marriage or simply the feelings that had grown without him even realizing it, Finn had to acknowledge the truth.

He was in love with Darby.

It had happened so easily and so simply.

He'd always imagined falling in love again would be a hard-fought war. A dark slide back into a relationship where his head battled his heart for dominance. Only it hadn't taken a battle at all.

It had taken one feisty woman with a sharp mind, a bright smile and a sense of determination that never failed to humble him. He should be unsettled—rationally he kept waiting for that feeling to kick in—yet as he stood there, watching the dogs romp along the shrub line, Finn knew nothing but peace.

Penny's sharp bark pulled him from his thoughts, but the warning was too late to do any good. Sharp pain radiated through his skull as something heavy hit the back of his head.

Before he could even register an attack, the world went black.

Darby puttered in the kitchen, the scent of the pound cake she'd won at the cake walk wafting toward her now that it was open. She'd just begun hunting for a knife to cut the rich treat when she heard the knock on Finn's door. In the rush to get the dogs out, she figured he must have forgotten his keys.

She had the door open before she could even register that neither Finn nor Penny, Lucy or Lotte stood on the other side.

Instead a small, slim form rushed inside, driving into her body with surprising force. Darby whirled backward, her arms pinwheeling as she tried to fight off the assault.

"You bitch!" the woman screeched.

Quickly shifting to the reality of what was happening, Darby struggled against the small body trying to pin her to the chair. Screams ripped from the woman's throat, expletives and sobs in equal measure.

Darby pushed at the manic form, unable to believe the woman's strength. She shoved and kicked, screaming in some hope of getting attention, if not from Finn then from one of his neighbors.

A hard bark echoed in the air, muted through the screen door that led to Finn's small patio. Darby didn't want to take her focus off her attacker, but the bark registered as possible help. Shifting her gaze to the door, she saw Penny up on her back legs, bumping her body hard against the glass. Slowly an idea filled her and Darby shifted her focus from fighting off her attacker to using the woman's momentum to get them moving.

With a deliberate shift in her weight, she slid off the back of the chair, using the force of their bodies to rush them toward the door, the woman screaming the whole time. "He's mine! You don't understand!"

Darby's arms tired under the continued assault and she weighed letting go of the steady pressure against the manic gleam in the woman's eyes. Darby had no doubt the woman had come there to kill her.

That knowledge had her pushing harder, digging deeper for the strength as she back-walked them a few more steps toward the patio door. Penny's barks grew more frenzied and Darby pushed one more shot of strength into her body, shoving as hard as she could at her attacker.

The force did little to stop the woman's forward momentum, but it was enough to give Darby a chance to tug on the door. She pulled on the knob, wrenching hard on the handle only to find it stuck. A hard sob fell from her throat as the woman leaped on her from behind, fingers clawing at Darby's face and neck.

The sob turned into a scream as pain registered from her attacker's assault. Darby kicked out from behind, scoring a slight hit when the heel of her boot connected with a shin, even as another round of pain radiated against the tight hold on her neck.

The kick was just enough to have the grip on her neck loosen and Darby grabbed blindly for the lock, flipping it and dragging on the knob.

Penny fell into the room in a rush of barks and growls and leaped on the woman, immediately stemming the assault and going to battle. Incoherent screams turned into shrieks as Penny pinned down her quarry.

Lotte and Lucy leaped over the low patio fence, their barks and growls a match for Penny's. In moments they'd surrounded the woman, a phalanx of protection holding her back and away from Darby.

They were there. They'd come to protect her. The knowledge had her legs wobbling. As Darby fell to the floor, she heard the sirens. Shouts wove in between the mechanical screams and two officers raced through the patio door on the heels of the dogs.

But it was Finn's haggard features, a trail of blood running down his forehead, that had her dragging herself off the floor in a renewed burst of strength. He stood on the other side of the patio fence and she raced to him, wrapping him in her arms.

"Are you okay?" she asked, shocked to feel how cold he was.

"Never better." His arms went around her, his innate strength still evident beneath the shaking of his limbs as he pulled her close.

* * *

Finn huddled in a thick blanket, Lotte on one side and Lucy on the other. Darby came next on the couch and Penny lay on her other side, her head in Darby's lap. Several RRPD members still managed the scene inside his house but Finn had been given strict orders to sit still while he held an ice pack to his forehead. He kept the pack on but refused to let go of Darby's hand with his free one.

He'd come so close to losing her. Just when he'd found her and discovered the depth of his feelings.

"Do you know who she is?" Darby's voice was hoarse but steady.

His town crazy woman, Lydia, had been removed a few minutes earlier. The medics had moved her, dealing with the bruise she'd sustained when Penny had knocked her over. Surprisingly, Penny had avoided biting the woman, using her strength to hold her still until Lotte and Lucy had added their support.

"Her name's Lydia. She lives in town and is a nuisance. Always calling the precinct for something or other. I never imagined she was dangerous."

"She's been sending the gifts?"

Finn nodded, confirming the details one of his deputies had managed to get from her. "I had no idea. I never would have suspected her."

"How could you?" Darby turned to him. "How would you ever know she was so dangerous? Or so deranged."

He couldn't. That was the simple fact. But it had been his choice to drag Darby into this mess in the first place. "There wasn't a way of knowing. But I should have thought before bringing you into this.

Before parading you around town as my girlfriend and making everyone think we were a serious couple. Instead all I did was show you off in the face of a deranged woman with an agenda."

"I entered this with open eyes."

"And you've more than kept up your side of things. But I can't believe I almost lost you."

She squeezed his hand, drawing his gaze to hers. "I can't believe I almost lost you, too. Which is why I have to tell you I love you. I don't care if you don't feel the same, I just need you to know."

The haze of pain that muddled his mind cleared in the face of her news. "It's funny you mention that. Something dawned on me just before I got bashed over the head outside."

"What's that?"

"I love you, too."

Joy filled the pretty blue of her eyes, a match for the warm, welcome smile that painted her face. "What are we going to do about it?"

Finn looked at their joined hands, their assembled huddle of dogs and the team of people that tromped through his condo. His life was crazy and complicated and he still had a killer to catch.

But none of it seemed impossible with Darby beside him.

"I say we keep being in love and figure out the rest as we go."

Finn wasn't sure who moved first—the room had begun spinning again—but it didn't matter the moment their lips met.

She was here. She was safe. And she loved him.

Best Finn Colton could tell, life didn't get a whole lot better than that.

Epilogue

"The rabbit died."

Finn's eyes widened, his shock clear as he stopped midway to tucking his napkin on his lap. "We're having a baby?"

Darby glanced at the dog that even now lay next to the stove, her gaze pointed upward at the meat loaf sitting in a pan on top. "I meant Lucy, silly. We had a successful breeding. The vet confirmed it today."

"Wow. Of course. That's great."

Something flickered deep in his gorgeous blue eyes. *Did he think* she *was pregnant?*

Darby wondered if she should say something, nearly discarding the words before she admonished herself. That was the old Darby. The woman who held back or felt like she couldn't express her true self.

All that had changed since Finn had come into her

life. It had been reinforced again a month ago when that deranged woman had attacked her in Finn's apartment.

Life was meant to be lived. And part of living was saying what you wanted and what mattered to you.

Finn mattered to her.

Their future mattered to her.

"Would you like to have a baby?" she asked.

"Wouldn't you?"

"Of course—" Darby broke off, trying to find the right words. "I mean, for a long time I'd put it out of my mind. I wasn't with anyone and dwelling on it wasn't going to get me very far. But now? With you? With how I feel about you?" She nodded. "I think about it."

"I think about it, too. I see the way you are with Lora and all I can imagine is you holding our baby."

"I imagine it, too."

Finn laid his napkin down and got up out of his chair. He came around the side of the table, dropping to his knee. Something dropped out of the bottom of her stomach as the gesture registered.

Something delicious and exciting, like the first dip of a roller coaster.

"I love you, Darby Gage. I love being with you and I love imagining a future with you."

"I do, too."

"Then let's make that future real. I want to be with you. I want to marry you. And I want to make a heap of babies with you."

She leaned forward and pressed a kiss to his lips, that roller coaster starting its next big ascent. Oh, how she wanted that future, too. More than she could have ever imagined.

But no matter how much she loved him, some things hadn't changed. "There's still a killer on the loose."

He nodded. "I know. But I'm not going to stop living my life. Living our life."

"I don't mean that. But we already drew the attention of one crazy person. Maybe we can keep our future to ourselves for a while?"

"A secret engagement?" He wiggled his eyebrows, his smile going bright. "Like a covert op?"

"Something like that."

"I like going under covers with you."

She laughed at the innuendo and kissed him once more. "Me, too."

"So, it's settled? You will marry me?"

The roller coaster crept higher. "Yes."

"And you'll have babies with me?"

It ascended a few more notches, reaching the peak. "Yes."

"Can we do that under covers thing?"

Darby laughed and stood, pulling him to his feet as the bottom dropped away once more. "I can't see any reason why we can't get started right now."

Finn tugged on her hand and nearly had her out the door when she pulled him back.

"What's wrong?"

She pointed to their plates. "If we leave that meat loaf on the table, it won't be there when we get back."

Finn shot a stern look at the dogs. "Lotte's well trained. She won't touch it. And Penny and Lucy are equally good."

"Lucy's eating for seven now," Darby reminded him. "It's hardly fair to tempt her like that."

Finn had the plates back on the counter and his hand around hers quick as a flash, dragging her toward the bedroom.

"You don't waste time."

"Not when I see what I want."

"And what's that?"

"You, my secret fiancée." Finn pulled her into the bedroom before stopping to pick her up. He whirled her around in his arms before pulling her against him, his lips pressed to her ear. "Only you."

Darby pulled him close and knew she'd received far more than she ever could have imagined. In two short months her life had changed in ways she'd only dreamed of. As she pulled Finn close, she reveled in their secret. And in the future that spread out before her as she waited to become Mrs. Finn Colton.

A future that was bright and shiny and sure to be absolutely wonderful.

* * * * *

LET'S TALK
Romance

For exclusive extracts, competitions and special offers, find us online:

 facebook.com/millsandboon

🐦 @MillsandBoon

📷 @MillsandBoonUK

Get in touch on 01413 063232

For all the latest titles coming soon, visit
millsandboon.co.uk/nextmonth

MILLS & BOON

THE HEART OF ROMANCE

A ROMANCE FOR EVERY READER

MODERN

Prepare to be swept off your feet by sophisticated, sexy and seductive heroes, in some of the world's most glamourous and romantic locations, where power and passion collide.

HISTORICAL

Escape with historical heroes from time gone by. Whether your passion is for wicked Regency Rakes, muscled Vikings or rugged Highlanders, avail the romance of the past.

MEDICAL

Set your pulse racing with dedicated, delectable doctors in the high-pressure world of medicine, where emotions run high and passion, comfort love are the best medicine.

True Love

Celebrate true love with tender stories of heartfelt romance, from the rush of falling in love to the joy a new baby can bring, and a focus on emotional heart of a relationship.

Desire

Indulge in secrets and scandal, intense drama and plenty of sizzling ho action with powerful and passionate heroes who have it all: wealth, stat good looks…everything but the right woman.

HEROES

Experience all the excitement of a gripping thriller, with an intense romance at its heart. Resourceful, true-to-life women and strong, fearless face danger and desire - a killer combination!

To see which titles are coming soon, please visit

millsandboon.co.uk/nextmonth

JOIN US ON SOCIAL MEDIA!

Stay up to date with our latest releases, author news and gossip, special offers and discounts, and all the behind-the-scenes action from Mills & Boon...

 millsandboon

 millsandboonuk

 millsandboon

might just be true love...

MILLS & BOON
MODERN
Power and Passion

Prepare to be swept off your feet by sophisticated, sexy and seductive heroes, in some of the world's most glamourous and romantic locations, where power and passion collide.

MILLS & BOON
Desire

Indulge in secrets and scandal, intense drama and plenty of sizzling hot action with powerful and passionate heroes who have it all: wealth, status, good looks…everything but the right woman.